ONCE, A KING ADORED HER . . .

▲▼▲

He stepped forward. "You know who I am?"

The black-garbed figure crouched like a spider before a blazing hearth. Roderic could hear the wind howl outside the building. "Who would not know the Heir of all Meriga?"

"I do not know you, Lady."

She laughed, a hoarse, pitiful laugh. "You are the first to call me that in an age, Prince. I am Nydia, and this dark place is my home." Her arms extended in a wide sweep. Where fingers should be, three curved digits ended in long claws.

▲

"Strong Arthurian themes thread their way through this novel . . . . an interesting story with intriguing concepts."

—*Kliatt* on *Daughter of Prophecy*

"An engaging and powerful tale of kingship, prophecy and friendship."

—*VOYA* on *Daughter of Prophecy*

ALSO BY ANNE KELLEHER BUSH

Daughter of Prophecy

PUBLISHED BY
WARNER BOOKS

CHILDREN OF ENCHANTMENT

ANNE KELLEHER BUSH

A Time Warner Company

WARNER BOOKS EDITION

Cover design by Don Puckey
Cover illustration by Thomas Canty

Warner Books, Inc.
1271 Avenue of the Americas
New York, NY 10020

A Time Warner Company

Printed in the United States of America

First Printing: January, 1996

10 9 8 7 6 5 4 3 2 1

For Josephine Putnam Vernon—
Josie, dearest of friends—
Your imagination fed my dreams.

Acknowledgments

The original incarnation of this book was the first thing I attempted after a writing hiatus of eleven years. My sincere gratitude goes to the members of the Stroudsburg Writer's Group: Charlie Rineheimer, Pat Knoll, Mitzi Flyte, Juilene Osborne-McKnight, and Christine Whittemore Papa for their long-suffering patience with my numerous drafts while I struggled to get it right. Carol Svec, Lorraine Stanton, and Nancy McMichael were particularly generous with their time and unstinting in their constructive criticism. Without the support of their love and their friendship, this book would not exist, and I wouldn't be a writer. Karen Lee, Lin Norsworthy, Betsey Massee, and Judith Warner were kind enough to give me readers' impressions. Betsy Mitchell finally got this manuscript pointed in the right direction. Special thanks also to Kathy Tomaszewski, who helped me keep my house and my sanity while I rewrote the book, and, last, but never, never least, to my children, Katie, Jamie, Meg, and Libby, for having accepted the fact that their mother spends more time than they do playing make-believe.

Bethlehem, Pennsylvania
May, 1995

CHILDREN OF ENCHANTMENT

Prologue

Gost, 74th Year in the reign of the Ridenau Kings
(2746 Muten Old Calendar)

The girl hovered, hesitant, behind the oak tree at the edge of the forest glade. Her patched tunic, all shades of green and brown and black, and bare, tanned legs rendered her nearly invisible in the shadows. She watched the wounded man lean his head wearily against the ribbed trunk of another ancient tree, his shattered leg at a rigid angle to his body.

The barest breeze ruffled his hair, gray as the steel of the dagger he clutched in one white-knuckled hand. Despite his age, which must be more than sixty, his back was as straight as the broadsword strapped across it. His leathery cheeks were pale, his lips thinned in a grimace, and he clenched his teeth to hold back another moan. It had been some time since his companion had ridden off in the direction of the fortress called Minnis Saul.

A black-and-yellow bee buzzed close to her ear. Thin needles of light penetrated the leafy canopy overhead, suffusing the whole glade with a green glow. A bird trilled once, twice, and was silent. Annandale gripped the rough bark. Life pulsed beneath her fingertips in steady, sweeping waves, and her heart slowed of its own accord as it adjusted to the tree's rhythm. She breathed in the sweet scent of the sap and clung to the tree's deep-rooted strength.

The man groaned, a low, animal sound deep in his chest, his brow furrowed with age and pain. She knew who he was. He was the King—the King of all Meriga. Abelard Ridenau. She had often watched him riding through the forest at the hunt. But this day, his horse had stumbled into a hidden sinkhole left by an uprooted tree, and the animal lay dead some feet away from the King, its neck broken in the fall.

She shifted uneasily as the echo of his anguish reached across the glade, licking at her like the tendrils of ghostly flames. A twig snapped beneath her foot and instantly he was alert.

"Who is it?" He pulled himself straighter and raised his dagger, the other hand reaching behind his head for the hilt of his sword. "Show yourself."

She flattened against the trunk. Now what? Her mother had forbidden her to speak to anyone who might invade the forest. She could try to run, but she had often seen the King throw his dagger with frightening accuracy at even the smallest prey.

"Go on, child." The rasp startled her even more than the King's realization of her presence. She turned, back pinned to the tree, and gasped at the sight of her mother's squat figure wrapped, as always, in dense layers of black veiling despite the late summer heat. Her mother never ventured so far from the safety of their remote tower.

"Mother?" she mouthed.

"Go on." The figure gestured awkwardly beneath her wraps. "You're eighteen. The time has come for you to meet your father, and for him to understand what you are."

Annandale peered around the tree. The King had risen into a partial crouch on his uninjured leg. His eyes darted back and forth.

"My father? The King is my father?" This time she spoke more loudly, and beneath Abelard's repeated command to show herself, her mother answered.

"You know he needs you."

Annandale swallowed hard. Questions swirled through her mind and were discarded, meaningless, as the tendrils of pain twined ever more insistently about her, as if she were caught in a spider's web. Uncertainly, she sidled around the sheltering tree. She glanced back at her mother, her heart pounding in expectation. Only once before had she healed—a messenger, riding hard and alone, who had begged for a drink of water, and a bandage to bind his arm. She would never forget how she had been drawn to that man, just as she was now to this one, not simply by the pain, but by the sense of brokenness, the overwhelming knowledge that something was out of order and the certainty that she, and she alone, had the power to set things right. *But at what cost?* whispered a voice in her mind. *At what cost to you?* Her gaze dropped from the King's rigid face to his leg, where the broken bones gleamed whitely through the torn skin and the fabric of his riding breeches was dark with clotting blood.

Abelard frowned as she appeared. Wary amazement washed over his face, but he did not relax his guard. "Girl. Who are you? Where did you come from?"

She pushed a lock of her long, dark hair back from her face, wishing suddenly she was dressed like her mother in protective wraps, or anything more substantial than her ragged, shapeless tunic. "From our tower in the forest."

"Put down your dagger, Lord King. He who lives by the sword, dies by it." Her mother's voice was a guttural croak. She stepped into the center of the glade, her black draperies slithering through the underbrush. "Would you cut your own daughter's throat, Lord King?"

At that, Abelard fell back, but he still clutched the dagger defensively. "This is my daughter? Who are you?"

"Don't you remember me, Lord King? You knew me well enough, once."

"Nydia?" he whispered. "Is it you?" The dagger fell to the ground as he extended his hand. "Why are you veiled so?"

"To spare my daughter—our daughter, Lord King—from the pain of what I've become. But no matter. I thought it time you learned what she is."

"Have you forgotten my name in all these years, Nydia?" Regret and something that might have been hope flickered across his face.

"Your name? Your name's nothing but a curse. Annandale will help you, and then we'll be on our way."

"Help me?" he repeated. He looked at Annandale. "Come closer, child. Let me see you." He spoke more gently this time, but his authority was clear.

Annandale advanced. The strands of pain felt as if they had turned to shards of glass, which burrowed deeper the closer she came. Her own leg began to throb; her own bones seemed to be perilously close to splintering beneath the fragile skin, where it seemed her own blood bubbled at the bursting point. Part of her recoiled from the pain, scrabbling back like a hunted animal. Mother, let this pass, she screamed silently, let me turn away, let me go home. What is this man to me?

But something else kept her walking forward, her shoulders squared, her chin high. It didn't matter that he was the King, or her father. Misery was stamped in every line of his body, and she could feel that misery, that pain, as though it were her own.

She sank to her knees beside him, more from need than from choice, and scarcely noted his reaction, though she thought he studied her face. He glanced up at Nydia and brushed one finger down the curve of Annandale's cheek.

She never knew what he meant to say. The agony overtook her instantly at his touch, racing through her body from her face to her leg. The pain was a communion more intimate than anything else she had ever experienced. She gasped and clutched for his hand. A thin blue light flared between them, clearer and purer than starlight, and in that moment, she knew her leg shattered, and her skin split. Her blood spilled out onto the mossy ground, even as his bones knit and his sinews healed and his leg was once again made whole.

As the light faded, her pain ebbed.

The King sagged against the tree, breathing hard, and Annandale released his hand. She rocked back on her knees, testing her leg, and found it, too, was whole. She felt curiously lightened, purified, as though she had walked unscathed through searing flames. The pain was truly gone, and with that knowledge came an exuberance so great, she looked at the King, her father, and laughed.

"Child," he whispered, tears gathering in his eyes. "What did you do?"

At once, she felt another pain, but this time a different sort. This time it was like a thin stream of water leading to a great pool. It tantalized her, unmistakably seductive, and slowly, she reached out to take his hand.

"Stop!" Nydia stood over them poised like a hawk. "You cannot, child. You're too young yet. Such a thing would kill you. His grief goes too deep." With her black-wrapped hands, she pushed Annandale back from the King.

Annandale scrambled to her feet, while Abelard and Nydia faced each other like a pair of old adversaries.

"Now do you have some idea of her worth?" Even muffled by the black shrouds of her draperies, Nydia's voice was venomous.

"Let me take her with me." Although the words themselves were a request, his tone shaped them into a command.

"The time is not yet."

"Then why did you allow her to help me?"

"I wanted you to understand."

The King rose, cautiously testing his weight on his now-sound leg. Annandale was struck by his height, by the breadth of his shoulders, undiminished by age. Only the wrinkles which ringed his eyes and the lines which extended from his hawkish nose down the sides of his mouth betrayed that the King was long past his prime. "What will I tell my men? A rescue party should be coming along quite soon now."

"Tell them anything you like."

"Any suggestions?"

"Tell them you met the witch."

"I asked you all those years ago if you were a witch." His smile reminded Annandale of an old lycat she'd seen once, set upon by a younger male, too weakened by age to defend itself, too battlescarred not to try.

"I never lied to you." It was as much an accusation as a statement.

"When will you send her to marry my heir?"

"You won't be there to see it."

At that, he raised his head. "Will you tell me what you can?"

Nydia threw back her head and stared just over Abelard's shoulder. The glade darkened imperceptibly as a stray cloud wandered across the sun. "You're planning a journey south."

"Yes. Next month. First to Arkan, then on to Ithan Ford in Tennessey Fall. There're rumors of rebellion among the Mutens in Atland—I intend to cement certain alliances."

Another long moment passed, and finally Nydia shrugged. "I see nothing. Nothing you don't already know. Come, daughter."

"Wait." The King's voice was hoarse with emotion. "Tell me how it will end."

Nydia shook her head. "It ended nineteen years ago, with the choices you—we all—made then." Decisively Nydia turned her back and grabbed Annandale's wrist.

"What happened to you?" he called when they were just at the edge of the clearing.

Nydia paused, and Annandale thought she might turn to

face the King and throw back her ragged veils. Instead she spoke over her shoulder, and her muffled voice was thick with unshed tears. "I've but paid the price of the Magic, Lord King. As did your Queen. As did Phineas. As will you."

Chapter One

Sember, 74th Year in the Reign of the Ridenau Kings
(2746 Muten Old Calendar)

Snow fell, white as the wings of the gulls which huddled beneath the gray stone battlements of Ahga Castle, steady as the measured paces of the guards who kept the watch. Bounded by walls of crushed rubble, five towers rose twenty-five stories above the cobbled courtyards, black against the pale gray sky, their squared precision testimony to an age and a knowledge long lost. Within the wide inner wards, the sound of the sea as it washed against the foundations was only a muted roar, and even the wind was still.

Peregrine Anuriel eased her way through the massive doors of ancient steel and stepped out onto the terrace of the central tower. With a deep sigh as the air cooled her hot cheeks, she ripped the white linen coif off her head, revealing her dark brown braids. She mopped at her forehead, then let the cloth flutter heedlessly to the pavement. Sweat stung her armpits, and her green woolen dress itched through her chemise. She balled both fists into the small of her back and arched backward. The low swell of her belly was thrust forward, and her pregnancy was abruptly more obvious. She stared up at the structure looming overhead, the downy flakes of snow feathering her dark lashes and thick black brows. The twelve days of New Year's were less than ten days away, and it seemed as if every resident of the castle, like a hive of mindless hornets, swarmed through the great hall at the bidding of Gartred, King's Consort and the First Lady of the household.

A sudden gust made the snow swirl about her. Its fresh salt tang was a welcome relief from the cloying odors of the evergreen boughs, the bayberry candles, and the dried herbs used to decorate the hall, the rancid smell of sweat and manure which clung to the grooms who had been pressed into service, and the heavy aroma of the roasting meats and baking breads which wafted up from the kitchens. Under ordinary circumstances, the sights and sounds and smells of the preparations would not have bothered her at all. But this year was different. She was five months gone with child, and the baby was not her only burden. Gartred cared only that the work be done.

It mattered nothing to Gartred that the child Peregrine carried had been fathered by Roderic, Abelard's only legitimate son, the child of his dead Queen and the King's acknowledged heir. It mattered nothing to Gartred that the child, if a boy, could, quite possibly, one day reign in Ahga. And it certainly mattered nothing that Peregrine herself might one day enjoy the very same honor Gartred enjoyed now. Gartred only cared about the King and the power her position enabled her to exercise over everyone in the castle.

"Peregrine? Lady Peregrine?" The stealthy voice pierced the quiet twilight, and Peregrine jumped, feeling a stab of guilt. If Gartred had noticed her absence, someone else had suffered the bitter side of the First Lady's tongue.

The door swung open smoothly on well-oiled hinges. An older woman peered out, her furrowed brow wrinkled, her round cheeks flushed, her hair swathed in a white coif and a pale blue shawl held close to her throat. Peregrine breathed a sigh of relief as she recognized Jaboa Ridenau, wife of the King's eldest son, Brand. With the exception of the Consort, Jaboa was the lady of highest rank at court. When she caught sight of Peregrine, she beckoned with one hand. "Whatever are you doing out here, child? You'll catch your death, and Lady Gartred—"

"—is not likely to consider that any excuse to shirk my duties," Peregrine finished the sentence. "Come stand a moment, Jaboa. It's so blessedly quiet out here, and calm."

With a backward glance over her shoulder, Jaboa stepped out onto the terrace, letting the door swing silently shut behind her. "It's cold."

"But so peaceful. Here." Peregrine wiped away the snow on the stone guard rails of the terrace. "Let's sit a moment."

Jaboa glanced around again, as though she expected the Consort to appear at the door, and reluctantly perched on the edge of the rail. Her cheeks were damp and little curls of graying hair stuck out from beneath her coif. Pine needles were caught in the folds of her clothes, and a twist of red ribbon was twined about her wrist. Jaboa closed her eyes and sighed. "You'd think that with the King gone to Tennessey Fall and Roderic away fighting this year, she wouldn't go to so much trouble. But no, the lady must have things just so. This is how the New Year's always been celebrated in Ahga, she says, and so that's the way it's going to be."

"As if she'd know," mused Peregrine. "She's only been here—four years? Five?"

"She's been here much longer, my dear. It will be sixteen years in the spring. It was the year Captain—well, now he's Lord Phineas—was wounded. I remember how upset the King was when he brought Phineas home, blinded—lamed—it was so clear he'd never ride to war again. And then a few months later, just when everything had begun to settle, he brought her."

"What could the King ever have seen in her?" asked Peregrine, holding out her hand to catch the snow.

"Who knows what men see? She was carrying his child—little Lady Elsemone. Gartred was, and still is, very beautiful. The King's eye for women—some say it will be his downfall." Jaboa shook her head and chuckled. "As if anything could bring him down."

Peregrine did not answer. In the time she'd been in Ahga, she'd had very little to do with the King. This year, the court had not even been back from the summer residence at Minnis Saul two weeks when Abelard had left on his journey south. She couldn't remember the last time she had spoken to him.

The King was her guardian of necessity, nothing more. If only the Consort could be the same. She watched the flakes drift onto her upturned palm, soft as a lover's kiss. She thought of Roderic again and brushed the snow away. Where was he? she wondered. Was it snowing in Atland? Was he warm and safe and dry? Or even now, was he in the midst of some battle, dodging razor spears, fighting the hideously deformed Muten hordes?

Peregrine shuddered. She had never seen a Muten, and she hoped she never would. She had heard the stories told around the hearths in Ahga since she had come to live there three years ago as a sixteen-year-old orphan, her father's lands and title forfeit as dictated by the terms of surrender imposed by the King after Mortmain's Rebellion so many years ago. If she had been a boy, Abelard would have allowed her to return to the fog-bound coast and gently shivering sands of her father's tiny estate on the very edges of the Vada Valley when she turned eighteen. She had thought when she had come here that the best she could hope for was marriage with some retainer of the King, her hand and her father's title reward for some service well rendered.

But now, she thought as she shifted her weight on the cold stone, now she'd had these last few months with Roderic, and she preferred not to think about the distant future. It was possible that the King might look favorably on a marriage with his heir—what need did Roderic have of great estates? And if this baby were a boy . . . ? Only let him come home safe and whole, she prayed to the One and the Three. Let him see his child's face. Let me lie with him once more. If only he'd send some word. But although messengers came and went from distant Atland with some regularity, there had been no message at all for her.

"Are you cold, child? We ought to go in." Jaboa stood up, brushing the snow off her gray skirts, flapping her shawl so that she reminded Peregrine of a fat, full-breasted pigeon.

Peregrine heaved herself to her feet, wondering if Jaboa, so long married, had learned not to miss Brand. "I suppose we must." She would have preferred to freeze in the still evening than return to the hot chaos of the great hall, where Gartred strode back and forth across the dais, blaring orders to anyone hapless enough to stray within hearing, no matter what their duties or their rank. Even Roderic's old tutor, iron-bearded General Garrick, had been pressed into service, forced to raise and lower the garlands decorating the mantels as Gartred snapped her fingers impatiently. Garrick had never looked submissive when he dealt with Roderic. Sudden tears stung her eyes. Why must everything remind her of Roderic? Even this courtyard—this was the very place she had stood on the day he had first noticed her. "I wish—" she began, and broke off with a little catch in her throat.

"Now, now. There, there. He'll come home. Don't you worry." Jaboa reached over and squeezed Peregrine's hand.

"If he'd only send me a letter—something, anything. Even just a line or two, to let me know he's all right."

"Tsk, tsk. Don't fret. That's the way they all are, even my Brand. Why do you suppose our high and mighty lady is so out of sorts? It's been weeks since she's had word from the King. Never you mind. Your prince will come home, and when he does, everything will be just fine."

"But, Jaboa—" Peregrine turned to face the older woman "—what if she sends me away like—"

"Oh, child, don't believe those tales."

"But it's not a tale, Jaboa, you know it isn't. She could send me away—me and my baby, both. What if she convinces the

King to marry me off before Roderic comes home? Then we might never see—"

"Don't you think he'd come looking for you? And the baby? He's none too fond of her. You know that as well as I."

"But he doesn't know, you see. I wasn't sure—before he left. So I didn't tell him about the baby. And now—"

Jaboa's faded blue eyes were soft with sympathy, and Peregrine remembered that, throughout the years, the maintenance of Meriga's fragile peace required Brand's absence from Ahga far more often than his presence. "And now Roderic has other things to think about. But, really, you mustn't fret. Brand will bring him home. I promise." She gave Peregrine's hand another gentle squeeze. "Now come along. It's getting much too cold out here."

Peregrine met Jaboa's eyes and was startled to see the merry expression.

"Besides," Jaboa said, leaning forward to whisper in Peregrine's ear, even though no one was about, "you don't want to miss the surprise we've brewed for my lady. Old Mag put—"

Sudden shouts drowned out the secret. Peregrine looked up and frowned. In the outer ward, men were calling for grooms, for a doctor, and before she could move, a horse and rider burst through the opened gate which led into the outer ward, followed by at least half a dozen of the guards on duty.

The rider slid off the horse and stumbled as his leather boots slipped in the snow. A groom dashed forward to catch the animal's bridle. Blood-streaked foam flecked the horse's mouth, as it shied and tried to rear, slipping and sliding on the snow-slick cobbles. With a curse, the man waved away the others who offered aid or escort, and Peregrine saw that he wore the uniform of the King's Guard. The lower half of his face was obscured by a matted beard, and his hair was plastered against his skull. His cloak was torn and splattered with mud, and he looked as if he had been in the saddle for many days.

He staggered toward them, ignoring the guards who called for the sergeant of the watch.

"Lord Phineas," the man cried, his face red and raw with windburn. Peregrine glanced at Jaboa. Was the man insane?

"Take me—Lord Phineas—at once," panted the soldier. "Take me, lady—must speak with him—"

Peregrine's heart seemed to stop in her chest. Was it Roderic? Was the messenger from him? She sprang to the door. "Come, soldier. I'll take you there myself."

"But—" began Jaboa. One look from Peregrine stopped her protest. "I'll—I'll just let Gartred know a messenger's come."

Peregrine caught at the soldier's arm as he heaved himself up the shallow steps, breathing hard, snow frosting his brows and beard. "Please, just tell me, is it the Prince? Does he live?"

The man paused, narrowing his eyes as if he'd not quite understood. "The Prince? I know nothing of the Prince, lady. It's the King. King Abelard has disappeared."

Chapter Two

Janry, 75th Year in the Reign of the Ridenau Kings
(2747 Muten Old Calendar)

"Lost? My father is lost?" The parchment scroll fell to the floor unheeded as Roderic Ridenau, eighteen-year-old heir to the throne of Meriga, stared at the messenger in disbelief. An unruly shock of light brown hair, silky as a tassel of wheat, fell across his forehead, and he swiped it back automatically. "Phineas expects me to believe that the King has just disappeared?"

The messenger, one of the special corps who rode the length and breadth of Meriga in the service of the King, twisted his gloved hands together, his shoulders shifting beneath his dark blue cloak. "Lord Phineas has sent out three regiments of the King's Guard to search."

Roderic sank onto one of the long wooden benches beside the rough-hewn council table, feeling as if the air had been punched from his lungs. He stared at the hide map of Atland pinned to the surface, as though it might hold a clue to the King's whereabouts.

On the opposite side of the room, his eldest half-brother, Brand, stood with arms crossed over the insignia of the King's Guard emblazoned on his tunic. "When exactly was it realized that the King was missing?"

"He was expected at Ithan Ford by Thanksgiven Day, Captain. When he didn't arrive by the fifth of Sember, Lord Senador Miles sent word to Lord Phineas in Ahga and Lord Senador Gredahl in Arkan."

"And?" asked Roderic.

"The King had left Lord Gredahl's holding in Arkan at the beginning of Vember, Lord Prince. He should have arrived in Ithan in plenty of time for Thanksgiven."

Brand gestured a dismissal. "That will be all for now. Tell the master of supplies to give you dry clothes and a place to sleep. We may need to talk to you again before we send you back to Phineas."

As the messenger bowed out of the door, Roderic looked up, the dismay plain on his narrow face, with its high, slanting cheekbones, his light brown brows furrowed above his gray-green eyes. Brand walked around the table, and stooped to pick up the discarded scroll. "Well, little brother. It's a fine coil we have here."

"What are we to do?" Roderic twisted restlessly on the bench and stared over Brand's head at the narrow window. Outside, sleet spattered the rippled panes of smoky glass, and the wind howled between the low stone buildings of Atland garrison.

Brand paused in his reading, his lips pressed tight in an expression which reminded Roderic of their father. Finally, Brand looked up, and concern flickered in the depths of his dark eyes. "We don't have a choice." He shook his head, and the protest died in Roderic's throat. "Right now, we don't have a choice."

Roderic stared at his brother. At forty-five, Brand was not only the eldest of all of the King's illegitimate children, but the Captain of the King's Guard as well. The King's Guard were the elite troops charged with the responsibility for the King's safety, and the Captain of the King's Guard outranked every other soldier in all the Armies of the King. Abelard trusted Brand as he trusted few others. Only Abelard's insistence that Brand accompany his heir had prevented Brand from going with their father on what should have been a routine tour of the Arkan Estates. Now, in the orange glow of the fire, Brand's face was closed and grim, his jutting hawk nose so like Abelard's looking pinched in his square-jawed face. His hair, clipped close about his temples, was more silver than black, and the stubble on his chin was nearly all gray.

He blames himself, thought Roderic. He got up with a sigh, hooked his thumbs in his belt and paced to the window.

The rain was falling in fat, steady drops, regular as the muffled beat of a funeral drum. The guards huddled at their posts, wrapped against the weather in heavy cloaks of olive drab, crouched over low braziers of smoking charcoal. He gazed over the walls into the dark mountains rising up, stretching off into the distance as far as he could see. Beyond the garrison walls, the land lay ravaged beneath the lowering sky. Here and there, the black, bare trees rose like twisted skeletons, reminding him of the charred bodies he'd seen too often in the course of this wretched campaign.

This was his first command, and he had hoped to make his father proud. Now, he wondered bitterly if Abelard would ever know. And what would Abelard's disappearance mean for him? He was the heir of Meriga, the only child of Abelard's dead Queen. So far, he'd yet to prove himself on the battlefield. How could he rule all Meriga?

He turned away from the window with another sigh and paced to the hearth, where the fire snapped and hissed.

"Stop that, damn it," Brand spoke over his shoulder.

"Stop what?" Roderic threw another log into the middle of the fire.

"That pacing. It reminds me of Dad."

Roderic swung his long, gangly legs over the bench beside his brother and tapped the scroll. "What do you think?"

"I don't know what to think. I suppose Dad could have been ambushed by Harleyriders—though they've usually retreated to the deserts south of Dlas by Vember. Maybe he met a Muten war party as he crossed into Tennessey on his way to

Ithan, or maybe there was some sort of accident." He looked at Roderic and shook his head again. "I just don't know."

"Phineas says he's called an emergency Convening of the Congress. Shouldn't I be there?"

Brand shrugged. "In theory, of course. The Congress will acclaim you Regent—which I suppose you already are. But in reality—you can't leave Atland, Roderic. Not now. Not until we get the upper hand in this revolt." The brothers lapsed into silence, both thinking the same thing.

The war in Atland was not going well. Roderic was charged with what he increasingly thought of as an impossible task—the defeat of the Muten rebels once and for all. The King had managed to quell the last rebellion, a dozen years ago, by a combination of diplomacy, tactical genius, and luck, when a particularly virulent form of plague swept through the Muten ranks. Impervious to all the diseases which afflicted the Mutens, the King's Army had easily overrun the enemy.

But both brothers knew that so far, his heir was not so lucky. It was simply that terrain and weather, as well as sheer numbers, were against them. The Mutens bred like rats, producing six and seven and eight offspring, and those who did not starve or die from disease, went on to reproduce the same way. They were vermin, and like vermin, impossible to eradicate.

A log split with a loud hiss, and Roderic was reminded of their last encounter, only a few days ago. The driving rain had turned the ground to a soupy sea of red mud, and his horse had slipped and scrambled for purchase, even as he shouted the order to retreat. Once again they had underestimated the number of the Muten forces, underestimated the ferocity with which the Mutens fought. He had clung to his stallion's neck, watching the foot soldiers scramble for safety beneath a volley of razor-sharp spears that whined above the wind. From his perch on a rocky promontory, he had counted the bodies, slick with gore, heaped upon the battlefield. Most of those bodies wore the colors of the Armies of the King. The cries of the wounded and the dying, the horns which signaled the retreat, joined in an eerie chorus, punctuated with the shouts of officers as they tried to marshal the survivors into some semblance of order. The memory of that sound made his blood run cold, and the realization that he was ultimately responsible for those deaths made his sleep restless. They had left Ahga four months ago, but it felt like four years.

Finally Brand spoke, and his voice was heavy with regret and self-reproach. "We've got to get you back to Ahga in time for that Convening, if we can. I reckon we've three months—at the most."

"Three months?" Roderic repeated. "That long?"

"If Phineas sent word to the estates when he sent the messenger to us, some of the Senadors haven't even heard the news yet. And with the weather, and this rebellion, there're too many Senadors that can't leave their estates. For example, Kora-lado can't get out of the Saranevas until spring. The Senadors on the eastern coast would be fools to try to cross the Pulatchians in the middle of a Muten revolt. We have time. But not much."

"Not much of what?" The door from the outer room slammed open and shut, and Reginald, another of Roderic's half-brothers, stood shaking the water off his cloak. He threw back his head and ran his fingers through his long, lank strands of sandy hair. His watery blue eyes were the only feature which reminded Roderic that Reginald was Abelard's son. "Not much chance of finding a woman to come out in this weather. Hell of a way to keep New Year's." He scratched his armpit and yawned. His clothes reeked of old sweat and damp wool.

Reginald had commanded the garrison in Atland for years, charged with keeping the peace between the Pulatchian Highlanders, the lowland farmers, and the Mutens who lived in the inaccessible mountain hollows of the Pulatchian Mountains.

Roderic knew his father had never questioned Reginald's abilities as the commander of the largest garrison in southeast Meriga. But in the last months, Roderic had begun to regard Reginald's slovenly habits and sloppy person with disgust, and he was beginning to think that perhaps Abelard had never really known what sort of man Reginald was.

Now Reginald reached across Brand for the flagon of wine leftover from the noon meal. "There anything left in here? Not much. Let's send for more."

"Sit down." Brand's voice brooked no disobedience.

"As you say, Captain," Reginald replied sarcastically. "Why the long faces? What in the name of the One's wrong with you two?"

Before either Roderic or Brand could reply, there was a loud shriek and the muffled sounds of a scuffle from the outer room. Brand rose with a curse and was across the room in a few long strides. He flung open the door. "What's going on out here, Sergeant?"

"What's wrong now?" Roderic hastened to his brother's side and looked over Brand's shoulder. Six or seven men-at-arms, brandishing weapons, all hovered around the farthest corner of the room. Warily, he slipped past Brand. "What is it?"

The duty officer pulled himself straighter and saluted. "Caught one of them, Lord Roderic."

Roderic tried to get a better look at the intruder, but in the shadowy corner all he could see was what looked like a pile of old clothes. "Stand aside."

"Careful, Lord Roderic! These things are dangerous," the sergeant warned, but he motioned to the men to step away. The soldiers obeyed, but they did not lower their swords.

Roderic peered through the tangle of legs and weapons and realized that the intruder was in fact no larger than a child. "Come here."

The bundle of rags shook itself like a puppy, and a clay-colored face emerged.

"It's one of them, all right," muttered the sergeant as the other men made noises of disgust.

"Shall I kill it, Lord Roderic?" One of the men-at-arms raised his sword.

"Hold!" Roderic stooped, gazing at the little face peering back at his from the shadows. One dark eye, above and centered between the other two, stared back unblinkingly, and he shuddered with revulsion. But the rest of the face was thin, too thin, the reddish skin stretched tight across the delicate bones, and Roderic realized that this was, indeed, a child. A Muten child.

He motioned the soldiers back. "Where did you say you found him?"

"Kitchens, Lord Roderic," was the reply. "Trying to steal food, filthy thing. We nearly cornered it there, but it was too fast. Led us all the way through the garrison, it did."

"Do you understand me?" Roderic spoke slowly to the child, who had not taken its eyes off Roderic's face.

The Muten gobbled a response and nodded.

"Why were you in our kitchens?"

The child made another series of noises and held out a thick crust of bread and rubbed its stomach with the other hand. Beneath the ragged clothes, its two secondary arms emerged and twitched involuntarily, the tiny appendages smaller than a human infant's.

"You're hungry." Roderic stared at the hand that clutched the bread. The fingers were bony claws, the skin dry and flaking across the swollen joints. He raised his hand without thinking, and instantly the child stuffed the bread in its mouth.

"It's got into the food!" cried Reginald. "Kill it."

"No!" Roderic turned furious eyes on his brother. "Can't you see it's starving? Let it—him—whatever it is—go." He turned away, feeling sick and sad. "Let it go."

"But, Lord Roderic—" began the sergeant.

"I said, let it go. I don't make war on children. Starving children, at that. Increase the guards around the food stores. But take this one to the gates of the garrison, and if any harm comes to it, the man responsible will answer to me." Roderic met the shocked expressions of the soldiers evenly. If he were ever to assume his father's position, he'd better start playing the role. He knew Abelard wouldn't have cared whether the child lived or died, but he was certain his father never let anyone forget who was King. Brand watched from the doorway. He pushed past the soldiers, who snapped to attention, and Brand gave a little nod of approval. "Come in here, Reginald. We need to talk to you."

"About what?" Reginald clumped into the room behind Brand, who shut the door as the child was led away.

Brand resumed his place at the table. "If you'd been here, Reginald, instead of in pursuit of a woman, you'd have seen the King's messenger come in—"

"From Ahga?" Reginald's raised brows were pale against his reddened skin.

"From Phineas."

"And what's he want? Updated body counts?"

"Be quiet, Reginald." Roderic leaned across the table.

"Ho! The kitten shows his claws. Old man's not pleased with the way things are going?"

"Dad's missing." Brand's glare expressed more clearly than words what he thought of Reginald.

Reginald's little eyes darted from Roderic to Brand and back again. "What do you mean, missing?"

"Lost," said Roderic. "Disappeared without a trace. Here—" He shoved the parchment across the tabletop. "Read it yourself." If you can, he added silently.

Reginald took the scroll and scanned it. When he finally looked up, his expression was serious. "So what should we do?" He spoke to Brand, but it was Roderic who answered.

"Get this situation under control, so I can return to Ahga as soon as possible."

Reginald snorted. "You're going to 'get the situation under control'? How?"

Brand cleared his throat. "We'll call for reinforcements."

"From where?" Reginald drained the dregs of the wine into a clay goblet. "Everyone's got their hands full—just who—"

"Amanander," answered Roderic, looking at the map.

Even Brand looked surprised. Roderic tapped the map. "You're right, Reginald. Everyone north and west is tied up in this rebellion. But Amanander has a full garrison at Dlas-for'-Torth and a clear march through Missiluse."

"And you think he'll come?" Reginald leaned back in his chair, swirling the wine in the goblet.

Roderic raised his head. His father had always relied upon his brothers; he would have to rely upon them as well. "What choice will he have? The kingdom is in jeopardy. He swore the same Pledge of Allegiance the rest of us have." A memory flashed through his mind, of his father's steady blue gaze and strong grip on his shoulder on the day that he, too, had knelt and sworn to uphold the kingdom and the King unto death. The words ran through his mind: I pledge allegiance to the King of the United Estates of Meriga and to the kingdom for which he stands, one nation, indivisible . . . Indivisible. With blood and sweat and sheer determination, the Ridenau Kings had forged Meriga into one nation after generations of chaos. And now the task had fallen to him. He met the eyes of both his brothers with squared shoulders. "What choice do any of us have?"

Chapter Three

The cold Janry wind wailed across the ocher sands of Dlas-For'Torth, whipping at stunted cacti. Even to the unaccustomed eye, the weathered rocks appeared to lie in long lines and right angles across the desert floor. In the eastern sky, the sun was a thin red crescent curving over the flat horizon, and the first streaks of gray and violet light blotted out the last stars.

Sand shifted across forgotten highways, blew relentlessly against the high, crushed-rubble walls of the desert garrison. It made a sound like the hollow rustle of dead leaves. Above the rooftops, white smoke spiraled in thin lines, then dissipated in the gusty updrafts. It was the only sign of human habitation at this lonely outpost established to protect the borders of the Southern Estates against the incursions of the Harleyriders.

In the middle of the dusty yard, two sentries rubbed their hands over a small watchfire and tucked the ends of their cloaks more securely against the cold. The watch was nearly over.

"Cold last night," commented the taller of the two as he laid his spear upon the ground and blew on his fingers.

The other nodded. "Messenger come in late, did you see?"

"I was patrolling the eastern perimeter all night, you know that. Where from?"

"Hard to tell. But I saw he wore the King's colors."

"Kingdom messenger, then. From Ahga?"

His companion's shrug was interrupted by the sudden pounding of hooves from the direction of the stables. A horse, nothing more than a black shape in the predawn light, burst into the courtyard, screamed in protest as his rider drew hard on the reins. "You, at the gate—open it!" The voice was imperious, impatient.

On the other side of the wide yard, the sleepy gatekeepers jumped to attention, tugged down the heavy crossbars, and pulled open the high, massive gates to let the dark rider out. A low cloud of dust was all that remained of his passing.

"Wasn't that—?" The grizzled sentry turned incredulous eyes to the other.

"Lord Amanander. Riding as though the wrath of the One were behind him."

The ruddy light cast by the rising sun brought little warmth. Amanander flexed his hands in the black leather gloves, the fur lining soft and warm against his skin. The stallion rode hard at his urging, hoofbeats muffled by the sand. He followed the straight line of an ancient roadbed, due south, his shadow growing darker as the red sun rose. His dark blue cloak billowed out behind him. He wore his black hair long, knotted at his neck in an intricate braid, and his face was shaved smooth despite the early hour. His square jaw and high cheekbones bore the unmistakable stamp of his father the King, but his eyes were so dark they were nearly black, and his brows swooped like crow's wings across his forehead.

An hour from the garrison he pulled the horse to a stop. The road lay in ruins: great chunks of ancient stone lay piled haphazardly like some giant's discarded toys, and here and there metal sheets, scoured free of paint and corrosion by the relentless sand, stood at twisted angles from rusted poles.

The wind tugged at his cloak. His horse whickered and stamped, its breath a great white plume in the dawn light. A barely discernible shimmer hovered just a foot off the ground. Amanander closed his eyes, and a thin line appeared between his brows. His lips moved silently, and the shimmer subsided. He touched his knees to the stallion's sides and flapped the reins. The horse moved slowly off the road.

At the base of a great pile of ancient brick, Amanander paused once more. He swung out of the saddle with practiced grace and tethered the horse's reins to a twisted metal staff sticking out of the sand. He gathered his cloak and bent his back to enter the concealed cavern. No one would have noticed it without knowing it was there. Once inside, he stood straight, his head nearly touching the low ceiling. His boots scraped across a tilted floor of a material which had not been made in Meriga in centuries. Insects scuttled out of the dust raised by his passing, and in the dark corners, bats stirred with a leathery whisper of black wings. A lone torch burned in a crude bracket.

In the far wall of the cavern, he pushed on a metal bar, and a heavy door shrieked open. Preserved by the climate, protected from the wind, faded white letters proclaimed in a language half-forgotten: RESTRICTED ACCESS. AUTHORIZED PERSONNEL ONLY. Amanander did not hesitate. A long corridor lay before him: the low roof and squared walls gave evidence that this was no natural corridor. Clumsy brackets set at intervals three-quarters of the way up the wall held torches which cast an orange light. "Ferad!" His voice echoed down the length of the corridor. "Ferad?"

With a sigh, he started down the corridor. Other doors were set in the walls; these he ignored. At last the corridor turned right. At the end of the hall he pushed against another door. It opened silently, smoothly on well-oiled hinges. A draft from some unseen crack in the ceiling brushed across his face. "Ferad?"

A figure hunched on a high wooden stool beside a rusted metal desk looked up. "I was not expecting you, my Prince. At such an early hour." A lone lantern flickered on a surface dull with the dust of centuries, the flame drawn back and forth by the invisible, nearly indiscernible breeze which filtered down from above.

"I had a message last night." Amanander drew the gloves from his hands, smoothed the supple leather and tucked them into his belt. His boots made almost no noise at all as he crossed the floor. He took another rudely carved stool and sat down on the opposite side of the desk.

The other looked up, and in the candlelight, three black eyes gleamed flatly like a lizard's. Amanander suppressed a shudder. He was used to the Muten, had known him more than fifteen years, but his initial reaction to Ferad's deformities was always repulsion.

"Well?"

"Things aren't going so well for my little brother in Atland. He requests aid. From me, of all people."

Ferad's third eye, set in the center of his forehead, stared fixed and unblinking. He had no sight in it, of course, none of them did, although the ruling families of the Tribes did have full use of the small pair of secondary arms which in Ferad's case dangled limply from his shoulders, lost in the folds of his robe. He set down his pen in the center of his parchment scrolls and shrugged. "So?"

"I want you to keep my father alive in my absence."

Ferad glanced at a low door in a dark corner of the room. "Alive, Abelard Ridenau remains a formidable threat."

"I don't want him dead yet."

Ferad's smaller arms quivered in involuntary response. "And if Phineas sends the Armies of the King to search? Ten thousand, twenty thousand men will take the field, with twice that number in reserve. Are you so sure you want to take that risk? Is revenge worth it?"

"Yes." The word was a hiss. "I heard him say I would never be King—not with Magic or without it—and I swear I'll make him live to see the day he regrets those words. I'll kill him with his own sword and I'll wear his own crown when I do it. But think of the confusion. No one knows whether he's dead or alive. There will have to be a regency. Roderic's just eighteen years old and he's surrounded by old men like Phineas, who've grown soft in the peace of the last twenty years or more. He's already run into trouble in Atland. What if the Senadors fail to support him? And there's my twin—"

"Are you so certain of Alexander?"

"We are one. I don't expect you to understand. From the beginning, we were one flesh. It was always so with us. Why do you think my father sent me to this godforsaken outpost, and him all the way to the Settle Islands? He thought to put the length of Meriga between us—"

"Timing will be all, my Prince." The Muten's voice was soft. "Don't forget the lessons Senadors like Owen Mortmain learned to their detriment—"

"My father had the witch-woman by his side then, did he not? She used her Magic for him. She even used it to ensure he'd have a son by his Queen when all of Meriga knew she was barren. If he can use the Magic to disinherit me, what's to stop me from using it against him?"

The Muten's face was inscrutable in the shadows. "And if you go to Atland, my Prince? What then?"

"It will enable me to take Roderic's measure. I've learned enough of the Magic for that. There's Reginald—I have good reason to think that he will be more than sympathetic for the right price. Once I'm there, I'll be able to gauge how much assistance he's likely to be. And then what would be more natural than that I accompany my little brother back to the ancestral home? When the Congress convenes, the Senadors—"

"Bah!" Ferad cut him off with a snort. "There is another way."

Amanander leaned across the desk. His eyes were like pools of water beneath a night sky, so black that light seemed trapped within their depths. "What are you talking about?"

"Intrigue is all well and fine, my Prince. And you may be successful—who am I to judge? But the West was beaten long ago, and even though certain factions may rise against the young Regent, there is no reason why any of them should support you over him. Let Roderic have the regency. For a time. There's something else you can discover in Ahga. You must find out Nydia Farhallen's fate."

"My father's witch? She's been dead for years."

"And you believe that?"

"He certainly had nothing to do with her since before Roderic was born. They say she used her Magic to help the Queen conceive a son, and then, consumed by jealousy, she took her own life. Personally, I think it killed her. That's possible, isn't it? Couldn't that have been the result of causing a life to come into existence?"

Ferad didn't answer.

"So you think Nydia may be alive?"

"There were many rumors concerning her fate, my Prince."

"I'm not so naive I believe those stories about Phineas getting a child on her. Do you?"

Ferad was silent. Finally he said, "She either died or disappeared before Roderic was born. Besides the Magic she had other gifts which made her invaluable to Abelard. They say he never looked at another woman from the day she walked into his court."

It was Amanander's turn to shrug. "He looked at Melisande Mortmain, didn't he? Long enough to get a son off her. And while Roderic may be grandson to the old Senador in Vada, I'd wager half this kingdom Owen'll not lift a finger to help."

"Forget Vada. Listen to me. You must find out if Nydia Farhallen bore a child. In all probability, that child would have been a daughter. And you must find that daughter and bring her to me."

"Why?"

"Nydia was a prescient. She could see the future. Why do you think Abelard was so successful? So long as he had her, none of his enemies could ever surprise him. But something must have happened between them. Abelard would never have sent her away voluntarily."

"So that makes it likely that she died."

"But if she did not—if she bore another's child—surely you know your father well enough to imagine his reaction to that?"

"Well, what if she did?"

"Listen, you fool. You play for high stakes at long odds, but there may be a way to even them. If you can find the daughter Nydia Farhallen bore, we will have the key to control the Magic—all Magic. We will have the power to do what even the men of Old Meriga couldn't with their toys and their machines and their technologies which very nearly destroyed the whole world.

"For the problem is not with the Magic. It is in the reaction caused by the Magic as the universe seeks to right itself. If we can find Nydia's daughter, our victory will be assured, for the child of a prescient is always an empath. By an empath's very nature, the imbalance caused by the Magic is corrected, even as it occurs. The empath need not know the Magic. One only need touch her. Think of what that would mean for both of us."

Amanander sat back. "So if we find this empath—"

"We will have the means to realize everything we've ever wanted. Anything the Magic can be made to do . . . anything you or I can think of will be within our grasp. We need but think it . . . I will drag those sanctimonious fools of the College to their knees, and you, my Prince—you will reign in Ahga more securely than any Ridenau before or since."

Amanander listened, eyes fastened on Ferad's face. An ugly flush darkened Ferad's deformed features. He had never seen the Muten so animated.

"But you must find her, Prince," Ferad went on in his whispery rasp. "I've worked all these years to discover another way to control the consequences of the Magic and it eludes me still. And now, with your father in our hands, every day which dawns is another risk."

"Then I have much work to do, if I'm to reach the point where I can use the Magic as I please."

"Are you suggesting I'm not to be trusted?"

"You would be content to be a tool, Ferad? I don't believe that. After all, tools break." There was something in the tone of Amanander's voice, something in the way he stared at the Muten, that made Ferad drop his eyes.

"I know you wish to use the Magic yourself, my Prince." Ferad's voice had a silky lilt. "But you realize it may take years before you know enough to challenge Roderic? Before this empath, if she exists, will do you any good?"

"Roderic will have more than enough to keep him busy. The country will be thrown into chaos. He can't be King—only Regent. And the pledges of allegiance are all sworn to my father. It's quite possible that more than a few of the Senadors can be persuaded that in order to keep the pledge they swore to my father, they should not support Roderic. And if he survives the Mutens, the Chiefs in the Settle Islands are always ripe for war against the mainlanders, and the Harleyriders will surely use my father's absence to try to settle old scores in Arkan. I do have time. If there's anything I've learned in all my years in this wasteland, it's how to wait."

"You like to think of yourself as patient, my Prince. But I

still say this move against the King was precipitous and may in the end prove our undoing. When will you leave for Atland?"

"One week."

"You must not linger in Atland long. You must go to Ahga as quickly as you can. I will see that my brothers who support our cause give you information which will enable you to bring this rebellion to a speedy conclusion."

"Why not simply ask my father?"

The Muten's eyes darted to the shadowed corner. For the briefest moment, something like fear flickered across the twisted features. Then it was replaced by something else, something hard and cruel, and Amanander narrowed his eyes, suddenly wary. "You don't think that's wise, Ferad?"

Ferad shrugged with calculated indifference not lost on Amanander. "See for yourself, my Prince."

Amanander drew a deep breath and rose to his feet. Without taking his eyes off the Muten, he crossed to the door and paused. "Not coming?"

"As my Prince commands." Ferad gathered the folds of his robe around his shoulders and scuttled across the floor, his uneven gait the result of old injuries.

The door creaked as together they stepped into a dimly lit cell. The long form wrapped in a dark cloak stirred as their shadows fell across the battered cot. Amanander hesitated on the threshold.

"What do you want?"

The power of that voice, the ring of absolute authority, startled Amanander. No one ever questioned Abelard Ridenau and no one ever thwarted him. Involuntarily, Amanander stepped backward and collided with Ferad.

"I want to talk to you."

"YOU!" Abelard leaped into a sitting position, turning and twisting with a heavy clatter of chains.

"Welcome to Dlas, Dad."

"And what do you think you'll get from me?"

Even in captivity, stripped of weapons and every friend, Abelard's vitality was palpable. Amanander forced himself to step closer.

"Right now I want information."

"If you think to force me to make you heir . . ."

Amanander laughed. "That's an old story, Dad, and one told too long ago. I've no interest in being your heir."

"You'll never reign in Ahga." Anger simmered through the King's voice like summer heat. "Nydia said—"

"Nydia. Nydia Farhallen. Your witch. Yes, let's talk about her."

"What about Nydia?"

Amanander thought he detected a subtle change in tone, a suspicious wariness that made him confident he had hit a nerve. "Is there a child?"

"No."

Across the dusty space the two men stared, black eyes locked on blue, and Amanander cocked one brow. "I think you're lying."

"Really?"

Amanander forced himself to think clearly. "Ferad?"

"My Prince?"

"Get it out of him."

In the gloom, Abelard raised his head, and Ferad gasped. "Fool! You would use the Magic with no thought at all—you could bring the roof down upon us."

"Then scurry back to your lair, Ferad," Amanander spat. "I'll try."

He heard the rustle of Ferad's robes over the broken tiles and drew a deep breath, sucking the stale air of the cavern into his lungs. He placed his fingertips lightly together and shut his eyes.

Once again, he heard Ferad's rasping instructions. "See in your mind how each equation builds upon the one before it—

comprehension of the greatest is dependent upon the comprehension of the least. Hold fast to that understanding—"

As if from very far away, Amanander heard Abelard's snorted, "What dumbshow is this?"

Amanander ignored his father. His breathing quickened imperceptibly, and in his throat a pulse beat a rapid tatoo. Beads of sweat threaded his forehead, and a deeper flush rose up his throat. The air within the cavern seemed to thicken, and the shadows darkened. Amanander muttered, shut his eyes once more, groping with his mind for the way to penetrate the defenses of Abelard's will, as a single drop of sweat crept down his cheek.

The air heated within the chamber as Amanander built the equations, each upon the next, stripping the guise of solidity from the form of reality, until he reached the place where conscious thought had shape. With one mighty effort, he reached across his father's mind, intent upon finding the chink he was certain existed in armor even so zealously guarded. But the defenses of Abelard's mind, the force of Abelard's will, was like a wall, smoother than glass, slipperier than ice, harder than metal, and though Amanander hurled every ounce of strength he possessed against it, nothing changed.

"Stop!" cried a voice, the voice of his tutor, and Amanander broke away, dimly aware that within the chamber the temperature had risen to a nearly murderous degree. "You are not ready, my Prince . . . you will kill us all."

Wrenched from the equations, Amanander sagged and fell to his knees, while the room spun and tilted on a dizzy axis. Abelard laughed.

Amanander staggered to his feet and stumbled out of the room, Ferad following, Abelard's derision stinging in his ears, sweat pouring off his body.

Amanander shut the door of the cell against that awful noise, and shut his eyes, drawing deep gasping breaths until his pulse stopped pounding. "Let him laugh," he said when he could. "Let him laugh for now. But I tell you, Ferad, by the time I have finished with him, I will see him beg and cry and plead with me for what remains of his miserable life. And then, we'll see who laughs loudest."

Chapter Four

"I tell you, you're mistaken." Reginald raised the flagon of ale to his mouth and took a long swallow. He wiped his sleeve across his lips.

Amanander grimaced at the smacking noises his brother made and tried to ignore the heavy stench of sweat emanating from Reginald's clothes. He considered ignoring Reginald. But his brother, though Amanander flinched at calling him that, was nothing if not stubborn and persistent. Probably an indication of that peasant blood he'd got from his farm-girl mother. "And I assure you, Reginald, I am not." As he stretched his long legs in front of the fire, he made a mental note to tell his serving boy to polish his boots more carefully. The thinnest film of oil attracted the worst layer of dulling dust.

Reginald hefted his drink with a snort. "You mean to tell me that in all the months we've been fighting in this godforsaken wilderness, just as we need something—anything—to break these four-armed dogs—all of a sudden, you show up with information you say will change the tide of this campaign? Roderic might believe that explanation, but do you really expect me to believe you just stumbled upon this information on the way here? Just by luck?"

Amanander avoided looking at Reginald. There was too much about this stocky, ham-fisted brother with stubbled chin and lank, thinning hair hanging around his broad face that repulsed him. And he certainly did not intend to explain how he got his information or his reasons for wanting a speedy end to the campaign to Reginald. Not yet.

Instead, he rose and pulled the tent flap open wider. The damp night air blew some of Reginald's stench out into the mist. Fog swirled, obscuring almost everything except the black smudges of the nearby tents. Even sound was muted. It was a perfect night for a raid.

Thin lines of light shone from underneath the closest tent, where Roderic labored long into the night, awaiting Brand's return and the outcome of the foray which Amanander sincerely hoped would be the last of the entire campaign. But Roderic always kept late hours for one so young. At the thought of Roderic, safely cocooned with Brand and the loyal soldiers of the King's Guard, a line deepened between Amanander's brows. Ferad had been more correct than Amanander wanted to admit. This would not be easy.

He had not been prepared for the youth who had greeted him with such cool appraisal in his light grey-green eyes. It was not insolence, far from it. In fact, in council, Roderic spoke only seldom, deferring to all his brothers, in a manner which would have bordered on the obsequious had it been any less sincere. But there was something in the way he carried himself, something in the lift of his head and the set of his shoulders, that spoke louder than any words and which rasped like steel over slate across Amanander's nerves. It was the assurance which clung to Roderic like a cloak, the certainty that he indeed was the heir of Meriga, and that, no matter how much more competent the others were, the land they fought to preserve was his; his and his alone. And even Reginald responded to this instinctively, while Amanander hung back and gritted his teeth.

Even now, while most in the camp slept, or took their ease, he knew that Roderic could be found poring over a map or a list of supplies, making endless calculations, studying the notes his scribe made from the reports of the scouts. It was unnatural that one so young should be so diligent. And it angered Amanander, for it confirmed his growing realization that young though Roderic might be, he would very shortly be a formidable foe. He had even tried, once or twice, to find a way into the youth's mind, as Ferad had taught him, but Roderic was so focused, and so intent, that such a thing had proven impossible.

He had considered killing Roderic outright, though he was so completely surrounded by guards, and so constantly in the company of Brand, or one of his lieutenants, that such an opportunity never arose. Besides, a murder would only rouse the Congress, and he could not yet afford to discount the Senadors' wrath. So Amanander had quickly come to the conclusion that Ferad's advice to let Roderic have the regency was sound. But forced to bide his time, that patience was most sorely tested, and he was determined that this foray into Atland would end as soon as possible. He had to get to Ahga and try to discover the fate of Abelard's witch.

But Reginald was speaking, and Amanander let the tent flap fall shut. " . . . if this fails?"

Amanander turned back with a thin smile. "It won't."

Shouts coming from the perimeter of the camp awakened Roderic out of a sound sleep. It seemed that he had only just laid his head upon the pillow, but he opened his eyes to a grayish, predawn gloom, and the realization that the stub of the candle he had left burning in the crude stone cup had long ago smoked away.

Months of campaigning had taught him to come instantly alert, and with one hand he reached for the boots beneath his cot, and with the other for the sword which hung on a hook just within his grasp.

"Lord Prince!" The guard who burst into the tent made only

the briefest bow and gestured wildly into the dawn. "The Muten leader—we have him—"

"What? Already?" Roderic did not quite believe what he thought he heard. He pulled his boots on and strightened his tunic. The guard did not have time to reply, for Brand's tall shape loomed in the opening.

He pushed past the guard, who snapped to attention and saluted. "Let's go, Roderic."

"Is it possible you found—" He paused over the foreign name. The early morning air was thick with dampness. Mist swirled around their ankles, and the breeze which ruffled his hair did not cool.

"Ebram-taw," Brand answered shortly. "We got him. The information Aman gave us was right. We brought him in with about thirty of his fellows. It looks as though our luck has finally turned."

Brand stepped aside and held open the flap of the command tent, allowing Roderic to pass in front of him. The tallow lamps added to the rank smell of unwashed men, horses, and sour ale. As Roderic's eyes adjusted to the light, he saw Reginald and Amanander already there, in chairs on the periphery.

Roderic sat down behind the rough wooden table which served as a desk as well as a council table. Usually he found Amanander's presence unnerving, but he was so excited at the prospect of this confrontation, he forgot him. He gripped the arms of the chair as the Muten was dragged in, heavy chains dangling from its wrists.

The men-at-arms threw him on his knees. He lay unmoving on the dirt floor and met Roderic's eyes unblinking. No one spoke for what seemed a long time.

Finally, his heart thudding in his chest, in a voice he hoped did not quiver, Roderic said, "Bring a chair for our guest."

The Muten spat in the dirt before the table when he was seated.

Roderic startled back by reflex. It was the first chance he'd had to observe an adult Muten so closely. His powerful primary arms were bound before him, the heavy steel chains glinting in the shadowy half-light. His small secondary arms were folded firmly across his chest, and Roderic was reminded that in the ruling families, these appendages were fully functional. The tiny hands were clenched in defiant fists. His skin was the terra-cotta color of raw clay, and his eyes were black and glared with unconcealed hatred. The third eye, above and centered between the other two, seemed to stare past and through him.

Involuntarily, Roderic shuddered. It was said that with that third eye, the Mutens could look into a man's soul and suck it out. He wore only leather trousers, and black, soft skin boots. His hair was long and gray, and his face was marked in deep lines cut into swirls and triangles on his cheeks.

Brand leaned down, spoke close into his brother's ear. "Dad knew this one well. He's the leader of the whole Southern Alliance of Tribes. I knew him as soon as I saw him, even though it's been a dozen years since he was brought before the King."

Roderic cocked his head. "So you are known to my father."

The Muten spat again.

One of the men-at-arms raised the butt of his spear and would have struck the Muten, but Roderic stopped him with a wave of his hand. "How long must we continue this, Ebramtaw?"

"Your peace is not ours." His voice was low and deep, and his accent fractured the words, but Roderic understood his speech.

"I will not debate you. Take this message back to your brethren. Either lay down your spears and swords by daybreak tomorrow, or—"

"You are a boy. We do not deal with children. Where is the one who calls himself King of all Meriga?"

"My father's of no concern to you. I am Prince of Meriga, and his armies are mine."

"Claim all the armies you wish. We are the Children of the Magic, and we do not call your father King."

"You lie, Ebram-taw." Brand spoke up. "A dozen years ago, the King of Meriga received your tribute and your pledge, and you promised not to raise arms against your neighbors or your King."

"We paid tribute that our women not be slaughtered."

"You have broken your pledge."

"We made no pledge."

"You lying, four-armed louse." Reginald swaggered into the center of the tent, thumbs hooked in his belt. The Muten flinched, but one small arm flailed out. Reginald caught it and gave it a cruel twist.

"Hold, Reginald." Roderic held up one hand.

Reginald turned to face his brother. "Nothing's to be gained from speaking with this vermin, Lord Prince. Let my men beat the spirit out of it. It's the only thing it understands."

Roderic looked from his sweating, red-faced brother to the Muten who sat as still as the thick air in the tent. "I'll consider that. But I must speak to this—this person before I decide."

Reginald's mouth tightened. "As you say." He stumped out of the tent, hand clenched on the hilt of his dagger.

Roderic watched him go, then looked at the Muten. "Shall we have peace?"

"There can be no peace so long as the son of the Ridenau sits in Alant-Jorja. You stumble in the dark, and see not with your two blind eyes. You take our land, you burn our crops so that our children starve and yours grow fat. You invade our sacred places, bring your herds to foul our sacred ground. You are people without souls or spirit. You are already dead."

Roderic leaned forward. He wanted desperately to understand this Muten, to end the fighting rather than drag the campaign on. The latest dispatch from Phineas set the date of the

Convening for the first day of Prill, and the beginning of the spring rains made for miserable conditions. "We Ridenaus brought peace—"

"You know your lessons well."

"I have no wish to slaughter your people, Ebram-taw. Could you not tell your brethren—"

"I am not your messenger. We are not your slaves. We are the Children of the Magic."

"Then use the Magic against us, Child of the Old Magic." Amanander purred from the shadows, and the hair on the back of Roderic's neck rose.

The Muten looked in the direction of the sound, and Roderic had the unnerving thought that he could see Amanander in the darkness. Ebram-taw answered so quietly, Roderic had to strain to hear him. "The Magic must not be used—"

"Must not?" Amanander flowed like a shadow into the center of the tent. "You cannot use it, though your lives might depend upon it." He laughed, low and cruel. "Go back to your warrens."

The Muten drew himself up, and the muscles of his arms and chest strained against his bonds. He sat on the crude camp stool as proudly as the King upon the throne of Meriga. "We keep the memories—"

"But can your memories keep us from your walls?"

Roderic was confused and disturbed by Amanander's words. There was an undertone, a meaning that Roderic could not quite grasp. "Do you know the Magic?" he asked the Muten curiously.

Amanander stood behind the Muten like a predator poised for the kill. "It's not enough to know it, is it, Ebram-taw? One must understand it."

"That is not for such as you to know."

"And not for such as you, either. For not one among your warriors can raise the smallest flame, shift the smallest pebble, bend the thinnest steel." He clapped the Muten's shoulder in a parody of comraderie, and even Roderic winced.

"Roderic—Brand—" Reginald burst into the tent. "To arms—the camp's attacked!" Blood ran from a wound on his leg. Brand reacted instantly. He drew his sword and ran from the tent shouting orders, with Reginald at his heels.

Outside, soldiers ran past the open flaps, and Roderic heard the clash of metal and the thunk of arrows and spears. The guards snapped to attention as he stood up.

"Stay here. Guard the prisoner." He beckoned to Amanander. "Come." As they reached the opening, Roderic hesitated and stepped aside.

Amanander smiled. "Always cover your back, little brother. Always."

Then they were in the midst of the confusion. Men ran past, hastily buckling on leather armor, unsheathing swords, or slinging quivers over their shoulders.

Black smoke billowed from tents set afire. Roderic stopped short and tried to assess the situation. Horses screamed, frightened by the fire, and the sergeants of the regiments frantically tried to rally their men into some semblance of order. His eyes watered from the smoke, and he coughed. In that instant, three white-painted Mutens attacked.

Roderic swung his broadsword blindly, dodging the vicious slash of the long razor-edged spears. One whistled through the air near his head. He ducked and fell to one knee, wondering briefly where Amanander was. His broadsword connected with legs, and a Muten fell screaming as the tendons were severed.

He whirled around and sliced his backstroke across another's midsection. As another puff of smoke blinded him, he heard Brand cry: "Hold!"

Roderic crouched, warily. A razor spear sang through the air. He blocked it, and with a swift motion, brought the Muten to its knees, the edge of his sword held against its throat. The razor spear clattered to the ground.

"Well done, Roderic." Brand materialized out of the hazy smoke, wiping his hands on his bloody tunic.

"Is it over?"

"Of course. They must have been trying to rescue Ebram-taw. I don't know what possessed them to try it—I suppose they thought to take us unawares."

"How many are still alive?" Roderic prodded the Muten with the flat of his sword as two guards grabbed it by the arms and jerked it up roughly. Behind the mask of paint, its three eyes stared fixedly, its feet twisting as they dragged it away.

"Lord Prince." One of the lieutenants saluted. "Captain."

"Well?" asked Brand.

"Thirty-five of ours dead. Twenty-three injured. One horse trampled."

"And them?" Roderic wiped the blood from his blade.

"It was just a small party by their standards, Lord Prince. Forty dead. Sixteen more captives."

"Where are they?"

"We've put them in the pen with the others, Lord Prince."

Slowly Roderic drew a deep breath. The light was no longer gray; through the mist, the flat red disc of the sun shone just above the tents. Red like the color of the blood on the weeds. He tried to ignore that thought and looked at the lieutenant. Blood stained his uniform, and a thin slash along his cheek seeped red droplets down his unshaven face like slow rain. Roderic stared, fascinated.

Time seemed to slow, drag, and he turned to look at Brand with a puzzled look on his face. But Brand was staring in the other direction, and Roderic panicked. He felt a desperate urge to regain his self-control. And then, as though something deep within had been released, some savage instinct he had only felt in battle or at the hunt, uncoiled itself, and his blood began to burn.

"Bring them here," he said through clenched teeth and thickened tongue. A kind of slow fire seeped through his veins, one that sparked and flared at the prospect of the prisoners, bound and at his bidding. "And gather the men." His voice sounded the same, but the words were heavy with threat.

He looked up to see Brand frowning. "What are you planning, Roderic?"

He avoided Brand's gaze, and as he looked away, he saw Amanander watching from the side of the tent. His dark eyes were hooded, but his mouth was curved in a thin smile, and in the weird light of the ruddy sun, his lips were coppery red. His hand curved over and around the hilt of his dagger, caressing it like a woman's flesh.

Roderic felt the sudden urge to smile back. "Maybe Reginald's right," he said to Brand. "Maybe these animals do understand only one thing. I'd like to find out." He gave Brand a smile that matched Amanander's. "Bring out the prisoner," he barked to the guards in the tent.

When the troops had crowded around the smaller circle of captives, Roderic stood with Ebram-taw in the center, who still stood straight and unbowed. "Well, Ebram-taw, I asked you before, I ask you again. Shall we have peace? Or shall your kind be wiped out?"

The Muten did not answer. Roderic caught a glimpse of the wary frown on Brand's face, but before it could register, that sight was replaced by Amanander's enigmatic smile. He signaled to two of the soldiers. One of the Muten captives was dragged out into the center. "Peace?" Roderic asked once more.

Again, the Muten did not speak. Without another word, Roderic signaled to the guards.

They raised their blades and began.

It seemed to him that they knew exactly what he wanted, although he couldn't remember giving the order. But that had to be impossible, he thought, in some rational recess of his mind that recoiled at the sight unfolding before him. He knew that though Brand stood shocked and horrified, his brother did not dare countermand his orders. Besides the urgent bloodthirst, there was a heady sense of his own power. It was like a ritual, a dance, a ceremony, for as each hacked and flayed and ruined body was dragged away, Roderic turned to Ebram-taw and put the question to him once again. "Peace?"

And at each silence, Roderic gave again the signal, and another wretch was thrown in the red-brown mire which soon was ankle deep. Finally, when only four remained alive, Ebram-taw, agony on his face and sweat pouring from his skin, shouted "Stop!"

Roderic shook his head. He felt dazed, drunk, as though the blood had satiated every appetite and left him sodden, stupid. The silence thickened. It seemed to be a tangible thing, one that crept and swayed with a life all its own, and Roderic knew that Amanander stood just beyond the inner circle. Something in him recoiled at the realization, and something else, some sense that this reaction was the true one, the right one, threw off the heavy, sickening feeling like a shroud. It seemed that the fog cleared then, though the mist was still as thick as ever, and the hot scent of the carnage before him was suffocating.

"Peace?" he asked slowly, wonderingly.

Ebram-taw, shoulders slumped, spoke in a hoarse and ragged voice. "Peace. I cannot kill my son."

Chapter Five

On a cold day at the beginning of March, Roderic left Atland garrison, riding beside his brothers Brand and Amanander at the head of the weary army. Reginald, as the commander of the garrison, stayed behind, charged with overseeing that the terms of the peace were honored. Roderic was only too glad to turn his back on Atland at last.

He preferred not to think about that terrible day when he had forced Ebram-taw to accept his offer of peace. The knowledge that he was capable of such cruelty was a greater burden than any other he contemplated on that long ride across the stark landscape.

He was silent and listless for the most part on the journey across the Pulatchian Mountains. He avoided Amanander's company altogether; there was something in Amanander's expression when their eyes met which reminded Roderic of the bloodlust he had felt when he had ordered the soldiers to do their terrible work. He knew that Brand watched him with concern. But he did not want to know what his brothers thought of him, and in his worst moments, he wondered what the people who had known him all of his life would think of him: his tutor, Garrick, who had taught him that honor was at least as important as strategy; Brand's wife, Jaboa, who had taught him that the weaker were to be treated with compassion, who had treated him like a son. He wondered what the scullions and stable boys would think, the ones who had been the playmates of his youth, from whom he had learned that birth is not the measure of a man's worth. And he wondered what Phineas would say.

Phineas—old and blind and lamed, who nonetheless was first among all his father's advisors, the one voice Abelard listened to before and after all the others, whom Abelard trusted as he trusted no one else. It had been thus for as long as Roderic could remember. Phineas never hesitated to say what he really thought. Phineas wasn't afraid of Abelard's wrath. What would he say to Abelard's heir, who had brought peace at the price of slaughter? What kind of prince—what kind of king—could he be?

And then there was Peregrine. He began to think of her more and more as the distance from Ahga gradually shortened. He remembered the first day she had caught his eye. He had championed one of the weakest of the scullions against the others, and he remembered the admiration he had seen in her eyes. But what would she think about this? He could imagine the disgust darkening her brown eyes, her full lips pursed in disdain. What sort of man would she think he was?

Once across the Pulatchians, riding almost due north, they followed the course of what had once been a mighty river, but now was nothing more than a trickle in the center of a deep gorge. The weather held clear, the spring promised to be mild, but nothing could lift the weight which seemed to hang like a brick around his neck. The villages they passed through were few, comprised only of a few rude shacks built by baked earth, with roofs of ancient metal, scoured bare by the ever whining wind.

Roderic remembered that his history tutor had taught him that before the Armageddon—before the Magic-users of Old Meriga had discovered the Magic and nearly destroyed everything in their attempts to make it work—once the Arkan Plains were vast fields, where wheat and corn grew from horizon to horizon in all directions, and the whole world fed on the bread of Meriga. Roderic found that hard to believe. The land which lay around him, stretching on for miles, was a wasteland of stunted, wind-whipped trees, the earth itself worn down in many places to polished bedrock. Beside the ancient highways, twisted pieces of corroding metal lay like skeletons along the road. Roderic shuddered at the ruin. How could the men of Old Meriga have allowed such a terrible thing as the Magic to be used? Had they no idea of the cost?

In the villages, ragged children stood in doorways, with dirty fingers in mouths full of rotted teeth. At the first such place they stopped, Roderic was so horrified by their plight that he ordered the food and blankets be shared with the villagers.

In a dry voice, Brand remarked that if the Prince intended to distribute goods at every place they passed, they would have nothing left for themselves for the long march back to Ahga.

Frustrated by the truth of Brand's observations, feeling helpless, Roderic dictated orders to his scribe for the relief of the villagers to be sent on to Ahga.

The scribe said nothing as he penned the Prince's words, though he looked at him with something like pity when Roderic finished.

"What is it?" Roderic picked up the pen the scribe offered.

The man only pushed the paper closer and said nothing.

"You look as if you want to say something. Well, speak, Henrode. Do you think I'm wrong?"

"Lord Prince, it is not for me to question your orders. It is not for me to offer counsel or advice."

"I'm not asking for either. Just say what you have on your tongue."

"Do you think there is more misery here, Lord Prince, than elsewhere in Meriga? There are those who live in the shadow of the walls of Ahga who have not much more than these. Will you order them fed as well? You will bankrupt the treasury and exhaust our food stores."

"But what else can I do? These people are my father's subjects. They look to me for protection. How can I leave them in such misery, without hope?"

"The Ridenaus never sought to alleviate people's suffering. That would be impossible. You fulfill your obligation if you preserve the peace of this land. That is your task, Lord Prince. Not to feed the hungry or clothe the naked. If you could rid these lands of the Outlaw Harleys, they might some day be able to provide for themselves. But there is no point in you giving them things which others will only take away."

In disgust, Roderic tore up the parchment and reached for his cloak. Outside, night had fallen, and in the black sky, countless stars glittered. Heaven itself is more populated than this lifeless land, he thought as he walked the perimeter of the camp, watching the fires of his men flicker in the dark.

Beyond the camp, nothing moved. A sentry came to attention and raised his spear. "Who's there?"

"The Prince Regent."

"Your pardon, Lord Prince," the guard answered, but his spear remained high until Roderic came closer and pushed the hood back from his face.

Roderic stood within the circle of the watchfire and held his hands over the flames. "It's cold tonight."

"Indeed it is, Lord Prince." The sentry lowered the spear and leaned upon it. "What're you doing out on a night like this, when you could be warm inside your tent?"

"It's not so warm inside. Besides, I've never seen a land like this."

"Nor did you ever want to, I bet."

"It's so empty." Roderic raised his hood and tucked the ends firmly around his neck.

"Empty?" The grizzled sentry snorted. "So much blood's been spilled on these plains, I wonder the old river don't run red with it. This is my twenty-seventh year in the army, Lord Prince, and I've spent most of them in places much like this."

"It's not the place I'd choose to be."

"This is better than some. Farther south, this turns into swamp, and you've no idea of what misery is until you spend a night breathing the stink from the poison pits. The mists hang in the air, and deeper in the desert, the beastworms hunt at night. Believe me, Lord Prince, cold and empty is not so bad."

Roderic nodded and continued on his way. The few shacks which made up the village were almost indistinguishable in the starlight from the rocks piled along the ancient gorge. From the low black shapes no light shone, no smoke issued, and nothing marked it as a place of human habitation. As Roderic stood and watched, a cry rose out of the dark, high and wailing, the sound giving voice to all the misery of that wretched place. It made the hair at the back of his neck stand up as gooseflesh rippled down his arms. Then, as suddenly as it began, it stopped, and the night was once more quiet under the silent stars.

Was it not for these that the Ridenau Kings had striven to unite the Estates of Meriga? he wondered. His father and Garrick and all his tutors had stressed repeatedly that a united Meriga was a stronger Meriga, a Meriga at peace. And yet what was the good of that peace, if it were only for the strong? A united realm was his birthright—Abelard had charged him over and over again to keep the kingdom whole. And yet, what was it that Phineas had said, one day, as Roderic had watched his father preside over the Court of Appeals? *"It is a sacred trust,"* the old man had said from where he lay, propped upon pillows on his litter on the floor. *"A sacred trust between you and your people, as sure a pledge-bond as any made between the King and the Congress."* Roderic looked out over the bleak landscape. He was, he supposed, as well prepared as his father could have made him for the task at hand. But what about this other trust, he wondered, this other bond, unspoken and unacknowledged by most? He had the unsettling feeling that little had prepared him for that.

He started to find a tall, dark shape standing by his side, well-wrapped against the weather.

"Sleepless night?" Brand's voice was muffled almost beyond recognition by the depths of the hood which covered most of his face.

"Brand." Roderic wondered why he felt so relieved to realize it was his oldest brother who stood beside him in the dark. "What are you doing out here?"

"Looking for you. A messenger came in from Ahga a few minutes ago."

"What now?" Beneath his cloak, his shoulders tensed involuntarily.

"The Senadors are beginning to arrive at the Convening. Let's walk a bit, shall we?" For a few minutes Brand said nothing. "We haven't had much chance to talk, you and I. Not since Amanander arrived." The soil crunched beneath their feet, brittle as old bones, and Roderic waited for his brother to continue. "Now that he's in his tent there're things I thought at first that Phineas should tell you—but I don't think it's wise to wait. The Convening is scheduled for the first day of Prill. Most of the Senadors are expected, and at this pace, we'll get there just in time. But I think you should know that Amanander may make a bid for the throne—and Alexander will probably support him."

"Why?"

"Because many years ago, long before you were born, Dad was contracted to marry a woman named Rabica Onrada—who died giving birth to the twins."

"But Dad never married her?"

"In some of the estates, and this is the sticking point, a contracted marriage is as legitimate as an actual marriage. If the Senadors who have similar laws rally around Amanander—"

"So there may be a fight when we get back to Ahga?"

Brand nodded. "If they all honor the oaths they swore when Dad named you his heir shortly after you were born, you should be recognized as Regent with no discussion, no question. But I want to warn you that might not be the case. And then there's Phillip."

Roderic paused and searched his brother's face. "You don't trust Phillip either?"

"Dad has seven sons—all older than you. It was a long time before you were born and Dad named you his heir. It would have been only natural for the others to have hopes."

"Not you."

Brand's face relaxed into a smile. "No. Not me. My mother was a kitchen maid—I've risen higher than I ever expected. But Amanander and Alexander, their mother was the daughter of a landed Senador. And Phillip—Dad married him off to old Jarone of Nourk's daughter—because his mother, too, was noble, the daughter of some Mayher. Some thought Dad should name Phillip his heir."

"What about the others? Reginald? Everard and Vere?"

"Vere ran off years ago. I doubt Dad even knows where he is. He might even be dead. Everard—his mother's family was well entrenched in the Dirondac Mountains across the North Sea. He has holdings there, and they're like the Pulatchian Highlanders, not much given to seeking outside company. As for Reginald—" Brand shook his head. Even beneath the shadow of his hood, Roderic could see that Brand's mouth was twisted in a bitter line. "It comes down to one thing. Dad had too many sons. The One knows he did the best he could by all of us—put me in the Guards, married Phillip to Nourk's daughter, put Alexander up in Spogan, Reginald in Atland. Everard's happy in the North Country. As for Vere, who knows? But—" Abruptly, Brand sighed. "I'm only telling you what I think you ought to know."

"And Amanander?"

Brand glanced over his shoulder. "I don't trust him. He's like a blade too well oiled; it gleams nicely, but turns too easily in your hand. I don't believe the story he fed us in Atland—that on his way to us, he captured a Muten war party who told him Ebram-taw's position, and then very conveniently escaped."

"Then how else could he possibly have known—"

"Just where to look for Ebram-taw? I shudder to think of the possibilities. But it all seemed just too convenient. We wanted, and needed, a speedy end to this rebellion. Amanander arrives and hands it to us on a platter." Brand shook his head. "It's almost as if he wanted to get to Ahga as quickly as we did, though why, I cannot say. He's said nothing to me to indicate that he might make a bid for the throne—but then, he'd be foolish if he did. But thirty years with men under extreme conditions have taught me to trust my instincts—and they tell me not to trust Amanander."

"There's nothing we can do at this point."

"No. But I thought you should know what you're walking into." A cold blast of air sliced through their cloaks and Brand shivered. "You'd better try to sleep. Good night."

He turned away, then stopped when Roderic spoke once more. "Brand. Any word of Dad?"

The expression on Brand's face reminded Roderic inexplicably of the King. Brand shook his head once more. "No. Nothing. Get some sleep. We have a long way to travel tomorrow."

He gave Roderic the briefest bow. Roderic watched him go, then followed, picking his way through the maze of men and supplies and animals.

And that night he dreamed. It seemed as if he walked in a gray silence through the shadowed halls of Ahga, beneath high-vaulted ceilings which in his dream stretched away into swirling mists. The corridors were full of gaunt, hollow-eyed people who stared in mute misery as he passed. The weight of centuries seemed to hang in the air, and yet he had the sense of enormous strength in the soaring walls, the firm foundations which had stood unshaken through the days of the Armageddon and all the years since. He wandered aimlessly, and yet he did not stop or pause, yet walked on, as though his feet had a will and a purpose of their own.

At last, he stood before the door of the King's bedchamber, a room which customarily was guarded. But the soldiers were not there to challenge him, and so he opened the heavy door and stepped inside.

The great chamber was dark. The King's bed, big enough for three men and their women, was covered in sheets, the heavy drapes drawn against the windows. The smell of dust was thick in the cold air. The fireplace, so high a man could stand in it, was empty, the costly tiles scrubbed clean. Above the bed, the jewels in the crest of the Ridenau Kings looked like common stones plucked from a riverbed, and even the gold lettering looked dull in the gloom. The place was like a tomb. And then he noticed a thin line of light under the door which led into the King's private study. He opened the door and stepped inside.

A fire burned brightly, and Abelard stood beside the hearth. "Dad!" Roderic cried.

The King smiled and held out his arms. Roderic noticed, in the curious detached way of dreams, that one arm ended in a stump, from which the flesh hung in red strands and white bone gleamed wetly. But he did not flinch from the King's embrace. "Dad, what happened to you?"

Abelard shook his head.

"When are you coming back?"

Abelard's smile changed from one of welcome to one of sadness.

"Oh," said Roderic. "You can't come back."

The King shook his head again.

"I miss you, Dad."

In the dream, Abelard was very tall. He folded Roderic in his arms as if Roderic were once again a small boy. Roderic felt the tremendous strength in his father's muscles. For a moment, he let himself relax in that embrace, and then the King pulled back. With a sweep of his remaining hand, he indicated the room, the wide desk covered with rolled parchments and dispatches, the framed maps of every corner of Meriga which hung on the walls. He drew Roderic out into the bedroom, and with another motion, pointed to the crest hanging over the bed. His father's broadsword, the bloodred stones shimmering in the unnatural light, hung in its scabbard over the crest. It was the sword his father carried when he rode to war.

Despite the darkness, Roderic could see the words on the crest as clearly as though the sun shone full upon them: *Faith shall finish what hope begins.* The King swung him around so that they faced each other. It seemed in that moment Roderic grew taller, so that he and his father were equal in height. Abelard's eyes seemed to burn into his brain, and the words on the crest echoed through his mind, as though Abelard had spoken them aloud. *Remember,* his father seemed to say. *Faith. Hope. In this, find your strength.*

Roderic smiled, though he could feel tears welling in his eyes. "I'll never forget you, Dad."

The King nodded gravely, sadly, and pointed to the door with the stump of his wounded arm.

Roderic woke up on the low camp cot. The light was gray, and the smell of morning was in the air. He dressed quickly and went outside. The camp was just beginning to stir. He watched for a moment—the men emerging from their tents, the occasional whicker of the horses as they were fed and watered. The smell of breakfast cooking wafted by on the slow breeze.

Faith and hope. Images of the dying Mutens, the starving children, clung to him like a miasma that even the new day could not lift. Such suffering made a mockery of platitudes.

What did any of these people believe in, what could any of the Mutens hope for? He knew what his father believed in—the sanctity of the pledge-bond, the indivisibility of the Union. Was that enough? he wondered. Or were they only faded words on a tarnished shield? He remembered the information which Brand had given him the night before and wondered if all the faith and hope in Meriga would indeed be enough for the task which lay ahead.

Chapter Six

"There now, Tavvy." Jesselyn Ridenau tucked the worn quilt up to her sister's chin, and patted Tavia's tear-streaked face. "You have a little sleep, and tonight, Everard will be here. And he always brings you a present."

The woman in the bed turned on her side and shut her eyes like an obedient child, despite the fact that she was more than forty. Jesselyn straightened with a sigh and met the eyes of the nurse who stood beside the bed on the other side.

"I'm sorry to have called you away from the infirmary, Rever'd Lady, but when she gets like that, there's no managing her."

Jesselyn nodded and slowly caressed Tavia's smooth cheek with her own work-worn hand. She touched her sister's long dark braids, which were streaked with gray. "You did right. I had to come back here anyway, just to make certain everything's ready for tonight." She glanced around the room which, though small and shabby, was as cheerful as she could make it. The curtains at the narrow window were bright yellow, tied back with blue ribbons, and the floor of scrubbed pine planks was covered with a rug braided out of scraps as colorful as they were varied. Dried flowers bloomed in an earthenware pitcher on the table which stood beside an empty cradle. "If there's nothing more, I'll leave you with her while she sleeps. She won't wake now for several hours."

The nurse nodded and picked up a woven basket spilling over with mending. Jesselyn shut the rickety door softly and stepped into the low-ceilinged hallway of what had been her home for the better part of her life in these eastern foothills of the Okcono Mountains. She leaned back against the white-washed wall and pushed a wayward strand of fine brown hair out of her eyes. She was more than tired—she was exhausted. She was barely thirty and felt sixty. There was so much to do between now and the time Everard was expected. She had no idea why he was coming, though she supposed it had something to do with her father's disappearance, which she had heard about just a week or so ago from a traveling band of laborers who followed the seasons in search of work. But her fatigue was not just a result of her brother's anticipated visit. Every day was like this—as more and more refugees streamed up from the South, and the sick and the old and the poor found their way to her door. Most of the time all they found was an easier death. *For the harvest is plenteous, but the laborers are few.* The old words of the ancient Scripture ran through her mind unbidden, as though by reflex. She smiled a little to herself. Renegade priest and excommunicant she might be, but she still knew her Scripture.

"Rever'd Lady?"

The voice, so soft that it might have gone unheard by any other ear, startled Jesselyn. The Muten woman stood hesitantly in the door as if she expected to be rebuffed, her face shadowed by the worn scarf she used to hide the ugly scars of wounds inflicted in childhood. Although Jesselyn accepted her story without question, and welcomed the woman as she did all who came to her, nevertheless she often felt inexplicably uneasy in the woman's presence. Jesselyn forced herself to speak as gently as she could. "Yes, Sera? Has my brother come?"

"No, 'm. We've found one of the Children in the wood—he's in a bad way. Could you come to the infirmary?"

At once, Jesselyn forgot any misgivings about the woman and automatically gathered the patched skirts of her worn clerical dress about her. "A bad way? Has he been hurt?"

"No, 'm. They said it looked like the purple sickness—" Before the words were even out of Sera's mouth, Jesselyn was out the door and running along the beaten dirt path toward the infirmary, completely disregarding the bitter March wind. There was no disease among the Muten population so deadly or so virulent. It was said that one could sit down to his dinner and be dead before he raised his hand to his mouth. If this truly were the purple sickness, the sufferer must be quarantined as quickly as possible, and it was dangerous for the Muten attendants to even so much as breathe the same air. "Mharri, Chas'n," she called as she stepped over the threshold of the long white building nestled among a stand of sheltering pines.

It was over. She knew as soon as she saw the looks on the faces of the Muten attendants. They had arranged themselves as far away as possible from the door of the inner chamber where the newcomer had been placed. The occupants of the low white cots stared up at her with frightened eyes. There was a sweetish smell in the air.

The Muten lay on the white bed, still and unmoving. Clearly he had died in agony, his back twisted and bowed in a convulsive rictus, his skin marred by blotchy purplish lesions from which red-tinged mucus still dribbled. Dark blood spooled down his chin from a corner of his mouth. Both of his secondary arms were splayed outward, his primary arms clenched in fists on his chest. Sighing, she leaned against the door frame as her two human attendants peered around her.

"There was nothing you could have done for him, Rever'd

Lady," whispered Mharri, her pale eyes in her ancient face soft with sympathy.

"No." The old woman was right. But why did she feel so defeated, as though this were one more burden laid across her shoulders, a burden which she had no way to bear? She looked around the cool white room. "The body will have to be burned—everything he touched will have to be burned." As she was speaking, she heard a new commotion outside—the sound of pounding hooves and eager shouts of greeting. Everard had come.

"Rever'd Lady?" One of the Mutens across the room gestured toward the water buckets. "Our supplies of soap and clean linen are very low. If we must see everything is washed, is it possible—"

"Of course. I'll see more are sent over from the laundry." Suddenly she felt very weary. There was so much to do, and so few to do it. "Only humans handle the body, do you understand?" She spoke more harshly than she intended, and instantly she regretted it. "I'm sorry," she said to no one in particular. "I'll be back to say the rites after I've seen my brother."

Later, as the sun slipped like a red disk behind the rounded western hills, Jesselyn stood within the circle of the firelight, and recited the ancient burial rites of the Muten tribes in a language liquid with vowels and meaning. The wind-whipped flames leaped high in all directions, obscuring the dark shape of the funeral pyre at the center.

Throughout the ceremony, she was conscious of Everard's reassuring bulk beside her, his very presence comforting in a way the old words could never be. As she lowered her arms from the final blessing, Everard shifted on his feet. He was a big man; beside him the Mutens were dwarfed and she herself felt child-sized. Of all her many brothers and sisters, only Everard contacted her. Her work among the poorest and the lowliest of the Mutens had made her a pariah among her own people. Abruptly she realized she had no idea what the reason for his visit was, or where he might be going. He had come provisioned for a long trip. As the crowd slowly dispersed, he tilted her chin up. "You look tired, Jessie," he said, breaking the silence.

She shrugged. "A lot has happened lately—refugees of the rebellion arrive every day from the South, sometimes as many as two or three dozen. It must be horrible down in Atland."

There was another long silence, and finally Everard plucked at her sleeve. "Come. A cup of hot spiced cider will do you good."

"I'm sorry. We've no spices—I traded the last of them to the Mayher of Bartertown to buy us a little peace."

"I brought you more. And don't worry—that lordling will not trouble you again. I encountered his minions on my way here, much to their regret." He put his arm around her shoulder and pressed her close to his side, and for a while she stood content. At last she drew away and managed a smile in the flickering light.

"Spiced cider sounds good."

As they turned to go, Mharri approached, her back bent beneath the ragged shawl she wore against the evening chill. "Rever'd Lady, great lord."

"What is it?" asked Jesselyn, preparing to ask the woman to wait until the morning. Out of the corner of her eye, she thought she saw Sera pause in the shadows, just beyond the periphery of the light.

"There's been no chance to give you this, Rever'd Lady. But the poor soul—he had this in a pouch around his neck. He was clutching it when he died. We found it when we carried him out to the pyre. It looks like the sort of thing the Children use for their messages." Hesitantly, she held out a hide-bound package, greasy and worn from much handling.

"Have any of the Children touched this?" asked Jesselyn sharply.

"No, Rever'd Lady. But before it was burnt, we thought you'd better have it. It does look as if it's come a long way."

Jesselyn nodded and took the package. "That would explain who the poor wretch was." She turned her face up to Everard. "Some messenger—bringing this to one of the Northern tribes, no doubt. We'll have a look and perhaps you'll see it gets to wherever it was to go."

Everard was like a mother hen, Jesselyn thought as she leaned against the high back of the one comfortable chair in the room which served her as sitting room and office and, if necessary, supply closet. She sipped at the cider he handed her. For a man so big and burly, he moved lightly, even gracefully. His eyes watched her closely, and though they had not lost that glint of humor, he looked as careworn as she felt. She closed her eyes and let the hot steam curl around her nose.

"Feel better?" He settled on the floor by the hearth near her feet.

"Much."

"You've had a hard time."

It was not a question, but she shrugged in response. "It has never been worse. The stream of refugees is nearly constant—we're always short of everything. If you hadn't sent those supplies a month ago, I don't know what I would have done. There's never enough food, enough clothing. I try to find them little plots of land, or settle them with some of the neighboring tribes, but—" She broke off, suddenly too exhausted to continue.

"You do good work, Jessie." For another long moment there was silence, while they sipped their cider, and the fire burned merrily in the hearth. He poked at the logs with a long iron. "Better open that message while I'm here. I'll take it with me if needs be when I leave in the morning."

With a start, she set her cup on the floor and pulled the packet from the pocket of her gown. In the confines of the room it stank of a sick man's sweat. Gingerly, she unwrapped it and removed several sheets of parchment. She leaned forward and read it with growing disbelief.

"Well?" Everard asked finally.

She held it out to him. He glanced at the parchment and shook his head. "You know I don't read Muten, Jessie."

"No," she said, beginning to tremble. "But look at the signature. It's from Vere."

"Vere?" Everard turned the parchment over. "I always wondered if that's where the poor bastard had gone when he disappeared all those years ago, during Mortmain's Rebellion. You were probably too little to remember—"

"I remember Tavia telling me, when I'd got a little older."

"So what does it say? Who's it addressed to?"

Jesselyn took the sheets back from Everard and peered at them with a wrinkled brow. "It's addressed to the Council of the Elders—the Pr'fessors—at the College."

"Vere moves in high circles."

"Indeed. This messenger was to take this to their place of exile—do you know where that is?"

Everard only shook his head.

"Let me see—it says—'To my brothers and sisters of the Council, I send greetings and the urgent wish that the recent unrest among the Lesser Children has not affected the tranquility of your lives. I fear this message will have just that effect. I believe I have found the traitor, Ferad-lugz, in the deep desert of Dlas-for'Torth. Our fears are justified that he has continued in the study of the Magic and at this moment poses a greater threat not only to the Ruling Council and the Children, but to the whole of Meriga itself. Despite the uncertainties of the present situation, I am sending my servant to you in the hope that you, having taken counsel, will be able to advise what the next course of action should be. I intend to follow my servant. However, due to the current troubles, my arrival may be delayed. May the Power which orders the Universe keep you in care. Vere.' "

Jesselyn looked up and stared at Everard. "We must see that the Elders receive this."

"Is it dated?"

She turned the thick parchment over. "Febry first. Do you think that you will be able to find a way to get this to them?"

"I hope so. But you'd better make a copy. The Elders aren't the only ones who must know what this message says."

At that she looked up, a question clear in her blue eyes.

"Roderic must know, Jessie," Everard said, trying to answer. "If this is something that may affect the whole of Meriga—"

"Bah!" She turned away, nearly crumpling the worn parchment in her hand. "Do you know what they call him? The Children, I mean? They call him the Butcher."

"Jessie—no matter what might have happened, he is, or will be very shortly, the acknowledged Regent of all Meriga—"

"And a fine beginning he's had. Have you heard the tale first-hand? I have, Everard, and it still makes my stomach churn. I see those poor creatures in my dreams—he ordered the skin peeled from their bodies—limbs hacked off slowly with blunted blades—how can you even stand the thought that he is your brother?"

Everard was silent. He got to his feet, poured more cider, and leaned against the hearth. "Perhaps the tales are exaggerated."

"That's what I wanted to think—until I met one of those who was there and was spared. Roderic may be the Regent of all Meriga, but he's no man—"

"You're right, Jessie. He's a boy—an eighteen-year-old

boy faced with one of the largest rebellions in living history, and Dad gone. I'm not excusing what he did in Atland, I'm only saying that perhaps it was understandable under the circumstances."

"Are you saying we should try to understand slaughter?"

Everard sighed. "I don't expect you to understand—"

"Oh, spare me the helpless woman lecture." She got to her feet and paced beside the fire.

"Have you forgotten that Dad disappeared somewhere in Arkan? That's close enough to Dlas to make me think that perhaps this Ferad had a hand in Dad's disappearance."

She paused and could not meet his eyes. "No. I didn't think of that."

"Then this is not just a matter for the Elders. This is a matter for Roderic, as Regent, and his advisors, if not the entire Congress." When Jesselyn was silent, he continued, "I'll take this message. I'll try to deliver it. But I think you must go to Ahga."

At that she stared at Everard in disbelief. "Are you mad? I can't go to Ahga. I'm under interdict—the Bishop will have me taken before the Council of Bishops and even Dad wouldn't be able to protect me. There's no way—"

"There must be a way, Jessie."

"Why can't you go to Ahga?"

"I'm on my way to Atland. Phineas contacted me and asked if I would assist Reginald in administering the terms of the peace."

"Assist? You mean make sure he doesn't break his word. He's another in the same mold as Roderic—even though I'll grant you I've never heard he's ever done anything quite so bad. But none of the Children trust Reginald."

Everard motioned her to sit. "It's not just Reginald. The Senador in Atland is old, and Phineas is counting on me to deal with the lesser lords—the Mayhers and Govners. Reginald's not much of a diplomat. So you see I can't go back to

Ahga. I'll make sure the message reaches the Elders, but you must go to Roderic."

"Couldn't someone else take the message? What about Phillip?" Even as she spoke, Jesselyn realized that Everard spoke the truth. Phillip was probably in Ahga already, and if the message truly was as urgent as Vere implied, there was no time to find out. And who else could be trusted? "Who is this Ferad-lugz?"

Everard shook his head, smiling as he acknowledged her capitulation. "I've no idea. I've never heard the name before, but that's not really surprising. You know a lot goes on at the College among the Pr'fessors that no one knows about, or understands. It's enough for me that Vere mentions the Old Magic, and the fact that this Ferad-lugz is a traitor to them. That could only mean one thing. Ferad's attempting to use the Magic for his own ends, whatever they may be. And think about it, Jessie. Think about what that could mean for all of us."

Jesselyn sighed. She walked to the window and stared out into the dark night. She could hear the slow beat of the hide-bound drums as the Mutens mourned the dead messenger, and the old glass felt cool beneath her cheek. "What if I just wrote a letter?"

"Stubborn, aren't you? I wouldn't suggest anyone cross these mountains if it weren't necessary. But the Mutens do know and respect you—where they won't one of my messengers—and the human population will respect you as a priest, while they most assuredly would not a Muten. If you think you'd have trouble getting into Ahga, what sort of difficulty do you think one of the Children would have? And besides, you aren't just one of the Bishop's minion priests—you're a Princess of the royal blood. You have every right to go to Ahga. If you notify Roderic that you are on your way, surely he'll send an escort for you."

"I'd have to bring Tavia. There's no one who can handle

her as I do, and she won't let me out of her sight on her bad days."

"How is Tavia? I didn't see her at dinner."

"Today was one of the bad days. After what she's been through, I can't say I blame her. But I can't leave her."

"Then you may well have to take her with you. Have you ever thought that a trip back to Ahga might do her good? I would go if I thought I could, Jessie. But the peace in Atland is too tenuous. I would not like to think those poor wretches died in vain." For a moment his shoulders seemed to sag and his eyes lost their customary gleam. "Under any other circumstances, I'd take the message to Roderic myself."

"You think you could stand his presence?"

"I'm sworn to go if he summons me."

"But—"

Everard held up his hand. "Peace, Jessie. He's the Regent. We're all sworn to obey him."

"I'm not." Jesselyn folded her arms and leaned her cheek against the cool glass. "I'm not, nor will I ever swear anything to him or to any man."

Everard nodded and drew a long breath. "Forgive me for saying so, Jess, but it strikes me you always were a trifle loose about keeping vows." He gave her a brief bow, stalked to the door, and yanked it open. Speechless, she watched as he nearly tripped over a small figure huddled by the door. "What are you doing?" Everard hauled the figure up by the scruff of the neck, and Jesselyn realized with another shock that Sera must have overheard their entire conversation.

"Sera. Why are you here?"

"My turn to serve, Rever'd Lady." The Muten cringed, holding up her scarf to hide her face.

Everard set her down, though none too gently. He let out a long sigh of relief. "Go on, get about your work." He turned back to Jesselyn as Sera scurried away. "Please, Jessie. Please do as I ask."

Silently, Jesselyn nodded, wondering why she felt she ought to follow Sera into the dark night.

Chapter Seven

At noon on the last day of March, Roderic, followed by his brothers Brand and Amanander, crossed the lowered drawbridge, and guided his tired horse through the ancient towers of the gates, into the first ward of Ahga Castle. Behind him, the weary army tramped through the winding streets lined with a subdued crowd of citizens. Sitting straight in the saddle, wearing his battle-scarred leather armor, Roderic met their grim expressions as evenly as he could. He did not blame the people. Their King, the man they had cherished and cheered and supported, with their blood and their gold and their own hopes and dreams, for more than forty years was gone. And yet there was no concrete finality of death—he had simply vanished, snatched away by some enemy even he had not had the foresight to anticipate. No wonder the people of Ahga were frightened. The heavy supply wagons lurched across the uneven pavestones, the low rumbling of their wheels the only chorus of welcome in those silent streets.

As they emerged from the shadow of the gatehouse into the outer ward of the great keep, Roderic looked up to see the entire household waiting on the steps which led into the inner ward. Above him, the great stables rose ten stories, with grooms and stable boys assembled on the rising curve of the entrance ramp. A long line of soldiers in the uniform of the King's Guard snapped to attention. A cheer rang out from the household, loud and welcoming, and behind him, he heard the flap of a standard. Out of the corner of his eye, he caught a glimpse of a blue, white-bordered pennant, emblazoned with the eagle of Meriga as it fluttered to the top of the gatehouse: his own standard, announcing to the world that the heir of Meriga was once more in residence. He realized with a start that for the first time his colors would fly alone above Ahga. He drew the reins, and a stable boy ran forward. With a tired smile, Roderic relinquished the horse to the boy. "My thanks," he murmured, beneath the cheers.

The boy ducked his head in an awkward, embarrassed bow and led the horse away. As other boys ran forward to take the reins from Brand, Amanander, and the officers of the regiments, Roderic tugged his tunic into place and threw his cloak over one shoulder. He was home, at last. But how different was this homecoming from what he had imagined on that autumn day when he had ridden off to war with Abelard's blessings ringing in his ears, his hand still tingling from the strength of Abelard's clasp. He did not return the favored son, the cherished heir. Now, he was the master of the massive structure which rose around them all, the highest towers soaring twenty-five impossible floors above the ground. And although he had known the day was coming, when all of Meriga would be his, somehow it had always seemed a part of some far-off, distant future, which even his imagination could not quite encompass.

He started forward, aware that he would be expected to assume his father's place immediately and wondering if he would have to answer for his actions in Atland to his father's council. He shifted his broadsword across his back, searching the crowd for some glimpse of Peregrine. He saw Garrick, smiling broadly, Jaboa, her face soft with welcome, her eyes fastened on Brand.

In the center of the top step which led into the castle proper, Gartred, the King's Consort, held the gold welcome cup, steaming with spices, in her hands. Phineas lay on his litter at her side, his lids closed over his sightless eyes, his scarred hands plucking restlessly at the blanket which covered him from chest to feet.

As Roderic reached the bottom of the shallow steps, the entire household bowed and curtseyed and Gartred raised the golden goblet. "Welcome home, Lord Prince." Her husky voice was a low murmur, and he had to bend closer to hear her. "I trust your journey was easy." She bowed her head, and her lowered lashes were dark crescents against her creamy cheeks. A scent, as heady as twice-fermented wine, rose from her skin. As he reached for the cup, the tips of their fingers brushed. He looked down and noticed that she wore a dark red gown cut so low that the tops of her areolas were visible. Automatically, he averted his eyes and scanned the women near her for Peregrine.

Gartred rose from her curtsey and caught his eyes once more, as though she knew whom he sought. "You look well, Lord Prince."

Her mouth was very full and very red, and a rope of pearls nestled in the hollow of her bosom. Despite his discomfort, his attention was diverted by the blatant display. "Thank you, lady," he managed, and he gulped the wine so clumsily that a little spilled over the edge, and one bloodred drop ran down the side.

She caught the drop with one long finger as it edged down the curve of the cup. Deliberately, a little smile lacing the corners of her mouth, she licked her finger with the very tip of her tongue.

Beside Roderic, Brand coughed. Roderic passed the cup to his brother and bowed. "Thank you," he said again, a little perplexed by her overt suggestiveness. The consort was twenty years or more his senior and, until this moment, had never behaved as though he were worthy of her notice. He stepped past her, glancing through the crowd once more, and finally paused in front of Phineas's litter. "Lord Phineas," he said with a heavy sigh.

"Roderic." Although the body was frail and the face scarred with old wounds, the voice was the same as he remembered—the voice of a man who knew his words would be obeyed without question. There was another tone, an undercurrent, as though Phineas struggled to speak over some emotion he could not quite suppress. "Welcome home, Lord Prince."

"I'm glad to be home." It was the first time Phineas had ever addressed him by the title of the heir of Meriga. Roderic paused, wishing he could throw himself on the old man's chest and bury his face in the blankets, as he had when he was very small and his tutors had seemed so harsh. He remembered the dream of his father. "I wish it were under happier circumstances. There's been no word, no sign, of Dad?"

"We must talk as soon as you are settled."

"As you say, Lor—"

"At your convenience, Lord Prince," Phineas interrupted gently, and with those words, Roderic understood just how truly different everything was.

He looked around. Brand was enveloped in his wife's embrace, the other officers surrounded by wives and children and friends. The courtyard was completely crowded now, men and horses and wagons all milling in organized confusion.

Garrick pressed forward, reaching for his hand. "Welcome home, Lord Prince. You look as if campaigning agreed with you."

Roderic's words of welcome faded as he stared at his tutor. Had he grown so much over the winter? Garrick seemed smaller, thinner, as though in the months of Roderic's absence, the tutor had somehow shrunk. Only his iron gray beard was the same, closely clipped about his mouth and chin with the old military precision. "I'm glad to see you, Garrick," he managed. He glanced away, into the crowd, and saw Amanander deep in conversation with a Senador. "Garrick, isn't that Harland of Missiluse?"

Garrick followed Roderic's line of vision. "Indeed it is. Those two spell trouble. And only yesterday Phineas got word that Alexander is on his way and expects to be here in time for the Convening."

As they watched, Harland drew Amanander apart, listening, with an inscrutable expression on his face. Amanander looked up just as Roderic glanced in his direction. Their eyes met and held, and Roderic was the first to break the contact. As he looked away, he saw Amanander smile.

Gartred materialized out of the crowd, blocking Roderic's path into the castle. "Allow me to show you to your chambers, Lord Prince. There've been many changes while you were away—I had them completely redone. In keeping with your new status, of course." She seized Roderic's arm. Out of the corner of his eye, he caught a glimpse of the swirl of a forest green gown, and he craned his head, hoping to see Peregrine. He was disappointed when he realized it was only a serving maid, who curtseyed and simpered in response.

The household pressed upon him, men and women of all ranks bowing and murmuring words of welcome, and Gartred pulled him forward, his upper arm held hard against her breast, her perfume as insistent as her flesh.

At last they stood before the door of the chambers which had been his since birth, in the eastern tower which faced the sea. Gartred looked up at him with a smile, her eyes long and slanting, and Roderic suppressed a shudder. Her expression made him feel as if he were a choice cut of meat on a platter. She stepped aside and let him pass.

He walked into the room and stared in astonishment. She had indeed been busy over the winter. The outer chamber, once nursery, then schoolroom, had been completely refurbished. Instead of the scarred table and mismatched chairs which had served his boyhood needs, a massive desk, ornately carved, dominated one end of the room. Behind it was a high-backed chair thickly padded and meticulously covered in leather. It looked like the sort of chair one could sit in comfortably for a long time. To the side was a smaller desk, with another chair, this one not as ornate, nor as elaborately covered, more serviceable and obviously meant for a scribe.

The scarred wooden chest which had once held his toys and more lately his ragged maps and tattered scrolls had been replaced with a cabinet fronted in precious glass which could only predate the Armageddon, and within it, he could plainly see long wooden chests and fine-tooled leather rolls.

Before the hearth, a new rug woven of costly shades of red and purple and black covered the floor, and fat cushions invited him to lounge in comfort. A low table place to one side of the hearth held a flagon of wine and two goblets.

Through the door which led into his bedroom, he could see that the hangings and the coverlet of his bed had been replaced as well. Everything was so new, so strange, he felt as though he did not quite belong. He took a few steps, peered further into his bedroom, and turned to see Gartred on her knees before the hearth.

"Will you take a cup of wine, Lord Prince?"

He did not reply. She poured a little of the dark red liquid into a goblet, and as she did so, he noticed it was one of the silver ones used at the king's table. He took the proffered goblet dumbly, still too amazed by the transformation of his rooms to speak.

"Well, Lord Prince? What do you think of my efforts?"

"I don't know what to say. You've gone to a lot of trouble—it's—"

"Still nothing like the King's suite."

"But I didn't expect—"

"You didn't expect everything to be the same as when you left?" She cocked her head and gave him another long-eyed smile. "Not after all—everything that's happened."

"Yes." Automatically he took a sip of wine. The taste lingered on his tongue. "I suppose it has."

She rocked back on her heels. "Shall I light your fire, Lord Prince?" Suddenly Roderic noticed how the late afternoon sun illuminated the fine wrinkles at the corners of her eyes, how the line of her jaw was marred ever so slightly by the shadow of a jowl. She's old enough to be my mother, he thought. Suddenly he understood the source of his discomfort. It was not the surprise of seeing his rooms so suddenly altered, nor the shock of seeing the change which had affected all the court. It was the behavior of the woman who knelt before him, her breasts threatening to spill out of her low bodice, her eyes shadowed by cosmetics, her lips artificially reddened. She's my father's consort, he thought; she might as well be my mother.

He banged the goblet down on the nearest available surface and gestured to the door. "No, lady. If you will call for my servants, I won't require anything else of you."

She rose to her feet, her full lip pursed in a pout. "But if there's anything you do require? Anything at all?"

"Perhaps there is one thing more. I didn't see Peregrine Anuriel outside—"

"Peregrine is about her duties, Lord Prince."

The rancor in her voice startled him, and her words did not ring quite true. "Surely her duties are not so demanding they would keep her from welcoming us all home?" He watched her face, suddenly wary. Gartred had never evinced any interest in him before.

Gartred's eyes narrowed. "There is no need to waste your time with an orphaned waiting woman, Lord Prince. Any lady in Ahga will be more than happy to keep you company—any lady at all."

The note of invitation in her voice was unmistakable. He took a step backward involuntarily. "I doubt I'll have much time to enjoy a lady's company. Any lady. Now, if you will order my bath? And send someone to attend me?" He bowed an unmistakable dismissal.

"As you say, Lord Prince." With another low curtsey calculated to display a vast expanse of bosom, and a loud swish of her skirts, she departed. The odor of her perfume lingered like the memory of a bad dream while he bathed and dressed, and clung to his skin for the rest of that long, long day.

It was very late when he finally returned to his rooms. A fire burned in the grate, and a cold supper of cheese and bread and apples lay on a plate before the hearth. He barely glanced at it. On his desk lay a pile of rolled parchments, demanding his attention. He fingered a few and his head gave another throb at the thought. Some required a reply, some only his signature, others a prolonged consultation with Phineas. He had been Regent of Meriga for one day, and already he understood why his father had so loved to escape to the comparative peace of their summer residence at Minnis Saul.

He walked into his bedroom and sat down on the edge of the wide bed. The quilts and the hangings were new, and he fingered the soft fabric, woven in dark shades of soothing greens and blues. The pillows were high and plump, covered in fresh white linen cases and scented with lavender. He wished he could bury his head among them and give himself up to sleep, but he knew he would only toss and turn if he went to bed. He was still restless after all the events of the day. The afternoon had been completely given over to conferences with Phineas and the other Senadors who comprised Abelard's council: the lords of Arkan, Mondana, Kora-lado, and Tennessey Fall. Two or three of the Senadors had requested private audiences; these, on Phineas's advice, he had granted. He'd had a brief, troubling conversation with his brother Phillip.

Phillip resembled Abelard so closely that Roderic had felt his heart leap when his tall blond brother had strolled into the council room. But Phillip seemed well satisfied with his wife and the estate she had brought him: Nourk, bounded by mountains and sea, her rich, fertile fields well protected by those natural borders. So long as Roderic respected Phillip's right to rule Nourk as he pleased, Phillip would support Roderic in the Congress. But their talk had been troubling because, when he had mentioned the need to fortify the garrisons in Arkan and the South, Phillip seemed reluctant to promise any troops, making vague noises of the Muten threat. Roderic remembered that at the very height of the uprising, when it had seemed that Nourk was likely to be invaded, Phillip had refused all offers of aid. It was a puzzle he had left with Phineas to ponder.

He had spent a long time in the council room, reviewing the state of the army, the reports of all the outlying garrisons, the latest messages from the royal administrators of Abelard's far-flung holdings. The hereditary holdings of the Ridenau Kings were vast, and when combined with the western territories which Abelard had wrested from Owen Mortmain, the Ridenau Estate was the largest single parcel of land in all of Meriga.

The fire snapped and a log split, raising a shower of sparks. With a sigh, Roderic got to his feet and threw another log onto the fire. It would be cold when the fire died.

A framed map above the hearth caught his eye and he straightened slowly to get a better look. It was an old map of Meriga, showing how it had looked before Mortmain's Rebellion. The rebellion had happened long before Roderic's birth and had brought Abelard a Queen, and the revenues of Mortmain's vast estate, the fertile Vada Valley. Mortmain lived on in disgrace, under the thumb of the administrator Abelard had sent to ensure that, as Abelard phrased it, his Queen's interests were protected. What that really meant, Roderic knew, was that Abelard's coffers swelled with Mortmain's treasure—treasure which had helped to finance the wars against the Harleyriders, and the Mutens. And to keep the other lords in check.

In the years which followed, Abelard had decided that the Congress, which had convened every year on the first of Vember, need only meet every other year. And then, as the wars on the Plains dragged on, it had seemed expedient to reduce the Convenings to every third year. Even after the Harleyriders had been driven back, into the deserts south of Loma and Dlas, expediency had given way to custom. And what that meant, Roderic had long ago realized, was that Abelard had even greater latitude in the exercise of his power.

And that power was his now. Roderic traced the old boundaries on the parchment and walked back into the study, seating himself behind the desk. Better see what was in store for him tomorrow.

He had never thought of his father as a tyrant. But Phineas had cautioned that some of the Senadors might find a focal point for rebellion in Amanander's claim to the throne. He sorted listlessly through the rolls of parchments, the ancient glass in the window behind his desk rattling in the wind. Lightning flashed over his shoulder.

The storm had broken around dinnertime, when the household had gathered in the great hall to celebrate his homecoming. The rain was mixed with ice and snow, and a bitter north wind whistled around the towers. Lights shone only sparsely throughout the city, and the sea, whipped into a frenzy, washed in frothy waves into the outer courtyard. At his place in the center of the high table, on the raised dais which dominated one end of the hall, Roderic had shivered. Spring was a long time coming this year.

Beside him, Gartred had smiled and murmured inconsequential nonsense, passing him the choicest cuts of the huge roast, the softest of the steaming loaves, the best of the stewed fruits and vegetables. She had ensured that his wine goblet was never empty, but Roderic found everything tasted the same beneath the reek of her perfume. Abruptly he had excused himself when the dancing began.

His head felt heavy on his neck, and the blood pounded in a slow throb in his temples. He slumped against the soft leather chair and picked up the first letter which came to hand. He broke the thin seal and scanned it. It was a request from his sister Jesselyn for an escort into Ahga.

Jesselyn. The name meant almost nothing. She had left when he was barely old enough to remember, dressed in the black robes of a priest, her mission to minister to the people who lived in the mountains between Ahga and the eastern ocean. But somehow her zeal had been misdirected, and she had become embroiled in a scandal which had involved Abelard, his old nemesis the Bishop of Ahga, and the Mutens. Jesselyn had been completely disgraced, placed under interdict, and forbidden to ever enter the "Holy City" of Ahga again. But now she sought to enter the temporal city, and he supposed he was within the bounds of his authority to override the Bishop's decree. His headache intensified at the thought of having to deal with the Bishop and the priests. Even Abelard had avoided the whole pack of black-garbed crows, dismissing them with a contemptuous wave. But he had never overtly challenged them, either.

And why, Roderic wondered, as he reread the letter. Why did she want to come home *now*? Didn't he have enough to contend with? He scanned the letter once more. She was maddeningly vague—hinting that she had some incredibly crucial information. What kind of information in the name of the One and the Three could she possibly have discovered in the eastern wilds of the northern Pulatchian Mountains? Abelard hadn't disappeared anywhere near there. He let out a deep sigh and threw the letter down. There was no help for it. He would have to provide the escort. And prepare to face the Bishop's wrath once the word got back to her, as it most assuredly would. He had never met the Bishop, but her battles with Abelard were legendary. Surely with the King gone, he could assume that the Bishop would take up the gauntlet once again. It had been that kind of day.

"Do I disturb you, Lord Prince?"

Gartred's voice shattered his reverie. He jerked upright. He had thought he had been firm but undeniable in his refusal of her favors. But he had no wish to antagonize her. She was not only Abelard's consort, but the First Lady as well, in charge of all the domestic cares a household the size of the court engendered.

"Is there something you require of me, lady?" He pulled the chair closer to the desk, glad that its bulk was between the two of them.

"I?" She gave a little laugh and a girlish shake of her head. "No, Lord Prince. You did not look yourself at the feast this evening—I thought perhaps you might need—"

"I need rest, Lady Gartred. I'm tired. I'd like to go to bed." Surely, he thought, such an obvious rebuff would deter her.

But Gartred only gave him another smile and advanced, the firelight softening the contours of her face, her dark eyes gleaming in the shadows beneath her lids.

He straightened, pressing against the high back of the chair, feeling stalked. She was beautiful, he acknowledged, in the way a rose is in the last days of its bloom when the bud has fully opened, and the first petals have yet to fall. The flickering light effectively erased all the tell-tale signs of age the brutal sun had revealed.

She leaned over him and gave his chair a playful little push. It spun on well-oiled castors to face her. He could smell the wine on her breath. She glanced over at the letter from Jesselyn lying face up by his hand. "A letter from the lady Jesselyn?" She read the letter before his wine-dulled reflexes could react. "So am I to expect visitors? You must let me know, Lord Prince. I would not want any of your needs to go unmet. Ever." His eyes were level with her breasts. She seemed to offer them like plump, white pillows, where he might lay his head. She traced the line of his jaw with the tip of one finger, and it reminded him of her gesture on the steps outside when her little pink tongue had licked the wine drop from her finger. He stared, fascinated, spellbound. Despite his initial revulsion, his body was beginning to respond. It would certainly be easier, he thought, to succumb, to take her to his bed. He was expected to assume all his father's responsibilities, after all. Why not a few of his father's pleasures as well?

He closed his eyes, forgetting all about Jesselyn and her information and the Bishop as Gartred pressed his face into her bosom.

"I know how to soothe a King to sleep," she whispered. "Your father was often restless at night."

A sudden image of his father entwined with this woman flashed through his mind. He pushed away from Gartred, and rose, shaking his head. "I'm sorry, lady. If I were to lie with you it would feel as though I'd lain with my mother. I think of you as the King's—I cannot think of you any other way."

An ugly flush suffused her face, and she raised one thin brow. Her eyes glittered. "You don't find me beautiful?"

"Without question, lady. But you aren't for me." He gestured toward the door. "Please go."

Her bosom heaved with suppressed rage. "I suppose you'll ask for that mewling, mealy-mouthed drudge. Don't think you'll find her. I'll keep her so busy she'll not have time for her brat, let alone you." As soon as the words were out of her mouth, Gartred realized her mistake. She clamped her lips together and flounced toward the door.

He caught her by the wrist, quickly moving to block her escape. "What are you talking about? What brat?"

"Let me go," she hissed.

"Tell me—has Peregrine borne a child?"

"Let me go or I'll scream. I'll disgrace you before the entire court—I'll tell them you tried to rape me—"

"Scream away. We're both fully dressed—"

For answer she ripped the thin fabric of her gown with her remaining free hand from neck to waist. Her heavy breasts swung free, pendulous as udders, and she raised her hand to rake her long nails across his face. He caught her wrist and pinioned both hands behind her back.

"Where is Peregrine? Answer me," he said. Something which reminded him of Atland was beginning to beat in his blood, a desire to pin her down against the floor and take her brutally until she gave him the information. She stared at him defiantly. By the One, he thought, sickened, that's what she wants.

He dropped her wrists as though they stung and turned his back. "You will take that wrap, the one on the chair by the hearth, and you will cover yourself, and you will never come to me alone again." He spoke over his shoulder, and out of the corner of his eye, he saw her moving to obey him. "Leave. I will deal with you tomorrow." But even as he spoke, he knew he would not have the time to even think of Gartred for many days.

She went with a last backward glare, and he waited until he heard the door of his antechamber close above his manservant's quiet, "Good night, lady." He closed his eyes. Old Ben would be discreet. When he was certain Gartred was gone, he opened the door and roused Ben. The old man leapt to his feet, looking guilty for having drowsed. "Lord Prince. How may I—"

"Do you remember the girl among the consort's women? Peregrine? The one with—"

"The thick brown hair, and skin the color of honey? You brought her here often enough, Lord Prince."

"Do you know where she is?"

The old man stared up at him, clearly perplexed by the urgency in Roderic's voice. He seemed to search his thoughts. "I—I do not know, Lord Prince. In truth, I haven't seen her since the day word came that the King had disappeared. But my duties are different when you aren't home, and I never thought—"

"Never mind. You know the kitchens, the servants' quarters?" The old man nodded and Roderic grasped his arm. "Good. Come with me."

"But—but—but where are we going at this hour?" stammered Old Ben, clutching Roderic's sleeve.

"To find Peregrine. And the child I think is mine."

Chapter Eight

"My lady." The soft voice from the shadows startled Gartred and made her jump, so that she knocked one knee against the rough stone of the battlements. The rain had ended and the wind had subsided, and she was too ashamed, too angry to return to her chambers and face the derision she knew she would see in her ladies' eyes. Hadn't they warned her? Hadn't they hinted, gently and often, that Roderic would never take her? That with the King's disappearance went the power she had exercised so long over all who dwelt in Ahga? She knew what they'd think, even if they didn't have the courage to say it. She'd be lucky if he let her stay First Lady after tonight.

Her knee throbbed. "Who is it?" she demanded. "Show yourself. How dare you frighten me?"

"Forgive me, lady." A tall dark shape coalesced out of the shadows, and in the gloom, she barely recognized Amanander. He stood still, almost unnaturally so, and she gave a little shiver.

"Lord Amanander? Is it you?"

He moved closer, so close his cloak brushed against her makeshift wrap. "Please. No titles, lady. I am sorry to disturb your thoughts."

She gripped the wrap closer to her throat, the fabric rough against her naked breasts. Pity this one wasn't Abelard's heir instead of that stoop shouldered, skinny boy. "You don't disturb me, Lor— Amanander."

"You seem upset. Is there anything I can do?"

Kill Roderic, she thought, and instantly quelled it.

He chuckled, a low sound deep in his throat, and she had the unnerving thought that he had heard her. "No," she managed. "Thank you."

"Do you enjoy the night, Gartred?"

What an odd question, she thought, though she automatically tilted her head in the manner she knew men found most attractive and answered him in her deepest, huskiest voice. "Only when I have someone to share it with."

She heard the sudden intake of his breath and felt the little thrill of power she always experienced whenever she had a man in her thrall. He touched her face. She expected warm flesh, but encountered something smoother and chillier than skin. He wore gloves, and the smooth leather sent a little unexpected shiver down her spine. She wondered what that leather would feel like against her nipples.

He chuckled again and turned her around to face him. She had another unnerving thought that somehow he had heard that last thought too. He slid his hand beneath the wrap, caressing the round swell of her breast. She stared up at him, entranced, feeling her nipples tighten in anticipation. He brushed one finger against the hard tip, and she moaned, swaying as her knees went weak. What's happening to me? she wondered. I'm behaving like an untried girl.

He bent his head and gathered her mouth to his, his skin as smooth and as polished as the leather, the scent of him a blend of leather and soap and something metallic. He twisted her nipple between two fingers, rolling and tugging it, sending little sparks of pleasure through her body. His tongue was hot and probing, stabbing every corner of her mouth. She could scarcely breathe. Abelard had been demanding but never brutal. There was a hard insistent edge to his son that excited her, incited her. This is what it would be like to be raped, she thought, forced down on hard stone, taken like an animal, penetrated in every orifice, humiliated and consumed and totally possessed.

Amanander drew back from the kiss. In the dark his eyes had an inhuman gleam, and Gartred felt more than a flicker of fear. "Whatever you wish, my dear." He laughed again, low and cruel, and then he was on her.

The kitchens beneath the great hall of Ahga were vast caverns, lit at that late hour only by rushlights set in sconces high on the walls. Sleepy scullions and kitchen maids stirred from their places beside the banked fires as Roderic and Old Ben passed by, and once or twice, a night-robed cook poked a sleep-swollen face from one of the cubbyholes which lined the walls. But no one emerged to challenge their passing, and Roderic hustled the old man through the kitchens and up the narrow steps into the quarters where the servants were housed.

"Where is she?" Roderic hissed as they paused in the long, dark corridor where the rooms were only partitioned by flimsy curtains. The dusty smell of age was thick in the air, and Roderic realized abruptly that for the ones who served those who reigned in Ahga, there was little luxury and few comforts.

"In truth, Lord Prince," whispered the old man, "I don't know—the maids are housed at the far end. She could be anywhere at all."

Roderic cursed beneath his breath. Peregrine was the daughter of a landed Senador. How had Gartred dared to treat her so? But there seemed to be no other way to find her. He'd have to go from room to room. With another curse, he started forward, intending to peer into the nearest room, when a huge man, bearded and naked from the waist up, emerged from some room perhaps halfway down the corridor.

"What do you think you're doing?" His face was creased with sleep, and his trousers were clearly those of the King's Guard.

"I'm looking for a lady," Roderic replied.

"Then you're looking in the wrong place, lad. Get out—before you disturb decent people at their rest."

A yawning woman peered out from another cubicle. Roderic groaned. It hadn't been his intention to rouse the whole house. "You don't understand—" he began.

"*You* don't understand," responded the hairy giant, hands on hips. "Who the hell do you think you are? Get back to your barracks, 'fore I report you to your commanding officer."

"What's your name, soldier?"

"Ha! What's my name to you, pretty boy? Get out of here, now, or I'll boot you out."

More and more faces, male and female both, were emerging from curtained openings along the corridor and Old Ben was tugging at Roderic's arm with increasing urgency. "It's the Prince," hissed a soft whisper, and Roderic glanced over into the eyes of a serving girl who had pleasured him years ago. He felt the blood rise in his face, as more and more faces pressed forward, and he recognized more than a few of them.

"Your name," said Roderic, as he gently but firmly disengaged Ben, "may mean nothing to me, but mine most assuredly will mean something to you. I am Roderic Ridenau, and my 'commanding officer' as you refer to him, has been lost in the field for some time now. And in his absence every soldier in the King's Guard, including you, answers ultimately to me." The people who crowded the narrow passage had fallen silent, staring in disbelief, and the soldier's mouth hung open. "Good people," Roderic addressed the gathering crowd. "I'm sorry to disturb your rest. But I came here tonight looking for a lady the consort—"

"Roderic?" A woman's voice, high with disbelief, rose

above the crowd, and as one, they all craned their heads. Men and women flattened against the walls.

"Peregrine?" He started forward, and then she was in his arms, her black-brown hair falling to her waist, her full mouth turned up to his. There was a ripple of nervous laughter and then a spatter of applause. She broke away from him, laughing with delight, and Roderic held her at arm's length. Glad as he was to see her, there was a difference in his feelings for her he could not quite define. "What's happened to you? Why are you here? Did the consort dismiss you?"

Before Peregrine could answer, an old woman broke through the crowd, a white-wrapped bundle in her arms. "It was the consort, Lord Prince. Because she carried your child, you see. When the news came about the King—the consort decided to get Peregrine out of the way. I think she thought to take her place—in your heart."

He looked down into Peregrine's dark eyes. "Is this true?" he whispered.

Peregrine nodded. "She sent me down to the kitchens—she wanted to keep me out of your way."

The old woman stood before him, and the bundle stirred and cried out. Peregrine reached out and took the baby. "This is your daughter, Roderic. I named her Melisande."

It was long after midnight when Roderic finally leaned back against the cushions beside the hearth. He could barely stand to look at Peregrine as he listened to the sorry tale she told, a tale which reminded him that he had not spared more than a thought or two for her the whole time he had been in Atland. A constant play of light flickered across her face, and her eyes were deep in the shadows. But he felt her watching him, knew that she had not taken her eyes off him since the moment she had seen him in the corridor.

" . . . and that's how you found me."

Her voice dropped off, and he stared, unmoving, into the fire.

"Roderic? What's wrong? Are you angry with me?"

"With you?" He looked up swiftly and shook his head. "Of course not. I'm afraid I'm not fit company tonight."

"It's Gartred, isn't it? I knew she was going to spoil things—I knew she'd spoil this homecoming for you—"

"Peregrine." He got to his feet and paced a few short steps so that he would not have to see the concern so plainly on her face. "This hasn't anything to do with Gartred. I'm very sorry that you should have suffered so. But this—" he gestured all around "—things are so different, this doesn't feel like home."

"I knew she shouldn't have changed your rooms." She raised her hands in a brief, futile gesture and dropped them back in her lap.

He felt a pang of pity and came a few steps closer. "I'm sorry about what happened. I didn't know. I wish you'd sent a message."

"I—I was afraid to approach a messenger—I was afraid the consort would take the baby."

"Take her?" Roderic frowned.

"Give her to some woman in the city who doesn't have a child—such things happen."

"By the One." He dropped beside her on one knee and touched her cheek. The texture and the color of her skin reminded him of honey mixed with cream, and he watched the pulse beat in her throat.

"You've changed."

"I didn't have a choice." His eyes followed the line of her bodice to her breasts, which rose and fell to the rhythm of her breathing. She smelled of lavender and rosemary.

She caught his hand and held it to her face. "I—I've missed you so much. All the time you were away, I thought of you—only you. And when Melisande was born, I hoped—" She looked down. "I thought maybe you'd have missed me, too. But you didn't even send a letter."

A vision of the butchered Mutens and the earth churned to a bloody mud flashed through his mind. He stood up and turned his head away. "I'm not the same as when I left here, Peregrine. I'm not sure you'd miss me, if you knew the things I've done."

For answer, she got to her feet and held out her hand timidly, as though she feared rebuff.

Beneath the thin cotton of her gown, her body was a dark, curving outline. He remembered all the nights he'd spent in her arms, all the long lazy afternoons, hiding from the consort and his tutors. His desire rose, first a hunger, then a demand. He pressed a kiss into her palm, watching her reaction.

She tightened her fingers around his and moved a fraction of an inch closer, her face tilted up. He bent his head and kissed her. There was not much gentleness in that kiss, but her passion seemed to match his own. She put her arms around his neck and thrust her hips against his. He held her tightly, the hard evidence of his need squarely nestled between them. They stood entwined for a long time, and then he picked her up and carried her to his bed.

He laid her on the pillows and felt for the lacings of her gown. She reached up to help his fumbling fingers.

He lifted his head and looked at her. "Do you want this, lady?"

"Roderic—" The word was a plea.

He caught her hands in one of his and looked squarely into her dark brown eyes. "I'm sorry I didn't write. I had no idea Gartred would do what she did. I want to make it up to you, I want to set things right. I don't know if I can offer you anything right now, Peregrine. I can speak to Phineas, but—but you aren't one of the kitchen maids and you've borne my child. I won't treat you as if you don't matter to me."

"Let me show you how I want to be treated." She undid her

bodice with one hand and placed the other firmly against his erection. Whatever tentative hold he had on reason was lost to him completely at that point, and any fuzzy half-formed notions he had of guilt or honor dissolved in the hot tide of passion which swept through him.

As the gray dawn broke over the sea, Roderic woke to find her head nestled in the hollow of his chest. Lazily, he nudged her awake. "Peregrine, the child—" he began when she opened her eyes.

"It's an honor to bear your child—you know that."

"Honor without substance is cold comfort." He rolled over on his back, staring at the ceiling, knowing she watched him with troubled eyes, remembering the long nights spent beneath these very sheets, the summer afternoons in the shadowed glades of Minnis Saul. She had suffered much for his sake in the last months.

"You've changed so much." She sat up, pulling the sheet close, and spoke over her shoulder, her eyes fixed on the scene outside the window where the gulls wheeled and shrieked. Her body had changed—her breasts were fuller, softer, her waist had thickened, and silvery lines etched paths on the skin of her belly and her hips. Her words surprised him. "Last night when you spoke to that soldier—I'd never heard you sound that way before."

Silently, he caressed the feathery tips of her hair, not knowing how to respond. What reassurance could he offer her, when there were so many decisions to be made, so many questions to be answered? The subject of marriage had not even been whispered, and that, too, was sure to raise a storm within the Congress, a storm he instinctively knew should be avoided for the present. To name Peregrine his consort was tantamount to announcing his intention to marry her, especially since he had no heir. What certainty could he offer her, when he was so uncertain himself?

She turned and he saw that tears had formed in the corners

of her eyes. "I don't want to leave you. I'd rather stay as the lowest scullery maid—"

He touched her mouth with one finger as he pulled her down beside him. "Of course you'll stay. I didn't mean to sound as if I don't need you. It's just I scarcely know how I fit in, let alone anyone else."

"What about Gartred?"

At the mention of the consort's name, his jaw tightened and his eyes narrowed. "I'm not sure. But I promise you, something will be done."

"Will you send her away?"

He shifted restlessly. That thought had occurred more than once in the last twelve hours.

Peregrine pressed closer, her hand straying lower, rousing and caressing. "I could be your First Lady."

He glanced down, surprised. Without the title of wife or consort, it was a position of only a little honor and many cares, one often bestowed upon some ancient female relative. As his body responded inevitably to her touch, he kissed her smooth cheek. "If you would be content with that, at least for a little?"

She lowered her eyes until her lashes brushed against his chest, and he was glad to see her dimples. "As you say, Lord Prince. Command me as you wish."

Alexander pressed his cheek against the cool panes of ancient glass and watched the fog rolling off the sea in thick, gray waves. The rising sun was no more than a paler splotch of gray over the horizon, and the gulls shrieked invisibly through the mist. He kept his face carefully neutral as he listened to his twin outline his plan for the taking of the regency.

His neck and shoulders ached, and his head throbbed with weariness. He had ridden all night, through the worst of the storm, in order to reach Ahga before the Convening, and he still wore his sodden clothes. Beyond the bedchamber, he could hear the harsh, tired voice of his bodyservant berating the castle servants as they fetched the water for his bath. The Convening wasn't until noon, and Alexander dearly hoped he would have a chance to snatch a few hours sleep. He stifled a yawn and reluctantly met Amanander's dark eyes.

Physically the brothers were identical in size and shape and form, and but for differences in style and dress, it would have been impossible for anyone to tell them apart. Alexander's beard concealed a mouth as sensual as Amanander's, and his dark hair was clipped close about his ears, a marked contrast to the intricate braids Amanander affected.

Amanander abruptly fell silent, and Alexander turned at the discreet cough. In the doorway which led to the bathing room, his manservant hesitated. "Well?"

"Your clothes are ready, Lord Alex. The castle servants are heating your water, and breakfast is on its way. Is there anything I can do for you, before I oversee the unloading of our packs?"

Alexander nodded, with a glance at Amanander. "Go to Roderic. Convey my greetings."

"Should I apologize for our late arrival, lord?"

Amanander snorted. Alexander nodded slowly.

When the door had closed behind the servant, Amanander made another sound of derision. "Apologize? Ahga is as much our home as it is his."

"But in our father's absence, Roderic is its master, is he not?" Amanander's boots made no sound as he stalked to stand beside his twin, and involuntarily Alexander drew back. "You do realize, don't you, that what you are proposing could be construed as treason?"

"Not if the Congress supports me."

Alexander sighed. "But that would require them to break the pledges they swore to Dad." When Amanander did not reply, Alexander swore softly beneath his breath. "Whose support can you count on?"

"Missiluse. Harland hasn't forgotten how Dad humiliated his father. He'll stand with us. And Reginald—we can count on him. As for Phillip, he's too fat in Nourk. He'll not stir himself either way."

"In order to nullify Dad's will you'll need the votes of two-thirds of the Senadors. Who else?"

"Ragonn. Mondana. Vada. Atland. All of them recognize the children of contracted marriages as equal heirs."

"By the One, Aman. Has the hot sun in Dlas addled your brains? Ragonn may support you, but what does he have to support you with? The army in Ragonn is Dad's army—they even fight under his colors. The lords of Mondana are among Dad's staunchest supporters, and always have been. Roderic's just been in Atland—the Senador's not about to forget—"

"That's where Reginald and Harland will be of use. They'll foment rebellion among the lesser lords in Atland, Tennessey, the rest of the South—the ones who'll be feeling the brunt of this new peace."

"Reginald? You mean to say he'll deliberately incite the lesser lords to rebel? He'll deliberately break the treaties he's just helped to make?"

Amanander's mouth folded into a straight line and he met Alexander's challenge with a raised brow. "Reginald will stand with us. He gave me his assurances in Atland—he has no wish to rule in the shadow of a puppet princeling. Don't you think he'd like more than that forsaken garrison Dad so generously bestowed?"

Alexander rubbed a hand across his face, scarcely comprehending the bitter sarcasm. His eyes felt gritty, swollen, as though the dust in the road had found a way beneath his lids. Although he had always known that Amanander believed the throne of Meriga should be his, the blatant scheming shocked him. "And Vada," he said, trying desperately to comprehend how far Amanander believed he could go, "Roderic is the old Senador's grandson. No matter what Mortmain thought of

Dad, do you really think the lesser lords there will march against Melisande Mortmain's blood?"

Amanander's eyes, fastened on the far horizon, were two dark slits. "And you?"

The question lay like a rock at the bottom of a still pond. Alexander swallowed hard. "I cannot break my oath."

Amanander did not even blink. For some reason the lack of a reaction made Alexander flinch more than if his brother had raised his fist. "And what of your blood?"

Alexander took a deep breath. How could he explain to Amanander the lessons he'd learned all these years in Spogan, wrestling with the Chiefs of the Settle Islands, keeping the peace between Mondana and Ragonn and the Chiefs, balancing the interests of Meriga against the Sascatch Tribes just beyond the northern borders? "I've seen too much blood spilled when men don't honor their oaths, Aman." He rubbed a hand across his eyes. It hurt him to disappoint his brother, for he knew that Aman had counted on his support most dearly. "Perhaps things have been different for you in Dlas. You've only the Harleyriders and the sand to deal with—in Spogan, I must balance the Chiefs and the lords, and the Sascatch—" He broke off. "I've seen what happens if one man breaks his word. I've seen tens of hundreds die as a result. I cannot break the pledge I swore to Dad—to uphold the kingdom—"

"Ah." Amanander faced Alexander, his face as blank as stone. "And yet you would countenance handing the regency to an untried boy—"

"Is he untried? I heard he acquitted himself well in Atland." Alexander met his brother's eyes and wondered why a chill ran down his spine.

"Oh, he acquitted himself admirably, if you find butchery admirable. Have you heard how he brought the Muten chief to his knees at last? He ordered fifty or more hostages tortured to death, one by one—had them flayed and hacked to death with blunted swords. You should have seen the blood spilt that day."

Alexander frowned. "No," he said slowly, "I had not heard. You were there? You saw this?"

"With my own eyes. Of course, it was only Muten vermin, and the Congress will not care, but—"

"If Roderic should prove to be an unworthy ruler, Aman, I will without hesitation support your claim. As undoubtedly will the others you've named. Perhaps we'll be able to bring together a coalition—"

Amanander turned away, but not before Alexander caught the curl of scorn which twisted his mouth. "I see what you've become, dear brother. You've become a peacekeeper—at any price. You forget how our father treated us—abandoned us, ignored us—"

"I remember how Grandmother dragged us off to the South when Dad banished her, and he let us go in order to prevent civil war."

"In order to prevent having to fight an enemy on his flank, you mean."

Alexander hesitated. He remembered the years spent in the Estate of Missiluse, remembered the Muten who had come to live in the highest tower of the keep. It was then that there had been a change in Amanander, but Alexander had always preferred to think that Aman had simply begun to mature, to become the man he now was. And what sort of a man was that? he asked himself. His mind veered away from the question. But there had been a change in their relationship, even though he wanted to deny it, and would have denied it still to anyone who asked. He only vaguely remembered the day their father had come for them, but he knew that was the day he had been afraid of Aman for the first time.

And he was afraid of Amanander now, he realized, afraid for some reason he could not articulate in any sane way. Perhaps he was only exhausted. He shook his head and took a deep breath. There was only one way to deal with the situation. He had to be as honest with Amanander as he tried to be with the factions in the northwest. "I see we remember events differently. But I cannot raise my hand against Roderic. The country is too unsettled—Dad's disappearance has caused shock waves from the Settle Islands to Atland. Unless and until Roderic shows himself to be unfit to rule, I am bound by my Pledge of Allegiance to serve him. As, I might remind you, are you."

Amanander gave him a hard stare. "I counted on you, brother." Alexander recoiled, as their eyes met. Whoever, or whatever, it was that glared out of Aman's eyes wasn't the brother he knew. Actually afraid, he glanced instinctively away, out the window. Outside, the sky was a uniform blank gray, as though the sun had been erased. "Very well, brother," continued Amanander, his voice cold as a cutting wind. "I will not raise my voice at this Convening, and I will not forget anything you've said to me this morning." Startled at the implicit threat, Alexander looked over his shoulder and saw that Amanander was no longer in the room.

Chapter Nine

The great hall of Ahga Castle was bright with the light of more than a thousand candles, and the voices of more than a thousand people rose and fell beneath the gentle melody of the music played on the mezzanine above. From his place at the high table, Roderic surveyed the hall, which was packed to overflowing with not only all the usual residents of Ahga Castle, but the Senadors and their retinues as well. Servants scurried between the tightly packed benches and tables, carrying trays and baskets filled with steaming food, or rolling great barrels filled with wine and ale and mead up from the cellars below the kitchens.

Brand sat at his left hand, Obayana, Senador of Kora-lado was placed at his right. Gartred had obviously understood Roderic's message of the previous night, for she sat three or four places away, between Amanander and Phillip. But no matter what he might think of her personally, Roderic had to admit that the woman knew her duties well. The seating of nearly fifty Senadors, who were as jealous of any privilege, and sensitive to any perceived slight, as the most petty matron, required the strategic genius of a General. If Peregrine were to replace her, her responsibilities would be formidable indeed.

Peregrine sat at a table just below the dais, the downy head of his daughter bobbing against her shoulder, the wine-flushed faces of the women nearby soft with smiles for the infant. He leaned back in his chair. Although the day had been as long as any he could remember, he was curiously exhilarated. The men who had always addressed him by name, or as "boy" or "son," now called him "lord," rose when he entered the room, and did not sit until he gave permission. It was his first taste of the honor given the King. No wonder Abelard had seemed to bask like a lycat in the sun.

The day had been full of unspoken tensions, but even Phineas was pleased that the Convening had gone as well as it had. Although Roderic had been worried that the incident in Atland would be raised, there had only been one tense moment, when Harland of Missiluse had risen to contend that Amanander should be Abelard's rightful heir. But even in his absence, the King cast a long shadow, and most of the Senadors seemed to believe that Abelard would return alive and well. Amanander himself had stayed notably in the background, coming forward in turn to kneel and swear the Pledge of Allegiance with the rest.

Beside Roderic, Obayana quietly sipped his wine, as he listened to young Nevin Vantigorn, the heir of the First of the Lords of Mondana. Old Niklas was dying and Nevin was sure to be confirmed as the new Senador by the time of the next Convening. Obayana's face was the color of the southern desert sands, and his eyes were dark and slanted in the manner of many in western Meriga. But about the man was a quiet alertness and Roderic sensed the man missed nothing. His fortress high above the Kora-lado Pass was one of the most impregnable in Meriga, and one of the most strategic, for it guarded the main trade route between the West and the rest of the country. Abelard had gone there for succor during Mortmain's Rebellion, and the bond between the two men had never been strained.

Roderic beckoned to the boy who stood behind his chair, and obediently he refilled Roderic's goblet. Brand paused in peeling an apple for his wife and murmured beneath the cover of conversation, "I'd like a few words, Lord Prince."

"Please, Brand. There's no need—"

"Perhaps not in private." Brand's dark eyes were full of meaning, but his face was carefully blank.

Roderic glanced around. Obayana was still engaged in conversation with Nevin. Roderic shrugged. "Well?"

"It's about the men in Amanander's retinue—the four who are his personal bodyguards." Brand hesitated, and Roderic narrowed his eyes. It was unlike his brother to search for words. "I've had complaints from some of the men in the barracks where they are housed—nothing specific, nothing of a disciplinary nature. So I sent my son to speak with them, to try to draw them out. I told him to report back to me any impressions he had—anything at all. I even sent them some of the best of the honey mead—" here he gave an apologetic shrug "—but according to Barran, they would not drink. They almost would not talk."

"Not at all?"

"Oh, they answered questions readily enough, but wouldn't say anything otherwise." Brand frowned. "Barran wasn't able to tell me anything specific. Finally I went to talk to them myself. I had the strangest feeling." He stared at Roderic, and in the candlelight, Roderic was amazed to see Brand still struggling to find the words. "It was as if—as if I did not exist for them, except when I spoke. As if they were in another place." He broke off and shook his head. "I am sorry, Roderic, that's the best I can do. But I must tell you this. My flesh crawled while I was in the presence of those men. If I did not know better, I'd say they weren't men at all. I've never felt anything like it—even touching a Muten didn't make me feel that way."

"You were afraid?"

Brand hesitated once more, and in that long moment, Roderic felt a touch of inexplicable fear. "Not for my life," he said finally. "For my very self."

Roderic stared at his brother. It was nearly inconceivable that Brand, who had led men into battle for more years than Roderic had been alive, should be afraid of anything which walked on two legs.

"But that's not all." Brand drew slow circles on the linen with his goblet. "Amanander has been asking a lot of questions. Not about anything you might expect. About a woman Dad was involved with once, a long time ago, before you were born. Her name was Nydia Farhallen."

"Nydia Farhallen?" Obayana leaned into the conversation, startling Roderic. "Forgive the intrusion, Lord Prince, but it's been twenty years since I heard that name."

"Indeed, Lord Senador," answered Brand. "It's been twenty years or more since that name was spoken beneath this roof. My father kept her at Minnis until . . ." His voice trailed off.

"Until what?" interrupted Roderic. "Why is Amanander suddenly interested in a woman Dad knew so long ago?"

"That's what I'd like to know." Brand stared out over the crowded hall, a faraway look on his face. "I remember her."

"Every man who'd ever seen her would remember her," said Obayana.

"Why?" Roderic was astonished by the wistful expressions on the faces of both men.

"Because she was beautiful." Obayana sipped his wine. "Oh, there are many beautiful women, especially here in Ahga, but the Lady Nydia surpassed them all as the sun outshines the stars. When she walked into the room, it was as if every other woman faded from sight. She was gentle and kind, but I don't think her beauty brought her any happiness. She often struck me as sad and more than a little lonely."

"She was pledge-bound to Dad," said Brand. "Ostensibly that was the reason he kept her at Minnis after he married your mother, Roderic. But everyone knew the real reason." Brand cocked an eyebrow at the question on Roderic's face. "He couldn't bear to be away from her. She's the reason he built Minnis—there was some suggestion from the Bishop of Ahga that Nydia was a witch. In fact, there was a trial right after Mortmain's Rebellion. He sent me to rescue her. I took her up to Minnis, and that very year he began the construction of the fortress you know. Minnis was just a hunting lodge before that. It couldn't have withstood a hunting party. Now it could withstand ten thousand men."

"At the least," said Obayana. "I have never been there, but I have seen the plans."

"All that for a—a consort?"

"She was never his consort," answered Brand. "Oh, it was clear she shared his bed. And while she did, he never looked at another woman. But then, right before you were born, there was some sort of quarrel, some falling out. I was gone in those years—fighting the Harleys in Arkan—and I never really knew the story. But by the time I came home, Nydia was gone from Minnis. And Dad never spoke of her again."

"Where did she go?"

"You know the high tower north of Minnis, the one that rises up over the trees?"

"The witch's tower?" Roderic nodded.

"It's said that Nydia is the witch who lives there." Brand shook his head.

"But why—why if Dad loved this woman, if she was so beautiful—why would she go there? And you say she was pledge-bound? What—"

"There was always something more to their relationship than either of them ever said," Obayana mused. "But it was generally believed that Nydia had a brief affair with Phineas and bore him a child, although Phineas has never by word or action confirmed that."

"Phineas?" Roderic could not contain his disbelief. This was too much information, too many mysteries all at once. He shook his head as if to clear it. "But why Amanander's interest in this woman? She's probably dead by now. And if

Phineas has never confirmed the rumor, perhaps his child died as well."

"I agree," said Brand. "But after Amanander is safely on his way back to Dlas—where you had better order him immediately—I think it might be wise to send a patrol up to the tower north of Minnis and just check out whatever might be there."

Roderic took a deep breath and let it out slowly. "Yes," he nodded at last. "Very well. And as for Amanander's guards—"

"I'll have them watched, Lord Prince."

Roderic looked beyond Brand at Amanander. Before him, the food on his plate looked untouched, but he reached for a large red apple from a bowl by his elbow. He glanced up at Roderic and his mouth curved into a semblance of a smile. He raised the apple to his lips, and as he opened his mouth to take a bite, Roderic thought he saw it move. Roderic gasped. The air seemed thick, as though the very nature of it had changed, as though it lacked the element to sustain life. He tried another breath; his lungs would not accept the air. He glanced around the table, and in that instant the feeling vanished, and no one else seemed to have noticed or been affected.

Amanander sat motionless, the thing held to his mouth. From Roderic's viewpoint, it appeared to be some small creature. He sank his teeth into it and red blood stained his lips. Roderic felt a chill of revulsion. He blinked.

Amanander smiled as he chewed and tossed the core of the apple into the bowl.

The babble of voices in the great hall could not reach the dank tunnels in the subterranean levels beneath Ahga Castle. The squat figure paused as it emerged from a tunnel, cocked its cloaked head, and continued to wade through waist-deep water. Light shone in a steady beacon from the heavy cylinder in its hand. Overhead, leathery wings flapped and sinuous bodies slithered as the darkness of centuries was penetrated.

Little splashes sounded here and there as small creatures hurried out of its way.

In the middle of the open cavern, the figure paused. Walls of broken, crumbling masonry rose to chest level. The intruder tucked the cold-fire lantern into the cloak's voluminous folds, and scrambled up onto the crumbling deck. It smoothed its wet robes and withdrew the lantern. It trained the beam in all directions in a wide arc, and instantly there was a scurry and a flutter of activity. Light reflected off the shattered surfaces of glass and tile centuries old. Satisfied, the Muten slipped through the old archway, where a flight of broken steps led up to the next level. An ancient sign, hanging at a crooked angle, proclaimed "CONGRESS." The Muten settled on the old staircase and, focusing its beam of light into the yawning abyss above, closed its eyes and began a low, crooning chant.

Fifteen floors above, Amanander paused on his way to Gartred's rooms. Although she had to be a bit bruised from his attentions of the night before, she had seemed quite amenable to his suggestion that they continue their relationship this evening. He hoped he had satisfied every one of her dark desires. He knew that she had his. Almost.

It would never have been his choice to take her on the cold rough stones of the battlement. But who was he to gainsay a lady's wishes? Certainly not when the lady was so willing as Gartred. At least she had been in the beginning. Toward the end, he had sensed a certain reluctance to experience some of her darker fantasies. But he never allowed second thoughts to interfere. And there were a few things he'd like to introduce to her tonight, a few things she hadn't even begun to dream of. Things better done in the privacy of a bedchamber, where her cries wouldn't be heard quite so readily, or if they were, easily dismissed. He had alerted his bodyguard to discourage any well-intentioned inquiries.

Now the mindcall sounded louder and louder in the inner recesses of his head, and he peered over his shoulder. The corridor was deserted, only a few candles burned in the sconces set high in the walls. He listened intently for another minute more, and then with a frustrated sigh started off for the steps, moving as quietly as a predator through the darkened castle.

He heard tired voices coming from the servants' quarters and the kitchens, and drew back into the shadows with a curse. But the servants were too busy with the monstrous task of cleaning up after the feast to notice him.

The mindcall burst impatiently in his brain, the summons loud and urgent. He shut his eyes and concentrated as Ferad had taught him, pulling the energy out of the dust motes which swirled in the air. He blasted a message back and was satisfied to feel the echo of the other's pain.

Finally, he threaded his way through the kitchens, past the weary scullions and exhausted maids, through the baskets and barrels of provisions, the shining utensils, the heavy pots and pans, and bunches of herbs hanging from huge hooks in the ceiling beams. On a bench in a low passageway, a scullion snored. Amanander glanced at him with contempt and continued on his way.

Beneath the kitchens were the crypts, where the bones of long-dead Ridenaus moldered into dust. A steady beam of light beckoned him on. His boots made a quiet shuffle across the uneven floor, and mice skittered and rustled as he passed. At the top of the steps, he paused. "Well?"

The Muten at the bottom jumped to attention. "Gr-Great Lord! My name is—"

"I don't care who you are. I know who sent you. What's wrong?"

"Why do you think something's wrong, Great Lord?" The Muten's voice was sulky, petulant.

For answer, Amanander reached down and hauled the Muten up by the neck of the robe. Its secondary arms flailed wildly, and it gave a muffled shriek. "I know something's wrong when your master sends a miserable runt like you into Ahga. Give me your message or I'll pry it out of your mind myself."

The Muten closed its eyes and swallowed. "Please. Put me down."

Amanander set the creature on the top step, so that he could stare it in the face. He felt the fear skitter through its mind as though the emotion were his own.

"My—my master bids you have a care, Great Lord. A messenger has gone to the Pr'fessors of the College—my master says the laboratory is discovered—"

"By whom? Who sent the message?"

"The one called Vere."

Amanander turned away with a curse. "Vere? That useless, sniveling, coward? Vere has discovered Ferad's whereabouts? Has this information reached the Elders at the College?"

"We—we—"

"We?"

"I—I don't know, Great Lord," the Muten whispered. "He—he reached the one called Jesselyn and died there of the purple sickness. But the one called Everard took the message—"

"Jesselyn? Jesselyn Ridenau? And Everard Ridenau? My brother and sister?"

The Muten nodded vigorously.

"By the One. And Vere? What of Vere?"

"He has gone, Great Lord. Into the desert, into the mist. My master—"

"Your master is a fool." He pushed past the Muten, and glared at the great crest of the Ridenaus carved into the granite of the closest tomb. "It is no longer safe for him to remain in Dlas—" Abruptly, Amanander broke off and slammed his fist against the stone. "And Vere—Vere must be found. Do you understand?"

The Muten nodded eagerly. "I will tell him, Great Lord." He turned to go, but Amanander stopped him.

"Wait."

The Muten cringed.

"I want you to wait. Depending upon what happens in the next few days, I may need to leave Ahga and go looking for Vere myself. I will need you to take the message back to Ferad."

"My brothers search for the one called Everard. My master says that when he is found, he will be slain. And the one called Jesselyn—she, too—"

"Good." Amanander turned on his heel, and the stone ground beneath his feet.

"Great Lord?"

"What will I do for foods? For warmth?"

Amanander did not pause. "Your people are accomplished thieves, aren't they? The kitchens are up this way. You'll do well enough, I'm sure." His voice echoed eerily as he faded into the shadows.

Silent as a wraith, Amanander made his way back through the shadowed halls, into Gartred's chamber. With a terse command, he dismissed her serving woman and waited until one of his guard had escorted the protesting servant out of the apartment altogether. When her surprised admonitions had faded down the corridor, he stripped and slipped noiselessly into the bed beside the sleeping Gartred. He was tired, for the little trick he had played on Roderic earlier had sapped more of his energy than he had been willing to admit. The information which the Muten had brought was unsettling, and he was beginning to feel the strain. He had to find out the answers to his questions about Nydia Farhallen.

He was becoming more and more frustrated. He had probed Gartred's mind readily enough and discovered that the hen knew almost nothing. Everyone else—Phineas, Brand, any of the Senadors—who might remember Nydia and have the information was too well-guarded in his presence. But perhaps Gartred might still be of service.

Deftly he tied both her wrists together above her head and tethered her hands to the bedpost. He bent over her breasts, lapping and nipping with tongue and teeth and smiled as she began to writhe and moan. When he had teased the nipples to hard, high peaks, he took a candle from the bedside table and dripped a little of the metled wax onto the sensitive flesh. She came awake with a little scream, startled to find herself bound, and then relaxed with a sleepy smile when she recognized his dark head. "Lord Prince," she murmured.

He smiled. That was Roderic's title, but he wore it better than Roderic ever would. For answer he clamped down on one nipple, raking it between his teeth so hard she gasped. Without further ceremony he thrust his thumb and forefinger into both her lower passages. She went rigid. "Not ready for me, lady? At dinner you were as eager as a mare in heat."

She moaned and arched her back a little.

He plunged into her mind as readily as he had her body, searching for something, anything that might be turned to his use. A name surfaced unexpectedly. "Jesselyn Ridenau?" He spoke the name aloud.

"Mmm." Gartred shuddered as he withdrew his hand and forced her legs apart, and reached again for the candle.

He remembered Jesselyn, a dark-haired child, gravely beautiful—some five or six years his junior. She had spent her childhood here—and at Minnis—in the years when Abelard kept the witch-woman by his side. Perhaps she would know Nydia's fate.

"You can talk to her yourself," Gartred grunted beneath his assualt.

Amanander pulled away. It was not uncommon for the mindlink to work both ways. "Ask her myself?" he repeated. "What are you talking about?"

"Jesselyn. She's on her way here. Isn't that what you just asked me? I thought you knew. She's got some urgent information for Roderic—he's sending a special escort for her tomorrow."

Abruptly Amanander sat up. Gartred writhed a little against her bonds, arching her back. He slapped her face. "Be still and answer my questions. When does he expect her?"

"Oh," said Gartred petulantly, "he's not bringing her here. He doesn't want to antagonize the priests. So he's meeting her at Minnis in another week or two, as soon as he can get away." She spread her legs a little wider, bucking her hips.

Amanander looked at her, scorn curling his lower lip. He would have to reach Jesselyn before the escort. He narrowed his eyes and watched Gartred tug at her bonds. He moved over her, and she relaxed, smiling eagerly. "I'm afraid I'll be leaving soon," he whispered as he tightened his grip on the candle, "and ordinarily, I wouldn't take the time. But you've been so helpful, my dear, I'm going to give you more than you ever dreamed you wanted."

Chapter Ten

The beach was deserted. Not even a gull flew across the empty expanse of the wide, blue sky, and the dark sea stretched to the horizon, the wind whipping it to little foamy peaks. The sun was warm, but the breeze was cool. Jesselyn pulled her cloak around her and gave a brief shiver as the covered wagon lurched to an abrupt halt. Just over the last rise was the toll plaza which marked the boundary of the hereditary holdings of the Ridenau Kings. Minnis was still more than another week's journey away, but once within the Ridenau lands, the long-maintained peace had encouraged the growth of numerous congregations, and it was no longer safe for her to journey on alone. Roderic's messenger had instructed her to wait for the escort here.

Above the water, weatherbeaten ruins rose, weird, indefinable, the remains of some forgotten city of long ago, and a crossroad ran straight across the beach down into the waves. Beneath the water, black shapes bore mute testimony to dwellings long forgotten.

"Are you warm enough, Rever'd Lady?"

The driver's question startled Jesselyn out of her reverie. "I'll be fine, Chas'n." His gray-bearded face was creased with concern, and she noted with alarm the deep circles which ringed his faded eyes. It would be a relief to reach Minnis. She nodded toward the back of the wagon, where Tavia lay sleeping under a thin blanket. "We had better get a fire going. I'll look for wood."

She clambered out of the wagon, her much mended clerical garments of faded black rustling around her bare ankles. Her clumsy shoes flopped awkwardly on the sand.

"As you say, Rever'd Lady." Chas'n hoisted himself out of the wagon. His old joints were stiff from the long journey, she knew, and she stifled the urge to offer assistance. "I'll try to get the fire started and see to the horses. It's as well we're stopping. They're about done."

Jesselyn nodded agreement. The air from the sea stung with a clean salt tang that reminded her of her childhood in Ahga and made her feel as though she were fourteen again. She walked to the water's edge, the sand shifting between her toes as it found its way through the patched leather of her shoes. According to the Mutens, the North Sea had once been a series of five fresh-water lakes, changed to salt when the Old Magic had caused the sea to break through the confines of the ancient channel. She halted some five or six paces from the waterline and stared into the distance. North lay the sea, stretching to the horizon for as far as she could see, and somewhere, off to the west, lay Ahga. It was one of those first spring days, when the air was soft with the promise of summer, and the warmth of the sun still a surprise after winter's cold light. She took a deep breath, savoring the clean, salt scent, mixed with the wild smell of the beach grass, and raised her face. Perhaps it was not so bad to be going home after all.

A thin wisp of smoke blew across her line of vision. She turned, surprised that Chas'n should have started the fire so quickly. The old man was nowhere in sight. Concerned, Jesselyn scanned the rocks, which lay in heaps, perpendicular to the shore line. A tall, bearded man sat on top of a low gray slab. He was smoking a long clay pipe such as the Mutens did. At her startled gasp, he rose to his feet and made her an awkward bow. "Jesselyn? Please, don't be frightened. I'm Vere—your brother, Vere."

Jesselyn stumbled back a few steps. Her initial reaction was to gather her skirts and flee to the wagon, but she controlled herself long enough to take a closer look at the tall, thin man before her. He wore a simple gray tunic, belted at the waist, patched gray leggings and soft leather boots. At his waist was a long dagger in a sheath decorated with intricate beadwork. His gray hair was long and streaked with white, his cheeks above his beard decorated with swirling tatoos in green and white and blue.

The tatoos convinced her. The patterns were familiar from the stories she had heard the Children tell, although she had never seen them. But she knew they delineated a member of the College, someone with access and knowledge to much that had been lost during the terrible days of the Armageddon. "Vere? Is it really you?"

"Yes." He advanced across the sand, his pipe held at his side, one hand outstretched. She took the hand he offered, and was struck by the delicate clasp of his long fingers. But the skin on those fingers was rougher than her own, and Vere's eyes, though shadowed by deep lines, were bright and piercing, the eyes of a man who saw across great distances.

"Are you going back to Ahga, too?" It was the first thing which popped into her mind at this most unexpected meeting with Vere, the brother she barely remembered. He had left Ahga sometime during Mortmain's Rebellion, had run away from the hopes and expectations of a father who never understood him, from the life he was so completely unsuited to lead. She had known for some time that Vere had gone to live among the Mutens, had been accepted as one of them at the secret College. But he had never contacted her, and she had never heard exactly where he was, for the location of the College was among the most jealously guarded of all the Muten secrets.

He smiled. "Yes."

"Have you heard?" she blurted. "About Dad? About Roderic?"

"That's what's brought me here. I see you come well equipped." He nodded in the direction of the wagon, where Chas'n had begun to haul out provisions for dinner, and Tavia had emerged from her cocoon and was staring at the water. "Is that Tavia?"

Jesselyn nodded, then put out her hand to stop him when he would have called out a greeting. "No, no, you mustn't. You'll frighten her. She's not like you remember. She's changed."

"Why?" Vere frowned. "What's happened to her?"

Jesselyn shook her head. "I scarcely know what to say. I have so many questions—so much has changed—I—"

"Jessie." Vere's thin mouth curved in a gentle smile beneath his beard. "I'm coming with you to Ahga—we have plenty of time to talk. Introduce me to your manservant."

She gathered up her skirts, and together they started back up the beach.

They had only gone a few steps when Vere said, "I wasn't strictly truthful. It's true I'm going to Ahga, but I'm here because of you."

"Me?" She stopped short.

"On my way back to the College, I met Everard. I'm grateful for what you did for my servant, Torach."

Jesselyn shook her head. "By the time we found him there was nothing I could do. I saw to his funeral, that's all."

"That's enough. But Everard told me you were on your way to Roderic—and I agree he must be told the content of my message to the Elders. I knew you'd have to come this way. So I thought I'd offer myself as an escort." Although he spoke lightly, Jesselyn noticed how his eyes ceaselessly scanned the road and hills around them.

Jesselyn frowned. There was more to his story than Vere

was telling. "Roderic is sending an escort, but perhaps now that you're here, I can go back."

"And not go to Ahga?"

"Surely you can't be eager to return. I always thought you were unhappy there, and I certainly have no desire to meet Roderic. None at all."

"Because of what he did in Atland?"

Jesselyn nodded.

Vere looked grim. "Our little brother might well live to regret that day. But I'm not certain that Roderic was truly responsible."

She stared at him in disbelief. "He gave the orders."

Vere motioned her on. "Come, Jessie. We'll talk after dinner."

The sun had set by the time their simple meal was finished and their utensils washed and stored away. The sky was a wash of lavender and pink and indigo, and the water lapped against the shore as gently as a sated suckling infant. The fire, fueled by driftwood, burned brightly. Vere stretched out his long legs and lit his pipe. Chas'n was already snoring in his bedroll, and Tavia had retreated to the high front seat of the wagon, where she sat murmuring a tuneless lullaby to her rag doll.

"How has Tavia managed the trip?" asked Vere.

"Well enough. I couldn't leave her, you see, and I thought—well, Ahga was her home, too, until she was married. I hoped when she saw it maybe something would remind her that there were happier days. . . ." Jesselyn's voice trailed off.

"Tell me what happened."

Jesselyn traced an aimless pattern of lines in the sand with the broken edge of a shell. "Tavia was married when she was seventeen to a son of one of the Arkan lords. I was only six, but I remember how beautiful she was as a bride. A year or two after that, she was traveling across the Arkan Plain to meet her husband. She was pregnant. They were attacked by Harleyriders, and the entire party was killed."

"And only she survived?"

"She was found a few days later." Jesselyn wrapped her arms around her knees and stared unseeing into the fire. "You know how brutal the Harleys are. The baby had been cut from her womb and left to die with the rest."

"How could she have survived?"

"No one knows. I have an idea, but—" Abruptly she glanced over her shoulder. Tavia rocked her doll, oblivious to their conversation. "I believe she must have been found by an empath."

Vere raised an eyebrow. "An empath? What makes you think so?"

"I've heard the stories the Children tell—that they have the ability to heal, to heal completely. And, on her body, although it was clear what must have happened, there are no scars, no marks of any kind. She is untouched. There isn't even any evidence that she was ever pregnant, let alone mutilated."

"Except the scars she carries in her mind."

Jesselyn nodded. "I guess whoever healed her wasn't strong enough to heal her mind as well."

"Such a thing would be impossible, I would think." Vere took a long draw on his pipe. "Empathy develops over time, but even the oldest and most experienced empaths have limits. If they spend too much of their energy at one time, they can die. And if Tavia was as wounded as you say, I would think the empath did the best she could and hoped that time would do the rest."

"She? You think it was a woman?" Jesselyn raised her brows in surprise.

"Empaths are almost always female."

Jesselyn shrugged. "I'm not sure whoever it was did her a

kindness." She glanced again at Tavia. Tavia was undoing the lacings of her bodice.

"What is she doing?" asked Vere.

"Watch."

He stared in fascinated horror as Tavia exposed one blue-veined breast and pushed her large brown nipple into the face of the doll. Drops of pearly, translucent milk made a spreading stain across its clumsily stitched face.

"Even her body weeps," murmured Jesselyn.

"And she never conceived again."

"What man would have her in her present state? You know as well as I do that it is no simple thing for a woman to conceive. I have lain with more men than I can count, and I have never borne a child. When Tavia lost her baby, she lost her only chance to have one. Only the Mutens—the Children—are able to bring more than one offspring into the world, and we humans are engaged in systematically killing them."

"It's a matter of resources, Jessie—"

Jesselyn tossed back her hair. "Spare me the lecture. Why do men always think that simply because a woman has another point of view, she can't comprehend a man's? I know that hatred is fueled by jealousy and greed and fear. But why can't we humans learn to accept the Children? They bleed the same color blood we do."

Vere did not reply. He stared into the leaping flames, puffing on his pipe. The fragrant smoke swirled about his face. Jesselyn wondered if she should have mentioned her thoughts about the empath. But why not? Vere was a part of the secret College. Empathy was an ability which passed from parent to child. After the Armageddon, during the Persecutions, the priests incited the mobs to burn such people, along with the Magic-users, as witches and servants of evil. It was said many had found refuge with the Mutens.

Finally Jesselyn spoke. "What made you run away?"

"I wasn't happy in Ahga, Jessie. Father—" here Vere

smiled at the ancient form of address used by the Mutens as a title of respect for the Pr'fessors "—Dad never thought much of me. I was the only one of seven sons who couldn't handle a spear or a sword, or even a staff. And while I was there, I never thought much of myself. So I decided to try to find a place I would fit in—where the things which mattered to me mattered to others, and I found it with the Children. What about you? You're a renegade, too, in your own way. What made you decide to set up the mission for the Children?"

"I was sent from Ahga to establish a congregation. And I guess I did. But the ones who made up my flock weren't the people I was sent to minister to, and so, when I refused to stop, I was placed under interdict by the Bishop of Ahga. That's why I needed an escort into Ahga. There's the possibility that if the Bishop catches me there, I could be imprisoned, or worse. Certainly I'd never see my congregation again."

"I've heard of the work you do." Vere shifted his position. "I was proud to be your brother." Their eyes met across the fire, and Jesselyn felt hers fill with tears. The breeze whipped a loose strand of hair across her face, and she brushed it away, pulling her cloak closer.

"I suppose we ought to sleep."

Vere nodded. "Go on. I'll keep watch for a little. In the morning, we should be on our way. This road goes straight to Ahga—we'll meet Roderic's escort on the way."

"But—I'm going back the way I came in the morning. You're here, and there's no reason for me to go to Ahga now," said Jesselyn.

Vere shook his head. "I'm afraid that knowing what you do, Jessie, even though that's not so very much, it may not be safe for you to go back."

"Not safe? The Children have never harmed me—even on our journey through the lands torn by the rebellion, I had no trouble. It's not the Children I fear."

Vere sighed. "There're some things about the Children you don't know. Have you ever heard of the Brotherhood?"

"No."

The silence lengthened between them and Jesselyn waited for Vere to explain. But finally, when he rose to his feet, all he said was, "You'll be safer in Ahga, Jessie. As safe as anyplace is likely to be." Troubled, she watched him pace across the beach and stand like a gray ghost at the dark water's edge.

Chapter Eleven

"And that's your last word?" Phineas spoke with such clipped precision Roderic looked from his brother Phillip to Phineas with surprise. He had never heard Phineas speak so coldly to anyone. Halfway down the long council table, Phillip glanced around the empty council room and stifled a sigh. At least, thought Roderic, he had the grace to look uncomfortable: shifting restlessly in the rigid confines of his chair, plucking at the wide band of gold embroidery on the sleeve of his flowing blue tunic with fingers heavy with rings of every description. Not only had Phillip something of Abelard's coloring, and Abelard's build, he had something of Abelard's presence as well. In the daily sessions of the Congress, among the more soberly dressed Senadors of the Arkan Plains and the war-ravaged mountain estates, Phillip with his bright blond hair and flamboyant clothes stood out like a swan among sparrows. A pity, thought Roderic, that Phillip apparently lacked Abelard's commitment to the unity of the realm.

Phillip's gaze darted from Phineas to Roderic and back. "Lord Phineas, please." He spoke with the slow, patient tone used with invalids, and Roderic writhed inwardly. How could Phillip so underrate Phineas?

"Try to understand," continued Phillip, "I know the perception you midlanders have—that Nourk is rich, with men enough to satisfy every demand. But we too have had to strengthen our borders against the Muten threat—Nourk has—"

"Nourk has ever held back," Phineas interrupted, his voice so dangerously soft that Roderic automatically straightened in his chair. "We only ask you for reserves. The Congress may have acclaimed Roderic Regent, but this country is far from settled. We only ask you for reserves, reserves to be held at Ithan Ford, in the event they are needed for the defense of Arken."

"But Ithan is much too far away for my needs. What if the Muten tribes in the North rebel? My own lands will be vulnerable. Surely you can't expect me to send men when my own situation may change at any time?" Phillip met Phineas's tone with a biting edge of his own. His blue eyes flashed and he looked so much like the King, something twisted in Roderic's chest. Abruptly Phillip pushed his chair back from the table, and Roderic noticed for the first time the hint of a paunch beneath his ornate robes. Life must be easy in Nourk for a man of fighting age to run to fat.

"The losses in Atland were heavy," answered Phineas.

"And why was that? I beg your pardon, Lord Prince, but perhaps it had something to do with your inexperience in the field. Or maybe your indifference to slaughter."

Roderic flinched and lowered his eyes. That day in Atland would haunt him for a long time.

Phillip stood up, placed his fists on the table, and leaned on the glass-topped surface. A bright shaft of light reflected off the glass, cutting across his face. "I renewed my Pledge of Allegiance. I will honor my oath if and when I must. But I will think long and hard before I commit my men." He looked at Roderic and inclined his head in a brief bow. "And that is my last word."

Phillip strode out of the room, his tunic swirling in rich folds around his ankles. When the door had closed behind him, Roderic stole a glance at Phineas. The old man's hands were laced across his chest and his lips were pursed. "We've never talked about what happened in Atland."

Phineas's eyes flickered and he drew a deep breath. "I don't blame you for the losses in Atland."

"That's not what Phillip meant." Roderic twisted his hands together. "It's the day Ebram-taw—the day I had—" He broke off and bit his lip so hard he tasted the salty-sweet tang of blood.

"Why did you do it, my son?"

"I don't know!" The answer burst from his throat, and he clenched his fists. "By Dad's throne, I don't know, Phineas. I don't understand why I did what I did. I guess—I guess I thought there was no other way."

"And perhaps there wasn't."

Roderic stared at the old man, not certain he had heard correctly.

"Perhaps there wasn't any other way to end it, Roderic. I'm not saying what you did was right—I can hear in your voice how wrong you thought it was. But every one of us—your father, Brand, even Phillip, the sanctimonious fool—have done things we are not proud of. Things we've lived to regret. There are always consequences, Roderic. Always. No matter what the choice."

Roderic spread the palms of his hands flat against the cool glass surface of the council table. Beneath his hands, preserved under the glass, were maps of ancient Meriga, so old that if they were ever moved they would crumble into dust. Sunlight made rainbow prisms on the walls, and his eyes fell on a grayed banner hanging limp and tattered in the corner. Legend said it was the flag of Old Meriga, and still barely discernible in the frayed fabric were thirteen stripes and fifty stars. What choices had the men of Old Meriga made that their children had lived to regret? "What are we to do?"

"About Phillip? Let him posture all he pleases. If we do need his troops, his oath will require him to send them. And if his conscience requires him to stir himself from behind his mountains and ride to war, so much the better. Phillip is hardly the one to talk to you about inexperience."

Roderic suppressed a smile. Nourk's natural defenses made the possibility of invasion remote, and Roderic could not recall a time when the Senadors of Nourk had called upon the throne for aid. Abelard had thought to bring Nourk's resources into the sphere of his control when Phillip had been married to the old Senador's daughter. But apparently, Abelard had been wrong.

The moment lengthened, and finally Phineas roused himself with a sigh. "Have all the dispatches we discussed yesterday gone out?"

"This morning." Roderic was glad to change the subject. "I never realized, Phineas, that so much of my time would be spent signing my name."

"Now you understand why your father, who loved to hunt, went so seldom to Minnis."

Roderic narrowed his eyes. "You don't think I should leave to meet Jesselyn." It was a statement, not a question, and Phineas was silent for what seemed like a long time.

"Jesselyn's message troubles me," he said at last.

Roderic rose and paced to the window, where the late afternoon sun had broken through the low-hanging clouds and the light glinted on the sea. The white sails of the fishing boats bobbed over the whitecaps. Less than a week after he had been acclaimed Regent, he could not deny that he had begun to think of the dark green forests and cool lakes of Minnis Saul with longing. Dispatches from every corner of the realm were pouring into Ahga, an unstoppable flood that carried no regard for youth or inexperience, only requests for supplies and men and justice—the King's justice to settle the endless disputes of a thousand competing interests.

As Phineas and Brand had anticipated, the Harleyriders who, for the last twenty years, had been more or less confined to the deserts of Loma and Dlas, had taken the opportunity of the Muten Rebellion to try and wrest back control of a greater portion of the Arkan Plains. Now they rode their shaggy ponies with greater and greater impunity, daring to press deeper and deeper into Arkan, into lands which had not seen the ravages of their raids for two decades.

During the three days of the Convening, Senadors, who had grown more or less quiescent under Abelard's firm grip, raised their voices experimentally, as if to test his heir, and acting under Phineas's advice, Roderic dismissed the Congress. With Roderic's confirmation as Regent, the reason for the emergency Convening had been addressed; there was no need, said Phineas, to continue. Daily more and more petitioners appeared in the outer wards, seeking a hearing at the King's Court of Appeals.

That very morning, Amanander had left for Dlas with orders to suppress the Harleyriders by whatever means necessary. Roderic had spent many hours with old Gredahl, the First of the Senadors of the Arkan Plains. The men of Arkan were tough and proud and bent the knee to few, but Roderic knew that among all the Senadors in the Congress, he could number them among his closest allies. But the men of Arkan could not stand alone, and Phineas had hoped to hear a firm promise of help from Phillip.

He hooked his thumbs in his belt. "It troubles me, too, Phineas," he said, watching the boats skim over the water. At this height, seven stories above the ground, even the largest of the fishing boats looked toy-sized. "And I don't want to antagonize the Bishop—"

Phineas waved a hand in dismissal. "She's old, Roderic. The fight went out of her a long time ago. But perhaps—" Phineas paused.

"Yes?" Roderic prompted.

"No matter, boy. Go to Minnis. After everything in these

last few months, you deserve a few days respite. Call for my bearers, please?"

"Phineas—" Roderic hesitated, unsure how to broach the subject he wanted to discuss. "Last night, Gartred asked me for permission to leave Ahga in order to visit Elsemone. Do you think I should let her go?" He had already told Phineas of the advances the woman had made and his discovery of how she had treated Peregrine and his child. Her request had come as a relief. Her daughter, his youngest half-sister, Elsemone, was married to the heir of one of the Lords of Mondana. It would be an easy thing for Gartred to ride with Nevin Vantigorn.

Phineas spread his hands. "Why not?"

"Then—"

"Say what you must, boy."

"I need a First Lady, do I not?"

Phineas nodded. "I suppose." He raised one eyebrow and tilted his head. "And you have someone in mind?"

"Peregrine Anuriel—you know, the daughter of—"

"I know who she is," Phineas interrupted sharply, so sharply Roderic was surprised.

"Well, I was thinking, you see. She's borne my child, and I thought perhaps, with my father's consort gone, I could make Peregrine the First Lady of my household, and then, perhaps—"

"Are you thinking of marrying this girl?"

Roderic cocked his head. "I—I thought it should be considered. Do you think Dad would object?"

What little color there was in the old man's leathery cheeks drained away. Phineas laced his fingers together and rubbed the palms of his hands together. "In the first place, you have no heir. And the subject of your marriage—" Phineas paused, obviously groping for words. Roderic narrowed his eyes. He had never seen Phineas so upset. "Make her your First Lady, if you will. The subject of your marriage—" Once more,

Phineas seemed to hesitate. "Must wait. Now, please. Call for my bearers. It's time we went down to the hall. The first of the Courts of Appeal is scheduled, and if you are intent on going to Minnis, we must try to hear as many cases as possible before you leave."

As he followed Phineas's litter down the stairs, Roderic pondered the strange reaction to the subject of his marriage. Perhaps, he decided, as he reached the hall, and saw the petitioners lining the walls, it was only a response to all that had happened in the last weeks. Enough had happened, he thought, as he assumed his father's place on the dais. Phineas was right. He would not broach the subject of marriage again. At least, he thought, as the scribe handed him a scroll pertaining to the first matter, not until he had something tangible to offer Peregrine. Gartred would go, Amanander had gone. The business of the government seemed well in hand.

He glanced up at the bearded faces of the merchants clustered before the dais. One held bolts of cloth, another a broken wagon wheel. Another was speaking in a low voice to one of the court scribes, gesturing with a scroll covered in many-colored seals. He nodded, more to himself than to the men before him, and the herald, gaudily dressed in the blue-and-white tabard embroidered with the Ridenau crest, stepped forward. With a loud cry, he announced the opening of the court. Roderic leaned back in his father's chair. The real work of his regency had begun.

Less than two weeks after his affirmation as the Regent of all Meriga, Roderic, with Alexander, Brand, Peregrine, and two companies of the King's Guard, set out for Minnis to wait for Jesselyn and enjoy a few days respite. As they cleared the outskirts of the city, Roderic spurred his mount on ahead, as he always had as a boy, and burst out of the city gates ahead of the rest. Before him, the road opened up into the wide paved roads of the open countryside, the rolling green fields and well-maintained farms which stood as testimony to the years of peace under Abelard's rule.

Just outside the city, he saw a crew working to repair the surface of the roads following the harsh winter weather, and Roderic raised his hand in greeting and stopped to speak to the workmen. It was these roads which had enabled his father and his grandfather to move armies and supplies across the great distances of Meriga, these roads which cut through mountains, arched over rivers, reaching across the wide plains straighter than arrows. His tutors had all emphasized the strategic and tactical importance of the highways, and Abelard had never begrudged the high costs of maintenance.

It was of some witch's brew, thought Roderic, as they continued on their way, that the ancient pavings had been poured, and he wondered if the men who had made the roads had known they were building their greatest legacy.

They had just remounted after stopping for a brief lunch, when Alexander nudged his mount over to Roderic. "A word, if you will, Roderic. When I go back to Spogan, there is a coil waiting for me. I hope you might have some insight."

"Me?" Roderic pulled at the reins so sharply that the horse whickered a protest. Alexander's face behind his beard was smooth, impassive; his eyes held an expression impossible to read. He knows about Atland, realized Roderic. He knows, and he wants to see what sort of ruler I am. "I doubt that I'll have any insight to offer," he said at last. "You know that region so much better than I."

Quickly Alexander outlined the current state of affairs in the Northwest, and as Roderic listened, a glimmer of understanding began to dawn. It came down to one thing. When Abelard had set a royal administrator over the affairs of the Senador of Ragonn, as punishment for his participation in Mortmain's Rebellion, he had upset the delicate balance of power in that region. So devastated by the effects of that rebellion was Ragonn, however, that the unablanced situation wasn't felt until now, more than twenty-five years later.

" . . . and I believe a full-scale war is inevitable, if things continue on their present course," finished Alexander.

"So we must find another way to balance the power than resorting to violence," Roderic replied.

Alexander looked surprised. "And what do you suggest?"

"Perhaps it is time to recall the royal administrator. Leave the troops in place, but I'll send out a dispatch to their commanding officer, ordering him to report to you. That will remove one thorn in your side, as well as give you more flexibility, in terms of men and resources."

Alexander was looking at him with wary respect. "Indeed, Lord Prince. It very well may." They trotted along in silence. Once more, Alexander cleared his throat. "There is another matter, Roderic. The M'Callaster, old Cormall, has a younger daughter, Brea. I'd like your permission to ask him for her hand."

"You want to marry her?" Roderic's mind raced furiously. Old Cormall had no sons, only two daughters by two different women. If Alexander married one, it was possible that he could inherit the title of the Settle Islands—and what would that do to the balance of power in the Northwest?

"Old Cormall's close to death. I think he'd like to see her provided for. No—" Alexander shook his head at the skepticism Roderic could not hide. "It's not what you're thinking. When one of the Chiefs dies without a direct heir, the contenders for his title must fight for it. I don't promise that I wouldn't fight for it myself, but it is no certain thing."

"And what about the older daughter?"

"Dierdre? A hell-cat if ever there was one. It'll take a better man than I to tame her." Alexander hesitated, and when he spoke again, his voice was soft. "I love Brea, Roderic. I'd take her if she had nothing but a shift on her shoulders."

"I will think on it. You understand that I must consult with Dad's Council over most decisions?"

Alexander nodded, a smile playing beneath his beard. "As you say, Lord Prince. As you say."

Chapter Twelve

They took the journey to Minnis in easy stages. Ever since Amanander had left, the whole atmosphere seemed changed. Roderic remembered the looks of relief among the soldiers of the King's Guard when Amanander and his four bodyguards had ridden out of Ahga.

On the last morning of their journey, before the towers of Minnis were visible, a party of men on foot stepped out from beneath the thick cover of trees and waited by the roadside until Roderic and his companions drew closer.

The leader of the group, a short man dressed in a much-patched tunic and trousers, a longbow slung over his shoulder raised his hand in a cautious salute. "Greetings. We seek the King."

Roderic exchanged glances with Brand. The Wildings roamed the northern forests between C'Nadia and Meriga, coming over the border especially in the summer. They were a solitary, nomadic people, who kept to themselves and lived off the land. Occasionally there were complaints of theft, but the Wildings so seldom went into populated areas, they were left alone for the most part.

"I'm Roderic Ridenau," said Roderic, as he guided his horse to the fore. "My father, the King, is away. I am his heir. Can I be of assistance?"

The man glanced over his shoulder at his companions, and cleared his throat. "We hope so, lord. It's the lycats, you see.

The winter was bad up here, and there's one that's taken to killing humans."

"It's huge, lord." Another man spoke up. "And it stalks us in the night—we've kept watch, but the thing is clever—it knows when our men are watching."

"It takes our children," said another, with a quiver in his voice. "Got my daughter—she was only four years old."

Roderic glanced again at Brand, who shrugged. Roderic suppressed a sigh. Even here, there were still responsibilities to be met. "Good people, we will do what we can. Tomorrow morning, before the sun rises, my men and I will go out to the hunt. Meanwhile, if you would come to Minnis this evening, around sunset, and give us more information about the beast—where it last hunted, where it's been seen—we will do what we can."

There were low murmurs of assent and gratitude, and with awkward bows, the men faded back into the trees.

"It must be bad," said Alexander. "I can count the number of times on one hand the Wildings have approached me in all my years in Spogan. Even when the Sascatch Tribes are on the hunt, the Wildings keep to themselves."

"I've caught glimpses of them now and again," said Brand.

Roderic nodded in agreement. "Sometimes, in the deep forest, I think I've seen them watching through the trees."

"Better a Wilding than a lycat or a Sascatch," said Brand.

"Indeed," said Alexander. "Wildings don't eat you for dinner."

The next day, Roderic rose before the sun and pressed a kiss into the tender skin beneath Peregrine's ear. She smiled in her sleep and snuggled deeper into her pillows. "Don't go," she murmured, and for a moment he hesitated. The thought of returning to her side in the warm nest of blankets was tempting, but then he sighed and reached for the clothes he had discarded the day before.

The Wildings' plea was serious. Once having caught the taste of human meat, lycats never hesitated to hunt and stalk such relatively easy prey. The soldiers of the garrison had confirmed that many lycats had been sighted in the forest surrounding the castle, and one or two of the beasts had even been seen from the walls of Minnis itself. The winter before last had been mild, and the past summer dry, resulting in ideal breeding conditions. As a result, there was a large hungry population roaming the depleted forest.

The rising sun whitened the mist as the hunting party rode out from the high walls of Minnis, and tiny drops of water condensed off the burgeoning canopy of leaves overhead. There was a wet, sweet scent in the air, a green scent, and the horses' hooves made a muted squish upon the damp earth of the forest trails. Roderic felt he belonged in these woods, beneath these trees, as though with his father's responsibilities came an appreciation of his father's pleasures.

There was a sense of rightness which hung about him, even as the sun rose and the mist dissipated, and the horses crashed through the green undergrowth. And this time, when his blood began to burn, and his senses seemed to swell with the fire of the hunt, he felt none of the shameful guilt he had known that awful day in Atland, no awareness in some inner recess of his mind that what he did was wrong. He swung his sword and threw his spear, and in the dark spurting blood, he felt somehow cleansed.

The hunt was not completely successful: in less than a few hours they had found and killed five of the beasts, but none so large as that which the Wildings had described.

The men rested as the sun pierced through the leaves with bright shafts of light, laughing and passing pieces of the fresh-baked bread and new-made cheese they had brought with them. Roderic lay on his back and listened to the others congratulate themselves and discuss the finer points of the hunt.

The day was pleasantly warm, yet the breeze which stirred the treetops was cool. As the men got to their feet, brushing leaves and debris from their clothes, Roderic rolled on his side and sat up. "Go on without me," he said, over their startled protests. "It's too late in the day for the lycats, and we are close enough to Minnis."

"But what will you do, Lord Prince?" asked the oldest of the lot, clearly bewildered.

"It's been so long since I had any time to myself, Teck. I shall be along shortly. Tell the Lady Peregrine that I'll want my dinner as soon as I bathe. And tell the duty sergeant I said you were each to have double rations of ale today, for all your pains."

They needed no more urging than that, and Roderic was left in peace. He leaned against a tree trunk, remembering how, as a child, he had often been afraid of the deep forest, the shadows beneath the ancient trees. His old terrors were all forgotten. Perhaps that was to be expected. Imaginary monsters paled in comparison to real enemies armed with razor spears.

He had just decided to go back when he heard the first of the thin cries. It was a high-pitched wail, and the terror in it was unmistakable. Roderic cocked his head and listened for the direction of the cry. When it came again, he swung up into his saddle and guided the horse at a quick trot through the dense underbrush.

The cry came again, and this time it was pitched with pain. He touched his spurs to the stallion's sides and crashed into a clearing, in time to see the largest lycat he had ever imagined standing on hind legs, against a partially fallen tree, claws extended. Its opened mouth revealed fangs at least six inches in length, a grotesque variation of the tabbies that haunted the stables and the kitchens.

The tree had long ago been struck by lightning, or toppled

by disease, for its trunk leaned over, and vines and a thick crop of tiny branches covered it like leafy hair.

The lycat crouched, poised to spring, and again, Roderic heard the high, thin wail of terror. Before he could throw the spear, however, the lycat pounced, and even as he aimed, the animal fell back, clutching a human child.

He came at a gallop, spear poised, and with one tremendous thrust, he buried it hard into the animal's side. The stallion screamed a challenge of its own to the red-and-brown spotted beast as they thundered past. Roderic pulled hard on the reins. The horse wheeled and reared.

With a jerk of its head, the lycat flung the child into the weeds at the base of the tree. Thick blood pulsed from a gash on the child's neck as he lay still in a crumpled heap.

The spear quivered deep in the lycat's side, but Roderic saw that he had missed a mortal blow by many inches. There was a bright burning hatred in the animal's eyes as it stood to take the measure of its newest prey. It stood, still as a stone, only its tail lashing. And then it threw back its head and roared, and Roderic saw the bloodstained yellow fangs, the pink jaws lined with double rows of teeth. The horse whinnied nervously as it caught the fetid stench of the carnivore. The lycat crouched, eyes on Roderic.

Roderic let the horse fall back several paces, wrapped the reins around one hand, and drew his short sword from the scabbard on his hip. As the animal sprang at the horse's neck, Roderic pulled hard on the reins, forcing the stallion to rear, and he slashed the edge of the sword through the lycat's throat. A heavy paw raked at his shoulder, and he felt the burn and sting as the sharp claws tore through his leather armor, piercing the flesh below. He managed to turn the horse's rump out of the way, so that the lycat fell with a thud to the ground. Dust rose in a cloud, and settled slowly. The last air escaped the lycat's lungs in a long, rattling sigh, and it went limp.

Still breathing heavily, Roderic leapt out of the saddle and flung the reins around the lowest limb of the nearest tree.

He wiped the sword hastily on his thigh. Forgetting the pain in his own arm, he grabbed the flask of water tied to his saddle, and hastened to the child, who lay just as the lycat had thrown him, like a discarded bundle.

The child moaned. He was a boy, about six or seven, a tiny dagger still clenched in a bloody fist. The wound in his throat gaped, bubbles of blood rose with each shallow breath.

Mercifully the boy was unconscious. Roderic looked around, wishing he had not sent the others on their way, for there was nothing he could do for the child except to try and take him back to Minnis. He had no idea where the Wilding camp might be. And yet, if moved, the boy was likely to die before they ever reached it. Kneeling, he placed one hand on the child's forehead. Already the flesh was clammy and grayish. The boy breathed in long, harsh gasps that ended in a rattle. Beneath the torn stripes of pink flesh and yellow fat, Roderic saw the gleam of white bone. It would not be long now.

He sighed and tore a length of fabric off the bottom of his tunic. He poured water on the rag and bathed the child's face. At the touch of the cool water, the child shifted feebly and moaned again. Roderic splashed more water on the rag, and held it to the child's lips, pressing it so a little water ran down into the boy's mouth. He adjusted his sword across his thigh and sat against the tree trunk.

The breeze ruffled his hair, drying the sweat on his face. Gently, he touched the child's back. The clearing was preternaturally quiet, except for the slow drone of the flies which had found the carcass and the rustle of leaves in the branches over his head. There was a difference between watching a man die in battle and a child die so senselessly. And then, unbidden, a vision of Atland rose before him, a vision of the helpless wretches who had died at least as painfully as this. Surely it had been no different for them than for this boy. And I was responsible, he thought, as surely as if I had wielded the dagger and the sword. How could I have done such a thing? How will I ever forget?

He dabbed once more at the child's face, and was about to lean back when some instinct brought him suddenly alert. The hair on the back of his neck rose. He crouched, left hand on the hilt of his dagger.

In the shadows beneath the trees across the clearing, a figure stood, slim as a young beech, dressed in a motley assortment of rags. Male or female he could not tell, but the person was smaller than he, and certainly looked no threat. "Come out," he called.

The figure stepped into the clearing and looked around as though to see who else might be watching. Roderic realized it was a girl, no more than his own age.

"The lycat's dead." Roderic gestured to the body of the fallen animal. "Come, there's nothing to fear."

As she came closer, Roderic saw that her clothes—a short tunic and leggings—were even more ragged than the ones he had seen the Wildings wearing, and clumsily patched, as though an unskilled hand had done the work. But perhaps, he thought, yesterday's delegation had deliberately dressed in their finest. Her feet were bare, though so dirty they appeared at first glance to be shod. Dark unruly curls fell in a rich mass about her face, bound back only by what appeared to be an attempt at a coif such as the ladies of the court wore. The pathos of this made him peer more closely at her. He caught a glimpse of a straight nose, cleft chin, and full, rosy lips before she bent her head away from him. He gestured to the child lying in the grass.

"Do you know him?" Roderic beckoned impatiently, for the girl seemed reluctant to approach. "Is there a camp nearby? Can you take word to your people, bring help?"

"I will take him." The girl's voice was low and sweet, with nothing of the northern burr of the Wilding's speech, and there was some familiarity of cadence which made him wary.

At this extraordinary statement, Roderic squinted up at her, as she stood silhouetted against the sun. "He's dying. You can't possibly take him anywhere. If your people are close enough and you will show me the way, perhaps we can take him on my horse."

"I will take him."

At this, Roderic rose. Perhaps the girl was a little simple. Such a thing was common he had heard, amongst the Wildings, who kept to themselves and were said to interbreed. She kept her face averted. He resisted the sudden urge to tug her chin around to look at him. "You can't."

"I must."

"The child's nearly dead—"

"And he'll die if you don't let me take him." This was spoken with such conviction that Roderic narrowed his eyes.

"You're nothing but a child yourself. He's much too heavy—"

"While we stand and argue, he is dying."

There was unmistakable truth to this, and Roderic stepped aside. She walked past him, knelt beside the boy, and a long shudder seemed to pass through her as she laid a dirt-smudged hand on the child.

"I told you it was bad," he said.

She raised her face, and he saw tiny beads of sweat had formed on her upper lip, across her forehead. She looked as though she were about to faint. He narrowed his eyes, wondering if it were some trick of the shadows that there was something familiar about her, something he ought to recognize. He leaned closer, and instantly she turned her face away, but not before he caught a glimpse of eyes a vivid and intense shade of blue.

"Not too far from here, there's a track through the wood,"

she said. "Do you know it?" She refused to face him, almost, he thought, as though she feared he might know her. But there had been no women amongst the Wilding party yesterday.

"It leads to a lake." He tried to see past her profile, but a lock of her thick hair had fallen down her cheek.

"His—our people are there. Take your horse. I'll stay with him."

Roderic hesitated. There was logic in her words, and yet the feelings she roused in him had nothing to do with logic. He realized with a start that he had no wish to leave her, that somehow to remove himself from her presence was to lose something precious yet so intangible it defied definition. There was something magnetic about this girl, something that appealed to him beyond reason or even simple lust. She had aroused him by her very presence, and yet his need to possess her was at once more compelling, and less explicable, than anything he had ever felt before. His flesh seemed to expand beneath his clothing. By an act of will out of all proportion to the situation, he turned to go, thought again and turned back. She had her hand on the child and was leaning closer over the still figure. He thought he heard another moan.

"Go!" It was a low, choking sound, and it spurred him on.

He mounted the horse and followed the trail. Originally it had been a road, for here and there black pieces of ancient paving lay revealed beneath the encroaching underbrush. The trail itself led directly down into the lake. He stopped on the sandy shore, looked around. There was no sign at all of any human habitation.

He had been tricked. With a curse, he jerked the horse around and the stallion reared and whinnied in protest. He crashed back through the wood, back to the clearing, and stopped. The girl and the child were gone. He clucked at the horse, and flapped the reins, and obediently, it moved slowly forward. The lycat's body was where he had left it, flies buzzing around its wounds and bloody jaws. He retrieved his spear.

Roderic guided the horse over to the tree. A slight depression in the long weeds, as well as smears of congealing blood, marked the place where the child had lain. He got off the horse and touched the crushed weeds. The blood was sticky. Some of it had formed a gelatinous clump, and flies crawled eagerly over it. His stomach churned with disgust. The girl could not have carried the child away. She might have been able to drag the body, but—

Roderic examined the ground for the marks of a body being dragged. There was nothing. Slowly, he straightened. The sun was at its height and sweat trickled down between his shoulder blades. The horse whickered and stamped impatiently. Absently Roderic patted its head as it nosed at him and snorted. There was something very odd about the girl. It was almost as though he should have known her—and yet, surely, yesterday had been the closest contact he'd ever had with the Wildings in his life. Slowly, still troubled, he mounted the horse. There was nothing more he could do—the responsibility for whether the child lived or died had been taken from his hands. He clucked, and the stallion turned eagerly for home. But the girl—why had she lied? She had seemed genuinely concerned for the child. Perhaps the camp was nearer—it was well known that the Wildings were extremely secretive. But surely, she should have needed help. Sighing, he shook his head and rode slowly back to Minnis, leaving the mystery behind him.

He knew something was wrong when he saw the soldiers on the walls cry out at his approach, and Brand himself came running to grasp his bridle. "What is it?" he began, but Brand cut him off without any attempt at ceremony.

"The escort you sent for Jesselyn arrived. She's dead."

Chapter Thirteen

Roderic stared at Brand in disbelief. "Dead?" he repeated. "How?"

Brand handed the reins to a groom. "Come with me. The sergeant of the company is in the hall—along with Tavia and Vere."

"Tavia? Vere?" The names meant nothing. Both brother and sister were much older, and long gone from Ahga, and their lives had never, for a moment, impacted upon his. He searched his memory as he followed Brand, trotting at his brother's heels just to keep up. Tavia had been wed to some Senador's son long before his birth, and some tragedy surrounded her. Abelard had mentioned her rarely, and always with regret. And Vere—Vere had left Ahga long ago, his name never spoken. He had gone in the chaotic days of Mortmain's Rebellion, and no one knew where. As far as Abelard was concerned, Vere might as well have been dead. But now he was here—turned up in Jesselyn's company, a name and a face so long forgotten surely few remembered him.

In the hall he was met by a scene which could only be described as organized chaos. Women from the kitchens ran here and there, bringing water and linen bandages, and on the floor in front of one high hearth lay a long bier covered in a plain white shroud.

On the floor alongside the opposite hearth lay another pallet, and here the women clucked and tripped over each other like a gaggle of geese. Soldiers in travel-stained uniforms sat in silent clusters, drinking and eating a hastily served meal. At the entrance, Roderic paused and laid a hand on Brand's arm. "What's going on?"

"Sergeant—" Brand motioned. A grizzled veteran limped forward, mud clinging to his boots. Roderic recognized him. He had fought long and hard in the service of the King, but refused to retire even though he had earned his respite many times over. He had volunteered to lead the escort.

"Sergeant Tom?" Roderic unbuckled his sword belt and handed it to a passing servant.

"Lord Prince." The old Sergeant's salute was as crisp as ever.

"Tell me what happened. How did my sister die?"

"We don't rightly know, Lord Prince. We found 'em all in a camp just near the toll plaza at the outermost boundary of the Ridenau lands. Lord Vere—we didn't know it was him, sir, until Captain Brand recognized him—he's bad wounded. The Lady Jesselyn, we found her lying in a pool of her own blood, her throat cut. And the other lady—Lady Tavia—she couldn't tell us nothing." He jerked a thumb over his shoulder, where Peregrine sat spoonfeeding a woman with long dark braids.

"You've no idea who did this?"

"No, sir. There was nothing to tell us anything. The Captain of the guard at the toll plaza, he was just as horrified as we were. If word gets round the country, he's like to have a panic on his hands. But the murderers made a real mistake. They left Lord Vere for dead. If he gets better, maybe he can tell you."

"What about Tavia?" Roderic looked at Brand.

Brand averted his eyes. "You'd better come see for yourself."

Mystified, Roderic followed his brother to the dais. Peregrine looked up with a troubled expression.

He bowed to Tavia and extended his hand. As his eyes met hers, his words of welcome died on his lips. The woman who crouched on the low stool stared past and beyond him, looking into some unseen unknown. She crooned tunelessly under her breath, and her eyes were blank and blue. Her face was pale and unlined, like a child's, and she clutched a bundle, vaguely shaped like a baby, to her bosom. Her garments were of rough homespun wool, and they stood out around her like bulwarks. "What happened to her?"

Peregrine glanced at Brand. "Maybe the shock," she said. "The shock of seeing her sister and her brother murdered."

"Then why didn't whoever it was kill her, too?" asked Roderic.

"The men say they found her in the wagon, just as you see her. She must have stayed hidden. Even if she knows anything, she'll never tell us in her present state." Brand hooked his thumbs in his belt.

"What about Vere?" Roderic stared at Tavia, trying to think of some way to penetrate her trance.

"I think he might recover," answered Peregrine. "He lost a lot of blood, but no vital organs were injured."

"Can he talk?" asked Roderic.

"He was in a dead faint when they carried him in," said Brand.

Roderic pressed through the crowd and knelt on one knee beside Vere's makeshift bed. The resemblance Vere bore to the King was so stark, his heart leaped. There was the same jutting hawk nose, the high cheekbones. But Vere's beard obscured the lower half of his face, and blood stained a rough bandage twined around his head. Roderic wondered at the intricate markings Vere wore on his face. He opened his mouth to speak to Brand, and in that moment, Vere's eyes fluttered open. His mouth moved, and Roderic bent closer. At the name Vere muttered, Roderic fell back.

"What is it," asked Brand. "What did he say?"

Roderic rose to his feet unsteadily and turned away, leaving Vere to the care of the nurses. "Amanander," Roderic said. "That's what he said. Amanander."

"He claims my twin murdered his own sister and tried to murder him?" Alexander's dark eyes flashed fire, and Roderic was reminded how alike the twins were. The hour was getting on to dusk. At last the hall had been restored to some semblance of order. Jesselyn's body lay in the little chapel, washed and decently wrapped in a linen winding sheet. Tavia had been led away in Peregrine's care, and now she sat over Melisande's cradle, rocking and crooning the same tuneless lullaby, refusing to be moved. Vere had been taken to a bedchamber, where he lay, fading in and out of consciousness. A messenger had been sent back to Ahga to alert Phineas, and another party of soldiers had gone out to ascertain if Amanander were indeed on the road to Dlas.

Roderic shifted uneasily in his chair. The wounds on his shoulder and upper arm throbbed; in all the confusion, there had been no time to tend them. He had begun to hope that he and Alexander were developing a relationship of mutual respect, and now the accusations of a stranger, whom Brand insisted was their brother, were placing this newfound trust in jeopardy. "Yes," he said finally. "That's what he said."

Alexander only glared, and Brand swallowed a long quaff of ale. "But why?" asked Brand. "Why would Amanander want to kill Jesselyn and Vere? Even if we believe what Vere says—and perhaps you misunderstood him, Roderic—what could possibly be the reason?"

Roderic glanced from Brand's troubled face to Alexander's angry one. "This wasn't just a visit. Jesselyn was coming for a reason."

"Which was?" demanded Alexander.

Roderic set his goblet down deliberately before answering.

"She sent me a letter—it was waiting for me when I got back from Atland. She said she had some crucial information."

"About what?" There was a dangerous look in Alexander's eyes, and Brand drew just a fraction closer to Roderic's chair.

"I don't know." Roderic felt Brand's presence and met Alexander's gaze levelly. "But it would seem that Jesselyn was killed because whoever killed her—and I'm not saying it was Amanander—didn't want me to have that information."

Alexander dropped his eyes. "That makes sense."

"Alex," said Brand, "you're closer to Aman than any of us. Did he—in any way—hint that he might be planning such a thing? Did you have any idea—"

"No!" Alexander swung on Brand, hand reaching for a weapon which wasn't there. Out of the corner of his eye, Roderic saw the soldiers positioned at the door come to attention, instantly alert.

"Hold, Alexander." Brand raised his hands. "I want no quarrel with you. But whoever murdered Jesselyn must answer for his crime. Don't you agree?"

Slowly, Alexander relaxed. "I'm sorry," he muttered, turning away. "The idea that Amanander would murder one of his own sisters is not something I care to contemplate."

"No," said Brand. "None of us wants to believe it."

Though likely all of us can, thought Roderic.

"Roderic?" Peregrine's soft voice interrupted any further conversation. "Vere's awake." She stood in the doorway, bloodstains on her white apron. In her arms she held a laundry basket of bloodstained linen. "He's awake and asking for you."

Roderic nodded at both his brothers. "Let's go."

In the sickroom, a fire burned in the hearth, and the windows were open to catch the breeze which ruffled the white curtains. A pot of broth hanging from a little iron tripod bubbled over the fire. A basket of clean bandages and a tray of unguents lay on the table beside the bed. When the men entered, the woman bending over Vere looked up disapprovingly. "You may have a few minutes, Lord Prince. That's all." She placed a bowl and spoon on a little tray and carried it out of the room with a loud sniff.

Roderic was relieved to see how much better Vere seemed. He was propped up against the pillows, and his head was freshly bandaged. He wore a clean white bedgown, and his beard had been trimmed. The varicolored tatoos on his cheeks were the only incongruous note. Vere smiled weakly at the sight of his brothers. "Brand, Alexander. And you—Lord Prince?" His voice was a throaty whisper.

Roderic strode to the bedside. "Please, call me Roderic. We're brothers, after all. Can you tell us who did this to you?"

Vere's gray-green gaze flicked past Roderic to Alexander and a look of great sadness came into his eyes. "Amanander."

"But why?" Alexander pushed past Brand and stood next to Roderic. "Why?"

Vere shook his head and winced. "Not now—can't—now. But Jesselyn—he killed her deliberately. . . ." Vere closed his eyes and his face blanched.

"That's enough," said the nurse. She stood in the doorway with her hands on her hips. "All of you, out. Now. He needs rest, or he'll never be able to tell you what you need to know."

Reluctantly, the men filed into the corridor. They stood in awkward silence outside the door. Alexander took a deep breath. "You know I must leave on the morrow, Roderic. But promise you will write to me with Vere's story—I must know why Amanander would do such a thing." Beneath his tunic, Alexander's shoulders seemed to sag. He walked away with the heavy gait of a much older man.

"Alex." Roderic reached out and grasped his arm. "I am sorry. I know you love him."

Alexander hesitated. Finally, he cleared his throat. "I want you to know I had nothing to do with what Aman did. I realize you may not believe me, but I had no inkling that he would kill anyone." In the darkened corridor, Alexander looked much older than his thirty-odd years. Deep pockets ringed his eyes, his mouth seemed dragged down by the weight of the lines carved into his face. "The murder of an innocent woman—I cannot condone—"

"Condone?" Roderic's voice sounded harsher than he intended. "That's too soft a word, isn't it?"

Alexander raised his head and Roderic saw the misery and the pride in his face. "I never intended to challenge you, Roderic. I do not want to be King."

"And Amanander?"

"I know you expect me to betray my brother—"

"Amanander must be found and brought back to answer for his crime."

"I agree, but—" Alexander hesitated, and Roderic watched the struggle on his face. "You don't know what you ask of me. He's more than my brother. I don't expect you to understand—I don't expect anyone who's not a twin to understand—but he's like an extension of myself. It used to be that I knew what he thought, and how he felt, even when we were apart. I admit I never thought he'd do anything like what he did, but—Roderic, you're eighteen years old. Can you understand why Amanander believes he should be King?"

"I'm not the King," Roderic said softly.

"No," Alexander admitted. "Not yet." He rubbed his temples as though his head ached. "Before I left for the garrison in Spogan, all those years ago, I swore to uphold the kingdom and the King. I don't know if I can do what you ask of me. If my brother comes to me, I'm not certain I can turn him over to you, even though I agree he should answer for his crime. But I will not give him succor, or aid him in any way, and I will, as much as I am able, assist you to find him."

"Alex." Roderic could not conceal the urgency in his voice. "You've got to tell us. Do you know anything about Amanander's plans? Anything at all?"

Alexander closed his eyes. "I can offer you no more."

"And in return for your help in finding Amanander?"

Alexander looked at the floor and then at Roderic. "I believe a man should do what is right without a price. What my brother has done is heinous." He shook his head. Roderic had never seen such agony in a man's eyes. "I can offer you no more."

Abruptly Alexander turned on his heel and strode away. Roderic started after him, but Brand stopped him with a touch.

"He knows something," Roderic insisted. "He knows more than he's telling us."

"I know," said Brand. "But let him go. He may not be a friend, but he's no enemy. We'll have to content ourselves with that for now."

Chapter Fourteen

Five days passed, days in which Roderic watched Vere struggle for his life. Although at first he had thought Vere not badly injured, Peregrine changed his mind, when she described the severity of Vere's wounds. But Vere seemed to heal quickly, much faster than Peregrine or anyone else expected. Roderic hoped he would be able to talk to him at length soon.

On a cool morning, after the brief service held for Jesselyn, Roderic and Brand watched as the plain coffin was placed on a cart. Her body was to be taken to Ahga, to be interred in the crypts which held the bones of the Ridenau ancestors. As the little procession trundled through the arched gateway, Roderic drew a deep breath. He was sad to think that he would never know Jesselyn, but he was more troubled by the circumstances of her death. "I've decided to summon the court to Minnis," he said without preamble. "After all, it's almost time for the court to come anyway. And I'd like Phineas to hear what Vere has to say. Vere won't be able to travel for some time, I think."

"Perhaps," said Brand, "we ought to go back."

"But Vere—"

"Vere is not your only responsibility."

Roderic shot a quick look at his brother. Brand's eyes were fastened on the dust cloud raised by the funeral procession.

He knew Jesselyn, thought Roderic. She was not just a name to him. He bit back the retort.

"Lord Prince," a maidservant interrupted the awkward silence. "Lady Peregrine sent me to fetch you. Lord Vere is awake and insists that he must speak with you."

Roderic tapped Brand's arm. There wouldn't be any point in quarreling with this brother whom both his father and Phineas trusted so much. "Come. Let's go."

In Vere's room, the windows were thrown open to let in the fresh air. A faint smudge barely visible above the tops of the ancient trees of the Great North Woods was the dark tower where the witch-woman Nydia was reputed to live, and Roderic was reminded once more of Amanander's queries about the fate of the witch.

They found Vere sitting in a chair by the window, shaking his head at a nurse, who was insisting that he be covered with a wrap. As Roderic and Brand entered, Vere held up his hands in mock surrender. "Peace, I beg of you! I'll cover up, I promise. Only leave me alone, mistress—your fussing will be the death of me long before the wind."

Muttering dire predictions, the woman left the room shaking her head at male stubbornness. Vere smiled at them beneath his beard. "Spare me from the good intentions of capable women."

"You look better, Vere." Roderic noted that his brother's color was much better, although he still seemed painfully thin, his shoulders knobby beneath the fine-spun linen of his bedgown. He tried not to stare at the intricate swirls of color on Vere's cheeks.

"I am better." Vere knotted his slender fingers in his lap and turned his head to look out the window, where the branches of the closest tree brushed the casement, twisted with the first pale flowers of the purple delvines. From the courtyard came the muted sounds of the garrison guard at their drills. The scent of the flowers wafted in on the breeze. "Better than I was when Amanander's men left me. They came in the night. We had no chance. They slit Jesselyn's throat, and thought to have cut mine as well."

"Why do you think it was Amanander's men?" Brand stroked his chin as he leaned against the bedpost.

"I saw him. He did not do the killing—he stood apart, silent. His arms were folded across his chest, and the wind whipped his cloak around his shoulders. He did not move—he did not even seem to breathe—his stillness was unnatural." Vere stared out the window, as if seeing it happen once again.

"It was dark," said Brand. "Could you be mistaken?"

Vere turned to look at his brother, and in the arch of his brow, the proud lift of his head, Roderic saw again the clear stamp of Abelard Ridenau. "There was no mistake."

"This has something to do with the information Jesselyn was bringing me, doesn't it?" asked Roderic.

Vere nodded. "Unquestionably."

"Do you know what that information was?"

Vere hesitated. "I will tell you what I can. But you must understand that I am bound by other vows—vows from which I have not been released—"

"If this has to do with Dad—" began Brand, crossing his arms over his chest. His dark brows knitted in a frown, and he lowered his head like an angry bull.

Vere shook his head. "I am not sure that it does."

"You must tell us everything," Roderic sat down opposite Vere and crossed his long legs at the knee.

"I will tell you what I can." There was a quiet note in Vere's voice which brooked no argument. "I am a tracker—there is no need for you to understand exactly what that is—suffice it for me to say that I have spent the greater part of the last years searching out ancient knowledge among old ruins. What I have found is of no concern to you, either, except that as I have traveled, I have also been searching for the whereabouts of a renegade Muten named Ferad-lugz."

Brand shook his head impatiently. "And what does any of this have to do with Amanander?"

Roderic took a deep breath and leaned forward. "This is no time for secrets if the safety of this realm is at stake."

"I will tell you what I can," Vere repeated. "Many years ago, Dad quarreled with his mother, Agara, and banished her from Ahga."

"Why?" asked Roderic.

"I can tell you that," said Brand. "The quarrel concerned the succession. She was determined that Amanander should be King after Abelard. He refused to name Amanander his heir—he was concerned that any son other than that of his Queen would be questioned by the Congress. Although Amanander's mother was contracted to marry Dad, she died before the actual ceremony could take place. And therein lies the problem—in some of the estates, a contracted marriage is as valid as an actual marriage, and in some of them, it isn't. You must remember that Dad came to the throne in the middle of a struggle with the Congress over the unity of the realm, and in Mortmain's Rebellion, the entire western section of the country tried to establish a separate kingdom. So Dad was afraid that if he named Amanander his heir, and then had a son by his Queen, too many in the Congress would support Amanander, and once again, there'd be the threat of a division. So Agara took Amanander and Alexander with her when she left, and together they went to Missiluse, to Eldred, Agara's cousin, and Dad's old enemy."

"It was while they were there—" Vere spoke up when Brand paused "—that Agara became involved with this Muten—Ferad-lugz, he was called—because she wanted to learn to work the Old Magic."

"Old Magic?" echoed Roderic. "Is such a thing possible?"

"Of course not," said Brand. "She was crazy by that time."

"It is more than possible." Vere gave Brand a cold stare. "I don't expect you to believe me, for the priests would have us all think otherwise. But Agara's intention to use the Old Magic and thus in some way force Dad to name Amanander corresponded with Ferad's own plans."

"And they were?" asked Roderic when Vere stopped.

"I do not believe I can tell you that without breaking my vows. But since that day in Missiluse—when Eldred was killed and Dad and Phineas were rescued, along with Amanander and Alexander—we have searched for Ferad without cease."

"Who's we?" asked Roderic. "What are these vows of yours? Who do you serve?"

"I serve the Pr'fessors of the College of the Elders."

"The Mutens," said Brand. He made a derisive sound. "I should have known you'd end up with them. By the One, Vere, enough of this superstitious nonsense. Next you'll tell us the real threat to the realm is the Old Magic."

"It is."

There was a long silence while the two brothers stared at each other, neither willing to capitulate. Finally Vere's mouth curved in a gentle smile touched with sadness. "I did not come to quarrel, Brand. And I did not come to seek approval of the way I have chosen to live my life. I came because, despite what you might think, I have never forgotten that I, too, am a son of Abelard Ridenau."

In the last, quiet words, Roderic heard a trace of longing for the acceptance he himself had so freely received from Abelard, the acceptance denied this son who had never equaled Abelard's expectations, and so had never been missed. He glanced at Brand, who had dropped his arms and leaned against the cold hearth. "Go on," said Roderic.

"I located Ferad's hiding place in the deep deserts near Dlas-for'Torth, but I was never able to penetrate his defenses. I sent a messenger back to the Elders. He died of the purple sickness near Jesselyn. She found my message and sent it onward with Everard, who was on his way south to ensure that the peace made by the Children after Atland was honored by all. By the time the Elders received it, I myself had arrived. The Elders told me what happened to Ebram-taw's people." Vere glanced at Roderic, and Roderic flushed. "When I knew the whole story—I decided to come north, to Ahga. I wanted to see Amanander if I could."

"Do you think Amanander's involved with this Muten, this Ferad?" asked Roderic, fighting to keep his voice steady.

"Without question." Vere replied. "Amanander was there, you see, when Ferad was teaching Agara the Magic. And Amanander was the focus of all her plans."

"And Amanander has been in Dlas for years," said Brand.

"Yes." Vere let the implication sink in.

"Tell me about the Old Magic," said Roderic. "What is it? What can it do?"

"Come now, Roderic." Brand gestured impatiently. "Don't you swallow this Muten pap, too. How can you stand to listen?"

"Don't you remember what you said to me about Amanander's men, in Ahga? What you felt when you went to speak to them yourself?" Roderic faced his eldest brother. "You said you feared for your very self—those were your words, Brand, not mine. We have to listen to Vere—Muten pap or no."

Vere was listening carefully. "I would like to speak more to you concerning these soldiers of Amanander's, Brand. But to answer your question, Roderic, the Old Magic can do anything the mind can conceive. The Old Magic is a series of equations—mathematical equations. When one can understand the equations, enough energy is generated by the human mind to change the physical world. One can therefore do anything one desires—including affecting the actions of others."

"What do you mean?" asked Roderic.

"That day in Atland—when you killed Ebram-taw's people—how did you feel? What were you thinking?"

Roderic hesitated, and he glanced at the floor. "I was wrong," he whispered.

"Yes," said Vere. "But at the time, how did you feel? Close your eyes—try to remember."

Obediently Roderic closed his eyes. The room was completely silent, even the whisper of the rustling branches against the window had stilled. It reminded him of the stillness that day, before the bloodlust had come upon him. "They attacked our camp. They were trying to rescue Ebram-taw. But there were too many of us, too few of them. Amanander had told us where to look for him. He said he had discovered the information on his way to Atland. He turned out to be right." From somewhere which seemed very far away, he heard the sharp hiss that was Vere's intake of air. "The fighting had stopped. I remember Amanander watching me, and then I felt as though I could not breathe—as though the air was too thick, like water. And then I felt this need—to shed blood—I remember even the sun looked red—"

"It was red," interrupted Brand. "It was the clouds."

"Why didn't you stop me?" asked Roderic.

"How could I?" Brand's face was dark with some emotion Roderic could not name. "You're the Prince. You were before all the men. I cannot countermand or question one of your orders in public. To do so would undermine your authority."

Roderic raised his head and stared at Vere. "Are you saying Amanander forced me to do what I did?"

"The potential for such violence exists in every man—and every woman, too, for that matter. Amanander simply reached into your mind, found that potential, and brought it to the surface. You normally control such feelings, except perhaps in battle."

"Yes," said Roderic, "that's how I felt. Just as though I were fighting for my life. But the whole time, I knew the battle was over—I knew the battle was over and I just couldn't stop."

"It is very difficult to fight such a thing. I have seen older and wiser men than you succumb," said Vere. "Anyway, that's why I've come. Amanander is almost definitely in league with Ferad, and Ferad is more dangerous than anything or anyone you can imagine. If Amanander ever masters the Old Magic—"

"Next you'll suggest that Roderic had better start studying it." Brand shook his head. "I cannot listen—"

"No, wait." The note of command in Roderic's voice made both the older men look at him. "At Ahga—at the feast when you told me about the men—I saw something—or thought I did."

"Tell me," said Vere.

Briefly Roderic described the sickening sight of the small creature in Amanander's hand—a creature fashioned out of an apple.

"You were tired," said Brand. "Probably confused what you saw. No one could do such a thing."

"Anyone could do such a thing—if they know the Magic," said Vere.

"Do you think Amanander has something to do with Dad's disappearance?" asked Roderic.

Vere shrugged. "I wish I could tell you for certain. The Old Magic is very powerful, but it requires years and years of study. Amanander is certainly able to affect people for some short length of time—but you must understand that the mind has its own defenses. For example, if you distrust Amanander, you are shielded to some extent. I would doubt that he knows enough to breach such defenses entirely. I wish I had spent time with him. I might have been able to gauge the extent of his knowledge."

"And Ferad?"

"I shudder to think what he has learned in all this time."

"Are there any limits to this Magic? Anything it cannot do?"

Vere nodded. "It is very dangerous and should not be used at all. The men of Old Meriga who discovered it learned that to their peril. The Magic brought about the Armageddon. You see, every time the Magic is used, there are consequences. For every action, there is an equal and opposite reaction. That is one of the most elementary laws of the universe, but the men of Old Meriga forgot. So while they experimented, and played with the Magic like a new toy, Meriga and the whole world fell apart around them. And then the priests rose up and marshaled the people, who of course had suffered terribly in the Armageddon. That's when the Persecutions began. Anyone who had any knowledge at all of science or mathematics or any form of technology was killed. The Mutens took to the hills for they were, as the priests claimed, the result of the Magic. Books were burned, ancient artifacts destroyed. And so we were left with very little to make our new world."

"But should then there not have been a consequence when Amanander worked his Magic on me?"

"There was—somewhere. That's what made the Magic so unpredictable. Consequences can happen anywhere in the world—a Magic-user on the eastern coast can affect something half the world away." The blanket slipped off Vere's knees to the floor, and he thrust it away impatiently. "And it depends, you see, on the degree to which the natural order is disrupted. But it was a long time before anyone made the connection."

Roderic folded his arms across his chest and considered Vere's words. He could almost hear Garrick's voice, patiently explaining: "Men don't fight over ideas, Roderic. Men fight for gold or wheat or cattle, or the land that sustains all those things. Men don't even fight over women, though quite a few might like to say they had. Ideas are only excuses. There never was a war presumably fought over ideas where the loser agreed to change his mind and therefore kept his wealth. Don't ever forget that."

Once more, Roderic was a boy of twelve, crude parchment spread before him, a cold gale rattling at the windows, a fitful fire in the unpolished grate. "Well, then," he had challenged, "what of the Persecutions? They fought about Magic, didn't they? How can you say it wasn't over ideas?"

The tutor had answered: "They fought because most people came to believe that men who controlled Magic would control the resources. And when the resources—the farmland, the water, the animals, became scarce, the men who did not have the Magic became frightened. And so the priests and the Bishops began the Persecutions."

He had rolled onto his back on the threadbare carpet, digesting that information. "Do you believe all that, Garrick? The weaponsmaster says they flew through the air in wagons which rode the wind, and that they used these roads for carts that went so fast no horse could ever keep pace. And he says that when they fought, they used—"

"It doesn't matter anymore," Garrick had replied flatly, changing the subject.

Garrick had diverted Roderic's attention to other matters, and he had never raised the subject of the Magic again, content to relegate the superstitious chatter of the servants to the stuff of dreams. The subjects Garrick decided did matter were more than enough to occupy his time and attention. But perhaps, thought Roderic, Magic did matter. "What do you mean, the natural order?"

"Let's say the Magic-user, with only the best of intentions, sought to bring rain." Vere gestured to the cloudless sky outside. "It is possible that out of the unseen vapor of the air, one could draw out the moisture to make rain. But on a day such as this, such a feat would require an immense expenditure of energy, and therefore, probably an immense disruption. Look outside. On such a day as this, there's no possibility of rain.

But, say, on a day where rain threatens, and the clouds have gathered, the manipulation of the combination of factors to cause the rain to begin to fall would be a fairly easy thing. So it depends."

"And Amanander? With his trick?"

Vere stroked his beard. "If what you say you saw is true—and I don't doubt you—" he held up his hand "—then Amanander may be even more dangerous than I thought."

"What do you mean?" asked Brand.

"Tell me about the guards."

It was Brand's turn to stumble over the words as he tried to describe the four bodyguards and the effect they had had on the men with whom they had come into contact. "What do you think of that?" he finished, with a challenge.

"The Magic is primarily involved with the reorganization of the fundamental elements of matter. But Amanander's interest is not in simply bending the material world to his will. Amanander seeks to control men's minds. He does control these guards of his—that's why they seem so unnatural. They are unnatural—they are men robbed of their will. And you—" Here Vere looked at Roderic. "He's found a way into your mind. Your youth played against you, Roderic. Older men are stronger. But if Amanander ever learns to perfect this, he will be a deadly, deadly opponent. It isn't just that he can steal a man's will. He might be able to use it."

"Use it? How? To do what?" asked Roderic.

"To absorb the energy of it. To add it to his own will." Vere paused, as if considering. "I can teach you certain exercises, spells, if you will, to increase your own mental shields. But Amanander is not quite so strong yet. He killed Jesselyn—that's one mistake. And he left me alive—there's another. Amanander is dangerous. But he's not invincible. Yet."

The word lingered in the air, and Roderic rose restlessly and paced to the window. He wasn't certain he liked the sound of Vere's spells. The dark shape just barely visible over the treetops reminded him of something else. Abruptly he turned back to his brothers. "Does the name Nydia Farhallen mean anything to you, Vere?"

Vere gasped. "Nydia? What has she to do with this?"

"We don't know," answered Brand. "Perhaps you can tell us. You knew her, didn't you?"

"Yes," said Vere, and Roderic saw the same faraway look in his eyes as Obayana and Brand when Nydia's name had first been mentioned.

"Why would Amanander be interested in her?"

"Because Nydia was far more than one of Dad's women."

"What do you mean?" asked Brand sharply.

Vere hesitated, clearly torn between two allegiances. "Nydia was a prescient. She could see the future—and she could work the Magic."

Brand swore beneath his breath. "And Dad believed this nonsense? No wonder he accepted her Pledge of Allegiance."

"Is she dead?" asked Roderic.

"He not only believed it, he relied on it," Vere answered Brand, then turned to Roderic. "I have no way of knowing if she's dead or not."

"The old rumors say Dad sent her away because she bore a child—Phineas's child."

Vere frowned. "A child? When?"

"Years ago," said Brand.

"Then you must go to that tower, as soon as you can, if you can, and find her."

"If we can?" asked Brand.

"I imagine if Nydia is still there and wants no company, that tower is impossible to approach. The Magic can be used to shift appearances, so what seems to be a straight path is in reality crooked, what seems like a thicket of impassable underbrush is in reality a clear path. Perhaps Amanander tried to go there himself, though I doubt he yet possesses the skill to challenge Nydia, if she is still alive. But I think that old rumor—of the child—is the key to Amanander's interest in Nydia. If there is a child, she will be the focus of Ferad's plans."

"Why?"

"The child of a prescient is always an empath. Never mind what that is—you won't believe me, anyway. But the empath is the key to controlling the consequences of the Magic. If an empath exists, believe me, Ferad—or Amanander—will try and get her."

"Her?" repeated Roderic.

"Empaths are almost always female. I have only heard of two males in all of history. Who they were is not important. But you must trust what I say, Roderic. I know it sounds absurd, I know it violates everything you've been taught. But you must believe me."

Roderic did not reply. This information was unbelievable—it was the stuff of legends and dreams. He understood why Brand scoffed, and yet—he could not afford to take chances. It would be a simple enough thing to go to the dark tower. It was no more than a few hours ride. But he could not go in search of Amanander himself, and the regiments of the King's Guard were already depleted by the search for the King. "You're a tracker, Vere. Could you find Amanander?"

"If he's rejoined his troops going to Dlas—" began Brand.

"I doubt that Amanander's going to Dlas," said Roderic. He walked to the window and stared out over the trees.

Vere's voice interrupted his thoughts. "I cannot search for Amanander for you. Much as I understand your need, I serve other masters. But I will go back to the College and ask the Elders to send you aid in the event that Amanander decides to use the Magic against you. I think it's likely, given all you've told me, that he will. Eventually."

Brand shook his head. "And in the meantime? We allow Amanander to go free?"

"We'll send our scouts out to look for him," answered Roderic. "But I'm not worried that he might be lost. If we don't find him, Amanander most assuredly will find us."

Chapter Fifteen

Vere left the very next day, striding out of Minnis with nothing more than the clothes he had worn, a walking stick, and a worn pack on his back filled with only the barest minimum of supplies. Peregrine shook her head at his leaving, saying that he was sure to open his wounds and likely bleed to death or be eaten in the wild. Roderic watched the easy, confident stride as his brother disappeared beneath the trees and doubted that her dire predictions would prove true.

Tavia was pliant and silent, crooning to the rag doll no more. She ate and slept and stared out the window all the day long, not responding to any human touch or voice. Peregrine, out of desperation, brought her a kitten, and Tavia sat stroking the little beast hour after hour, staring into some bleak place where no one else could follow.

A messenger arrived from Ahga, bearing dispatches and the news that the court would arrive within a day. Roderic sifted through the documents and tried to concentrate, but the dark tower seemed to call to him, insisting that he stare at it over the trees. He spent a restless night, tossing and turning beside Peregrine. Before dawn broke, his mind was made up. He would not wait for Phineas. He would go to the dark tower as soon as he could.

At misty daybreak, he ordered horses made ready, and with only one companion, Brand's son, Barran, rode out ostensibly to the hunt. He seemed to have a preternatural awareness of his surroundings: the feel of the horse's muscles beneath him as he galloped along the forest paths, the twigs and dry leaves which crunched underfoot, the falling petals which drifted into his hair. The damp leaves had a musty smell, faintly sweet. As the sun rose higher, they paused by a lake to eat. "Where are we going, Lord Prince?" asked his kinsman. Barran was actually Roderic's nephew, but they were so close in age, Roderic thought of Barran as a cousin.

"You're going to wait for me, Barran. I'm going to the tower."

"The dark tower? Where the witch lives?" Barran actually crossed himself in the superstitious gesture the priests made against evil and clutched the iron cross he wore around his neck. "Roderic, are you mad? I can't let you go there—my Sergeant would have my head and my father would have the rest."

Roderic had been expecting that. He tossed the core of his apple into the lake, and it sank without a sound. "It isn't a question of your letting me, Barran. Your orders are to wait for me—I have no intention of taking you any closer than we are already."

Barran raised his head. He was only twenty-one years old—he had pledged allegiance in the service of the King's Guard nearly six years ago. He grinned. "Do you want to wrestle for it?"

Roderic grinned back and shook his head. "Those days are gone. I won't be long."

"No, Roderic. I'll come with you—I must. Surely you understand that? If I can't keep you out of danger, I can't let you walk into it alone."

Roderic considered. "Very well," he said at last. He got to his feet and shook out his cloak. "It's not much further."

The forest was quiet, unnaturally so, the closer they came to the tower. It was as if they were the only living things beneath the trees. Roderic peered at the ground, searching for signs of some animal's passing. There were none. At last, the sun was at its height. The light filtered through the leafy branches, casting odd shadows on the ground. Roderic stretched in his saddle. He was getting tired. They had been riding more than five hours. Surely they should have been there by now.

He signaled to Barran to dismount. The grass was the color of emeralds, as soft as moss, and suddenly a bone-weary exhaustion made him stumble against the horse. The stallion whickered a protest and stepped aside. Barran was yawning unashamedly. "We'll rest." From some rational part of his brain, he was astonished to hear how he slurred the words.

Without further prompting, they rolled in their cloaks and slept. The next thing Roderic knew, he was being shaken awake, and there was a frantic urgency in Barran's voice. "Roderic, Lord Prince, for the love of the One, wake up. The wind's changed: it's in the north and the sun is gone."

He started awake, still groggy, his head full of dreams he could not name. He sat up and looked around. A cold wind was beginning to stir the leaves, and the sky had darkened. Clouds had formed while they slept, and the gray underbellies hung low and threatening. "We'd better get back." Roderic shook his head to clear it and leaped to his feet.

Like men in a dream, they fumbled with the horses and finally were mounted and ready to ride. The wind blew harder and the leaves rustled a warning.

"Let's go!" Roderic cried above the wind as the first drops of rain touched his cheek.

"It's ice! Roderic, this shouldn't be—it's too late in the year for weather like this!" cried Barran above the increasing whine of the wind. The drops stung and Roderic shivered, unable to answer as the full fury of the storm broke upon them. The horses reared and neighed. Fighting both weather and animals, they finally brought the horses under control.

"We should seek shelter," Roderic managed.

"I can't see where I'm going," shouted Barran.

Stumbling like blind men, they led their horses on foot through the driving sleet. "I think I see something," Roderic called, as he peered through the wildly dipping branches.

"Roderic!" Barran cried.

Behind Roderic there was a loud crash and a horse's scream. Roderic turned, trying to see through the weather. "What is it?"

"My leg—it's—"

"I can't hear you."

Roderic led his horse back to see Barran fallen by a log lying across the forest floor.

"My leg," Barran said above the wind. "I heard the bone snap."

Roderic rubbed his hands together and hunched his shoulders against the cold. "I'll put you on your horse," he shouted above the wind. He managed to put Barran on his skittish mount. His face was twisted in pain. Roderic looked at the leg and saw the white edge of bone through the raw edges of torn flesh and ragged fabric. "You've done a job there, Barran." He tied the horses together, swung up into the saddle behind his kinsman, and put Barran's head against his shoulder.

Barran sagged. "It's bad, Roderic." His hair was plastered against his head. His lips were thin with pain.

"We'll look for shelter."

Blinded by the driving storm, trees bending low and slashing at their faces, the icy sleet pounding through their cloaks, they emerged into a clearing at the very base of the dark tower.

"Roderic? Not here, surely?" cried Barran.

"We must," Roderic answered. "We must have shelter. We can't go on." He dismounted as carefully as he could, and Barran slumped forward across the horse's neck. Roderic bent his head and ran up the great stone steps to the heavy carved doors. He wrapped his wet hands around the icy handles and pushed, then pulled with all his strength. The door would not budge. He pounded with both fists. The door shuddered. He raised his voice and cried "Open!" as loud as he could, and again there was no response. At his back, the wind howled in renewed fury and the horses huddled together in the little clearing. Roderic had raised his fists again when the doors swung open with a loud creak of the ancient hinges. He narrowed his eyes and squinted into the darkness.

A slight figure, wrapped in a shapeless garment made out of an odd assortment of varicolored rags, stood in the center. "I am Roderic, Prince of Meriga," he gasped above the weather. "I seek shelter for my companion and my animals."

The figure bowed and stood to one side, motioning him to enter. "What about the horses?" Roderic peered through sleet. Something about the way the figure moved told him she was a woman. For reply, she gestured again, motioning him to bring them inside as well.

"My man is injured. We need a fire and something to bind his wound," he said as he turned away to lead the horses into the dark space beyond the door. The figure nodded and inclined her head.

Slowly, Roderic guided the horses up the slippery steps. Barran had slumped forward across the saddle in a faint. Roderic looked around as he stepped over the threshold. The place was ancient, the ceilings vast and cavernous. Corridors led off from the back and sides. The floor was dull, broken squares of black-and-white marble, and the columns holding up the ceiling were webbed with cracks, clumsily patched. The windows, which once had held great panes of priceless glass, were covered over with planks of wood, and little light penetrated the gloom. He stood between the horses, shivering, for a moment. Then Roderic eased Barran off the horse, cradling him in his arms. "He's hurt badly," he repeated to the woman. "Please, is there a place I can let him rest?"

"What comfort we have, you are welcome to, Prince,"

rasped a voice above them, too deep for a woman's, too soft for a man's. Roderic craned his neck around, and on a wide sweeping staircase, another figure crouched, swathed in black garments from head to toe. Roderic squinted in the dark, trying to see. "Carry him above, Prince," instructed the voice, "and follow me." It turned, moving ponderously, and he heard a curious rustle and click as it moved up the steps.

Roderic looked at the woman standing silently by in her multicolored rags. "Lead on."

"But, Lord Prince," Barran said, in a weak whisper, "that's the witch."

"Would you rather bleed to death here?" Roderic hissed between clenched teeth. Barran was heavy and Roderic was beginning to feel the strain in his arms. "We have no choice."

"Come, Prince, and fear not." The raspy voice floated down from a great height.

The woman gestured toward the steps. Roderic hoisted Barran again and started up the steps, acutely conscious of the presence of the woman following. The place had once been beautiful, he thought, as he concentrated on getting up the wide, shallow steps. They led in a broad arc to a graceful balcony, and in the rushlight, he saw the squat, black form of the witch in the corridor. Halfway down the corridor, the woman touched his sleeve. She gestured to a room off to the side. Roderic entered, somewhat hesitant. To the side was a low bed, covered in furs, and a small fire burned in a primitive hearth. He realized that, like the central keep of Ahga, the place had been built in the days when the heat came from furnaces in the cellars, blasted through pipes in the walls. She indicated that he should put Barran down.

He looked at Barran's white face. She touched his hand, a brief, fleeting caress, and inexplicably, his fear and suspicion ebbed. With newborn confidence, he put Barran on the bed. The woman gestured to the door.

"Come, Prince," came the hoarse whisper.

Roderic hesitated. Barran lay on the low bed with his eyes closed, his breathing slow and ragged.

"Prince." The whisper was seductive in its call. With another backward glance, Roderic started down the corridor in the direction of the voice. At the end of the corridor, he paused before a great wooden door.

"Prince."

He pushed the door open and stepped into a warm, brightly lit room. Once this room had been walled with windows on two sides with great panes of precious glass, but now all four walls were hung with tapestries. These were as finely wrought as anything in Ahga. The threadbare furnishings looked as though they, too, had once been covered in rich fabrics, for the wood was carved in intricate designs which could only predate the Armageddon.

The black-garbed figure crouched like a spider before a blazing hearth, her hands extended over the flames. He could hear the wind howl around the building, but in the warm chamber, the storm seemed far away. He stepped forward. "You know who I am."

She turned, and for a moment he thought he saw dark scales on the flesh of her hands before they disappeared beneath her garments. "Who would not know the heir of all Meriga?"

"I do not know you, lady."

She laughed, a hoarse, painful laugh. "You are the first to call me that in an age, Prince. You have your father's courtesy, if not his face." And she laughed longer, as if that struck her even funnier.

"Have you a name?"

"I had two names," she said, "once, long ago."

"And now?"

"I am Nydia, and this dark place is my home." Her arms extended in a wide sweep and the veils across her face moved.

He caught a glimpse of something which did not look quite human.

"Thank you for your hospitality." Roderic inclined his head.

She laughed again, and the flesh crawled at his neck.

"Well you may thank me, Prince, and well you will pay."

He frowned. "Pay?"

"Never mind," she rasped. She raised her arms, and this time, he did see her hands. Where fingers should be, three curved digits ended in long claws. The flesh was dark and scaled, and he drew back involuntarily and shuddered. As he recoiled, she clapped her two hideous claws together, and the slight-figured girl appeared in the door. Even as Roderic turned, the witch beckoned, and the girl, her head still lowered, hurried to the witch's side. One slender white hand emerged from the shapeless garment, and the witch made an impatient gesture, gripping the girl's fabric-covered forearm instead of the bare hand. Roderic narrowed his eyes as the witch muttered something he could not understand. A chill rippled through the room, and gooseflesh prickled his arms and neck. He opened his mouth and found his movements constricted and slow, as if time had lengthened. His clothes dried on his back, and where the fabric had been ripped in the storm, it mended in an instant. The moment seemed to condense, collapse somehow, into an ordinary pace.

"What sort of payment do you want?"

"Sit. Eat. Refresh yourself." She indicated a table set with two goblets and bowls of late spring berries and autumn nuts.

"What's happening to Barran?"

"His needs are well met."

"I'm going back to get him." He turned to leave.

"Not yet, Prince."

Again he heard that low croon and his hand suddenly felt frozen, as though all the heat had been leached from the flesh, and he pulled back from the doorknob, just in time, as it glowed white with heat. He flinched. "What manner of woman are you?"

"I am not a woman at all," she hissed again. "And you will leave only when you have agreed to my terms."

"What terms?"

"Not yet. Sit and eat."

He was across the room in three strides and seized her by the throat. The flesh was soft and felt like sponge through the fabric, and he grabbed her with all his strength. She threw back her veils and his grip faltered as he stared at the horror before him. Her face was inhuman. Her eyes were hooded and yellow like a reptile's, the pupils long, black slits. She had no nose, only a pointed snout and long, yellow teeth, dripping saliva. Her flesh was scaled and black, reflected green in the firelight. He dropped his hands as a wave of nausea rose in his throat.

"Since you insist, Prince, we will discuss it now."

She moved off and covered her face again. He again heard the curious click beneath her skirts and realized it must be her feet against the floor.

"What do you want?"

"You will marry my daughter."

Automatically, Roderic's eyes fell on the girl standing nearly motionless before the hearth. "What?"

"Yes," she hissed. "If you want to leave here alive."

"You cannot hold me."

"Can I not?"

He tried to draw a breath to answer her and a wall of flame engulfed him where he stood. The fire licked his boots and singed his hair. In another instant, it was gone, leaving only the stink of burned hair.

"Do not doubt my power, Prince. It is as real as the heat of the flames."

"But I cannot marry your daughter."

"Why not?"

"The woman I marry must be—"

"Of highest birth, of bluest blood."

Roderic nodded.

"My daughter is all that."

"I cannot marry her."

"You fear she resembles me, perhaps. Well. Let me lay that fear to rest." She turned to the girl standing so quietly beside her. "Roderic, Prince of Meriga, this is my daughter, Annandale."

The figure came forward into the firelight, still swathed in her shapeless rags. Roderic caught at her arm and pushed the hood away from her face. He drew his breath as she raised her eyes to his. He knew her, then, as the girl in the wood.

At first glance, she did not strike him as beautiful.

And then, as the firelight flickered across her features, he realized that she was more than beautiful, that her beauty defied every description he could conceive. He was Prince and soldier, not poet, and his father's court attracted many beautiful women. But there was always some flaw, some aspect that was not perfect, and therefore gave character or charm or counterpoint to the face. But in this girl's face, as she looked up at him, with eyes of deep and vivid blue, there was no flaw. Her face drew him in as he looked upon it and seemed to grow more beautiful the more he stared. It was in some way indescribably balanced, as if this face were the pattern from which all others are drawn, as if all other faces were only endless variations of this one.

He felt some reverberation in his flesh where he touched her echo up his arm and spread throughout his body like a warm breeze in his blood, even as he watched a blush creep up her throat.

Annandale felt the heat rising in her cheeks. Modesty might have made her drop her gaze, but curiosity had the better of her. She stared, unabashed, into the eyes of the young Prince. How, she wondered, could anyone think him Abelard's son?

Surely they saw the leanness in his frame, the long muscles curving smoothly over narrower shoulders than the king possessed. His face was thinner, too, the cheekbones less well defined, the nose straight and tipped at the end, nothing like Abelard's hawklike beak. And even his coloring—green eyes and light brown hair—suggested another sire than the King.

But the set of his shoulders was like the King's and the arrogance of his lifted brow like him as well. His mouth was curved in an expression of both disbelief and disgust, as though the thought of touching her turned his innards. With something like desperation, she glanced at her mother, knowing even as she did so that the thickness of her mother's veils barred any kind of wordless reassurance.

She swallowed hard and looked back up at Roderic. This was the man she had been born for, and he was looking at her as if she were a rotten piece of offal flung from the rudest kitchen. Fear shuddered through her. What would her mother condemn her to?

"Lord Prince." Her voice was like a bell, and he knew immediately that she was indeed the girl in the wood who had taken the child the lycat had injured. What had happened to that child?

Roderic lifted his eyes away from Annandale's face to stare at her mother. "She's a witch just as you are. I can take her, but I can't marry her."

"Then let me show you what you will wreak upon your father's land." The witch drew back from the fire and indicated its depths.

As his mind reeled in automatic denial, he saw himself, held hostage by the witch's magic, unable to move or break her spells. He saw Brand and Phineas order frantic searches, all come to nothing. He saw the Congress and the Mutens and the Harleyriders rise in rebellion. He saw a country torn apart, bleeding and vulnerable, split into a hundred different regions. He saw a great army rise and sweep Meriga before it like a dry leaf in a wind. He saw soldiers with dead men's eyes march across the land, and even the Harleyriders fled in terror before them. He saw children spitted and women torn and men die slow and sickening deaths. On the enemy's shields they bore a device of a triangle with a sidelong crescent like curved horns at the top. He saw his brothers die in a last disastrous battle, Phineas forced to serve Amanander, his sisters raped and skinned. And Annandale—this girl who stood before him, so small and vulnerable and somehow pure—he saw Amanander thrust himself upon her white, fragile body, and nausea rose in Roderic's throat.

He looked at the witch. "Is this about Amanander?"

"Already he sows chaos across the kingdom, leaving a random, scattered harvest for you to reap. All these things will happen if you do not leave here. Like a beast bringing death in the night, it comes, seeking to crush all Meriga in its jaws. Even now, it stirs; the birth pangs are well along. The time is not of my choosing. Fourteen nights ago, Amanander came to the doors of this tower, seeking entrance. He came with four companions, dark riders all, five men, one purpose."

"Amanander came here? For the girl?"

"He came looking for me, but if he had found my daughter, he would have taken her if he could. I have little strength left. The years have weakened me; my own time nears—I can protect her no longer. The only chance you have to prevail against it is to take Annandale, marry her, and keep her as safe as possible."

"Where did he go?"

"West. West to Alexander. And, he hopes, to succor. Listen to me, Prince," the witch hissed. "I seek to save your realm. Far more's at work here than you will ever know."

He looked down at the girl, who stood perfectly still. "Are you one of her enchantments?"

"She is as you see her."

"What word have you to give me that I can trust?"

"Go to Phineas. And he will tell you that you must marry her, and that you must keep her safe—guard her with everything you have, Prince, for she is your father's hope and the Magic's key."

"Phineas? How do you know Phineas?"

"You cannot begin to imagine how much I know."

"You will let me go?"

"As long as you take my daughter."

"And Barran?"

She shrugged. "What use have I for him? See for yourself." She pointed to the door behind him.

Barran stood leaning against the door frame. His face had color in it, and he seemed weak, but both his legs were whole.

"Barran!"

"Roderic."

"Your leg?"

"My leg's fine."

"The bone was shattered—I saw it myself."

For answer, he shrugged. "You must be wrong, Roderic. I don't remember."

Roderic looked back at the witch. "More enchantment."

"You know nothing of enchantment, Prince."

"I'll take the girl. I can give you no other promises. And we will ride now."

"Roderic," said Barran, "the storm's still bad."

"We ride now." Roderic looked down at the daughter. "We go to Minnis, lady. We have no time to pack your tricks."

Annandale broke away from his grasp. This was too much. This boy—this man—he didn't understand yet what was at stake. She had felt the evil come knocking when Amanander had stood before the door, and the thought of leaving the safety of her mother's side terrified her more than she could stand. She sank to her knees before her mother. "Mother—no, don't make me leave you. Please, he doesn't know—he doesn't understand. He doesn't know how to keep me safe. Don't make me go with him—"

Nydia pulled back with something that sounded like a snarl. "Your time has come." Nydia shook away her daughter's reaching hand impatiently. "Tell Phineas I have discharged my pledge-bond to the King. Go, child—my part in this is over. I want no more to do with it. My price is paid."

Annandale gasped, a deep sobbing breath that caught in her throat, and Roderic softened unexpectedly. Whatever machinations had taken place between the witch and his father, this girl seemed as innocent as he, and the witch's claim that Amanander would have any interest in the girl was enough to make him determined to get answers. And if the only way to get them was from Phineas, so be it. "Come." He pulled her to her feet and propelled her past the witch. "Now."

She stumbled beside him, tears streaming down her cheeks, stopping to glance behind, as though she didn't quite believe even as it happened that her mother would send her away. At the bottom of the wide steps, the horses stood as they had been left, but they, too, were dry. "Open the doors," Roderic ordered Barran.

Annandale bolted from his grasp. "Mother!" She stared up at the figure which crouched at the top of the steps like a fat spider, her arm stretched out in supplication.

Roderic extended his hand to draw her away, when Nydia spoke once more, and in the faltering voice, Roderic heard what could only be sobs. "Child, you know this is not of my choosing. Look for me in your heart—the bond between us can be broken only by death."

"Promise me, Mother." Annandale's voice broke over the last word. "Promise you will not use the Magic against yourself—"

"My time is finished, daughter. Let me go in peace."

Stricken, Annandale stared at the figure above her. "Promise me!"

"How can I raise my hand against myself, child? Don't you think I, of all people, have learned that the will of the One is not to be gainsaid?"

There was a silence, and finally, Annandale turned away. Once outside, Roderic lifted her up and placed her on his saddle. He swung onto the horse behind her. "Now which way?" he asked less to Barran than to himself.

The girl before him roused with a soft sigh of resignation, and so deep a pang went through Roderic, he frowned, wondering why he should feel her pain as if it were his. "Minnis is this way," said Annandale. She shrank against Roderic's chest as they once more rode into the forest.

"Stay close and go slowly," Roderic said. The sleet had softened into a light rain, but night was falling. The sky was dark and the wind cold. Annandale put her hand upon the reins and guided the beast through the darkening forest, and the falling rain, back to the walls of Minnis Saul.

Her body was pressed against his, hip to hip, thigh to thigh, shoulder to shoulder in the saddle, and even as they rode through the wet dusk, a curious warmth gradually spread throughout his whole body, so that soaked to the skin as he soon was, he was as comfortable as if they rode at noon in summer.

Chapter Sixteen

When they reached Minnis, grooms gathered quickly to help them down out of the saddles and into dry shelter. Roderic stalked across the courtyard, into the main hall, with Annandale at his heels, noting from the wagons crowded into the courtyard, and the increased number of people, that the court had arrived in his absence.

"I want Phineas," Roderic said to the first person he met.

"At once, Lord Prince," the servant replied.

Roderic looked around for Peregrine. "Get the Lady Peregrine now," he ordered another.

"As you say, Lord Prince."

He looked down at Annandale, standing wet and still in her tattered rags. She was looking around the hall with great interest, and he realized she had probably never seen so many people in one place before. Fleetingly, he wondered what she would think of Ahga. Roderic frowned as she looked up. "Don't move." He was gruffer than he intended, and he saw hurt flicker across her face.

"Lord Phineas will receive you whenever you wish, Lord Prince." The first servant bowed. Close behind, came Peregrine.

"Roderic! We've been so worried." She flung her arms around him. Roderic pulled her arms away from his neck and indicated Annandale with a nod.

"See to the girl."

Peregrine looked at Annandale in amazement. She was a ridiculous and pathetic sight in her wet rags. "Who—"

"Never mind. Find her something dry to wear, feed her if she wants to be fed. And give her a place to sleep."

Peregrine stared.

"I am going to change my clothes and then I will be with Phineas. You may send a tray to me there."

"As you say, Lord Prince."

Roderic left them, changed in his chambers, and went to Phineas. He pounded on the door, and an astonished servant opened almost immediately.

"Lord Prince?"

"Phineas," he pushed past the servant. "Phineas!"

"Roderic, what's happened?" The old man was lying in his bed, sheets drawn up to his chin, thin wisps of gray hair fanned out across the linen pillow.

"I want answers and I want them now, and you will not try to cajole me."

"Roderic, what's wrong?"

"The high tower north of here? Do you know it?"

"Know it?"

"The witch there knows you. She told me to ask you why I must marry her daughter."

"What happened today?"

Roderic paced back and forth by the side of his bed. He had never been so angry. "I went there today. We were caught in the storm, and by the work of some demon, we ended up on her doorstep. Barran was badly injured, and we sought shelter. And so I met the witch. She told me I must marry her daughter. She wouldn't let me leave until I promised to take her with me—"

"She's here?"

"Yes, she's here. That—that—monster wouldn't let me leave without her. What is she?"

"What do you mean? The witch—"

"I want the truth, Phineas. What is she?"

"She possesses the knowledge of the Magic of Old Meriga. But the daughter is here?"

"With Peregrine."

Roderic stopped pacing and stared as Phineas turned his head into the pillow. He watched as slow tears leaked from Phineas's ruined eyes and dripped onto the linen. "It is true, then," the old man muttered. "It will be as she foretold."

Roderic touched Phineas's shoulder and felt the thin, brittle bones beneath the woolen bedgown. "What are you talking about?"

"It is true, Roderic." Phineas raised his tear-streaked face. "You must marry this girl. She is the bride your father intended for you."

"That cannot be."

He shook his head. "It does not matter that you do not believe. Roderic, there is a letter for you among my private papers. Your father wrote it for you the day you were born, and told me to see you received it on the day this girl came to you. Let me send it to your chamber. It will take my servant some time to find it."

Roderic drew a deep breath and rubbed his hand across his face. "My father arranged this?"

"Yes."

"Is this what you meant when you said the subject of my marriage would have to wait? Why didn't you tell me then? Why have I known nothing about this?"

"It did not seem as if the time were right to tell you. These last months have been so fraught with peril, and with everything else—I did not know the time or the manner of her coming."

Roderic hit the bedpost with his fist and the whole frame shuddered. "I cannot believe this would be wise, Phineas, for me to marry a—a ragged outcast of some inhuman monster."

"Read the letter, Roderic. Perhaps it will tell you what you wish to know."

"And if it doesn't?"

"Then you must make your own decision based on what you believe best."

"What do you think?"

"I know that the King wanted you to marry her. I know that the King wanted her son to follow you to his throne."

Roderic had no answer. He stalked away to his chambers to eat the food Peregrine sent, and to wait upon the letter his father had written. The storm was finally over, and the sky was clear. He saw the stars through his window, opened the casement and leaned out.

The wind once more blew gently from the east, and slow drops fell from the eaves with a gentle *tap-tap* to the ground. The leaves whispered and rustled in the night air, and the peace which lay upon the land was at painful contrast to the war which raged within his heart.

"Roderic?" Peregrine startled him and he jumped. "Forgive me, is everything all right?"

"What do you want?"

"What happened today?"

"I don't want to talk about it."

"You seem angry."

"I am angry."

"Who is that girl?"

Roderic laughed sharply, shortly. "If Phineas is to be believed, she is my bride. The next Queen of all Meriga."

"That waif? She—she doesn't even have clothes on her back—who is she?"

"What will it matter?"

"Roderic, I don't understand—"

"You don't understand—hah. Do you think I do?"

"But where does she come from?"

"From the halls of hell."

"Roderic, you aren't making any sense."

"If it's sense you want, get out."

"Why are you angry at me?"

He was sorry, then, and held out his hand. "Forgive me. It's not your fault. It has nothing to do with you."

She took his hand, and he pulled her close. "I was frightened for you out in that storm," she said. "I was so worried."

"Were you?" He pulled her hips against his and loosened the pins which bound her hair. It fell in a heavy dark brown mass down her shoulders and her back, and he twined his hand in it and pressed it against his lips. She wrapped her arms around his neck and leaned into him. He bent his head and kissed her long and slowly. Her mouth opened and her breath was sweet, her lips soft and willing. "Are you finished for the evening?" he asked against her ear.

"Yes."

"How convenient." He kissed her mouth again. They sprang apart at a knock upon the outer door. "What is it?"

"Lord Phineas sends you this letter, Lord Prince," was the reply.

"Leave it on my desk," he said.

"Is it important?" Peregrine asked as he drew her to him once more.

"Not as important as this." He caressed her breasts through the fabric of her clothes. She closed her eyes and moaned softly.

"Is it about the girl?"

"What girl?"

"The one you brought."

"Forget her. She's not important, either." He led Peregrine to the bed and they left their clothes in heaps on the floor. When they were naked and he ran his hand up her thigh, something curious happened. He remembered the feeling of Annandale's arm beneath his hand in the tower room of the witch, so clearly that it might have been her flesh he touched.

He froze. Peregrine stretched beneath him like a cat, drew her hands across his shoulders and caressed the muscles of his upper arms. He bore down upon her, and the memory of Annandale's body pressed against his in the saddle intensified and blotted out Peregrine.

She whimpered, guided his hand to her breast and pressed the palm into her flesh. He bent his head, took her nipple between his teeth and listened to her make soft sounds as she writhed against his hips. He nuzzled the soft skin of her throat as he eased into her, and a vision of Annandale's face, exquisite in its symmetry, filled his mind. As he gave himself up to the driving rhythm of lovemaking, the woman beneath him had eyes of drowning blue, and a body which sent waves of heat through him. And as his body shuddered in its final release, the woman who clasped his hips with her thighs was not the woman whose name he bit back from his lips.

In the early morning, before the first light, Roderic woke from a deep sleep and went immediately to his desk. He lit a candle and saw the envelope with his father's thick scrawl. He hesitated, then picked it up. The paper was yellow with age. He broke the King's seal and opened it.

It was dated the day of his birth.

The salutation said, "My son."

A chill swept down his spine as he looked at the handwriting, so familiar, written so long ago. He read it in disbelief.

My son—

You lie in your cradle not 12 hours old, and your mother lies on her bier. She died to give you life, but you are strong and healthy. Word has reached me from the forests of Minnis Saul that this day another child was born. She will be your bride in the fullness of time. Much was risked to bring the two of you to birth, and much will depend upon the two of you. If Phineas has given you this letter, I must believe that you are King, bound only by the law of Meriga and the good of the realm. Her name is Annandale, and her mother is Nydia of the Tower of Minnis Saul. I hope and pray that you decide to marry her, for the fate of all Meriga and all that I have lived my life for depends upon the decision which you must make. I cannot imagine under what circumstances you are reading this. I only ask that you believe me when I tell you this is perhaps the most important decision you must make, and I bid you choose as I would wish.

The letter was signed with his father's signature, bold and unmistakable. Roderic sat down in the chair. The fire had died down in the night and he threw another log on the hearth.

"Roderic?" Peregrine stood in the doorway, wrapped in a sheet.

He held out his arms and she snuggled on his lap. He held up the letter. "This doesn't answer anything."

"What is it?"

"It's a letter from my father, written on the day I was born, for me to read in the event of his death."

"What does it say?"

"My father wants me to marry her."

Peregrine sat up. "Well, who is she?"

"Her name is Annandale. Her mother's name is Nydia—she's the one who lives in the high tower north of here."

"The witch."

"Yes."

"Are you going to do what the King wants?"

He pressed her back against his shoulder and buried his face in her hair. The fragrance of apple blossoms filled his nostrils. "I don't know."

"You mean you'll consider it?"

"I have to consider it. My father wants me to marry her. He makes it clear that it's my decision, but he says—here, I'll read it to you. 'The fate of all Meriga depends upon the decision which you must make.' Now. What does that mean? And then there's—" He stopped. He wasn't sure what had happened yesterday. The visions the witch had shown him were fading like a half-remembered dream.

"When will this happen?"

He tilted her chin and looked into her dark eyes. "Peregrine, does this grieve you?"

She shifted her eyes and bit her lower lip. "I knew you would marry someday."

"But?"

"It doesn't make me happy to think this must end."

"Surely there have been others. Perhaps one will even do for a husband—my father would want—"

"No. There've been no others."

"Why not? We've sworn no vows. I thought surely—"

"No. No others."

"But—"

She pressed her face into his chest and he thought he felt her tears. When she looked up, her eyes were wet. "I wanted—I thought—if I bore a child, I wanted it to be yours, not another's."

"Peregrine." He had no other answer. He rocked her in his arms. "Do you want to return to your home? If you want to leave, I understand. Perhaps Jaboa could take over—" He felt the words like the sting of a whip, even as they left his lips, and he knew he'd said the wrong thing.

He felt her stiffen and the tears spilled out and ran down her face. "You're thinking of replacing me already? Is that what you want? I thought my home was here."

"No. No, that's not what I want. I want you to stay with me, but I don't want you to be hurt. You know that when I marry I must take a vow of fidelity until my heir is either born or named."

"So when will you marry this short-skirted witch-spawn?"

"I must marry someday."

"And her?"

"I must do what I believe to be best for the realm."

"And is she best?"

"I don't know." He looked her full in the eyes. "You're very important to me, and nothing will change that. If we should have a son, it's possible I could name him my heir, but—"

"But we have no son—only Melisande, and if you marry this—" She stopped. "I will try not to interfere in this."

He was torn and confused. He loved Peregrine as friend and companion, and he had no wish to lose her, or to cause her pain. He wanted to assure her that nothing would change, but the memory of last night's lovemaking stopped the words in his throat, and he felt drawn to the stranger like a salmon to the river that spawned it.

So he kissed her because he did not know what else to do, and he carried her back to bed. He tried to remember how his father had handled the numerous women who had borne him children, and he realized with a glum sense of dread that he did not know. So he went through what he hoped were appropriate motions, and all the while, he was haunted by the specter of Peregrine's grief.

Chapter Seventeen

He could not sleep again after that. He rose as the light changed from gray to gold and tucked the covers carefully around Peregrine's sleeping body. He dressed in the clothes he had worn yesterday. Except for smudges and creases, nothing suggested his ordeal. He picked up his boots and carried them to the outer room and sat in the chair to pull them on.

The hair prickled at the back of his neck as he looked at first one, and then the other. They were his oldest boots, scuffed at the heels, the stitching pulled loose and the leather almost worn through at the toes. He ran his fingers slowly over the surface. The boots were whole, as they had been when new. The stitching was perfectly in place, the leather across the toes as thick as when it was first cut. It was not even as if some master had mended them, for while human hands could have replaced the stitching, they could never have fabricated leather where it had been worn away.

He put them on reluctantly.

He stopped by the kitchens and took a mug of hot cider and half a loaf of bread and went to the barracks where he knew he'd find Brand. The men-at-arms were washing at the stone tub outside the low wooden building, and they straightened to attention as he approached.

"Lord Prince," they said in a ragged chorus.

Roderic nodded. "Good morning. Where's Captain Brand?" he asked the nearest.

"Inside, sir."

"Thank you."

Brand was shaving, standing bare-chested in his spotless cubicle when Roderic entered. He stopped, and force of long discipline brought him to attention as Roderic entered. "Lord Prince."

"I came to talk about yesterday."

Brand picked up his razor and turned to the mirror. "What about it?"

"Have you spoken with Barran?"

"What did you think you were doing, Roderic? He's a good soldier, and the One knows I'd trust him with my life, but he's only one man. If you'd encountered any real danger out in those woods, what did you think he could've done about it? What if you'd met Amanander?"

"What did he tell you?"

Brand twisted his face to the mirror and did not reply. Finally, he wiped his chin with a linen towel. "He told me a story I'd say was the ravings of a madman, if I hadn't heard it come from my own son's mouth. Nonsense about the witch and the tower and a lost princess. What do you have to say about it?"

"It's true."

Brand swore beneath his breath and turned to face Roderic. "You listen to me. I'm only the Captain of the King's Guard, and you're the Regent of Meriga. But I'm sworn to protect you with my life, and before you make that any more difficult, you listen to me. Forget Vere and his Muten nonsense—"

"What about Amanander and his men? You saw them—are you going to tell me that was nonsense, too? And Jesselyn—our sister—is dead because of him. If he can kill his own sister, he can kill all of us." Roderic put the mug down and waited.

With a shake of his head, Brand picked up his shirt. "But, Roderic, think. If the Mutens had the Magic, why haven't they used it against us? Does what Vere said make sense? You don't know Vere the way I do. He was always the odd one, poking around under the castle, wandering in the tunnels, looking at books. When he finally ran away, to tell you the truth, he wasn't even missed. All right, Amanander's guard did frighten me. But there are only four of them, Roderic, four, against our thousands. And the Congress—yes, there are some malcontents, there always have been. Yes, Missiluse is a problem, as well as Senifay and a few others. But don't you see? You can't go chasing after shadows. Vere's stories are better used to frighten naughty children."

"Two weeks ago, Amanander was at the witch's tower."

Brand paused in the middle of pulling his shirt over his head, and his face suddenly lost its exasperated scowl. "He was?"

"With his four companions. They didn't get in—apparently no one gets in unless the Witch wishes it. But Vere was right. They did come for the girl. Nydia said they went west. I think they must have gone west to Alexander."

Deliberately Brand smoothed his shirt and tied the laces. When he raised his face to Roderic, his mouth was set and grim. "Care to join me at practice?"

Roderic nodded. "Very well," he said. "Why not?"

In silence, they walked to the practice fields. The sun had risen above the trees, but the morning air was chill. In the shadows beneath the trees, patches of white frost lay on the ground. Despite the splashes of spring color, the temperature had dropped below freezing in the night.

They chose swords from the weaponsmaster, and Roderic tested the balance of his as they faced each other across a marked-off square. That was another lesson he was unlikely to forget. His father had insisted that, unlike many lords, who would only use their own weapons, made and balanced for them alone, Roderic learn to use any sword with ease.

Around them, many men faced off, and their swords rang

together with hollow clangs in the crisp air. They saluted briefly, and the blades met in a loose arc.

"So you think he went to Alexander?"

Roderic shrugged and attacked. "Where else?"

"Mmm." Brand grunted an assent, blocked the blow, and riposted right.

Roderic dodged, and circled, point raised.

Brand swung the sword at Roderic's midsection and he backed away. He feinted to Roderic's right and attacked again to his left. "And now?"

Roderic brought his own blade up and under and caught the hilt of Brand's sword in his. Brand shoved him back, and retreated as Roderic attacked with a series of blows to his unprotected legs. He tripped, rolled to the side and came up crouched in a fighting stance. "I'll send messengers to the Lords of Mondana, the commanders of the garrisons and the toll plazas. Perhaps we'll be able to apprehend Amanander before he ever reaches Alexander. Two weeks is not so very long."

Abruptly Brand lowered his sword and leaned upon the hilt. Roderic lowered his own blade and looked around. All the others were engaged; no one was paying them the least attention. "Look, Roderic, forgive me for speaking to you as I did. It's just, well, sometimes I think of you as a son, rather than a brother. And my Prince. It's not for me to tell you what to do, or how to govern."

Roderic nodded slowly. He needed Brand, needed the advice and counsel of this eldest brother who had served their father for so long and so well. He had been foolish to venture out without a bigger escort, and he had thoughtlessly risked Barran's life as well as his own.

"What will you do about the girl?" asked Brand.

Roderic hesitated. He knew that Brand's words carried a certain amount of truth, that Brand was level-headed and utterly loyal, that Brand would sooner cut his own throat than lead him astray. He wanted to ask Brand about Nydia, what he remembered about her, how long she had been at Ahga and at Minnis. But perhaps it was better to discuss such things with Phineas. It had not appeared last night that Phineas would simply dismiss such questions out of hand, as it seemed Brand would. "I don't know," he answered honestly. "I accept your apology." He handed Brand the sword. "Thanks for the practice."

Roderic walked back to the hall deep in thought, feeling more alone than he ever had, knowing Brand stood watching him with a troubled expression. "Has Lord Phineas awakened yet?" he asked one of the serving maids.

"I shall see, Lord Prince."

He sat down on a wooden bench by one of the hearths and leaned his chin on one hand. What should he say to Phineas? he wondered. Is this girl your daughter? How did one confront any man about a child he might not even know he had? Was it possible to think that Phineas would have lain with anything so hideous?

"Lord Prince?"

The voice made him jump. Before him stood a kingdom messenger. His cloak was spotted with flecks of mud, and a faint sheen of sweat shone on his forehead. "What news?"

"Message from Ahga, Lord Prince." The messenger gave a brief bow and offered a wooden tube. The seal had been done in haste, for the wax was smeared across its surface.

Roderic picked at the seal and pried the scroll from its cover. He read the contents in disbelief. "An earthshake in Ahga?" It was from the commander of the garrison of Ahga, the division which protected the walls of the City. He could hardly understand the scrawl. "What does this say—the west wall of the city collapsed?"

The messenger nodded. "In three places."

"Three places? Is any of it left standing?"

"Most of it was demolished, Lord Prince."

"Was anyone hurt?"

"There wasn't time to make an accurate assessment before I left, but I would estimate several hundreds."

Roderic waved a dismissal. "Thank you, messenger. Get some rest."

The man made another bow. "As you say, Lord Prince."

He rolled the parchment and placed it back inside the tube. Ahga had not been invaded in over twenty years, and the people were bound to be nervous. If the Harleyriders should hear that the walls had been breached, they might even try a raid. He rubbed a hand across his forehead. There had not been an earthshake in Ahga since the Armageddon. Was this an omen of what was to come?

"Lord Prince," the maid servant bobbed a curtsey. "Lord Phineas can see you now."

Roderic forgot the situation at Ahga as he read his father's letter to Phineas. "There." He threw the paper like a challenge down on the table. "Could you please explain this? Why does my father want me to marry the daughter of a witch? What is the fate of all Meriga, and why does this affect everything he ever lived his life for?"

Phineas drew a long breath. "Your father had some dealings with the woman—I know that."

"Dealings? That's not what I hear. I hear she was pledge-bound to him—that she was something called a prescient, and that he relied on her to work the Old Magic for him. And I hear that the daughter I brought here last night is yours."

Phineas did not reply, and Roderic pressed on. "And what were you to my father that he should banish the woman and keep the man who betrayed him by his side?"

"I was the Captain of the King's Guard."

"You?"

Phineas straightened his bent frame painfully, proudly. "I

was not always as you see me now, Roderic. Once I too was young and tall and strong. And the King loved me like a brother."

"What happened?"

"What may happen to anyone who lives by the sword. I was terribly injured in a battle. But the King brought me back to Ahga, and when I recovered, valued my counsel so much he gave me the honor I have now."

Roderic stared at Phineas, trying to understand why he had the sense that there was far more to the story than Phineas admitted. "Why did you weep last night when I told you the girl had come?"

"Nydia warned the King of impending evil, before you were born, which could be overcome if you married her daughter when you came of age."

"What evil? Magic?"

"There was only one kind of evil which your father understood. The dissolution of the kingdom was the worst thing that could happen, and something he would seek to prevent—at all costs."

At all costs. Those words echoed in Roderic's head like a mourning bell. And marriage with a witch's daughter was the price he was expected to pay. "This makes no sense to me, Phineas."

"I am certain Nydia must have shown the King the future, even as she showed you. I do not know what he saw, but it could not have been very different. He never spoke of it, except to say that if for some reason he was dead when she came to you, I should do all I could to urge you to marry her."

"Did you ever see this witch?"

"Yes."

"What did she look like?"

Phineas turned his head away, though not before Roderic saw his mouth work. The silence grew louder. "She was very beautiful." His voice was a hoarse whisper.

"That's what you all say." Roderic rose restlessly and paced over to the window. The wind swirled the leaves around the trunk of the ancient tree, and he was reminded of the storm. Involuntarily, he shivered. "So now what? Should I marry this—girl, or whatever she is, and risk offending anyone with a marriageable daughter? What if she's really a monster like her mother?" He did not wait for an answer. "And now, now I must return to Ahga today or tomorrow at the latest. I've had a dispatch—there was an earthshake just after the court left. The west wall of the city collapsed."

"Earthshake?" Phineas sat back and frowned. "This is troubling. There has not been an earthshake in Ahga since the Armageddon."

"Maybe that witch brought it on us with her Magic." Roderic picked up the letter and folded it carefully.

"Amanander." Phineas whispered the name, and his wrinkled face was as pale as the bleached linen pillows behind his head.

Roderic stared at the old man. "What made you think of him?" He related his conversations with Brand and Nydia. "So those orders will go out today. We will find Amanander. He cannot have disappeared without a trace."

"Abelard did."

The silence in the room was suddenly charged, and Roderic felt as if a heavy hand had wrapped around his throat. "Amanander—he had something to do with Dad's disappearance," he whispered. "You think so, Phineas?"

"I'm afraid to even consider the possibility."

"Do you think he's still alive?"

"Abelard? No."

"But why conceal—?"

Phineas moved his head on the pillow, shifting right and left as though seeking an answer in the darkness before his eyes. "Perhaps to throw us all off guard. With the King missing, you can't be crowned for seven years. All the allegiances to you are sworn in the name of the King. And if enough could be convinced that the kingdom would be better served by another . . . ?" He let his voice trail off. "And it would buy Amanander time, time to find Nydia, and the girl."

"Do you think we'll find them?"

"I think Abelard will be found. Dead, most likely. As for Amanander—"

"If we don't find him first, he'll move against us all. I intend to send word to Alexander that Amanander is likely on his way."

"Good. But as far as the girl is concerned, Roderic, you do realize that no matter whether you ultimately decide to marry her or not, you must make it clear to the entire household that she is under your personal protection."

Roderic hesitated.

"It would be better if her identity could be concealed."

"It's too late for that, I'm afraid. I shall see that she is watched."

"But you must protect her as well. Not only from Amanander. Your father may have had reasons which you might never know, and you may not decide to accept his choice, but he would not want her treated poorly if he believed she should be your Queen."

"When have I ever allowed anyone in this household to suffer?"

"But you are often gone and superstition is strong. How do you think the servants, the priests, will react?"

Roderic folded his mouth into a narrow line at the mention of the priests. "I see."

"And furthermore, if Amanander is interested in her, for whatever reason, we must assume the girl needs to be protected. Have you talked to the girl at any length?"

"No." Roderic's voice, even to his own ears, sounded childishly sulky.

The sunlight shone through the few wisps of Phineas's hair

and surrounded him with a golden aura. "Roderic, you've done well so far and your father would be proud. Don't allow your anger and your fear to interfere with your ability to make this decision."

Roderic looked down at the table and was shamed. "Nydia may have been beautiful once, but she certainly isn't now. It is hard for me to believe this is the marriage my father would make for me."

"Will you at least speak to the girl?"

"After I have washed and changed. But I must go to Ahga. I'll leave her in your charge, Phineas. The servants are more afraid of you than they are of me." He went to the door, opened it and looked back at Phineas. "Phineas—is she your daughter? Is she?"

Phineas turned his head in the direction of Roderic's voice, and his shoulders shook with a suppressed sob. "Oh, my son," he answered in a breaking voice, "would that she were. Would that she were."

Roderic ordered Annandale to attend him in the late afternoon when the golden spring light filtered through the brilliant leaves and the first of summer's warmth lingered in the air. He was not sure where he should confront her. The gardens and the hall were too public. He knew he would feel too exposed if he took her into the forest, and he had no wish to seek her in whatever place Peregrine had found for her.

Peregrine escorted her as the servants arrived to kindle the fire against the night's cold. He put down the book he was pretending to read and leaned back in his chair, trying to ignore the way his pulse had begun to pound. "Thank you," he said to Peregrine. "You may go."

She threw him an angry look and flounced away with a loud swish of her skirts. He waited until the door was shut and the servants gone, and in the interval, he looked closely at the girl who stood before him.

She wore a brown dress, clean and patched, and her dark hair was covered with a short white veil. The sleeves were too long, the bodice ill-fitting, and the skirt ended just above her knees. Her legs were bare, and she wore heavy felt houseslippers, such as the housemaids did. Obviously, Peregrine had not opened her coffers. And then, he remembered that he had not asked it of her.

"Your name is Annandale."

"Yes, Lord Prince." Her voice was low and sweet, each word like the note of a bell.

"Look at me." She raised her head and he felt a leap in his chest at the sight of that extraordinary face. Some part of him had said he was mistaken: that her beauty was a trick of the witch or a fool of firelight—but with the sunlight streaming full across her face, there could be no doubt.

Her mouth was neither full, nor thin; her nose neither long nor short. Her chin had the shadow of a cleft, her cheekbones high and round. Her eyebrows were dark and arched over her blue eyes—eyes as blue as the Northern Sea on a clear day. Her skin was smooth and tinted with a hint of rose.

It was a face so beautiful that looking at her was a pleasure to be savored, like that of a rare jewel or a good meal, or a harp perfectly tuned. He literally had to tear his eyes away.

"Your mother expects me to marry you."

She dropped her eyes and a deeper pink stained her face. "Yes."

He was growing more and more uncomfortable. "I'll be brief. I've not decided what I'll do with you. You will stay here with the rest of the court, and when it is time, you will accompany us to Ahga. It is the seat of the Ridenau Kings—my family has ruled in Ahga for hundreds of years, long before Meriga was united. I leave tomorrow: I do not expect to see you again for some time."

"As you say, Lord Prince."

He was amused and somehow touched at that answer. "Who taught you to say that?"

"Lady Peregrine said that was the proper response to any request you might make of me."

"Did she give you those clothes?"

"No, Lord Prince."

"Who did?"

"The chief cook."

"Why the cook?"

"It is where Lady Peregrine placed me to serve."

"Oh, she did? Indeed." He would speak with Peregrine. "You have been in the kitchens, then, this day?"

"Yes, Lord Prince."

"Doing what?"

"Peeling potatoes."

"Potatoes? Let me see your hands." She held out two small, white hands, tipped with short, rosy nails. The skin was soft and supple. "You don't look as if you've ever peeled a potato in your life."

She met his eyes, and he saw a flicker of humor in her eyes. "I have peeled more potatoes in my life than you have in yours, Lord Prince."

"Have you? And what else have you done?"

"Whatever my mother required of me."

"And what was that? Stealing dying children?" He meant to be amusing, but tears came to her eyes and she looked away.

"It wasn't like that, Lord Prince. You don't know what you're talking about."

He cleared his throat. "I shall speak with Peregrine. I don't want a prospective bride peeling potatoes."

"Prospective bride?"

"I have not ruled out the possibility of doing what your mother wished. But I must consider the effect such a marriage might have on the entire kingdom."

"I understand, Lord Prince."

There was a long silence while she looked around the room and he looked at her. "One more thing.

"You may be in a difficult position. The old legends about the Magic, the Armageddon, are often repeated among the castle servants, and they believe them. It is possible that there are some here who will be afraid of you." He realized as he said it that he was half afraid of her. "And because of that, try to do you harm. I want you to know—" He cleared his throat, and began again. "You may appeal directly to me if you should have any kind of trouble with the rest of the household." She smiled at him and he took a deep breath. He had not felt so tongue-tied with a woman since he was fifteen.

"Thank you, Lord Prince."

"Here, take this." He handed her a silver ring which had been the Queen's. It had lain in his trunk for as long as he could remember, and it was poorly made and insignificant. The stone was a small white pearl. "This is not a bridegift, or a token of a promise. Do not assume anything by this. But I am often away, and if it should happen that you are in some danger, send this. And I shall come. You may go."

For a moment she stared at him, and he was surprised. He had expected her to obey him, unquestioningly, as did everyone else in the household. "Is there something wrong?" he asked at last.

"You may not wish to marry me, Lord Prince, and that may well be your decision to make. But believe me when I tell you you ignore my mother's warning at your peril." She dropped a graceful curtsy, as practiced as any of the ladies of the court. "Thank you, Lord Prince. We shall see what kind of protection this brings." Clutching the ring, she moved toward the door.

Shocked, he could only stare. As she opened the door, he managed her name. "Annandale."

"Lord Prince?"

"We shall speak again."

"As you say, Lord Prince." She bowed her head and was gone. He unclenched his fists and forced himself to take a deep breath. He called for Peregrine, and when she came, he was sorting his papers into a pack.

"What are you doing?"

"I'm going back to Ahga tomorrow."

"Why?"

"There's been an earthshake in Ahga, Peregrine. Don't worry. I'll be back as soon as I can. I must see about any left-over business from the Convening as well. It is a bit early for us to be here. Have you forgotten?"

"No, of course not. Are you angry with me, Roderic?"

He did not answer the question. "And another thing, Peregrine. Get that girl out of the kitchens. She's no scullery maid."

"Well, what is she, then?"

"Did you ask her?"

"I asked her what she could do, and she said she was willing to do whatever needed doing. Cook was complaining that one of the maids ran off, and another had a bad burn and couldn't work, so I put her where I thought we needed her. Have I done wrong?" She looked at him defiantly.

He softened. Nothing would be accomplished by antagonizing Peregrine. "Can't you have her with the women who tend to Tavia?"

She dropped her eyes and swallowed. "I—I could."

He turned back to the desk and shook his head. "Have you looked at her?" He stared off into space, seeing again that unearthly face.

"Of course I've looked at her."

"And what do you think?" He was looking at the desk and did not see her throw the book. It hit him squarely on the back of the head and fell in a flutter to the floor.

"Just like a man!" Peregrine had tears in her eyes and her

face was red. "You all think with your cocks and balls and never with your brains. Just because she's beautiful—"

He drew her into his arms and held her while she sobbed against his chest. "In that case, I think about you a lot."

"Don't try your charm on me!"

"Peregrine, I know this isn't easy. But I expect you to treat this girl like a guest. Do you understand?" He hugged her tightly.

"I'm sorry I hit you with the book."

He kissed the top of her head. "Can we talk about Annandale?"

"If we must."

"I want you to watch her closely. Keep her under your personal supervision as much as you can. And you must watch the household as well. Let me know if you see or hear anything."

"Like what?"

"The girl may do us harm. And she may be in some danger herself. There's always the servants. They may carry tales to the priests. My father had enough trouble with the Bishop of Ahga. And I have concerns about the household, too."

"What do you want me to do?"

"Come to me immediately. I have told the girl to come to me as well. I want it made clear that I will deal harshly with anyone who threatens her unprovoked."

"I see."

"All right?"

"Roderic, I knew you would marry someday. It isn't that I'm jealous—it's just that she—I thought you would take as your bride the daughter of some great Senador—"

"Why do you talk as if I had made up my mind? I know nothing about this girl—almost nothing, at any rate. And I don't like what I do know. This is not a decision I will make quickly, or lightly, or—" and he thrust his hips against hers "—in bed."

She pulled away. "I will make the arrangements for you for tomorrow."

"Thank you."

"Do you—do you want my company tonight?"

"Bring me a tray for dinner. I want to go to bed early tonight—I leave at dawn."

"As you say." She smiled and he was glad to see her dimples.

"Peregrine?"

She paused in the door.

"Find her something else to wear? Please?"

She folded her lips in a prim line and made a little face. "As you say, Lord Prince."

Chapter Eighteen

Once he had left Minnis, Roderic found it easy to forget Annandale, and he was glad to read in the tone of Peregrine's letters that even she relaxed as the weeks went by and nothing changed. With Brand's words ringing in his mind, Roderic threw himself into the task of supervising the repair of the damage done by the earthshake.

But when the repairs to the walls of Ahga were nearing completion, when the plans of the defense of the city in the event of an attack were made, when the dispatches were read and answered and he had returned to Minnis, Roderic, although he tried to ignore her, was aware of Annandale. It would have been impossible not to have been aware of her. Glimpses of her hovered just at the corner of his vision: the curve of her profile, the lift of her hand, the flash of her skirt. His body responded involuntarily to her and he felt her absence as keenly as he did her presence.

He was not the only one affected; wherever she went, everyone—men and women and children—stopped and stared for the pure pleasure of looking at her. But that was little comfort to his distraction.

As she had promised, Peregrine placed Annandale among the women who cared for Tavia. She was always surrounded by others whenever Roderic saw her, and he made no attempt to see her alone. He knew she spent time with Phineas, and that the old man seemed happy since her coming. And he knew she sometimes sang with the harpers in the long evenings after the last meal. He never stayed to hear her sing: he had a hard enough time keeping her face and form out of his mind. He did not want her voice haunting him as well.

Annandale kept to herself for the most part, said little, and stayed in the background as much as she could. Peregrine did not mention her name; Roderic chose not to ask.

So the summer wore on. Roderic paid careful attention to the dispatches from the outposts. He was troubled when all the commanders from the garrisons and toll plazas leading into the west reported nothing of Amanander. Messengers arrived daily from all parts of the realm, but no word came from Vere, and nothing new was learned of Abelard. Roderic's dreams were sometimes darkened by the specter of soldiers with dead men's eyes, and one day, he sketched from memory the crest he had seen in Nydia's flames. He hid the paper in the back of his desk and tried to shut such seemings from his mind.

As Mid-Year passed, and Gost approached, Roderic brooded more and more upon the impending question of his marriage. Sooner or later the court must return to Ahga. Sooner or later, he would have to decide. He had always thought that this would be a subject for discussion, even lengthy negotiations. Now it seemed that Abelard had never intended that there be any question at all. What did his father owe the witch that his son should pay such a price? Phineas refused to answer any more questions, pleading ignorance.

One day, as he sat with his scribe, Peregrine asked to be admitted, and asked him to come with her.

Roderic frowned. He was in the middle of a delicate negotiation of water and mining rights between two equally powerful Senadors in neighboring estates, who each invoked ancient and apparently opposing laws. "Must I now, lady?"

"It concerns the Lady Annandale."

"Oh?"

"And your sister."

"Tavia?" Roderic put the pen down, and followed where she led. "What's going on?"

As they climbed the steps of the tower where Tavia lived, Peregrine explained: "She was upset today. I think her kitten scratched her. Anyway, we tried to soothe her and Annandale came in and put her arms around her, and Tavia started to cry."

"And you took me away from my work for that?"

Peregrine stopped on the middle of the staircase. "Don't you understand? Tavia never cries. She makes some unearthly wailing noise, but she never cries. She never sheds tears. Annandale put her arms around her, and it was like someone broke through a dam. Come on."

She held her finger to her lips as she gently pushed the door open. "Listen."

Roderic heard a voice, softly singing:

"Hush, my baby, sleep, my baby,
Day is dying in the west,
Gently, gently, night is falling,
Day is ending, time to rest.

"In the south the winds are blowing,
Softly, softly, warm and sweet,
Hush, my baby, sleep, my baby
Father watches as you sleep.

"In the north the winds are blowing,
Fiercely, fiercely, brisk and chill
Hush, my baby, sleep my baby,
Mother warms you, so be still.

"In the east the winds are blowing,
Quickly, quickly comes the dawn,
Hush, my baby, sleep, my baby,
Soon the moon and stars are gone.

"In the west, the winds are blowing,
Night is falling, time to rest,
Hush, my baby, sleep, my baby,
Slumber safe on mother's breast."

Roderic closed his eyes and leaned against the wall. The notes were pure and clear and true, as he had known they would be, and he felt one more stone in the wall he had tried to build between himself and Annandale crumble into dust. As the song faded away, he opened his eyes. "Let's go in."

They peered around the door. Annandale sat beside Tavia, who was curled on the bed, eyes closed, tears still seeping down her cheeks. The pillow beneath her face was wet.

Annandale's head was bowed, and she held one of Tavia's hands in both her own.

"Annandale?"

She looked up, and Roderic stared in amazement. Her cheeks were streaked with tears, her eyes still brimming over. On her face he saw anguish and mortal fear.

"Is she sleeping?" Peregrine tiptoed over to the bed.

"Come with me, lady." His voice was brusque.

Immediately, Annandale disentangled her hands and wiped her face with a linen square. She looked up at Peregrine.

"I'll stay with her." Peregrine nodded.

Roderic stood aside and let her precede him down the steps. "This way." He led her to his study and gestured an abrupt dismissal to the scribe. When the scribe had gone, clutching his bundle of pens and parchments to his bony chest, Roderic nodded at the chair. "Sit."

She obeyed.

He looked her over suspiciously. She seemed calm, though her face was damp. "What have you done to my sister?"

"I soothed her to sleep."

"Why was she crying?"

"She has much to cry about."

"Such as?"

Annandale looked at him as if he had suddenly spoken another language. "She has known great grief."

"But Peregrine says she never cries."

"I cannot speak to that, Lord Prince."

Her answer struck him as evasive. He crossed the room and caught her wrist. "If you have harmed my sister—"

"No! No, Lord Prince, I swear! I cannot harm her. I only tried to comfort her with a song my mother sang to me when I was small. It's a lullaby."

Roderic saw the fear in her eyes, and for no reason he could have articulated, he believed her. He dropped her hand: he had no wish to renew the memory of that first touch. "We shall see."

"I promise you, Roderic, she is not harmed."

"You used my name."

"Forgive me. I know I have not your permission."

The silence in the room grew until Roderic thought he heard the beating of their two hearts. She looked so small and vulnerable. She twisted her hands in the fabric of her gown. He noticed then the ugly orange color. Peregrine was still trying to minimize her beauty.

She looked up, and he swallowed hard. "I swear I did no harm, Lord Prince."

He closed his eyes and tried to steady his breathing. The blood in his veins was hot, and he felt himself grow hard. It would be so easy, he thought, to reach out and take her. "Are you a witch?"

"No."

"I want the truth."

She shook her head. "I know nothing of the Magic, and I have never harmed a living soul." She held out her hand. "I don't know how to make you believe that."

"Neither do I." He moved away from her to lean against the empty hearth. There was another long silence.

"Are you well treated, lady?"

"Yes, Lord Prince."

"Are there any problems?"

"No, Lord Prince."

"And Peregrine?"

"The Lady Peregrine is kind."

He looked at her gown and smiled. "Indeed. Do you enjoy it here?"

"It is very different from what I am accustomed to."

"What do you do all day?"

"I sew. I sing. I read."

"You read?"

"Yes, Lord Prince."

"And the rest of the household?"

She hesitated for the fraction of an instant. "They are kind. I have no complaint."

"Truly? All of them? Are you certain?"

"They talk about me—where I came from, why I'm here."

"You expected that, though, didn't you? I did."

"They stare, sometimes."

"Sometimes? I don't wonder."

At that she blushed and lowered her eyes. His gaze fell on her hands, which still twisted nervously in her lap. "You wear the ring."

"You did not say not to."

"No."

"Do you want it back?"

"I told you under what circumstances I wanted it back. Has anyone noticed it?"

"No."

"Are you certain?"

"Only Phineas. He felt it when he took my hand one day."

"Did you tell him I gave it to you?"

"Yes."

"And what did he say?"

"He seemed well pleased."

"Did you know I have a letter from my father? He wrote it the day I—we were born. Did you know we were born on the same day?"

"Yes, Lord Prince."

"Am I to believe we were born for each other?"

She raised her head and looked at him, and he thought that in the proud set of her chin, in the arch of her brow, she looked as royal as any of Abelard's get.

"It is true, lady," he said, after another silence, "that I am drawn to you for some reason I do not understand. But why should I marry you? You know nothing about the running of a household like Ahga, do you? If I marry you, it means there must be a First Lady. I don't want to live in a house of quarreling women. I know my father wants me to marry you. But why?"

There was another pause. And then she said: "Why not?"

"I beg your pardon?"

"Why not marry me?"

It was Roderic's turn to stare.

"Are there objections? Another candidate?"

He searched his memory. Except for Peregrine—and that was a candidate of his own choosing. He could not remember that Abelard—or anyone else—had ever mentioned his marriage. "No," he admitted.

"Then why not?"

Because I don't trust you, he wanted to say. You frighten me with your unearthly beauty. When I am with you, I am like a man lost in a desert, panting for water. He pushed that thought aside with effort and spoke slowly, haltingly. "Your mother showed me a fate worse than anything I ever imagined in my bleakest nightmares and said you were proof against it. But nothing, nothing I've ever been taught, nothing I've ever encountered, prepared me for you. The day I found you there was an icestorm in the middle of a spring day, and the night I brought you here an earthshake brought down the walls of Ahga. Was that a natural earthshake, or did your mother's Magic have something to do with that? Was it a result of my bringing you here? What am I to believe?"

She stood up. "I cannot tell you what to believe, Lord Prince. My mother used the Magic to make the storm to bring you to the tower. But I can only assure you that the earthshake was nothing in comparison to what the Magic can do. Neither you, nor the King, nor Phineas, nor all the Senadors understand what can happen. So the question is not why you should not marry me. The question is can you trust the word of a woman?" She inclined her head in a brief, graceful bow and was gone before he could even think of an answer.

That afternoon, after a long session with Phineas and the emissaries of the two Senadors, Roderic held up his hand to Phineas's litter-bearers when they came to take him from the room and told them to wait outside.

Phineas sat quietly as they left, and then he said: "Is there something you need to discuss with me, Roderic?"

"Yes. I think you know what it is."

"Your marriage."

"Exactly."

"It's been almost two months since you brought her here. You've had time to get to know her and to watch her among the court. What do you think?"

"There's been no trouble with her. But I keep coming to the same question. Why? Why should I marry her? Why did my father choose her for me?" He looked out the windows into the green expanse of the gardens. "And I still don't feel I really know her."

"That's been your choice, has it not?"

Roderic glared, knowing Phineas was right. "I suppose."

"You've avoided her, Roderic."

"Yes."

"Why?"

Roderic ignored the question. "There's been no word from Alexander about Amanander. No one has seen him, heard from him. Phineas, have you heard of anything odd happening in the realm? Anywhere?"

He frowned. "What do you mean by odd?"

"I don't know—anything not—usual. Like that earthshake in Ahga—that wasn't normal."

"Why do you ask?"

"I haven't told you all that happened that day. The witch—she showed me a vision in the flames, what would happen if I were not to return from that place."

"Yes, so you did say."

"That vision haunts my sleep—it was worse than any nightmare—and the most frightening part was that she said the only chance I had to overcome it was if I married the girl."

"I see."

"She said war would rise in the four corners of the country, that I would be beset on all sides and at once, and that only with the help of Annandale was there a possibility for a victory."

Phineas said nothing.

"I don't know what to believe, Phineas. If Dad knew something like this would happen, why didn't he warn us? And you didn't see the witch, and you can't see the girl, Phineas. She has the face of a—when I am with her, I cannot tear my eyes away. What Magic is this?"

"Why do you think it's Magic?"

"Because no woman is that beautiful! She has a beauty beneath the skin; it draws me like a magnet."

"It may not be Magic, Roderic."

"What else could it be?"

"Perhaps it is nothing more than what you see. I cannot answer your questions. I know your father believed it was imperative you marry her. If you do not, and the King returns, I would not want to answer to the consequences."

"But, Phineas." He sank into one of the chairs and raked his fingers through his hair. "She doesn't even know how to run the household—Peregrine must remain here as First Lady. She brings me no land, no men, nothing—not even clothes on her back. And that day in the witch's tower, that day was not the first day I saw her. In the spring, some Wildings asked me to hunt a lycat that had taken to killing their children. I killed that lycat, but not before it had harmed a child. The child was nearly dead, and she—Annandale—she took the child."

"What do you mean, took the child?"

Roderic explained the events of the day he had slain the lycat. "There," he finished. "What do you think of that? She tricked me. What happened to that child? What do you think she did with it?"

"What do *you* think she did with it?"

Roderic stared at the old man. The question was unanswerable. "I don't know," he said grudgingly.

"Lord Prince." A maidservant peered around the door. "Lady Peregrine requests your presence in the Lady Tavia's chambers at once."

"Now, we'll see," he said to Phineas. "You wait here." Not waiting for an answer to any of his questions, he pushed past the maid and took the steps two and three at a time. "Peregrine? Tavia?"

They stood by the window, side by side, Peregrine's arm around Tavia's waist.

At the sound of Roderic's voice, they turned. "Roderic," Tavia said. Her voice was hoarse, and she had changed. She was no longer so young looking; her face had lines and wrinkles, and she looked almost as old as Brand. But her eyes were focused on him and no longer stared past and through him into some place he could not follow. She smiled broadly and stepped forward, arms outstretched.

"Tavia?" Roderic could not believe his eyes.

"Thank you for your care." Her smile made her face beautiful and inexplicably reminded him of Annandale's.

He drew Tavia close, wondering, and looked at Peregrine over the top of Tavia's head. "How did this happen?"

Peregrine shook her head. "I have been here maybe three or four hours, since you sent Annandale away, and she woke just now, as you see her."

He held Tavia at arm's length. "How do you feel?"

"As if I had walked from darkness into light." She turned to Peregrine. "I don't know how or why, but when I woke from that last sleep, it was as if I woke from the grave." She laughed. "Is it not wonderful?"

"Do you remember anything?"

The smile faded and she reached for his hands. "I remember it all. But it's over, and I'm alive, and—Roderic, I feel as if the sun has risen after a long, long night."

He thought he would never forget the wonder and the disbelief of that day. His sister declared herself hungry and in need of a bath, and as the servants were sent scurrying to fulfill her wishes, Roderic stumbled, almost in a daze, back to the council room where Phineas waited.

"What has happened?"

"It's—it's Tavia. She's herself again."

Phineas said nothing.

"I don't know what's happened, but Annandale was involved in some way, I know it."

"How?"

"She was last with her."

"Is Tavia harmed in any way?"

"Oh no, far to the contrary. She's better than ever." Roderic gave a short laugh. "If this is Magic, perhaps we need it after all."

Roderic opened the door to call for the litter-bearers, and as they lifted Phineas to carry him out, he held up his hand and the men paused in the doorway. "I made a mistake once, Roderic, a very long time ago. It was the worst mistake I have ever made, and everything which I have done, or has happened to me since, is a result of it." He faltered, his voice breaking with emotion, and Roderic waited, stunned. "I, too, distrusted a beautiful woman—a woman who was more than beautiful, whose beauty was like a sword, it cut so deep. I was afraid of her, I was afraid of myself, of the way she made me feel." Phineas took a deep breath and went on in a rush. "If I had ever been able to love her as much as I wanted her, things might have turned out so very differently than they did."

"What do you mean?" Roderic asked, struggling to imagine Phineas as a young man, in love.

Phineas shook his head. "Only that the King might still be with us, and that I might have been a much happier man." He motioned the litter-bearers to proceed.

As they were taking him up the steps, Roderic spoke softly. "I make no promises, Phineas, but I will try to know her better."

Tavia joined them in the hall for dinner that evening, and ate and talked and laughed with such energy that Roderic was amused just watching her. After dinner, he tried to excuse himself as usual, but Tavia caught his arm and begged him to stay for the singing and dancing. There was not much he could say.

Roderic settled back in his chair, allowed himself to be coaxed onto the floor by both Peregrine and Tavia, and then, pleading exhaustion, he was about to make another excuse when the King's Harper, Rordan, stopped him. "Lord Prince," cried the harper in a voice that carried into every corner of the room, "will you not honor us yet a while longer?"

Roderic paused, hoping he wouldn't be expected to sing.

"In honor of the Lady Tavia, I would sing a favorite song

of your father the King. It is one Tavia heard often in these halls."

Roderic gave a short nod and a shrug and sat down. Rordan smiled and seated himself on a low stool and struck a few chords on his harp. "We are fortunate, too, Lord Prince, that there is a lady of the court whose voice does justice to the second part."

Roderic's heart began to pound as Annandale rose to stand beside the harper. Rordan smiled up at her, and she down at him, and Roderic shifted in his chair. The harp's music rippled like liquid silver, and Rordan's voice was deep and resonant as it filled the hall:

"I must away, love, I can no longer tarry,
This morning's tempest I have to cross,
I must be guided without a stumble
Into the arms I love the most.

"And when he came to his true love's dwelling,
He knelt down gently upon a stone,
And through the window, he whispered lowly
Is my true love within at home?"

Annandale took a breath and he tensed as her voice spilled like a waterfall over the company:

"She raised her head up, from her down soft pillow,
She raised the blanket from off her breast,
And through the window, she whispered lowly,
Who's that disturbing me at my night's rest?"

The harp's music fell like the crystalline water of a mountain stream, and Roderic realized how little he had really known of his father. He had never heard this song played before.

Rordan's eyes never left Annandale's face.

Roderic felt the blood pulse in his veins, a heat which centered in his groin and grew with each heartbeat. Annandale raised her eyes and as her voice and Rordan's entwined like lovers, Roderic's eyes held hers across the space which separated them.

"And when the long night was passed and over,
And when the small clouds began to grow,
He took her hand, they kissed and parted,
Then he saddled and mounted, and away did go."

As the court applauded with whistles and claps and quite a few suggestions of what sort of entertainment they might like to have next, Roderic held out his hand and beckoned. "I never heard this song before, Rordan, and yet you say it was one of my father's favorites?"

"Indeed, Lord Prince, it was. But after your lady mother the Queen died, he only wanted to hear it in private. And he did, almost every night."

"Why? Why only in private?"

"It made him weep, Lord Prince."

Roderic turned to Annandale. "Your voice is as fair as your face."

She blushed. "Thank you, Lord Prince."

"Did Rordan teach you that?"

"No, Lord Prince."

"Where did you learn it?"

"It was one of my mother's favorite songs. She sang it all the time, until—" Her voice faltered and she looked down at the floor.

"Until?"

"Until she could sing no more." Slowly she raised her eyes to his, and tears laced her lashes, clinging like pearls.

Desire, and something more, something stronger and

deeper that he had ever felt before, made him clench the arms of his chair. More than anything else, he wanted to take this woman and make her his, only his. Every other woman he had ever known seemed to pale and fade, even Peregrine, in the face of the feelings this strange, sad girl roused in him. If they had been alone, nothing would have kept him back. "Will you dine with me tomorrow noon?"

"Tomorrow. Oh, I—"

"Is there a problem?"

"Peregrine—Lady Peregrine—has arranged for a picnic."

"Indeed?"

"Yes, but if you—"

"Not at all! Another time perhaps. Enjoy your expedition." He got to his feet and held his hand out to Peregrine. "Come, I'm tired and want my bed." As he led Peregrine from the hall, he could feel Annandale standing as he had left her beside the chair.

Chapter Nineteen

The day following Tavia's recovery was cold and rainy, and Roderic was certain there was no picnic. But rather than find Annandale and repeat his invitation, he abruptly decided to return to Ahga. It was easy to plead the press of business, although he knew Phineas saw his excuse for what it was. He stayed away a little more than a month, and as Gost faded into Tember, in a tangle of sweltering days and sleepless nights, he knew he should return. It would be his last possible chance for a respite.

In the fields bordering the highway, the farmers tended their crops, the trees hung heavy with fruit, and the land lay like a ripe peach under the warm sun. The sky was clear and very blue. Roderic's party camped in a stand of trees by a rushing stream. Roderic looked up at the sky as he lay on his blanket, and watched the stars wheel in their orbits, listening to the sounds of the night creatures calling through the trees. He took his turn that night, keeping watch over the rest as they slept. He crouched beside the fire, and a deep sense of peace pervaded the sleeping camp. A stick broke suddenly, sending up a shower of sparks, and he looked up and saw a star shoot across the sky. It left a trail of light. He stood up and watched it blaze into the eastern horizon. Momentarily, the sky was black once more, and then, as though the star's light had been dispersed and diffused, the first light of day brightened the sky

He had been running away, he thought suddenly, running away from something he didn't want to understand. No, he corrected himself, not something—someone. The circumstances surrounding their meeting were so fantastic, so unbelievable, he had a hard time comprehending the fact that the girl existed, let alone that he should marry her. The Magic Vere described was the stuff of stories, and yet, that was countered by the evidence of his own experiences, and Brand's. Brand's advice to let the girl stay, to let things go on as they were and devote his energy to the kingdom was countered by Phineas's insistence that he should marry her as soon as possible. He understood a little why Annandale should be protected from Amanander; there was something so fragile and unsullied about her that just the thought of her in Amanander's presence made him shudder. But that same indefinable quality frightened him, too. Those eyes of hers—so large and clear and blue—appeared to look all the way through him. He didn't like to think what she might see.

Something else about her eyes tugged at him, something familiar. He didn't want to trust her, didn't want to let himself give in to the undeniable attraction he had for her. He wondered what Phineas had meant—that he had distrusted a beautiful woman and so had made a terrible mistake? Did he refer to Nydia? What could possibly have changed Nydia from the beautiful woman every man remembered into the monster she now was? Had her beauty been a disguise all along?

He shook his head, disgusted with his own thoughts. I'm behaving just as Brand feared. A bird twittered on the branch above his head, scolding, and the rising breeze stirred the campfire. He hooked his thumbs in his belt and bent to roll up his blanket. It was time to travel on.

From her window in the eastern tower, Annandale watched the comet streak across the sky. It disappeared into the west just as the first light of dawn broke over the trees. She shifted the baby's head against her shoulder. Silky wisps of dark hair tickled her cheek. The child stirred, whimpered, and was still.

Melisande was teething. Her gums were swollen and sore, the tooth buds just visible beneath the skin like tiny pearls. During the day there were more distractions, more hands willing to help and hold and soothe. But in the night, the pain intensified, and now these vigils had become a habit.

Annandale sat down once more in the rocking chair. She tucked the blanket closer around the baby's shoulders. Her own gums ached and throbbed in a constant flux of pain and relief. She leaned back against the chair, shut her eyes, and listened to the rising chorus of birdsong.

Behind the chair, the door opened. "Is the baby all right?" Peregrine spoke in a sharp whisper.

Annandale took a deep breath and braced her shoulders against the abrupt blast of Peregrine's jealousy. "She's fine. She was in some pain last night—I don't think the medicine did much—"

"That's what my mother always used on the children at our estate." Peregrine swept over to the chair, her lips tightly pressed together, but her expression softened as she gazed at her sleeping daughter. The two women's eyes met, and with a sigh, Peregrine dropped hers and turned away. "I want to hate you, you know."

"I know." Annandale cradled Melisande close, reveling in her buttery, caramel scent.

"He went away because of you." Peregrine stared out the window as though she could summon Roderic back by sheer force of will. "And I have no idea when he'll come back."

"But he will come back."

Raw emotion emanated from Peregrine in slow, hot waves—pain born of jealousy and fear. "It isn't fair." In the shadowy room, Peregrine's face was a pale smudge. "Why should he come back to you? Why should you be the one to marry him? What have you ever done—?" Her voice faltered and Peregrine broke off.

Annandale looked away. Peregrine's pain was like a snake, twining and twisting in her gut. "I'm sorry."

Peregrine gave a little laugh. "For some reason I don't understand, I believe you. It's another reason I ought to hate you, but how can I? Even my baby prefers you to me."

"That's not true." Annandale rose and came to stand beside Peregrine. "She loves you. You're her mother—" A sudden pang made her break off as she thought of Nydia, alone in the tower, left with her grief and pain and regrets. Her voice quivered as she tried to finish. "Nothing can break the bond between a mother and her child."

If Peregrine heard the break in Annandale's voice, she ignored it. "But you can make her stop crying when no one else—not even I—can."

Annandale drew a deep breath and, with a shudder, murmured a silent prayer to some unknown source of strength. Almost immediately, her own pain ebbed away, and with a sigh, she controlled her emotions. Her mother had warned her, time and again, not to reveal who and what she was, under any circumstances. "I—I have always had a way with small creatures," she said after an awkward silence.

Peregrine shook her head. "It doesn't matter. I ought to be glad you're so good to her. Even if Roderic wants me to leave after—I know you'll take care of Melisande."

"He may not decide to marry me."

Peregrine snorted softly. "Not decide? He's made the decision—he just doesn't know it yet."

A shadow of Peregrine's pain shivered through Annandale. With only the greatest effort she fought back the impulse to reach out, seize the pain, and make it her own. The promise of the exhilaration of its dissolution whispered seductively through every cell of her body. Instead, she whispered, "I am sorry."

Derision crossed Peregrine's face. "What have you got to be sorry about? It's not your fault that you're the one his father wants him to marry. Roderic's always done what his father wanted him to do." She faced the window. The wind had picked up and the trees rustled as the rising sun tinted the puffy clouds orange and pink and gold in the pale gray sky. "I remember the first time I saw him. I had just come to Ahga—he was only fourteen, but he was all the serving maids talked about. He was always so kind, they said, but he's his father's son . . . an eye for a pretty girl already. I saw him in the courtyard. The other boys were teasing one of the scullions—he was fat and slow, and always the butt of their jokes. But that day Roderic stepped in front of him and dared them all."

"What happened?" Annandale shifted the sleeping baby in her arms.

"Just then the King happened by, They all scattered, even the scullion, all of them but Roderic. He faced the King and took his punishment—"

"But why was he punished?"

"Fighting's forbidden. Teasing isn't. The King set him to shoveling out the stables. And Roderic did just as he was told, but by the way they looked at each other, I knew they understood each other completely. He really was his father's son, but not in the way the maids all meant. He saw me watching, and I tried to duck out of sight, because I thought he wouldn't want anyone to see him shamed, but he smiled at me and winked. I think I fell in love with him then."

Annandale placed the baby in her mother's arms.

"I knew," Peregrine continued, her cheek against the baby's wispy hair, "I knew that someday a woman would come—that he would marry. I thought I would just go away. I didn't think it would be so hard."

"To leave?" prompted Annandale, sensing that as Peregrine spoke of her feelings, some of her pain diminished.

"To hate." Peregrine clutched the baby close and turned to

leave the room. As if from very far away, there was the distant sound of shouts and the clatter of horse's hooves pounding across the cobbled courtyard. "They're here." Peregrine walked to the threshold.

"I knew he'd come back," Annandale said.

"But not for me," replied Peregrine. "He's come for you."

When Roderic opened his eyes, Annandale was sitting on the bed next to him, adjusting a veil around her head. A pile of bloody linen lay in her lap, and his bedroom was in semidarkness. Roderic lay for a moment staring up at the wooden bedframe. He blinked. He remembered riding into the courtyard, remembered the shouts of welcome as the household came running to greet him. He remembered the stable boy's grimy hand on the bridle. He had started to dismount and the horse had reared unexpectedly. He remembered falling backward, out of the saddle. The rest was blank. He raised his head, expecting pain, and was surprised when he felt nothing. "Annandale."

"How do you feel, Lord Prince?" She tensed, as though poised to flee.

"What happened?"

"The horse shied as you were dismounting. You fell and hit your head."

"My head?" He felt cautiously around the back of his head, expecting to feel a bruise or a wound. He rose up on one elbow. A bloodstain soaked the pillow. He sat up and frowned. At the back of his head, his fingers encountered matted, sticky hair, but nothing else: no scab, no soreness, nothing. He looked from the pile of bloody linen on Annandale's lap to the bloodstains on the pillow. "Where did all this blood come from?"

She kept her eyes down. "You were hurt."

"Why do I feel nothing?"

She averted her face and finished adjusting her veil.

"Annandale?"

She looked at him with such naked, unclouded fear, he was confused. Scarcely believing what he did, Roderic pulled the veil off her head. He touched her hair and stared in disbelief, for it was sticky with clotting blood. He held out his blood-stained fingers. "What is this?"

She drew a quick breath and she twisted her hands in her lap. "I could not let you die!" The anguished words burst as though torn from her throat. "I don't care what you think of me—I could not let you die!"

"Let me die?" He wanted to touch her again, wanted to touch her so badly he clenched his hand in a fist and reached around to the back of his own head instead.

"You were very badly hurt—"

"What kind of witchcraft is this?"

She shuddered at the word. "It isn't witchcraft at all. It's—it's what I am."

"What you are?" he echoed, even as he remembered Vere's words. "An empath? That's what you are. My brother said—" What had Vere said? *"You won't believe me if I tell you."* Roderic sat up straighter. The mattress dipped and Annandale leaned closer involuntarily. Immediately she drew back. "Vere—one of my older brothers—said you were an empath. But he didn't tell me what that meant." Roderic took her chin and forced her, gently, to face him. "So you tell me. Just what is an empath?"

"An empath," she said, so quietly he had to strain to hear, "has the ability to heal—to heal completely. I didn't tell you because I was afraid. My mother warned me never to tell anyone, not even you."

"Why?"

She gave a little shrug and a sad smile. "She told me the story of how she came to be at Minnis—how the Bishop of Ahga threatened to have her burned as a witch. Empaths, too, are considered witches by the Church."

"You healed Barran's leg that day in the forest. And Tavia. You had something to do with Tavia getting better, didn't you?" When she nodded, he asked. "How can this be?"

With her head cocked like a child reciting a lesson, she said, "There is a balance to the body and the mind. When the body or the mind is injured or ill, I can restore the balance by taking on the injury or the illness. The other person is left whole, restored."

"So you took my injury on yourself?"

She nodded.

"Let me see."

She bent her head and gently parted the tangled, blood-matted curls. He peered at her scalp. On the white skin a wide angry red mark was fading even as he watched. "That's all?"

"That's what's left."

He sat back. "Do you feel the pain?"

"It doesn't last very long."

"But—but it must last long enough. And you do this willingly?"

"I must. The healing would not happen if I did not will it so."

"I have never heard of such a thing." He looked at her in wonder and disbelief.

"Another empath healed Tavia long ago."

"How can you know?"

"Because when I touched her, I could feel the residual pain echoing through her mind. She was attacked by the Harleyriders and left for dead. What was done to her—there is no other way she could have survived such a thing."

"But why did that empath not heal her as you did?"

"The ability has limits. I cannot make the lame to walk or the blind to see. There is a limit to how much energy I can expend at any one time before I too am spent. If I overstep my limit, I will die."

"And this has nothing to do with the Old Magic?"

Once again, she twisted her hands together. "It was the Old Magic that made us."

"What do you mean?" He forgot his wariness and gently disengaged her hands.

"Long ago, before the Armageddon, the men we call Magic-users sought to bring an end to all the mortal sicknesses which plagued humanity. In those days, people got sick—"

"Got sick? They ate and drank too much?"

"No, not that. You know, the Mutens have the plague they call the purple sickness? It kills within hours, but it never attacks humans. In the days before the Armageddon, there were many sicknesses like that, sicknesses which did attack humans, which would attack us still. But the Magic-users changed us. They used their knowledge and deciphered the instructions each of us carries within the tiniest units of our bodies, the instructions which make us what we are. But when they did that, there were consequences."

"Of course," Roderic muttered as a chill went down his spine.

"With their experiments, they did all sorts of things. That's how the Mutens came to be, and why humanity is impervious to disease—now, we only die from injury or old age. And also, there were others who were even more different, yet who appeared like everyone else. They could see the future, as my mother could, and their children were like me—they could heal."

"So the priests—"

"Are right, in their fashion. The Magic did bring about the Armageddon. But we—the prescients and the empaths—we are not evil."

"The child—the child in the wood, that day I killed the lycat—what did you do to him?"

"I healed him and sent him on his way."

"He was almost dead."

"He was the worst I'd ever tried to help. But children are amazingly resilient—they are easier to heal. And each time I do this, I'm strengthened and better able to help the next person."

"So there are more like you?"

"A few, perhaps. I don't know. So many were killed in the Persecutions. My mother told me never to let anyone know. She said the priests would burn me if they knew."

"Then why did you tell me?"

She bit her lip, and would have twisted her hands together, but he still held them. "Because—because I did not want secrets between us."

"My father knew what you would be?" he whispered.

She nodded.

He lifted her chin with the tip of his finger. "I see." Their eyes met and held, and suddenly, he was acutely conscious that they were alone, that the bedroom was shadowed and very private. Dust motes danced in the thin beams of light which penetrated the drawn curtains, and time seemed to slow, to stop. Only the thudding of his heart told him that the minutes were passing. This gift of hers must be the reason Abelard had chosen her to be his bride. And no wonder. What need had he of land, of men, of horses? What were any of those things beside the extraordinary ability this woman possessed? She could keep him alive and whole and healthy until the country was united and settled once again. Surely this ability alone would be enough for Amanander to want her, and yet, Vere said she had something to do with Magic, too?

"Annandale." For the first time, he realized how easily the syllables of her name slipped off his tongue, how they lingered in his ear like a caress. "What happened to your mother?"

"I cannot say." This time she did wring her hands nervously, and he caught them both together and held them, gently imprisoned between his. Her skin was as soft and unblemished as Melisande's, smooth as the finest silk velvet.

"You said no secrets between us."

"She used the Magic. She used the Magic in a way it must never be used. And so she became as you see her."

What had Vere said? The natural order? Magic violated the natural order? "She violated the natural order? And because of what she did, she became that—that—" He stumbled over the words. "That's why she looks the way she does. Then why—" he hesitated, uncertain how to phrase his question. "Why didn't you heal her?"

"She wouldn't let me." She would not look at him, but in her voice he heard such sorrow, such grief, he felt tears well in his own eyes. "That's why she went about veiled all the time, you see. So I wouldn't see her and wouldn't touch her accidentally."

"But why not?"

Annandale shook her head and shrugged, a helpless, hopeless little gesture, her fingers spread wide. "She didn't think my healing would work—the Magic is not only dangerous, you see. What makes it dangerous is that there is so much about it we can't understand. And the more we meddle—" She shrugged again. "My mother wouldn't let me help her."

A tear rolled down the curve of her cheek. Roderic reached out, drawn by an impulse he could not explain, and drew his fingertips down the path of the tear. Instantly, a thin blue light flared, and Roderic jerked his hand away. He drew back, biting down on his lip until he tasted blood. "If this is not Magic—not witchcraft—I don't know what to call it."

He rolled off the bed, away from her, wishing he could control the pounding in his chest. "Go. Change your clothes. Attend me in the hall." She rose to obey him, the bundle of bloody linen spilling from her arms. "No wait." He stopped her with a shaking hand, his emotion seething in a conflicted jumble of wonder, desire, and fear. "Who—who else saw me fall?"

"Everyone."

He swore beneath his breath. "You'd better bind some of that around my head. The One only knows what they'll think of this—no one had better know. Come." He sat in the chair by the hearth while she wound the strips of bloodied linen as artfully as she could around his head. "All right," he said when she was finished. "Go."

He waited until he heard the soft click of the outer door closing. Questions swelled in a chorus, doubts dancing through his mind. The intensity of his feelings alone frightened him. He touched the back of his head again, felt the stiff linen where the blood had dried. Whose blood, he wondered. His? Or hers? Part of him wanted to call her back, and part of him wanted to send her away, back to the forest tower, back to the monster who had been created out of her own Magic. At the thought of Nydia, he froze. Annandale said it was the Magic that had made her mother like that. Annandale said the healing had nothing to do with the Magic. But what if she were wrong? The witch herself had refused to let her daughter touch her. But the witch had said Annandale must be protected, and he was beginning to understand why. He looked beyond the walls to the forest looming as far as the eye could see in all directions, and suddenly, it seemed that Minnis was vulnerable in some way he couldn't name. I ought to get her back to Ahga, he thought suddenly . . . back to where she can be behind higher walls than these. . . .

He thought of Phineas, so certain, so sure that he should marry Annandale. He had never had a reason to doubt Phineas. And he had never had a reason to doubt Abelard. He got to his feet, cautiously holding the bandage to make certain it was secure. With a tug, he opened the curtains and the noon sun streamed freely into the room. He gathered his resolve about him like a cloak and opened the door to the outer chamber. "Ben."

At once the old man was on his feet, offering a tray of fruit and bread and wine. "Did the lady help you, Lord Prince?"

Roderic froze in the doorway, and his hand automatically went once more to the bandage on his brow. "Help me? What do you know about that lady?"

Ben pushed past him gently, set the tray down on the table by the window, and proceeded to plump the pillows and smooth the bedcover. "Haven't you noticed, Lord Prince, the difference? Since you brought her here, I mean? But then," he continued, opening a chest and laying out clean undergarments, "you've been so busy this summer, perhaps you haven't."

Leaning against the door frame, Roderic watched the servant work. "You're right. I've been busy. So tell me. How are things changed? For the better? Or the worse?"

The old man raised guileless eyes. "To be near her is like—like finding the warm spot by the fire, like coming into a bright room from a dark night. She's kind, Lord Prince, kinder than anyone I've ever known."

"Kind in what way?"

"She cares, Lord Prince. Cares about everyone from the greatest to the least." Ben hesitated. "I remember her mother. The priests, the Bishop, tried to burn her, you know. But there was no evil in the Lady Nydia. She was only beautiful. I think the old hags were jealous, myself. They were witches, if you ask me, not the Lady Nydia. And here at Minnis, the children—"

"What about the children?" Roderic watched the sunlight fall full across old Ben's seamed face.

"They know, children do. The children all love the Lady Annandale. You've been so busy, Lord Prince, you don't see. But the children have a sense about right and wrong, and there's no more evil in the Lady Annandale than there was in her mother." Ben held out two tunics. "Which would you prefer, Lord Prince? The green or the blue?"

Roderic ignored the question. He stared out the window, beyond the room. From his place by the door, he could not see the herb garden laid out in precise squares of sage and basil and rosemary and thyme, but the sultry air was heavy with the scent of the heat-drenched herbs. He fancied he could hear the buzzing of the bees in the tall stalks of lavender. He kept his eyes fixed on the blue sky. "What would you say, Ben, if I told you my father wanted me to marry her?"

"I'd say he was a wise King, Lord Prince." The old man placed the blue tunic on the bed beside the underlinen and shook out a pair of clean trousers. "This belt, Lord Prince?"

Roderic smiled. "Then what would you say if I said I was going to do as he wished, Ben? If I said I was going to make the lady my wife?"

Ben paused in humming a little tuneless song. "Then, Lord Prince, I'd say you'd chose well."

Chapter Twenty

Tober, 75th Year in the Reign of the Ridenau Kings
(2747 Muten Old Calendar)

Steam drifted from the surface of the bath, sweetly scented with the essences of roses and lilies. Annandale leaned against the high back of the porcelain tub, listening to the excited chatter of the women in the dressing room, Tavia's laughter ringing out over Jaboa's gentle murmur. Her dark hair had been washed hours ago and now was piled on top of her head in a careless knot. Little tendrils trailed over her shoulders and floated in the water. The wedding was less than one hour away.

The candles threw huge shadows on the tiled walls of the bathroom, and on a wooden stand in the corner, the dark blue silk of her wedding dress shimmered. It was the most beautiful gown she had ever owned. Its simple, careful cut clung to the lines of her body, yet it was completely plain, without embroidery or any other adornment. A cool breeze blew from the partially opened window, and she shivered as the air touched the back of her neck. She crouched lower in the water and wondered if it were only the autumn chill which made her shiver.

In the six weeks since the day she had healed Roderic and revealed her secret, she had not been alone with him once. Since the court had returned to Ahga, she had not seen him at all, even at dinner. But always, since his healing, guards were present, four of them, following her from place to place, even posted outside the room in which she slept. She might have thought herself a prisoner, but her movements were in no way restricted, and they treated her with utmost deference and unfailing courtesy. She had realized that this was Roderic's first attempt to protect her from a harm he did not yet understand.

She shut her eyes, remembering how she had cradled his head when he had lain unconscious in her arms. She had sensed the uncertainty born of his youth, his fear of the threat posed by Amanander, the awful weight of the responsibility the King had bequeathed him. His doubts were an attempt at self-preservation. If only she could break through those defenses.

She remembered how smooth his hair was, how it had fallen across his brow so that he looked more like a child asleep than a man injured. She remembered the weight of his body in her arms, the implicit strength in the long muscled limbs, and not for the first time wondered how it would feel to have his body pressed against her. "Are we born for each other, lady?" he had asked her. If only he knew just how true that was. She closed her eyes and sank down deeper in the tub, the water up to her chin, praying to whatever gods existed that their will might include some happiness for them both.

A discreet tap on the door roused her. "Annandale?" Tavia's voice was muffled through the thick door. "It's time—the Bishop's here—we must dress you."

Quickly, easily, the women got her dried and dressed, unpinning her hair and letting it fall in a dark cloud across her shoulders and down her back. "You've chosen well, child." Jaboa smoothed the creases from the dark blue silk where it fell in shimmering folds from Annandale's hips to puddle on the floor.

The door opened with a slam, and Peregrine peered into the room, her hair covered with a filmy coif of sheerest linen, the keys of the household jangling in a heavy mass on her belt. "The Bishop's waiting. Is everything ready for her?"

Tavia and Jaboa exchanged another glance and Annandale

nodded, hoping her face reflected a composure she did not feel. Nervousness dampened her hands and she clenched them tightly into fists, not wanting to stain the silk gown. "Yes, thank you, lady." Her throat was dry, her voice a whisper.

Peregrine neither answered nor looked at Annandale. She pushed the door open farther and stepped out of the way, tugging her skirts aside with a gesture which might have been a curtsy.

Tavia offered her a reassuring smile. But there was no more time for reassurances, for the Bishop of Ahga lumbered into the room, her heavy scarlet cloak flapping off her bony frame like broken wings. She paused just inside the doorway, blinking as though the light blinded her. "The bride is ready?"

Her voice was hoarse and weary with age. Annandale stared, amazed. This was the woman who'd ordered her mother burnt as a witch—not once, but twice? Who'd dared to defy the King himself in his own city? Whose enmity was the reason the King had built the fortress of Minnis Saul?

The Bishop's face was webbed with wrinkles, her brow so deeply furrowed the lines might have been etched by a chisel. "The bride," she repeated.

"I'm here," answered Annandale. She faced the Bishop across the room, as compassion for this aged wreck of a woman who shuffled across the floor with bent back, a battered leather case clutched in one age-spotted hand, replaced her apprehension at meeting this old enemy of her mother's. Annandale stretched out her hand, instinctively responding to the woman's acute loneliness running like a river through a deep channel, carving the striated rock bare and vulnerable.

The old woman paused a few feet from Annandale, her eyes narrow slits, and on her craggy face, Annandale recognized a ruthless, relentless pride. This woman would never bend, never yield. She held to her stubborn belief in an outdated creed with all the tenacity of a tree which clung by bare roots to the rock which ensured its death. Annandale dropped her hand and curtseyed, bending her head submissively. The Bishop might lack the spirit for another challenge to the temporal power of the Ridenaus, but there was no forgiveness in her. Briefly, Annandale wondered if there ever had been.

The Bishop coughed, clearing her throat, and the women all jumped. She fumbled with the worn clasp of her case and reached inside, withdrawing several yellow sheets of brittle paper. It was ancient, rare, and precious. Her mother had described it often enough. The print predated the Persecutions and Armageddon. The edges of the paper were ragged and torn, and even as they all watched, the ancient scripture crumbled between the Bishop's fingers into dusty flakes which scattered in a random swirl upon the floor. Jaboa and Tavia gasped, both reaching in a futile attempt to catch the paper as it fell.

The Bishop had not taken her eyes off Annandale's face. In the craggy hollows of her face, intractability carved the map of some deep and secret pain. The Bishop's faith had betrayed her, offering an empty hope and an incomprehensible promise. The ache which ate upon the Bishop was her own empty heart, feeding upon itself. Soon it would be gone.

"Girl," the Bishop rasped. She made a brief gesture with her hand which might have been a blessing.

"Lady Bishop," gasped Tavia, from her knees, her hands full of the dusty scraps, "the scripture—"

"It doesn't matter. Do you think I don't know the words?" the Bishop muttered. "I know the words. Come." She swept a glance over Annandale and paused. "Do I know you, girl? Your face . . . it seems I ought to know you," she muttered, more to herself than to the women in the room. "Well. No matter. I know the words. Come." The Bishop turned, the hem of her heavy scarlet cloak sweeping the fragments of the scripture into a swirl of dust. Silently, Annandale followed, her heart aching with the Bishop's grief.

* * *

On the dais, Roderic fiddled with the gold buckle on his belt and fingered the design on the scabbard of his dagger. Phineas lay on his litter, his lids closed over his sightless eyes, his hands clasped loosely across his chest. He might have been sleeping, but the faint smile which lifted the corners of his mouth betrayed him. Roderic knew Phineas wouldn't smile if he knew what Roderic was thinking, that he would marry this woman, this girl, this—this witch, his mind whispered. He would do as Abelard had wished, but he couldn't stop thinking of her as something not quite human.

Out of the corner of his eye, Roderic caught sight of Peregrine, her belt heavy with the keys bright against the background of her drab green gown. With a quick pattering of steps, punctuated by the clink of metal against metal, she marched to the dais to take her place. Her lips were pinched, her face was pale, and he realized that she had lost weight in the last months. Something like regret stung him, that she should suffer on his account. I made her no promises, he thought, and instantly knew he was wrong. Peregrine's pinched face was like a ghost's, haunting his waking moments.

Then he forgot about Peregrine, for the trumpets blared from the musician's mezzanine, and Brand, dressed in the full regalia of his rank, escorted Annandale to the dais.

Most of the ceremony was a blur in Roderic's mind, but he noticed that Annandale wore a gown of dark blue silk which finally did her beauty justice. Her hair was long and unbound and fell in dark waves below her shoulders. The only ornaments she wore were the rings which had been the Queen's—one of sapphire and one of pearl. He stood before the entire household, with her by his side, and took her hand. The pressure of her palm sent a reverberation like the beating of a muffled drum through his body. He remembered the light which had flared between them when he had touched her cheek the day she had healed him, and his mind went to later, after the ceremony, when they would be alone. He had not touched her or been alone with her since that day.

In the light of the hundreds of candles throughout the hall, her face was nearly incandescent. She looked up at him and her smile made his heart falter in mid-beat. Then the Bishop was speaking the sonorous words of the wedding vows, the ancient words which bound her to him more surely than the wishes of the King. He pushed the plain gold wedding ring on her finger, the one visible link in the chain.

They did not sit long at the wedding feast. Roderic rose, after only an hour and one of the three courses, and held out his hand to Annandale. She rose obediently, and the assembly exploded in cheers and ribald shouts. She put her hand in his, trustingly, like a child. He led her through the halls and up the stairs, into the chambers which had been prepared for them. By previous arrangement, guards blocked the company from following.

The chambers were the ones which Gartred had occupied: wide, graceful rooms near the top of the eastern tower which overlooked the sea. A fire burned in the great hearth of the outer room, and the air was scented with the bridal herbs strewn among the logs. The rooms had been completely redone in the last weeks, and now blue carpets covered the wooden floors, the curtains at the windows were of fine spun white linen that reminded him of fog, and the bed hangings were soft velvet of blue and white.

Roderic left Annandale in the outer chamber with a brusque: "You may call for your women, lady." Perhaps it had been a mistake to have nothing to do with her all these weeks. His self-control was like a brittle shell; he could feel it cracking all around him. He went to his dressing room, where his personal things had been moved that day, and stripped, leaving his clothes in a heap. He went into the bedroom, got into bed and snuffed out the candle. He did not wait long.

She entered, her bare feet making little noise on the soft carpet. She paused by the side of the bed. Roderic kept his back to her. "Come to bed, lady. It has been a long day for both of us."

"Roderic?" She said his name hesitantly. It was the first time she had so addressed him, except for the day in the audience room and at the ceremony that evening.

"Yes?"

"Will you not look—" She stopped. Before he had a chance to react, she moved to the other side of the bed and stood beside him. The full moon shone through the window, and she was bathed in a silver aura. He could not tear his eyes away from the outline of her breasts moving beneath the thin cotton of her gown. "Do you find me so repulsive?"

He studied her for a moment, a smile tugging at the corners of his mouth, pressure building in his loins, and he could not deny his need any longer. He held out his hand. "No," was all he could manage.

Roderic wrapped his arm about her waist and pulled her up beside him on the bed. She quivered as he lifted her chin with his finger. He bent his head and kissed her, for the first time, on the mouth.

No other woman had ever affected him as she did with that one kiss. When he finally lifted his head, he too trembled. "Forgive me, lady," he whispered, for he knew he had hurt her. It was not her he wanted to reject, it was the whole unbelievable circumstances surrounding her.

She reached up and smoothed a wayward lock of hair back from his face. "I wish—" she began, and stopped, biting her lip.

"What is it?"

"I wish I could make you believe I would never do you harm." Her eyes filled with tears, and in that instant, he felt a depth of sorrow unlike anything he had ever known. "I know you're afraid," she whispered. "So am I."

A raw tide of emotion swept through him, longing and need and fear, and over and under and through it all, he felt an acceptance at once so complete and unconditional, his heart seemed to swell inside his chest. He took her face in his hands and looked her full in the eyes. "I will make you my wife—" He hesitated, searching to put into words feelings he had never known before. "By the throne of my father, I will trust you with my life." She closed her eyes and raised her mouth to his.

He pulled the gown off her shoulders and away, until she was naked, and he saw that her body was as perfect as her face, as if drawn by some architect with steady hand and perfect rule. He cupped a hand around one breast and flicked the pink nipple gently with his thumb. She rolled so they lay facing each other beneath the sheet. She reached out, touched his face, drew the tip of one finger down his chin, to his throat, and across his chest. She drew her fingers through the hair on his chest, like a comb, and continued down. His skin flared as if each nerve had only been partially awake before her touch.

He took her hand in his, before she could continue lower; he did not trust his control. He brought his hand beneath her neck and caressed the fall of her thick, dark hair and pressed her back. He threw the pillow to one side so she lay flat beneath him, and she opened her legs and wrapped one thigh over his hip.

He began to ache with desire. He kissed both breasts and took one taut nipple in his mouth and sucked until she moaned. She spread her legs wider and the head of his throbbing penis pressed against her hot, wet flesh. Involuntarily, he thrust forward and encountered resistance. She drew her hands down his back, cupped his buttocks, and arched beneath him. He thrust again, and again encountered resistance. Through the red haze of desire, he lifted his head. She was a virgin. Of course she was. She had spent her life in near seclusion. He lifted up and away from her. "Annandale."

She opened her eyes and smiled. "Don't stop." Her breathing was as ragged as his own.

"I don't want to hurt you. This—"

"You won't—please—"

"You don't understand, sweet." His body ached to the bursting point; he could not trust himself. "If we do this now, there'll be no pleasure in it for you—here, let me have your hand." He wrapped it around his pulsing shaft and guided it up and down. In only a few strokes, his breathing quickened, his body shuddered, and his seed spilled onto the sheet. He opened his eyes. "Forgive me. I've wanted you too long and too much—that would have happened as soon as I entered you and there'd be no release for you."

She had not let go her hold on him. She rose up on one elbow to lean over him. "Don't you think I have wanted you, too?"

He smiled and took her hand away. He drew her close and kissed her long and hard, and as they pressed together, he felt again the first stirrings of desire. With his immediate demand satisfied, he concentrated all his effort into pleasing her. He turned her over, holding her close within the curve of his arm. Beneath the heavy fall of her hair, he planted light, teasing kisses from the nape of her neck to the small of her back. He drew slow circles around the firm mass of her buttocks, nudged her thighs apart.

With a deep sigh, she rolled over in his embrace. Roderic raised his head, and she reached down to hold his face with trembling hands. The force of his own desire overwhelmed him—never had he wanted a woman so much, never had he wanted so much to give her pleasure. It was as if he could feel her need as his. With lips and teeth, he teased the soft skin of her inner thighs, then gently, he parted the swollen lips between her legs and tasted the faint, salt moisture of her desire. She groaned as he probed with slow, deliberate strokes. She twined her fingers in his hair and tugged.

He eased up her belly, exploring with lips and hands and tongue, and this time, when he positioned himself between her thighs, he knew he could bring her pleasure. She arched her back, offering herself, and he pressed forward gently, easing in a little more with each thrust.

"I don't want to hurt you."

"It won't matter." She arched against him urgently, drawing him in. Her breath was hot against his ear. With one short, quick thrust, he broke the membrane and penetrated. She gripped his shoulders. Her body felt like a hot silk sheath. "All right?" he murmured against her throat.

She took his face in her hands and looked into his eyes. Hers were dark in the moonlight. "Please. Don't stop." They found a rhythm that matched, and she moved beneath him like the sea, and as the pace increased, she sought his mouth with hers. She was his, all of her, and he had never felt so complete, or so one with any other woman. Bound together at lips and loins, they moved toward the same place, faster and harder, and when he felt her body tense and then relax, tense and then relax, he let himself go. She stifled a cry against his shoulder. A little later, he lifted his head. They looked at each other and smiled.

They spent the rest of the night entwined in each other's arms. Her body molded itself to his as if they truly were two halves of one whole. They slept, finally, as the moon sank in the night sky and the air grew chill.

He woke near dawn to see her standing at the window, watching the sea in the gray half light, and held out his hand. "Come back."

She turned, clasping her nightgown to her breasts, and he saw she had been weeping. "What is it, sweet? What's wrong?" She closed her eyes and wiped her cheeks and came to lie beneath the covers next to him. "Can't you tell me?"

"I was thinking about my mother—" She shook her head and turned away.

"What about her? Do you want me to send a messenger—?"

"No!" She shook her head violently. "Leave her in peace . . . do you think she would want anyone to see her the way she is?"

He did not try to understand. He said nothing more, but gathered her in his arms, kissed away the salt tears, and held her until she slept.

Chapter Twenty-one

Annandale opened her eyes. A long shaft of morning sun slanted across the bed, and she saw that the sky outside the window was a bright, clear blue. It must be very late. She turned her head. Roderic still slept, his face pillowed on the palm of one hand, a lock of his light brown hair falling across his face. With a gesture which was becoming automatic, she reached out and smoothed the hair off his face. He stirred and mumbled something, then settled back to sleep.

With the very tip of one finger, the lightest of caresses, she traced the line of his cheek down to his stubbled jaw. They had been married two weeks, and in that time, she still found it hard to comprehend the depth of the communion between them.

With the sharing of their bodies came an intimacy deeper and more profound than anything she had ever imagined. He felt it, too, and she knew that some of the doubts and suspicions which he harbored had been assuaged. The rest would fade with time. Each time they came together, she felt his loneliness, his uncertainty, fears which ran so deep within even he was unaware of them. She knew just how much he loved the King, how much he wanted to succeed in Abelard's place. She knew as no one else could the weight of the burden he bore, a burden which could only increase.

She pushed thoughts of the future away, for a dull sense of dread nagged at her awareness every time she thought of what would come. Her mother's warnings echoed over and over in her mind. Sooner or later, Amanander and the Muten Ferad would come for her. It was inevitable. Time and again, her mother had cautioned her, time and again tried to make it clear that in the final analysis, whatever happened would be up to her. But would she be strong enough to resist, she wondered? Would she possess the strength of will necessary to hold off an assault upon her very self? And all the King's men would be helpless to assist her in any way at all. She gazed at Roderic, at his gentle, vulnerable mouth, softened in sleep, and tried to believe he understood the threat.

Suddenly, with a little sigh, he opened his eyes. "Good morning."

She smiled back, pushing aside all thoughts of the future, and turned to kiss the hand he raised to lay against her cheek. "Shall we ride today, Lord Prince?" They had spent the better part of the last two weeks in bed, and she sensed a growing restlessness. Much as he lusted for her, and she for him, he was used to a much more active life.

At once his eyes lit up, and he tightened his grip on her hand. As he moved closer, she evaded him and sat up. "The day is half over. I'll get our breakfasts—you dress."

He rolled over on his back, and she felt a tug of desire at the sight of the flat lines of his belly, the smooth curves of the muscles of his chest and arms. According to Nydia's descriptions of the King, Roderic was leaner than Abelard had ever been, his coloring completely different, and she wondered why everyone else failed to see how little Roderic resembled the King. Perhaps, she thought, it was because people saw only what they wanted, or expected, to see.

He caught her wrist as she walked past the bed to gather the clothes he had discarded the night before. "Wait. Are you very hungry? Could you wait to eat?"

She shrugged, a little mystified. He looked as excited as a child, and a little of that excitement seeped into her as well. "I could wait for a little while. Why?" she asked, smiling as the feeling grew. "What do you have in mind?"

"Let's go to the beach."

"Now?"

"Why not?" He sat up, the sheet falling away, and she felt her cheeks grow warm. "Come here." He pulled her against him, lifting her up onto his lap as easily as if she were a child, and he nuzzled her neck and earlobes and her breasts. "But then again, perhaps we should just—"

Laughing, she pushed him away. There was strength in his embrace, strength in his love. "I'll have them pack us a basket. The day is beautiful—there will not be many days left like this." She nodded at the window.

He glanced outside, and a shadow crossed his face. "We've been lucky so far."

A chill went through her, something she could not explain and could not name, and she rose to her feet. "Yes," she said as she bent to gather up their clothes. "We've been very lucky."

The hour was close to noon by the time they rode into the country outside of Ahga, her inevitable guard following at a discreet distance. When they came to a little stand of trees which bordered the beach, he swung off his horse, and helped Annandale off hers. Roderic tethered both horses to a tree and reached for the basket of food. The leaves above them were all shades of red and orange and gold, and through the trees came the heavy sigh of the waves as they rolled against the beach. "I used to sneak away and come here every chance I could," he said. "Then they learned where I was."

"Did you have to stop coming?" she asked as she gathered up her skirts. A light breeze rustled the leaves, and she caught a whiff of a foul odor. She turned in the direction of the sea.

Roderic smelled it, too, for he looked over his shoulder. "Something must have died nearby. Come on. I'll show you where I'd hide when they came looking. It won't smell on the beach." He held out his hand and led her through the trees. But the closer they came to the beach, the stronger the odor became.

The trees thinned out, and a stretch of white sand opened up before them. Annandale was a little behind Roderic, for the path was narrow and overgrown, and so she only saw him stop at the edge of the beach. A stronger breeze ruffled his hair, and this time she gagged on the stench.

Roderic stared at the beach, eyes wide with disbelief.

"What's wrong?" Annandale caught up with him, peered around him, and the words died unspoken in her throat. The beach was a wreck. All along the shoreline, broken chunks of granite lay scattered like a child's forgotten toys. They were covered with dead fish and sandy seaweed, as if they had been flung from the bottom of the sea. Waves broke over the debris, as though the water would wash it all away. Hundreds of gulls swooped and shrieked, feeding in a frenzy over this unexpected feast.

"What could have happened here?" he muttered, looking first one way then the other. "Last summer there was the earthshake—but I'd no idea that this—"

"Roderic." Annandale touched his arm. "This wasn't caused by an earthshake last summer—this was caused by Magic."

He sat down on a rock at the edge of the sand. Clouds of flies buzzed and swarmed over the reeking corpses. "What are you talking about?"

"This happened recently. Look—" She pointed across the

sand, where blank-eyed fish stared sightlessly on and between the blocks. "These aren't even picked clean. This must have happened just within the last few hours. Look," she said, pointing to the sand where the nearest block lay, "the sand is still wet. Somewhere, for some reason we may never know, someone used the Magic. And this was the consequence."

"Then—why hasn't someone come and told me this happened?" He looked like a child struggling to understand.

"You said no one comes to this beach—that's why you liked it. You said that the rocks—these blocks—beneath the water made it impossible for fishing boats to come close, and that the water was very dangerous. And it's Vember. We're nearly a half hour's ride from the city. Who would come?"

"So—" he shook his head as if to clear it "—what happened here? How could this happen without noise, without some sign?"

She looked around. "Does anyone live near here?"

He glanced back up the path and answered her with his silence.

"No one ever knew how the Magic worked, Roderic," she said, gently.

"Could your mother have caused this?" he asked, suspicion giving his voice a hard edge.

"No." She shook her head emphatically.

"Why not? How do you know?"

"My mother had me to help her."

"Help her? You told me you don't know the Magic." He remembered what Vere had said. "My brother said that you—empaths—are the means to controlling the Magic. If you don't know it, how can you control it?"

She hesitated only the fraction of an instant. "It's difficult for me to explain these things, but I will try. But let's go back to the clearing? Perhaps we could eat there?"

He picked up the basket. "Let's go. I can't stand to look at this anymore."

Once they were settled in the little clearing where the horses were tethered, Roderic reached into the basket and portioned out the food. They were both hungry and for some minutes they ate in silence. Finally Annandale said, "When I heal, some part of me, deep inside my mind, knows how things are supposed to be. When I focus my thoughts on the person I want to heal, I see that person whole and healthy and complete, in harmony with the world around them."

Roderic tossed his apple core over his shoulder to the horses and nodded. "Go on."

"The Magic is like an injury to the way the world is supposed to be." She gestured with her hand, searching for the words. "And somehow, I don't know how, the same part of my mind understands and knows how to heal the injury. So if my mother wished to use the Magic, she and I would focus on whatever it was she wanted to do, and—" She broke off in frustration. "I'm a channel, a conduit for the energy of the Magic. I don't know how, and I don't know why. I only know that's what I am."

"So if someone wanted to use the Magic, all they would need is someone like you—" He raised his head and stared into the trees behind her. Understanding began to dawn. So this was why she feared Amanander. "I've told you about Amanander—how he killed Jesselyn, how he believes the throne should be his. We've had no word from Alexander, nor from any of the garrisons to the west. There's been no trace of him at all."

"If I were willing to help, then that sort of destruction—like the beach back there—wouldn't happen. But I must be willing, Roderic. It must be a conscious act on my part. And I would never be willing to help Amanander." She raised her face to the sun and took a deep breath. Here, beneath the open sky, on the leaf-strewn grass, surrounded by the trees, that part of her she could not articulate felt far more nourished and secure than she ever did behind the walls of Ahga, built of the rubble of human hopes, mortared with human tears. "I know this all seems like madness to you."

Roderic smiled ruefully. "What would you think, if you were me?"

"Think of it like this." She hugged her knees to her chest beneath the spreading skirts. "See that tree? That one, over there—see how different it is from its neighbor? And yet they're the same sort of tree . . . their leaves, their seeds, their wood, it's all the same. You can separate the parts, even carry them away, but each tree is a whole thing in and of itself. And that is what the universe is: a whole thing, made up of millions and millions and millions of pieces, but whole and complete in and of itself. And for some reason, part of me is able to comprehend that pattern, whatever it is, and keep it whole."

"Is there nothing you can't heal?"

She cocked her head, considering. "Pain which is self-inflicted. The Bishop, she was the saddest, loneliest person I have ever met, but there was no easing her. And Peregrine—" She broke off, sensing at once his discomfort at the mention of his First Lady's name.

"Has it been all right? Has she treated you well?" He sat up, nearly spilling his wine. "I can't send her away—she's the mother of my child—"

Annandale smiled sadly. "It's not easy for her, Roderic, loving you as she does. But she's another I cannot help. Her pain is both her shield and her sword. It cuts both ways, such a weapon. But I think it would be cruel to send her away."

He reached across the blanket and drew her close. Beneath his tunic, she could hear his heartbeat, and immediately, hers adjusted to his rhythm. There was strength in him, like the trees, rooted deep in the essence of his being. But there were wounds there, too, little ones, scars he carried and never knew he had. "I wouldn't have her make trouble for you." His fingers caressed her cheek, her hair, and he breathed deeply as though he would inhale her. "My dear, dear love—this is what your mother meant—about Amanander, why I must keep you safe." She nodded against his chest. "There's been no trace of him at all," he repeated against her hair.

"Except maybe that ruin on the beach."

"Amanander isn't the kind of man to give up." He tilted her face up to his. "What makes you think he couldn't force you to help him? What if he said he would kill someone if you didn't help him? Could you stand by and watch someone die in agony, knowing you could stop it in an instant?" His hazel eyes held hers, and in her silence, he had his answer. "If he's disappeared, there's a reason. I hope I'm ready for him when we find him." He clutched her closer to his chest and bent his head down to hers. "I'll never let anything happen to you," he whispered, his mouth against her ear. "I swear it. Amanander won't get within a hundred miles of you—I'll keep you safe, always."

"It may not always be possible to keep me safe."

He lifted her face to his, hands buried in the thick tresses of her hair, and tried to coax a smile from her. "I have but to give the order, and ten thousand men would stand between you and whatever would do you harm. I shall never let anything happen to you."

The tears in her eyes did not match the smile on her lips. She touched his cheek again, and beneath his bravado, she felt the calm certainty that something waited—for them both.

She turned to face the far horizon in the north. "I think we'll hear something of your brother soon. Very soon."

When they reached the castle, a groom came running to take the reins, and a servant dashed across the courtyard just as Roderic was helping her off the horse.

"What is it now?" he asked wearily.

"War, Lord Prince." The man breathed hard, from either exertion or fear. He pressed a worn and muddy dispatch into Roderic's hand. "In the north. Your brother, Alexander, is under siege."

For a split second, Roderic looked stricken. Then he ripped open the seals and scanned the parchment in dismay. "Summon Phineas and Brand. I will be in the council room in fifteen minutes. I want ten kingdom messengers, and tell the stables to have horses saddled and ready to go within the hour. Tell my scribe to be in the council room, as well."

He bowed his head. "As you say, Lord Prince."

"Send a message to Ariad, head of the grain merchants. I want a representative here within two hours."

"At once, Lord Prince."

"That's all. You may go."

The servant practically vaulted across the courtyard. Roderic turned back to Annandale, and his indecision was plain on his face. "I don't want to leave you." He touched her cheek.

"Must you go?"

He hesitated. "Let me talk to this messenger. Perhaps it won't be necessary."

"Roderic!" Brand called from the steps which led into the inner ward. "The messenger is in the hall."

"Let's talk to him now." With Annandale at his heels, Roderic followed Brand into the castle. In the hall, a knot of perhaps a dozen people clustered near one of the great hearths. A kingdom messenger lay spent on a pile of furs hastily pulled off the benches. His uniform was in tatters, covered in mud, his shoulder was bound with a bloody bandage, and crusted rags covered another wound on his thigh. Peregrine knelt by his side, a goblet in her hand, a bowl of water on the floor next to her.

Annandale clenched her fists together and sank down on a bench some distance away.

"Will you be all right?" asked Roderic, holding her hands in both his. "Let me talk to him—I'll have him moved to private quarters, and then—" Their eyes met, and she nodded. He was beginning to understand, she thought, how it was for her.

"Messenger." Roderic dropped down on one knee. The man opened his eyes; his breathing was labored, and his breath was foul.

"You—the Prince?"

"Yes. What can you tell me of my brother's situation?"

He coughed painfully, and Roderic looked at Peregrine, who shook her head. "Betrayed." His voice was a hoarse whisper.

"By whom?"

"The Chiefs. Complete surprise. He trusted them. He sought peace—a new treaty—"

"Take your time."

"No time left." The messenger groped at Roderic's tunic. "He sent out five of us—I alone made it through the lines. He is on Sentellen's Island. I took this—" he gestured weakly to his arm and legs "—when I ran into a scouting party in Mondana."

"They have attacked the Lords of Mondana as well?"

"The whole Northwest—they have set fire to the Forest of Koralane. You will have difficulty moving into the region."

"But why? What happened?"

The messenger's dark eyes seemed to glaze. "Alexander was working to heal the ancient breach between the Chiefs and the Lords of Mondana. But someone betrayed him . . . someone turned the Chiefs against him. The treaties fell apart and Alexander was trapped on Sentellen's." He fell back in a faint, and beads of sweat formed on his forehead.

Roderic looked over his shoulder at Brand, who shook his

head. "Have him taken to one of the rooms above. See to his needs as best you can, Peregrine."

"As you say, Lord Prince." She kept her eyes down and would not look at him.

Roderic sighed and got heavily to his feet. He waved the spectators away with an impatient flick of his hand. He glanced at Annandale and motioned her closer. "What do you think?" he asked Brand as Annandale came to stand beside him.

"We should get up there as quickly as we can," said Brand.

Roderic glanced at Annandale. "I would rather not leave Ahga if it can be helped."

Brand made an exasperated noise. "Will you excuse us, lady?" He dragged Roderic to a hearth across the hall. "So now you intend to sit by the fire and hold your wife's hand?"

"I didn't say that, Brand. It's just that—"

"Just that you've been married not a month and the thought of leaving her tears at your heart."

Roderic glanced around the hall. If anyone was paying them any attention at all, they were concealing it well. But the walls themselves had ears; he knew the servants gossiped and that there was little they didn't know. "I have to protect her, Brand. She is very special—"

"I agree. But who else can go and settle a dispute between our brother and the Chiefs and the Lord of Mondana? Who else has the authority? And didn't you hear the messenger? Someone betrayed Alex. Who do you think that someone might be?"

Roderic met his oldest brother's eyes evenly. "Amanander's name was the first to occur to me, although I can't quite believe Amanander would betray his own brother."

"Why not? He might have told Alex something of his plans, and if Alex rejected them—don't you think Amanander is capable of turning against anyone who might stand in his way?"

"Yes," Roderic nodded slowly, "I do."

"Then let's go get him. Let's end this now, once and for all. And then we can all grow fat together here beside the fires."

Roderic glanced away. What Brand said made sense and yet, he didn't want to leave Annandale's side. But between Phineas and Garrick, and the garrisons of the city and the castle, she should be safe enough—especially if Amanander were in the North. "But the Forest of Koralane is burning. Our overland access is cut off. How quickly can we muster the army?"

"The standing divisions will be ready within the week," answered Brand.

Roderic gazed beyond Brand's head at the crest of the Ridenaus, the faded banner proclaiming the ancient motto: *Faith shall finish* . . . The words echoed in his mind even as his brain formulated the answer. "We must cross the Saranevas at the Koralado Pass and go up the coast. And we'll pray that snow hasn't closed the passes, or we'll have the devil's own time getting there."

"We'll be almost completely cut off from our own reserves."

Roderic looked at his brother. "Not we. You must go to Mondana—someone's got to fight that fire and attack the Chiefs on their flank. That will open up the overland supply route. And I will send a messenger on ahead to the M'Callaster and try to open up negotiations with the Chiefs. We've got to have a clearer understanding of what's happened."

Brand gave Roderic a long look. "Are you ready for this?"

Roderic glanced across the room at Annandale. She met his eyes and nodded, her eyes wide with love and something else, something he wasn't sure he understood. A look passed between them, and suddenly Roderic wanted nothing more than to hand the charge of Alexander's rescue over to someone—anyone—else. Garrick and Phineas were old men—too old, surely, to protect his precious bride. And then Brand cleared his throat and folded his arms across his chest, waiting for his answer, and once more, Roderic was reminded that he was the Regent of Meriga, charged with preserving the union of the estates. He squared his shoulders and tried to speak lightly. "It's like everything else. It really doesn't matter whether I'm ready or not."

Chapter Twenty-two

Febry, 76th Year in the Reign of the Ridenau Kings
(2748 Muten Old Calendar)

The oars dipped and rolled, carving a channel into the inky water. Silently as wraiths, the boats moved across the surface of the bay. Before them, the black cliffs of Sentellen's loomed higher and more forbidding as they approached the island under a shrouded sky. Roderic shifted uneasily in the bow of the boat, as the white flag of truce fluttered in the breeze. A cold drizzle stung his cheeks and trickled down his neck beneath his leather armor and his tunic. He was accustomed to the discomfort, for the march through the Saranevas and up the thickly forested coast of Ragonn had been plagued with driving rain and bitter cold. By the time they arrived on the shores of Ragonn, the defense of Sentellen's had broken, and Alexander and his men taken captive by the M'Callaster and the Chiefs. All that was left for him to do was try to negotiate a peace, and Alexander's return. And that, from what he understood, was going to be no small task. The Chiefs were demanding Alexander's blood. But why? he wondered, as he adjusted his cloak, pulling it tighter against his throat. What had Alexander done to arouse the ire of men with whom he had lived so long and so peacefully? There was something about the whole situation he found unbelievable.

In the midst of his musings, Roderic felt the man beside him touch his arm. He started. "Yes, Havil?"

"Up there, Lord Prince. Do you see them?"

Roderic raised his eyes to the shoreline, squinting to see a mass of men waiting. "I do. That's the Chiefs?"

"That's their welcoming committee." Havil grunted and hunkered down once more, pulling his hood lower over his face.

Thank the One for Havil, thought Roderic. Havil had been Alexander's second-in-command at the garrison at Spogan, a levelheaded, experienced administrator and soldier, utterly loyal to Alexander. He had met Roderic's army on the northern shores of Ragonn and had already proven an invaluable asset in dealing with the aged Senador of Ragonn and his sulky heir. Lewis of Ragonn was one of those who had risen against the throne during Mortmain's Rebellion. Although Roderic understood in principle the urge which had made Abelard keep the rebellious lords so firmly under his thumb, Roderic wondered if his father had ever considered the legacy of mistrust he had left for his heir.

But men like Alexander and Havil went a long way toward healing the breach, and Roderic wondered again and again what could possibly have driven the Chiefs to rise against Alexander. Everywhere was evidence of Alexander's even-handed treatment of the opposing interests which vied for control in the North.

"Not much longer, now, Lord Prince," murmured Havil as he hunkered down beside Roderic in the bow of the boat.

Roderic murmured an assent. There had been no sign, no word of Amanander. No one had seen him, no one had heard where he had gone, or what he had done. It was as though he had vanished into the forests surrounding Minnis.

Roderic found this profoundly disturbing. He had expected some word, some evidence of Amanander's presence and the fact that there was nothing, although he had quizzed both Havil and the Senador's son, suggested that Amanander had never been there.

The walls of the cliffs seemed to rise perpendicularly out of the sea. The hollow echoing of the surf grew louder, and Roderic realized it was the waves battering at the base of the giant rocks. Roderic drew a deep breath and held it. With Amanander's disappearance, Alexander's rescue was paramount. He could not believe that Amanander had not tried to contact his twin, and now, coupled with the urgency to return to Annandale, he needed to resolve this conflict as quickly as possible. He needed Alexander's insights in order to end the breach once and for all. Too much time had been wasted already.

He forced his cramped, cold legs to relax as the crews brought the boats through the swirling breakers to scud on the sand of the narrow strip of beach beneath the cliffs. He wiped the mist off his face with wet leather gloves and leapt clumsily out of the boat, where he stumbled on the sand. All around him, the other men splashed through the shallows. Havil touched his arm and pointed.

Roderic looked up. Above them, a mass of men waited: tall, burly men, wrapped in lengths of patterned wool, furs draped around their necks. A burst of rain fell as though the heavens opened, and the wind blew harder. They stared at each other, and then the silence was broken by one of the men in the forefront of the mass. "Ridenau Prince?"

The words might have been curses. Roderic pulled his shoulders straighter and adjusted the short sword he wore at his hip. "I am Roderic Ridenau."

"M'Callaster awaits."

With a jerk of his head, the Chief indicated the steps carved into the massive face of the rock wall rising above them. Roderic glanced at his men, and Havil nodded. "Very well."

The crowd parted, and here and there Roderic caught the flash of metal, of gold and silver and enameled jewelry at throats and on bare upper arms. Some of the men were naked from the waist up beneath their plaids and seemed oblivious to the damp, whining wind. And to a man, they were armed with swords and daggers, the leather sheaths finely tooled and worked in intricate designs. He met their eyes, and they did not look down or break the stare; he was reminded again that the Chiefs of the Settle Islands did not acknowledge the supremacy of the Ridenau Kings, and that the M'Callaster scorned his place among the Senadors in the Congress.

He gazed up at the high, forbidding cliffs and he realized what sort of struggle Alexander must have put up in order to repel the attackers. He straightened his shoulders and met their gazes evenly as he passed by.

The path wound up the beach, to the very base of the black cliffs, and Roderic realized that steps cut into the wet stone were the only route up the face of the wall. A crude rope banister provided the only handhold. He glanced down at the faces staring up at him, suspicion and hostility evident in each one. One by one, as they climbed the face of the cliff, they would be easy pickings. He saw Havil glance over his shoulder at the men behind them, and he set his foot on the bottom step with renewed determination.

He felt the weight of the eyes staring as he climbed.

Higher and higher they climbed, wending their way up the path. In places the stone was cracked and broken, and he was forced to tread carefully, clinging to the frayed rope. The faces below faded into pale white moons, and only the colors of the plaids distinguished one man from another. Roderic felt a momentary spasm of dizziness as he looked down. Then his vision cleared and he looked up.

At the top, more men waited. They looked much like their fellows below, yet here and there, Roderic spied bandages, white against the weathered skin. The fortress of Sentellen's was where Alexander had withstood the siege.

The walls of the fortress, heavy crushed stone, bore marks of fire, evidence of a prolonged struggle. Inside the gates, the fortress itself bore silent testimony to the last battle. It looked as if the attackers had fought their way inch by inch, and

Roderic wondered what ferocity had driven the Chiefs to fight for Alexander's life with such determination.

His practiced eye swept over the fortifications. Alexander had been wise to withdraw here. Perched high above the sea, Sentellen's was inaccessible by almost every route, save the long road leading down presumably to the village. He wondered, fleetingly, why they hadn't come through the village.

Another sudden cloudburst saturated his cloak. Water ran down his face and dripped beneath his clothes, running down his back in cold rivulets. Involuntarily he shivered, and their guide noticed. "Don't care much for our weather, Prince?"

Roderic shrugged, refusing to be baited. They crossed the open courtyard in silence, Havil following close at Roderic's heels as they approached a low round, wooden building.

"That's called the hodge, in their language," Havil said.

"Silence!" barked the escort.

Roderic stopped in the middle of the courtyard. He resisted the urge to finger the hilt of his sword, but he looked up into the giant's gaze levelly. "We do not come as your prisoners. We come under a flag of truce, to parley."

He heard the low mutter of his men behind him, the shifting feet as the cloaks moved and hilts were touched. The giant narrowed his eyes and dropped his gaze momentarily.

"M'Callaster waits," he repeated.

"Then take us to him," said Roderic.

A low mutter swelled through the crowd as the men advanced. The guards who flanked the doorway of the hodge came to attention as they entered, and Roderic saw the rainwater beading on their cloaks, their swords.

Within the hodge, their clothes began to steam. Water dripped in growing puddles onto the floor. Around a circular stone hearth, several men crouched, alternately warming their hands and gnawing on meaty bones. Flasks stood at their sides, and Roderic felt his mouth water as the smell of the food reached his nostrils.

Their escort cleared his throat. The men broke off their conversation, looked up, and began to talk all at once, gesturing wildly. A clear voice cut through the babble. Roderic understood the word "Silence!" more by the tone in which it was spoken than the word itself. The voice was young, younger than his own, a boy's not yet broken into manhood.

"M'Callaster," said the giant in his slow and heavily accented speech, "the Ridenau Prince comes to parley."

Roderic gave Havil a glance and slight head shake, and did not speak. The men gathered around the fire conferred for a moment amongst themselves, and then that same clear voice spoke. A slight figure who sat across the stone hearth made an impatient gesture of dismissal, and the rest of the men rose to their feet reluctantly.

As the others filed slowly out the door, that high voice spoke again in clear and unaccented Merigan. "Which of you is Roderic, the Ridenau Prince?"

"I am." Roderic squinted in the smoky half-light provided by the flickering fire and the lanterns hung high on the walls. Who could this boy be?

"Very well. Irconnell, take his party to the guest house and treat them as is fitting."

As one man, the others obeyed, and Roderic nodded a reassurance to his men, standing his ground as the boy rose and walked slowly around the hearth toward him.

"Sit down, Prince."

Roderic was puzzled. The speaker sounded young, too young, and yet it was clear that the others, battle-scarred warriors all, deferred to him. He seemed to be at ease speaking Merigan, as well.

"Who are you?"

The boy gave a short laugh and sat down on a low camp stool.

"Are you the M'Callaster?"

"Sit down, Prince. Care for a drink?"

Something about the tone of voice made Roderic look more closely at the youth sprawling before him. "You're a woman."

She grinned. "You have a good eye."

"I have a good ear. Where's the M'Callaster?"

She stood up and made a mocking bow, sweeping her hood off her hair as she did so. A thick fall of red-brown hair was revealed. "I'm the M'Callaster."

"I see." Roderic did not see at all. He had never heard that the M'Callaster of the Settle Islands was a woman.

"Do you now, Prince?" She raised her eyebrow and settled down on the stool again, sprawling her legs before her as he had never seen a woman of the court do. Her eyes went over him as boldly as his might over a maid. "What do you think you see?"

Roderic wet his lips. He loosened the fastenings of his cloak and swept the wet garment off his shoulders. He pushed his sleeves up his forearms and settled on a stool near the fire. "Lady—M'Callaster—I admit, you are not what I expected. I expected—"

"A man."

"Yes."

The fire flickered over her face, and for a moment Roderic thought he saw something like regret wash over the sharp features of her face. "My father died last summer. Maybe you heard? So now you must deal with me."

Roderic inclined his head courteously. "May I know your name, lady?"

"Deirdre. But save your pretty manners, Prince. Your brother's life hangs in the balance."

Roderic shifted in his seat. "But why?"

She made a soft sound of derision, as though she spoke to an idiot. "Why?"

She looked about thirty, Roderic thought, though in the flickering light of the campfire, it was difficult to guess. Still, her dark eyes had fine lines about the corners that even the flames could not soften.

She got to her feet. With slow, measuring steps, she circled. She was nearly as tall as Roderic, and she carried herself with a swagger he had never seen in a woman. "How old are you?" The question was sudden.

Roderic looked straight ahead and did not meet her eyes. "Old enough, lady."

At that she laughed. "Old enough for what? It's easy to see where you were raised."

"I was raised to protect and honor women."

"I was raised to protect myself." She completed another circle and took a long pull at her flask. "I will tell you I was surprised to receive your message. I thought that, given the treachery of the Lords of Mondana, you'd have other things to occupy your time."

"Treachery of the lords? What are you talking about?"

She wiped her mouth. "Come, Prince. Koralane had value to you and your merchants as well. The tender ladies of your court will shiver this winter if the furs from the North can't be brought into the capital. I'd have thought you'd be busy bringing the lords to heel."

"You think the Lords of Mondana burned Koralane?"

"Well, you don't think we'd do it, do you?"

He stared at her. "We received pleas from Mondana, asking for aid. They didn't set the fire."

"They lied."

"I don't think so. People who commit acts of treason don't usually call for an army to come to their rescue."

"It was a trap."

"Lady, I beg your pardon, but you don't know what you are talking about. I sent three divisions into Mondana to fight that fire—an army larger than anything the lords could muster. And why would they set the fire?"

"Why would we?"

They stared at each other, and finally she looked at the hissing flames. "So what do you want of me?"

"I came for my brother."

"Alexander." The word could have been a curse.

Roderic shifted his position, trying to read the expression on her face. Perhaps, finally, some of his questions would be answered. "Why? What happened? In all honesty, I thought your people respected Alexander. What made you turn against him?"

"He violated the most sacred tenet of our code, Prince. The one which says that we protect the innocent and honor the women. And I'm not the only one who wants his blood. I'm just the one who wants him most."

"What has he done?"

She gave a harsh snort of a laugh. "You have sisters, do you not, Prince? Have you any that mean anything to you, other than as pawns to marry off to some lord or another?"

He nodded, thinking of Tavia.

"I have such a sister, Her name is Brea. She's not like me; she's young, soft, sweet. The kind of woman you Ridenaus prefer. Alexander came wooing her, with words as slick as honey, presents of every description from places I haven't even heard of. And he asked me for her hand—"

"Yes, I know he loved—"

"Let me finish." She stabbed the furs with her dagger and it stuck upright, hilt quivering with the force. "She was like one bewitched. She didn't even see other men, though there were two who'd loved her since childhood. So I gave my permission. And shortly after that, they were wed."

Roderic stared.

"I heard her screaming. But, frankly, I thought it was bridal nerves. Brea always was a bit skittish. The next day, her women found her in the center of a bloody bed. She was alive, if you want to call it that. Alexander had disappeared. I won't say what he did to her. He left her pregnant, and now she moans and claws at her belly, as though she'd like to rip the child from her womb, or as though some monster eats at her from within. She hasn't spoken a coherent word since that night." She looked up at him with narrowed eyes, and the fire he saw in them was no reflection of dancing flames. "According to the code by which we live our lives, any man who harms a woman in such a way shall pay with his life. Now. Do you want to tell me why I should let him live?"

Roderic shook his head. "But Alexander loved your sister. I know he did. He spoke to me for permission to marry her . . . he had no intentions of harming her."

She leaned forward, her elbows on her knees. "That's not all. He tried to pit brother against brother, Chief against Chief. He threatened to tax our liquor, our wool, the furs we bring to the mainland. He went from holding to holding, from island to island, leaving chaos in his wake. Are you sure I wouldn't be doing you a favor?"

"Did you know he has a twin?"

Her jaw dropped. "A twin? And I suppose you expect me to believe that this evil twin is responsible for everything that's happened?" She laughed and her scorn was obvious. "Do you really expect me to believe that one, mainlander?"

"I do," Roderic replied. "Because it's the truth."

For a long moment she stared at him, measuring and appraising. "Something tells me I ought to be believing you," she said slowly at last. "But—but why? Why and how would a brother turn against a brother so?" She shook her head. "Of all the bonds we honor in these islands, Prince, the bond of blood's the deepest. It's death to any man who raises a hand against his brother—"

"He's already turned against his sister," Roderic interrupted. "He killed my sister, Jesselyn, a holy priest of the Church. If my own soldiers had not been sent out to meet them, my brother Vere, who was traveling with her, would have bled to death from the wounds inflicted by Amanander's men. Yes," Roderic said as Deirdre gasped and shook her head a little in protest, "so you see, lady? It is more than possible that Amanander has spread his mischief across your lands."

"But why?" demanded Deirdre.

It was Roderic's turn to pause and gaze into the heart of the flames leaping within the stone circle. He shrugged. "When it happens, lady, as I know it must, even here, among you islanders, why does any brother turn against his own?"

"Usually they both want the same thing."

"Yes. Well, in this case, what Amanander ultimately wants is the crown of Meriga. And he asked Alexander to support his bid for the throne, and Alexander, who is an honorable man, as you all thought until these last months, refused to break the Pledge of Allegiance he had sworn to our father, and the one he was required to swear to me."

"It never made sense to me," Deirdre admitted after another silence. "But the laws of my people required—"

Roderic held up his hand. "I understand. We are both bound, you and I, by words and law. And so is Alexander. He is not the man to break his word. I know he isn't."

Deirdre sighed. "It won't end so easily, Prince. I might believe you, and I do, but my people—" She paused and cocked a brow. "My men will not."

Roderic nodded grimly. "We must work together. There are more pieces to this puzzle than either of us know. I came here in good faith, lady, for your father served my father faithfully and well. There is an oath which binds us—our interests are the same, ultimately. I've no wish to continue the bloodshed. There are too many questions we cannot answer alone. And I must settle this as quickly as I can, because if what I think has happened here is true, then the woman I love may be in danger even now. I give you my word, lady, that I will not leave until the peace is established once more."

"Your word!" There was derision in her voice. "You are the brother of an oathbreaker. You expect much."

"I give you the word of the Prince Regent of Meriga. Remember, there is an oath which binds us, lady."

For a long moment she hesitated, and Roderic watched as emotions warred across her face. Finally, she rose to her feet and held out a blanket. "Here. Take off those wet things—wrap yourself in this. I will send for dry clothes for you."

It was his turn to hesitate. He was wet to the skin, and he had little wish to negotiate naked under the bemused scrutiny of this woman.

"Oh, go on." She laughed. "I doubt even a Prince has anything I haven't seen before, and besides, I've always found men much easier to deal with when they are naked." She winked, as though he knew she'd read his mind, walked to the door and spoke a few words to the guards.

Amused, despite his situation, he stripped the wet clothes off and with a quick motion wrapped himself in the blanket. She did not turn away. "Sit." Her tongue flicked over her bottom lip. "Will you drink?"

"Water, please."

"In this weather?" She handed him a flask. When he put it down, she leaned back against the piled furs. Her hair, so thick and lustrous it seemed a living thing in the firelight, fell over her shoulders. Her dark trousers clung to the lines of her thighs, and her hands looked strong and capable. The backs were as scarred as his. She was so different from Annandale, indeed from any other woman Roderic had ever known, and yet there was a potent vitality about her which appealed to him.

"If I am to convince my people, you must tell me everything you can about this twin of Alexander's."

Briefly, Roderic told her about Amanander, Jesselyn's death, the fruitless search.

"I remember your soldiers coming to ask about the brother

of yours," she said as a knock on the door interrupted them. She got to her feet and retrieved a bundle of clothes from the guard. With a puckered frown, and a calculated expression in her eyes, she dropped the bundle in Roderic's lap. "But I did not realize that he so closely resembled Alexander we could all have been fooled."

Roderic unwrapped the bundle. Inside were clothes: linen underclothes, a short tunic woven in varying shades of green and blue, woolen trousers, and a short woolen cloak of the same tartan Deirdre wore. "At the time he disappeared, he didn't look like Alex. Alex has a beard—Amanander doesn't. Alex's hair is short—Amanander wore his long and oiled. Amanander has a distinctive taste in clothes—Alex dresses like a soldier. But all those things are easily altered, and otherwise, the brothers are identical. And as for your sister, Alexander told me last year he loved her. He asked me for permission to marry her, and he spoke like a man in love. Alexander would never have harmed your sister in the way you describe." But Amanander might, thought Roderic, if he believed his twin had betrayed him.

"And the man I'm holding here isn't the man who's caused all the trouble?"

"No, and if he were, we'd have a different issue to settle between us. I want him, too."

She stared into the flames. "And the fire?"

"I beg your pardon?"

"You say the Lords of Mondana didn't set the fire in Koralane? That they appealed to you for aid?"

"At the same time we heard from Alex."

"And he was besieged here—" She rose. Roderic heard her speaking to the guards outside. "You may speak with your brother." She took a deep breath, her mixed feelings plain on her face. "He'll be here in a few minutes. I want to warn you—" She broke off and Roderic looked at her with concern. "He is not well. I don't believe it was the effects of the siege alone, nor do I want you to think he has been treated badly, for we don't treat our prisoners of war cruelly. But your brother is a sick man."

She gave a brief bow, picked up a dark red-and-blue cloak, and was gone in a swirl of plaid. Roderic rose and dressed mechanically in the clothes he had been given, turning her words over and over in his mind. His thoughts were interrupted as the door banged open and two guards carried in a prone form on a fur-covered stretcher.

"Alex!" He jumped to his feet.

The man on the stretcher bore little resemblance to the man Roderic remembered. He was thin to the point of starvation, hot with some fever. His black beard was long and tangled, a stark contrast to his white face, and sweat beaded his forehead. Shocked, Roderic knelt by his side and whispered his name. "Alex? It's me, Roderic. I've come to take you home."

Alexander plucked at Roderic's sleeve with skeletal fingers. "Roderic? Forgive—"

"There's nothing to forgive."

"You should not have come."

"You're my brother. Should I have let these people kill you?"

He opened his eyes. "Roderic—"

Roderic tried to suppress a sigh. There was no point in forcing Alexander to talk when he was clearly so weak. "It's all right, Alex. We can talk later."

"No!" He gripped Roderic's arm with frantic claws. "Roderic, there's no reason why this should have happened. Old Cormall's dead. Died last summer. I never had a chance to ask for Brea's hand. I wanted to ask Deirdre, but—"

"Alex, we'll talk later."

"No! There's no time. Where's Brand?"

"In Mondana. Trying to get through Koralane. The lords say the Chiefs set it on fire; now the M'Callaster says they did no such thing, that it must have been the lords. Did you know that?"

He sank into the pillow. "I have had such dreams." His voice faded, and he stared vacantly at the beams of the ceiling. "Dreams of fire reaching to the sky." His eyes focused, and he struggled to sit. "Koralane burns—Roderic, it makes no sense. It would be as if you poisoned the earth around Ahga. The Chiefs would never burn Koralane. It is their life—they need the forest as much as they depend upon the sea. And neither would the Lords of Mondana. To do so would be utter madness."

Roderic pushed him gently back against the blanket. "Then if the Chiefs and the lords didn't set it on fire, who did?"

Alexander wet his dry, cracked lips and spoke so softly Roderic felt rather than heard the name, "Aman." It was less than a sigh.

"Amanander?"

"He comes to me in dreams, stalks my sleep."

"Alex, you've been sick."

"This is not raving, I swear it. I've had such dreams, Roderic, of great fires, and—and—Dad."

Roderic gripped Alexander's shoulder, searching his face for the truth. "What about Dad?"

"I don't know. I see him on a throne—I know Aman wants me dead."

The automatic denial died on his lips. Roderic remembered Annandale's words.

Alexander met his eyes, and in that moment a recognition passed between them. "You think Amanander's behind this, Alex." It was a statement.

Alexander closed his eyes and nodded wearily. "Yes. I refused him, you see. I refused to help him win the regency, and so he turned against me." A tear crept out of the corner of one eye and streaked down his narrow, too thin face. "I should have told you this at Minnis."

"Alex, you need to rest."

"Listen to me. Amanander wants the throne."

"I know that. Here, I'll call for the men—"

"Damn you." Alexander clutched at Roderic's tunic, and Roderic would never have thought a dying man had so much strength. "Listen to me. He won't stop until he has it—I was wrong not to tell you after he killed Jesselyn."

"Tell me what, Alex? I knew then he wanted the throne. So did Phineas, and Brand."

"You don't understand!" He gripped Roderic's hand in both of his with such frantic urgency the knuckles cracked. "Listen. When we were younger than you are now—twelve—our grandmother quarreled with Dad. She wanted him to make Amanander his heir, and when he refused, she hounded him until he banished her."

"What does this have to do—"

"She got her hands on some old books—books which went back before the Armageddon—books of Magic, she said. And she tried to learn how to use it. When she was banished from the court, she went back to Missiluse, and she took us with her."

"What happened?"

"She and my uncle, Eldred, they found a Muten. I don't know where or how, but they wanted the Muten to teach the Magic to them. And he did—or he started to. Dad came down after her, finally. Amanander overheard Dad tell her that it didn't matter whether she knew the Magic or not, that Amanander would never be King, not with Magic or without it. And Amanander never forgot that. Aman knows the old Magic is real—he's seen it work, and he did begin to learn it."

Roderic gently disentangled his hand from Alex's clawlike grasp.

Alexander looked at him with burning eyes. "He was pleased Dad sent him to Dlas—it would save him a great deal of trouble, he told me. Roderic, that's not all, please, listen." Tears ran down his face. "I should have told you everything.

Aman has convinced Reginald to join against you. And Reginald—"

Fear, pure and black and hard as the cliffs of Sentellen's cut through Roderic like a blade. "What about Reginald?"

"Reginald is poised to break the treaties you signed last year with the Mutens—to rally the lesser lords of Atland and Missiluse—Roderic, don't you see what he's done?"

"Yes," he whispered finally, when he could speak. "I do."

"I just don't know where he's gone. . . ." Alexander's voice trailed off.

Roderic looked down at his weary brother. The room was so quiet, he could hear the incessant drip of water from the eaves, and the snap of the fire beneath Alexander's ragged breathing. "I do," he said, grimly. "I think I know exactly where he has headed and I understand exactly what he has done. The question now is only can we undo this mischief in time to prevent the worst from happening."

Chapter Twenty-three

"And what about my cattle?" The M'Cullen's bellow was a challenge that reverberated through the thin frame of the hodge. Roderic groaned inwardly as the expressions on the faces of the men crouched around the hearth changed from those of grudging cooperation to avid interest.

"Not the time nor place to worry about your cows," snorted the M'Cooley as he tipped back a wineskin.

"How many cows d'you think you had?" jeered a red-bearded giant across the room.

"Cares more for his cows than any man of us," added the M'Clee, close by Deirdre's side. He picked his teeth with a dagger and spat into the fire.

"That's cause he diddles 'em." The red-haired chief reached for the mead.

Across the room, the M'Cullen began to rise, and Roderic glanced at Deirdre. She appeared to be listening patiently to the exchange, but as the M'Cullen began to move, his face distorted with rage, she grabbed the dagger away from the M'Clee and threw it. Roderic tried not to cringe. The blade went through the hem of the M'Cullen's cloak, pinning him to the floor.

"Now." Deirdre cleared her throat. "I agree the matter of your cattle is serious, M'Cullen." She used the formal address. "But now is not the time or the place. You know as well as I that such matters are to be brought before the jury at the

Mid-Year Meet." The Chief opened his mouth to protest, and she held up her hand. "I will hear your grievance later. Not now. Not before this honored guest." With a sweep of her hand, she indicated Roderic.

There were low mutters among those clustered closest to the M'Cullen, and Deirdre sighed. "Think, you fools—d'you want the mainlander to see us divided? You show him our weakness." She shook her head and waved her hand. "Go on now—the day is late, and I smell dinner. We'll meet once more tomorrow. Early."

There were groans from various sides of the fire, and as Deirdre rose to her feet, the door of the hodge opened, and a mud-spattered messenger, accompanied by two of the nearly naked warriors, stumbled inside.

At once there was silence. "Messenger?" Deirdre asked even as Roderic recognized the colors of the King's Guard.

Roderic rose and held out his hand and the messenger pressed the worn dispatch into his hands. "What news?"

"Koralane, Lord Prince," replied the messenger. "Koralane is saved. The forest no longer burns. Your brother Brand sends you this news." He gave Roderic's hands another squeeze and a look full of meaning.

"See to his needs," Deirdre broke the silence. "Take the messenger, clothe and feed him, treat him as our own."

A thousand questions danced on Roderic's tongue, and he bit his lip as guards approached the messenger. "Read the dispatch, Lord Prince," the messenger replied to the look on Roderic's face, as Deirdre's household guards tapped him courteously on the shoulder. "It will explain much."

Roderic waited until the last of the Chiefs filed out of the low doorway of the hodge. As Deirdre reached for one of the jugs of mead, Roderic tore open the seals, his frown deepening with each line.

"What's wrong?" Deirdre eyed him over the rim as she swallowed a long draught.

"The messenger spoke truth. Koralane is saved. But the Lords of Mondana blame you—the Chiefs—and they want blood. Brand suggests we ride to Spogan—you, a few of the cooler heads among you—and there negotiate a peace. Otherwise—"

"Otherwise it will be war."

"Yes." Roderic took the jug and swallowed. The liquor burned all the way to his belly, where it settled with a pleasant warmth.

Deirdre looked at him with something like amusement. "I thought our island liquor was too strong for you, Prince."

He put the jug down, wiping his lips with the back of his hand. "Too strong? No. But someone needs to keep a cool head—I don't understand why you haven't all killed each other long ago."

"Ha." Deirdre gestured dismissively. "It's just the way things are. None of them mean most of the things they say, Prince. For us, what we say is so much noise. It's what we do that counts."

"But tempers are so thin—"

"They're like complaining old women. They blather on and on because it pleases them. You don't understand what was really said."

Roderic looked at her. "Explain."

"Well." Deirdre shrugged. "When the M'Cullen mentioned his cows, he knew as well as everyone that it was not an issue here—it meant that we were on home ground, so to speak—that the treaty you have offered us is acceptable, at least to the M'Cullen. And they were getting bored. None of us are used to sitting still so long, Prince. They're usually drunk or passed out if they stay in one place this length of time. You'll see."

"And what about this?" He waved the dispatch in the air.

"We'll ride to Spogan in another week or two. And if it's to be war, it will be war. But it will not be of my choosing."

Slowly, Roderic nodded and sank down on the furs. He

reached for the remains of the noon meal which had been brought to the hodge, tore a hunk of meat out of the haunch of the roast and bit down, chewing thoughtfully.

"What's wrong?"

Roderic looked up at her. Had it only been a week? They might have known each other all their lives, so easily did they seem to read one another. He trusted her implicitly to maneuver her quarrelsome kin. The real negotiations took place between the two of them.

"Tell me."

Again he hesitated.

"Come." She hunkered down beside him and lifted the jug to her lips. Thunder rolled suddenly across the bay, echoed off the cliffs. "What's wrong? Your mind wasn't here this afternoon. Are you worried about your brother?"

"Alex? No." Roderic shook his head. "I know you are doing all that can be done for him. It's the other—Amanander. I don't know for certain where he's gone, and that troubles me more than I can say."

"Where do you think?" She stretched out beside him on the thick furs, her long body lithe in the firelight, less than an arm's length away.

Rain pounded harder on the roof as his eyes ran over her. Suddenly Annandale seemed very far away.

"I think he's gone to join forces with my brother Reginald in the South . . . and that he intends to march on Ahga. My wife is there, you see. And Amanander wants her." He was suddenly conscious of Deirdre's closeness.

She wet her lips. "She's very beautiful, your wife?"

He nodded.

"You think you'll be a while in Spogan, and you're afraid he'll attack your city while you are away?"

He fixed his eyes on the leaping flames. "Yes, that's always a possibility. I thought for certain we would find him here. I never thought he would disguise himself as Alexander, nor masquerade so successfully."

"Listen," she said. The silence seemed to thicken between them tangibly. "Why don't you send her away, out of harm's reach? The Ridenau holdings are vast, are they not? Surely there's someplace safe and protected she could go. A place he wouldn't expect to find her. Send the messenger out in the morning. Once you know she will be safe, you can concentrate on the task at hand."

Roderic nodded. Deirdre's words made sense. Even if the Chiefs were pacified, there was still the matter of the Lords of Mondana. He had an opportunity to build a lasting peace in the Northwest, to secure Alexander's work, and perhaps begin to heal the enmity of centuries. But if he were to leave, if the King's Army was to withdraw, there would be certain war, and he would be drawn into it once more. "Yes," he nodded slowly. "There is such a place. Minnis. I'll send her to Minnis." He reached for another hunk of meat and heard her moving around.

He looked up to see her standing naked in the corner. Roderic averted his eyes and got another chuckle. "What's the matter, Prince? Never seen a woman before?"

Roderic looked back, ready with a retort, when he saw her body. Her torso was crisscrossed with more scars than his; one breast was missing completely. "Why have you been so cooperative?" he asked instead.

She pulled a linen shirt over her head. "Because," she squatted beside him, "it's in my best interests to settle this as well." She seized his face in her hands and kissed him, long and hard on the mouth. "What a pretty Prince you are."

For a moment, taken off guard, Roderic felt his body respond, then he pulled away and sat up. "No, lady."

"What?"

"I cannot—"

"Cannot? You looked more than capable to me."

"I've taken a vow of fidelity until my heir is either born or named. And just as I honor my word to you, so I must honor the word I gave my wife."

She did not seem rebuffed. She settled back on her haunches, stroking her chin. "A pretty lady of the court, I iamgine?"

"Very pretty."

"Can't hold a dagger?"

"Only to cut her meat."

She laughed again, got to her feet, and turned away. "You send out your messenger. We still have much to discuss on the morrow."

"One question, though, Deirdre. How has it happened that you have the title of M'Callaster?"

"My father had no sons," she answered as she pulled a clean tunic over her head. "My kinsmen gathered like dogs at his dying, but he would not name an heir. And so, when the Challenge for the title was called, I entered the combat."

"Didn't anyone object?"

"I beat all who objected in the combat." She laced her breeches. "Our ways are very different from yours, Prince. My only hope is that I will bear a child, so that I might hand the charge of my kin down to one of my own blood."

"Is that why—"

She sat down on the other side of the fire and pulled on her boots. "I kissed you because I want you. If you'd got a child on me, so much the better." Suddenly, her voice was fierce. "I won this right, Prince, by the strength of my arm, with the shedding of my blood. It was no deathbed gift. I fought harder for my inheritance than you or any other man ever fought for yours." She reached for her dagger and fingered the hilt.

Roderic watched the flames, doubting he could agree. "Don't be so certain, lady."

Behind him, he heard the door scrape across the floor. A sudden gust of wind made the fire dance. He looked over his shoulder to see Deirdre holding the door open as she slung her plaid over her arm. "Come," she said with a wink. "Let's put our cares aside for a little. The boys are spoiling for a fight, and it's sure to be a good one."

Chapter Twenty-four

Ahga Castle
March, 76th Year in the Reign of the Ridenau Kings
(2748 Muten Old Calendar)

The chatter of the women gathered in the great hall was cut short abruptly by the approach of a manservant. Annandale looked up from her sewing and waited as the man bowed deeply in front of her, offering a wooden message tube. "From the Lord Prince, lady."

Annandale smiled her thanks and, setting the fabric down, took the message. The women were conspicuously silent as she broke the seals and read the letter. She looked up into Tavia's anxious face. "Everything's fine. Roderic arrived in Spogan safely, and he has every hope all will go smoothly." Annandale smiled.

The women breathed audible sighs and turned once more to their tasks. Tavia mopped the perspiration off her face with a linen square. "Bring us something to drink," she called to the servant, who hovered just out of earshot. "By the One, I can't remember a spring so hot. Does Roderic mention the heat?"

Annandale glanced down at the thick sheet of parchment covered in Roderic's now familiar scrawl. The heat he mentioned had nothing to do with the temperature. A rosy blush suffused her cheeks.

Peregrine sniffed and reached out to steady Melisande, who was beginning to take her first toddling steps. "And does he say when we can expect him home?"

Annandale shook her head. "No, he doesn't. The Chiefs and the lords are old enemies."

"Then may I suggest, lady," said Peregrine, her mouth drawn tight, eyes fixed on the chubby toddler, "that we go to Minnis as soon as we can? The heat grows worse each day—surely there is no reason to tarry."

Annandale glanced once more at Tavia, who exchanged a pointed look with Jaboa. As Jaboa leaned forward with a question for Peregrine about Melisande, Tavia shrugged. "If another message comes from Roderic, my dear, surely Phineas will see it reaches us. It has become unbearably hot this season—the castle is beginning to reek already."

Annandale hesitated. It was true that since the end of Febry, the days had been increasingly, unseasonably hot and that all the inhabitants of the castle and the city suffered for it. The women had gathered here in the hall at this unaccustomed hour in the hopes that the huge windows would invite a breeze off the sea—a disruption in schedule which seemed to annoy Peregrine no end. But in the last months, it had become plain to all the women that far more than the heat made Peregrine's temper so thin. "Let me speak to Phineas." Annandale got to her feet. "I know it's unpleasant. I know we would all be more comfortable at Minnis. It's just—"

"We understand, dear," Tavia said gently.

With another glance at Peregrine, who still avoided her gaze, Annandale folded up her needlework. She got to her feet, trying to smooth out the creases in her rumpled linen gown. It was the lightest garment she possessed, and it stuck to her upper body like a second skin. She crossed the wide polished floor of the great hall, and as she passed the double doors which led down to the kitchens, she fancied she could feel the heat rising from the great ovens. She followed the long corridor up the narrow stairs to Phineas's rooms. She knocked.

The servant who opened the door looked startled to see her.

"It's the Lady Annandale, lord," he said, bowing her into the room, where Phineas lay propped up on his litter, surrounded by neat piles of parchment. His scribe paused in his writing, and Phineas held out his hand. "Come in, child." He waved a dismissal to the scribe and the servant. "You've read Roderic's letter?"

Annandale waited until the servants had left, then she crossed the room and took his hand. His residual pain filtered through her body, and momentarily, a pale blue light flared between them. Phineas sighed imperceptibly, and the lines on his face eased. "Thank you, child," he murmured. "Now. Sit. We must talk."

"Peregrine wants to take the court to Minnis."

Phineas nodded slowly. "It is as well, then."

Annandale looked at him, startled. "You agree?"

"Roderic sent me a letter, too—directing me to send you to Minnis. Amanander has vanished again. He has no idea where he might be, and Roderic believes that you will be better off there. We will send you there quietly, with just a small party of men as an escort. If Amanander is foolish enough to attack Ahga, he won't find you here." Phineas paused and cocked his head. A few seconds passed, and then he said: "But you don't want to go?"

Annandale shook her head and spread her hands before she realized the futility of the gesture. "And I cannot say why exactly." She felt in the pocket of her apron for Roderic's letter. "I don't like leaving you."

"It's more than that, isn't it?" Phineas prompted gently.

"Yes. But I don't know why." An uneasy feeling nagged like a toothache every time Peregrine mentioned Minnis. There was no rational explanation.

There was longer silence broken only by the call of the seabirds as they swooped between the towers. "Is it your mother?" Phineas asked.

At the thought of her mother, tears formed in the corners of her eyes. "I try not to think about my mother. Sometimes I can't—can't quite feel her, and I wonder if she's dead. She's so alone, with no one to comfort her or share her grief."

"Could that be it? Why do you hesitate to go?"

"Perhaps. I just don't know—"

"My dear, when Roderic returns, he'll want to go there." Phineas reached over and patted her hand. "I miss him, too."

"Yes, I know." She got to her feet and paced to the window, where a sluggish breeze ruffled the curly tendrils which escaped her coiled braids. It was much too hot for a coif. "How is the campaign going?"

"The campaign is over in all but name. As soon as Roderic can restore some measure of peace to the Northwest, can forge some treaty between the lords and the Chiefs, he'll be home. It's not so easy, you see. There's no more stubborn a lot than the Chiefs of the Settle Islands, and the Lords of Mondana have their own grudges against them. And there are still resentments left over from Mortmain's Rebellion."

"Mortmain," she echoed. "That's when it all began, wasn't it, Phineas?"

He opened his mouth, and she saw his features harden into place, as though he pulled on a mask. He was going to deny her, she knew, when suddenly the mask dropped away, his sightless eyes shifted behind his closed lids, and his mouth twisted with a grief long suppressed. "It began long before that, child."

"Then, if the campaign is over in all but name, what concerns you so?"

Phineas flushed, then grew pale at her uncanny perception. "Whatever do you mean, child?"

She knelt beside his litter and took his hand. "I see the messengers come and go. I see the directions in which they ride. Not all go north and west. Some go south and east. What is it, Phineas? I can feel what you feel. You're worried, too."

Phineas turned his head away from her on the pillow. "It

may not have been wise for Roderic to go to Alexander's rescue. Things in Atland are very unsettled. I have had a letter from Everard—Abelard's third son—do you know the name?" When she murmured assent, he continued: "Last spring, I asked Everard to go to Atland, after the rebellion was put down, to ensure that the treaties were adhered to, that the Senadors and the lessor lords did not upset the balance of that tenuous peace."

"Why Everard?" she asked. "Isn't one of the brothers—Reginald—there already?"

"Yes," Phineas admitted. "But from the tone of Reginald's dispatches, while he may be a fine soldier, I don't believe he's anything close to a diplomat. Everard's mother's family—Abelard met her when he was on a brief campaign in the Dirondac Mountains—have always maintained a cordial relationship with the Muten Tribes in their part of the country."

"You thought Everard might be able to help maintain the peace?"

Phineas nodded. "But it seems that even Everard is unable. I have begun to think that something more is at work, though I cannot put my finger on the problem." He sighed. "I have written to all the Senadors—as well as the garrison commanders—asking for status reports. And the answers I'm getting back are troublesome, because they don't agree."

"So something is going on?"

"I have begun to think so."

"When Roderic does come back, he'll have to go away again."

Phineas patted her hand. "I'm afraid so, child. But perhaps this time, he could take you with him. It would be wise, I think, to call a Convening of sorts—perhaps at Ithan Ford. Thank the One we can trust young Miles. After all, if you two don't spend any time together, there will never be an heir."

She knew he meant to joke, but his words alarmed her. There was more truth in that statement, and more importance attached to it, than either of them wished to admit. Abruptly she asked: "Roderic has no inkling, does he?"

"About his parentage? No. As I told you before, until you came, Abelard and I were the only ones who knew the truth."

"Has anyone ever considered what would happen if Amanander were to learn the truth? If everyone learned the truth?"

"I've never spoken of it to anyone, except you."

"But what if Amanander ever discovered that Roderic was the Queen's son, but not the King's?"

"That's not something I care to contemplate."

"But Amanander does have the better claim. He is Abelard's son, not Roderic. It's not just what Amanander would do were he to discover the truth. I think Roderic might renounce the throne if he thought it were the right thing to do."

Phineas sat bolt upright, wincing as his old bones creaked in protest. "That is a possibility I never considered."

"I have not my mother's gift, Phineas. I cannot see the future, but I feel things—and I don't like what I've been feeling lately. The thought of going to Minnis makes my blood cold, and I have no reason to think there's anything wrong at all."

"I think you miss Roderic." Phineas smiled. "Go to Minnis, child. The change will do you good. Write him tonight, tell him you will do as he asks—I'll see the message goes out at dawn. He only wants to protect you. When I know he's on his way home, I'll come there myself. And if you wish, I can order a scouting party to go to your mother's tower and make sure she's all right."

"No." Annandale shook her head. "I know she wants to be left in peace. She's owed that, at least."

Phineas shrugged. "As you wish child. It's your decision. Believe me, you'll likely be safer at Minnis than anywhere else. The walls of Minnis have never been breached."

* * *

Never been breached. The words echoed over and over through Annandale's skull as the heavily encumbered party trundled along the forest road. Even here, where the plowed fields gave way to the thickly forested countryside approaching Minnis Saul, the unseasonable heat was intense.

Sweat ran down her back, and her coif was a tight, confining stricture around her face. In the wagon behind her, she heard Melisande's querulous wail, a cry of boredom rather than one of distress.

Annandale's head throbbed. Her joints ached from the nights spent on the road and her back itched. She had no comfort to offer anyone. Peregrine's voice rose among the babble of the women, sharp and complaining, an unconscious echo of her daughter's.

The sun hammered across Annandale's shoulders as she stared ahead at the rigid backs of the small regiment of the King's Guard who served as their only protection on the journey north. There had not been many troops to spare, but surely, she reassured herself, such a thing was unnecessary. Even the Harleyriders had never penetrated so far into the Ridenau domain. Old Garrick, his back ramrod straight despite his years, guided his horse at an easy jog over to her side.

"Not much longer now, Lady Princess." He spoke cheerfully, but Annandale could see the exhaustion which ringed his eyes and the sweat stains which marked his clothes.

"I shall be glad of that," she answered. "I cannot wait for a bath, to sleep in a proper bed."

"This heat's the worst I can remember. Not even in Missiluse, in the swamps—well, maybe it was worse, but I was a younger man then." A drop of perspiration ran down the bridge of his nose, and he wiped it with an impatient hand, swiping away a fly. "And the bugs! By the One, lady, I think this year we'll go after them with bow and arrow."

Annandale nodded. She did not envy those who had been left behind: Phineas, his scribes, the soldiers of the garrison, and the servants. And surely, surely, the heat which hung like a miasma over the trees could not last here in the North Woods. "How much farther?"

"To Minnis? We will be there by nightfall, lady. I have sent a messenger on ahead; they will have our dinner and our baths waiting."

"Thanks to the One," she breathed. She roused herself from her heat-induced stupor and smiled. Garrick was a good man, she could sense his loyalty to his King and to Roderic, his adherence to the rigid code Abelard had demanded of all who followed him. Garrick, too, had had a hand in shaping the prince.

She breathed a heavy sigh of relief as the walls of Minnis rose before them a few hours later. The rough gravel road opened up to the high narrow gates, and though those gates were open, no guard was visible upon the ramparts of the high towers before them. Garrick reined his gelding beside her. "Is there a problem, General?" she asked.

"I'm not sure, lady," he replied, frowning at the keep. "I don't see the guards—surely they have not become so lax—"

"It's the heat, General Garrick," interrupted Peregrine from her perch beside the wagon driver. She shifted the heavy child in her arms. "Probably they watch from the shade—look there—I see a guard." She raised her arm and pointed, and Annandale, following the line of vision, caught sight of a thin dark shape above the top of the wall. A cold sliver of fear and loathing sliced through her—a reaction so strong it nauseated her and took her breath away. She pulled hard involuntarily on the reins, and her horse shied and whined a protest.

"General—" she stammered. "General, we must turn back—"

"Turn back?" He stared at her as though she had suddenly taken leave of her senses. "Turn back from Minnis? Lady, the heat affects us all—we will be fine once we arrive."

"No!" She caught his arm, and this time his horse nickered and her mare pranced. "We must not go—"

The walls of Minnis loomed closer and closer. The deep shadows at the base of the structure seemed like inky pools in which terrible things writhed and swarmed. The nausea grew, snaking through and around her, comprised of fear beyond all reason, and complete and utter despair. Without another word, she leaned over her saddle and vomited into the road.

"Lady, dear lady," cried Garrick. "Lady Peregrine—Lady Tavia, Lady Jaboa, please, come here—" He called back over his shoulder, gesturing wildly, and caught at Annandale's reins, forcing the mare to halt.

Sweat beaded her forehead and laced her upper lip, and her skin was clammy. She was vaguely aware of Tavia helping her from the saddle, of the other women clucking and chirping amongst themselves. They helped her into the shade of the covered wagon and placed a damp cloth on her head. With a jerk, the wagon started forward. Annandale struggled to sit up. "No, no," she said weakly, but firm hands pushed her back.

She struggled away from the women, crouched in the opening and peered over the high front seat of the wagon behind the driver. The gates of Minnis swung wider, and the guards marched into the outer ward, the dust of the road swirling in a cloud about their feet, the wagons lurching behind them.

"Lie back, dear," urged Jaboa.

"Leave me be!" she cried, and knelt over the seat. Her blood turned to ice at the sight of the tall man dressed all in black who stood on the steps in the center of the gate which led into the inner ward. She heard Peregrine gasp, saw Tavia turn white. As the driver reined the team of horses to a halt, Annandale forced her way onto the seat of the wagon in time to hear Garrick demand: "What is the meaning of this?"

But the man on the steps ignored Garrick, and instead strode unerringly to the wagon where Annandale sat stricken.

He extended his hand, and Annandale saw he wore leather gloves so finely fit they might have been a second skin. "Lady Annandale? I'm so pleased to make your acquaintance. Allow me to introduce myself. My name is Amanander."

Chapter Twenty-five

His voice was like the leathery scuttle of a large insect across old parchment, and his eyes were flat and very black, as though they trapped and absorbed light within their depths. Deep within, her internal impulse to heal fluttered, ready to right the balance this man so dangerously tipped.

This was the man who wanted the throne of Meriga so much, who, if ever it were possible, would kill Roderic with no more thought than he might a flea. This man was the result of Abelard Ridenau's singleminded insistence that the future be hammered into a form shaped by his desires, irrational and unjust though they might be. Amanander and his thwarted ambition was like a knot upon a tree, and her healing impulse flared and wavered. This was a blight beyond her ability, and despite her fear and her revulsion, pity for him stirred deep within. And this was the man who should be King. She understood in an instant why the Magic was wrong, what happened when one man's will was brought to bear upon the eternal order.

She paused only a moment before she accepted his hand. When she stood before him on the ground, she raised her chin and their eyes met and locked. Something flickered in those inky depths, some vestige of the man he could have been, and for a fleeting moment, Annandale thought there might yet be hope. Then something else replaced that momentary gleam, something blacker than the color of his eyes and harder than obsidian, something which would swallow her pity whole. For the first time in her life, she was truly terrified.

She struggled not to flinch as Amanander traced the back of his hand down the side of her face to her jaw. "By the One, lady, you are fair. The fairest thing I've ever seen."

"Lord Amanander." Garrick had dismounted and now he strode up beside the taller man, his thumbs hooked in his sword belt, his shoulders rigid. The sheath of his dagger slapped against his thigh, and his footsteps raised small puffs of dust. "What's the meaning of this? Where is the garrison commander?"

Amanander's expression did not change as he slid his eyes off Annandale's face. She felt as if she'd been released as his relentless stare fell on Garrick. "He's indisposed, General Garrick."

"Why aren't you in Dlas?"

Amanander drew a deep breath and turned his eyes back to Annandale. "I had other plans."

"What other plans?" Garrick's hand slid over his dagger, pulling and tugging at it as though he'd like to remove it from his sheath, and out of the corner of her eye, Annandale saw the soldiers of the King's Guard come to attention, slowly reaching for the weapons they wore at their belts.

Amanander held up his black-gloved hand, beckoning. Immediately, dark shapes coalesced out of the shadows around the walls, tall and slim, soldiers dressed in black leather armor, who bore broadswords. The sight of those guards made the breath stop in her throat and for a terrible moment, she thought she might vomit once more. Then the feeling passed as the King's men drew closer together, muttering to themselves, and Amanander extended his hand to Garrick. "My plans don't concern you in the least. However," he continued, turning to look at Annandale, "they do most assuredly concern you, my dear."

Annandale drew herself up and met his eyes with the same defiance as Garrick. "I very truly doubt that, lord."

"Do you?" He raised his left eyebrow a fraction. "We'll see, my dear."

"Don't take that tone with her, you insolent puppy." Garrick said. "You must—"

In less than a breath, Amanander was upon him, his hand wrapped in the fabric of Garrick's tunic. "Little man, remember to whom you speak. 'Must' is not a word used to princes." He gave the older man a shake, and Garrick pulled away, his shaking hand clenched around the hilt of his dagger.

"I insist that you take me to the garrison commander."

Amanander narrowed his eyes. "As you say, General." Before anyone could move, or react, Amanander thrust his dagger into the space between the old man's ribs. Garrick's eyes widened in shock and terror, and Amanander pulled the blade out. "Give him my regards."

As Garrick's body crumpled into a heap, Amanander wiped his dagger on Garrick's cloak. Amanander resheathed the dagger.

There was a silence, complete, shocked, broken only when Tavia, leaning out of the wagon, Melisande cradled in her arms, spat in the dirt at his feet. "You despicable monster. I'm ashamed to think you're my brother."

Amanander raised his face, his mouth twisted with disgust, his dark eyes cold and flat as deep water. "Your brother?"

Annandale touched Tavia's hand and gave the older women a little squeeze. "This is your sister Tavia, Amanander. Don't you remember her? She was there when Jesselyn died. She was forced to watch while you killed her sister. Will you do the same to all of us?" asked Annandale, wondering at her own bravado.

For the first time uncertainty flickered across Amanander's face. Amazed, she realized her words had confused him, caught him off guard. But how? she wondered. Why?

Then he was speaking, his speech clipped as though he sought to cover up his lapse. "I offer you all the opportunity to change your allegiance, my dear. And if you do, I'll welcome you with open arms."

"And if we refuse?"

His eyes narrowed. Something licked at the edge of her awareness, a mental tap, and Annandale recognized with a shock that Amanander was attempting to use the Magic. Energy surged again, stronger and faster, but less focused, and Annandale realized that Amanander was still no master of the art. She took a step backward, shut her eyes and braced herself against the onslaught. All around her, the weapons of the King's Guard clattered to the ground, and some of the men fell screaming to their knees, holding their heads. "Stop it, Amanander," she cried. "You can't win."

Amanander nodded, his thin mouth curved in a chilling semblance of a smile, sweat beading his forehead. "So it's to be war between us, lady. As you will." He made a quick motion and the dark soldiers closed in upon the King's men. "Take them to the guardhouse. Gartred—see to our guests."

Annandale heard Peregrine's soft gasp, and a short, full-breasted woman swept up, clad in a long gown of fine-spun linen, so light and airy it seemed made of mist. Her lips were very red and her hair, which fell unbound to her waist, was long and straight and dark as Amanander's. She looked Annandale up and down as though she were a prize mare and put her hands on her hips. "Even Roderic's brat?" She gestured to Melisande. "Even that?"

"Even that."

Gartred nodded. "Come with me, all of you."

"Gently, Gartred," warned Amanander. "This lady is our most honored guest."

Gartred threw a look at Amanander, dark and full of meaning, and Annandale was instantly aware of resentment and jealousy.

Gartred made an impatient noise, and together, followed by Peregrine, who cradled Melisande close, they walked into the fortress of Minnis Saul in the shadow of the walls which had never been breached.

The candle flickered in the dark, wavering uncertainly as a cool breeze blew through the window. Amanander's boots made no sound at all as he stalked into the room and paused just inside the threshold. Gartred stopped brushing her hair and smiled at him over her shoulder from her seat in front of her dressing table. "You're late, my prince."

The hollows and the arches of her face were lit dramatically, giving her features a depth and a beauty they did not in reality possess. Amanander watched her turn back to the mirror and resume brushing, her hair crackling under the strokes of the brush.

"Reginald sends good news. Although the Senador in Atland refuses to forget his Pledge of Allegiance, the lesser lordlings there are ripe for rebellion."

"And what about Everard? Isn't he a thorn in Reginald's side?" Gartred asked, watching Amanander in the mirror. She put down her brush and leaned closer to the glass, examining the feathery lines at the corners of her eyes. She picked up a glass jar full of scented cream.

Amanander waved a hand in dismissal. "That fool? Everard continues to believe the best of people. He can't see what's happening beneath his very nose. With Harland in Missiluse on our side, and the lesser lords in Atland and Ginya, Reginald's attack on Ithan will come at just the right time." He met her eyes in the mirror and smiled. "All our plans are coming to fruition. There's only one thing." He placed his hands on her shoulders and she leaned back, rubbing her head against the bulge in his groin. "Stop that," he said impatiently. He went to the window and stood looking out over the gardens. In the distance came the low rumble of thunder, and a sudden flash of lightning illuminated the budding branches of the trees. The weather was about to break. "I must find a way to see that Roderic's little bride will help me."

Gartred made a little sound of protest and replaced the crystal lid. Her surprise was evident on her face. "Can't you force her?"

Amanander did not glance her way. He doubted he would ever be able to explain to the hen that there were certain things one couldn't accomplish by force. "No. I can't."

"You mean she must be willing?"

Amanander gave Gartred a stare, and she shivered. "I've explained this to you more than once. The empath must give consent—the Magic will not work any other way."

"Then use it without her."

"Only if I must."

"But, why—"

"Don't be stupid, woman," he snarled, his rage finally getting the better of him. "We have to find a way to compel her consent, and then we may use the Magic as we like. Surely you don't think I would be so foolish as to use the Magic to bring me the throne, only to have it destroy half the country, as it did in Armageddon. Even Ferad hesitates. Why do you think he's been content to wait and bide his time?"

Gartred rose to her feet, her garments swirling and floating like mist, and went to stand beside him in the shadows. "Forgive me, Lord Prince. I know there's much I don't understand."

Her use of that title brought a grudging smile to his lips, as it always did. "Even if she will not consent to help use the Magic, her ability will be useful to us in the coming months."

Gartred raised her eyebrows, and he knew she didn't dare ask him the obvious question.

The knowledge of her fear satisfied him. "In the coming

battle, my dear. Surely you understand that Roderic will not surrender without a fight?"

"Of course," she answered. "You mean her healing—but that must be done willingly, too, no?"

"From what I have learned from Ferad, the empath's very nature makes it nearly impossible for her to refuse to heal. Pain is intolerable to them."

They lapsed into silence, standing side by side. Thunder rumbled once more in the distance, and the first few fat drops of rain fell with a loud splash on the windowsill.

The knock on the door startled Gartred. "Who's that?" she asked sharply.

There was a silence, and then the low voice of the guard answered. "May I enter, lord?"

Amanander glanced over his shoulder, one eyebrow raised in surprise. "Enter."

The door swung open, and one of Amanander's special guards stepped into the room, holding Peregrine Anuriel by the upper arm. "This prisoner requests to speak with you, lord." The flat monotone sent a chill down Gartred's spine as always, and she glanced up at Amanander. His reaction surprised her even more.

He smiled, a genuine smile of welcome, and bowed courteously. "Of course, lady. Lieutenant, take the lady to my sitting room. I'll join you in a moment."

"What do you want to do with that little drudge?" demanded Gartred as she folded her arms across her bosom. "Why—what—"

"Silence!" He raised his hand as if to slap her, and she shrank away, a bitter scowl twisting her features. "That little drudge, as you call her, may be very useful to us. She may love her dear Prince Roderic, but she hates—she despises—his little wife. And she might have some use—but I won't know that unless you keep your mouth shut. Do you understand me, my lady? Or must I gag you or knock you senseless?"

"How do you know all this?" asked Gartred with a sidelong pout. She knew he was more than capable of beating her senseless, for she had seen him do it to servants who'd displeased him for far less.

"Because I might not have been able to reach that little witch, but that one—" he jerked his head in the direction of the sitting room "—is an open book for anyone to read. Let's see what she has to say, shall we?"

Hatred burned bright in her eyes as she stared at him, then she dropped her eyes and clenched her hands together. "If I must."

"Then come, my dear. We mustn't keep the lady waiting."

Standing beside the cold grate, Peregrine was startled when the two of them walked back into the room. They were so perfectly matched, and yet so opposite, the plump, bosomy woman in sheerest white, the tall man all in black. Gartred took a chair in the corner, folded her hands and dropped her gaze. Peregrine glanced nervously at Amanander. "Will you not sit, lady?" His voice was soft and not unpleasant, she thought, low and resonant, like a great bell.

Another flash of lightning split the night sky, and thunder echoed in the distance. He smiled. "Please."

She slipped into the chair he indicated, a deep chair with a high back and arms. In it, she felt protected, as though she might sink into its soft depths and be hidden away from his dark eyes, which seemed to probe her own. "Thank you for seeing me at this hour."

"I'm happy to oblige you in any way I can, Lady Peregrine. How may I be of service?" From the corner, Gartred made a sound which might have been a hiss, and Amanander shot a look in her direction.

Peregrine drew her upper lip between her teeth. This was

the man who was Roderic's sworn enemy, the man who wanted Roderic's throne. This was the man who thought he should be King. But maybe, she thought, they were all wrong about him. Tavia said that he had killed Jesselyn and tried to kill Vere, but maybe she'd been wrong. After all, in the state Tavia'd been in, who could say? And besides, he certainly didn't look very threatening as he leaned back in his chair, crossing his long legs. A little smile played at the corners of his mouth, and she thought he looked a little—sad. "I know that this means war between you and Roderic."

Amanander raised one eyebrow and made a little sound of protest. "That will be his choice, lady. I am hopeful that we will be able to work out our differences peacefully. Without further bloodshed."

"Nevertheless," she said, "I know that we are all hostages, should war be inevitable. And I came to ask you to send my daughter, Melisande, away. Please. Let her go—I'll do anything—help you any way I can—"

"You would betray your Prince?" Amanander spoke softly, guilelessly.

"I don't see it that way," she stammered, her words tripping over each other. "I only need to make my baby safe—surely you understand?"

"Of course, Lady Peregrine. Of course I do. May I call you Peregrine?"

"Yes," she answered, twisting her hands in the fabric of her gown. "You may."

"It's a beautiful name. Very unusual."

"I was named for my father. He was an unusual person."

"Oh?" Amanander cocked his head. "How so?"

She stared at him in surprise. No one, not even Roderic, in all the time she'd been in Ahga, had ever asked her anything but the most cursory questions about her youth, her family. She understood Ahga was the center of the country, the center of everything. Nothing that happened outside of it was ever as important as what happened inside it.

"You look surprised," he said when she did not answer.

"I—I cannot believe what I see in you." She raised her chin as another flash of lightning illuminated the room, and far away, a distant peal of thunder echoed. A fat drop of rain fell upon the sill. She shivered as the wind howled around the building.

Amanander rose and crossed to the window. "Don't let the storm frighten you. It's beautiful, I think, rather like music. Listen." He held up his hand.

As if on cue, the wind gave a mournful wail and the rain began to fall faster. Thunder rolled like a great drum, and just as she met his eyes, lightning cracked and the room was lit by its bluish glare. Her heart began to beat faster. He smiled again and pulled the window shut. The latch clicked as it fell into place like the spring of a mousetrap. When he turned back, he spread his hands. "I know what the others have told you about me," he said. "I know what Roderic believes."

"They say you want the throne."

He did not answer her immediately, but a pained look crossed his face as though her words had hit a very sore spot. "I took an oath of allegiance. We all do—you know that?"

Mute, she nodded, waiting to hear him continue. His voice rose and fell with a lyrical rhythm, so entrancing, just listening filled her with a curious pleasure.

"And in the oath of allegiance, we swear to uphold the kingdom and the King, with our lives, if we must." He was watching her face very carefully. His eyes pinned her to the chair, and the sound of his voice was like a caress, deftly coaxing all thoughts from her mind. "And sometimes, inevitably, what one man perceives to be in the best interests of the kingdom is not so perceived by others." He paused, and she found herself waiting, willing, wishing for him to continue. He gave her just the merest suggestion of a smile. "I know you love Roderic. I know he is the father of your child. I know she must mean more to you than even life itself."

Peregrine nodded.

"I know you would never, ever, wish any harm to come to her. And I know that it must grieve you greatly to know what her father is capable of doing."

"He—he had to marry," she managed.

"Marry?" Amanander looked surprised. "Oh. I was speaking of Atland."

"Atland?" Peregrine felt as though a warm mist had pervaded her entire body. The rain had settled into a steady drumbeat, and the thunder had faded to a low rumble. The candles burned steadily, and the room was filled with their hot, waxy scent.

"Atland. Of course he told you. It must have shocked you greatly to think that the father of your child could be so cruel—"

"Cruel?"

Amanander's voice unfurled like a velvet cloak. "He didn't tell you?"

"Tell me? Tell me what? What happened in Atland?"

"I would rather not speak of it."

Peregrine craned her neck around to Gartred, sitting quiescent in her corner. "What? What happened?"

Amanander shrugged. "He tortured the Mutens to death. And their deaths were neither easy nor clean. That's how he brought about the peace there. That's why it's so tenuous. You see, my dear, even Phineas knew that Roderic's not really capable. And when I saw with my own eyes what he did, and how callously, how cruelly he did it, I knew that if I were to honor my oath, I had to oppose Roderic's taking the throne."

Peregrine shifted in the chair, sinking deeper into the high cushioned back as Amanander continued, lulling, soothing, explaining. The rain had ended, long ago, and somehow, the window was open once more and a soft breeze, tender as a lover's caress, fluttered over her skin. When he touched her, she stirred, frightened, opening her eyes, gazing into the darkness she could not fight. "Melisande," she whispered. "Melisande."

He smiled, a slow, gentle smile, which spread across his face as easily as the last drops of rainwater slid down the windowpanes. "Of course we'll send her away. This is no place for a child—not your child. But you do see, you do understand, how very much I need you? How much I need your help?"

She stared at him, mesmerized. "Annandale," she murmured. "I can tell you what she is."

"Yes?"

She wasn't certain if he actually spoke. "She's—she's a witch. No one's supposed to know, but the servants all talk. She worked her Magic on Tavia, and on Roderic, too. He was never the same after that. After she uses it, she's weak. You could make her use her Magic. And when she's weak, maybe she'd help you then."

"Yes." The word shivered through her and she pressed her eyes closed, giving herself up to the dark. When he reached for her, her bones felt disconnected from her flesh, so that she hung as limp as a ragdoll in his embrace. She scarcely knew that Gartred had come forward, had drawn the coif off her head and pulled the pins holding her braids in place. She let the hands hold her, feel her, touch her. She gasped when she felt the air on her breasts and realized that somehow she had moved from the antechamber to a softly lit bedroom, where the windows were opened to the cloudless, moonlit sky, and the insects chirped a chorus. She was naked and she twisted around, her mouth shaping a protest, but Amanander was there, easing her down on the yielding mattress, drawing her breast into his mouth, even as Gartred loosed the bindings of her underlinens. She was floating, falling, giving in to searing sensations, powerless to resist. She arched her back, offering herself up to the intoxication of it, as another mouth, another tongue, encircled her other nipple. Peregrine moaned, wrapping her arms around both dark heads, spreading her legs to both sets of questing hands. This was where she belonged, beloved, cherished, not the cast-off of a puppet princeling. As readily as an unpleasant dream, all thoughts of Roderic and Annandale vanished, while above her, Amanander and Gartred chuckled with shared delight.

Chapter Twenty-six

It was close to dawn when the voices roused Annandale from fitful sleep. She opened her eyes, momentarily disoriented. Jaboa slept fully clothed on the other side of the great bed, and between them, Melisande was curled in a little bundle, her tiny fist securely tucked in her mouth. With Tavia and Jaboa, Annandale had whispered late into the night, mulling over their predicament, at last explaining her ability, half-afraid of their reactions. But they had only listened, and when she was finished, Jaboa had gathered her in her arms as if she were no older than Melisande, murmuring words of comfort and support. Now Annandale sat up, listening to the heavy tramp outside the door, the rough voices of men, the softer answering tones of a woman.

As the door swung wide, Tavia bolted upright from the hearth rug, her dress creased, her coif askew. "What is it?" she asked, even as Peregrine stood on the threshold.

In the grayish light, Annandale saw that the girl's gown had been laced carelessly, that her lips were swollen and purplish, like overripe fruit. Deep shadows smudged the delicate skin beneath her eyes, and her coif was crumpled carelessly in one hand. "Peregrine?" whispered Annandale, afraid to wake the baby. "Are you all right? What's he done to you?"

Peregrine came closer. There were reddish marks on the creamy skin of her throat, and she moved slowly, languorously, as if through water. “Melisande? Is she with you? Give her to me. He’s going to let her go.”

“Go?” echoed Tavia, getting to her feet. “Go where? With whom? What happened to you last night? Are you all right?”

“Amanander’s going to let you leave?” Annandale tried to hide the revulsion she felt as Peregrine came nearer. There was a smell about the woman, a musky, salty odor, and with a start, Annandale recognized it. It was the smell of lovemaking, the smell of sex, of hot bodies pressed together, of the sticky fluids binding them together.

Peregrine’s eyes flicked over Annandale, hatred so clear her gaze was like a whip. “Not me. Melisande. He’s going to let her go. And you, Tavia. You’re going to take her.”

Tavia put a hand on Peregrine’s arm. “How can you trust him? You saw him kill Garrick last night. This is Roderic’s child. Her life means less to him than Garrick’s did.”

Peregrine’s face did not change expression. “Get ready. He’s going to let her go.”

All three women exchanged glances.

“All right,” said Tavia softly. “Tell him we’re getting her ready. Go on.” She gave Peregrine a little push out the door, and with a venomous glance at Annandale, Peregrine went.

Annandale looked at the other two with fear in her eyes.

“What do you make of that?” asked Jaboa as Melisande whimpered and stirred.

“Amanander seduced her last night,” said Annandale. “He must have promised her Melisande’s safety in exchange for her cooperation.” She looked out the window, where the sun was rising over the treetops. The heat had forced an early spring, and the forest was in full leaf. Why Tavia? Amanander had not been able to hide his shock. She had surprised him with her presence. Was it only that she was a reminder of Jesselyn, or was there another reason?

The door shuddered under a sudden blow, and Annandale pulled the pearl ring off her finger. “Here,” she said, holding it out. "Take this, Tavia. Take the baby and get to Phineas. Tell him to send this ring to Roderic. He must not come here unaware."

Tavia nodded, placing the ring in the bosom of her gown as Melisande began to cry. "I'll do my best."

"It's our only chance," said Annandale. "You have to try."

A merciless sun beat down on the ramparts as Amanander, flanked by Gartred and Peregrine, watched the little party leave the shelter of the garrison walls. Tavia clutched the child to her breast, her face stoic. She did not glance back, her eyes fixed on the back of the black-clad guard who guided her horse away from the shadowed walls. They headed south down the gravel-covered road, toward Ahga and freedom. And death, thought Amanander, smiling inwardly. He glanced at the two women by his side. Gartred's mouth had the self-satisfied smirk she always wore when she found their love-making particularly satisfying. She had enjoyed their escapade with Peregrine last night very much, though he thought she was more pleased with the thought of debauching Roderic's woman than the sexual pleasure it gave her. Peregrine stared after the diminishing figures, disappearing now beneath the cover of the forest, her fingers white-knuckled as she gripped the battlements. He touched her cheek with the back of his gloved hand and chuckled when she flinched. She had been horrified when she had awakened before to find herself in the midst of one of his more exotic plays. But he had tapped deep into the well of jealousy which had festered in her for a long, long time, and her protests hadn't lasted very long. Besides, she had given him an excellent idea.

It pleased him to think that Roderic's woman, Roderic's child, and Tavia, whom he thought of as Roderic's sister, were all so totally lost. Three down, he thought, employing the parlance of ancient Meriga, as Ferad sometimes did. One to go.

The thought of Annandale, naked and helpless beneath

him, completely at his mercy, as Peregrine had been the night before, gave him the beginnings of an erection. He breathed deeply, enjoying the fantasy.

". . . shall we, Lord Prince?"

How like the hen to interrupt his most pleasurable thoughts. "What?"

She met his eyes calmly, a spark of amusement deep within. He knew that sometimes, more times than he liked to think, the mindlink between them enabled her to catch a flavor of his thoughts. "I asked you if you had any ideas as to how to force the little wife to your service."

He smiled at Gartred, good humor restored. "As a matter of fact," he said, "Peregrine gave me a wonderful idea. I can't wait to get it started."

"Are you going to share it with us?" asked Gartred, as Peregrine glanced at him with surprise.

"Force her to heal," Amanander began, and in the bright hot light of the noonday sun, he outlined a plan so diabolical in conception it made him smile just to think of it. Peregrine had proven her worth already.

Under the shade of the trees, the air was cooler than in the brutal glare of the open road. Tavia rocked Melisande, murmuring as the child twisted and squirmed. Melisande was a healthy toddler, and she did not understand why she should have to stay on the gently swaying horse. The shadows deepened beneath the trees, and Tavia grew concerned. "Sir." She leaned forward in the saddle. "Are you certain this path will take us to the road to Ahga?"

The guard did not reply. He had not said one word all morning, not since she had first seen him in the courtyard, not since they had mounted the horses Amanander had provided, not since they had ridden from the fortress. She wondered if he were one of the garrison guards Amanander had corrupted to his own use, or if he were a recruit from somewhere else.

There did not seem to be many guards at Minnis, and Tavia suspected that a fair number of men had elected to join their commander in death, though whether by choice or by default, she couldn't say.

Debris crunched underfoot, and the branches of the trees reached out like twisted fingers, grasping arms to tangle in her hair. As the morning wore on, deeper and deeper into the forest they rode. Melisande fussed, then slept. Finally, as the sun was beginning to dip down in the sky, Tavia reined her horse abruptly. Melisande woke and began to cry. "Soldier, we have to stop. The child needs food, water, dry clothes. And I need a rest."

With a grunt, the soldier swung out of his saddle. He turned, looking at Tavia with a blank stare. Hastily, Tavia slid out of her saddle as best she could while encumbered by Melisande. She set the squirming child on the ground and reached across the saddle for the pack tied across it. She fumbled with the bindings and finally worked it open. Except for a folded blanket, and a few stones to simulate the weight of equipment, it was empty.

"By the One," she breathed, as understanding dawned. Swiftly she scooped up the baby and turned to grab the reins. The horse whickered and stamped a protest at her awkward treatment, and the soldier, as though galvanized, drew his sword and advanced.

"Please . . . I beg you . . ." Tavia panted, trapped between the soldier and the horse. She sought to escape sideways, but the animal blocked her path. She feinted right and the soldier followed with stumbling gait, his sword trembling in his hands. Sweat had broken out across his forehead and poured down his face. In spite of her fear, Tavia had never seen anyone sweat so profusely. He swung, a clumsy stroke that missed Melisande's little head by inches, and Tavia scrambled backward into the animal's flank. The horse dodged, and Tavia saw her opening. She gathered her skirts in one hand

and, clutching Melisande around the waist, broke into an awkward run. Her heart pounded, and the forest seemed quiet, far too quiet.

Abruptly the path ended in a chasm about twenty feet deep. She muttered a curse she never thought she knew. Melisande squalled. "Hush, child."

Behind her the soldier crashed through the underbrush and she turned as the man broke into the clearing. He shambled, a weird sideways run, his sword weaving unsteadily before him. "Please . . ." She held her hand in supplication as the child squirmed against her hip, her little face twisted.

The soldier approached, sword raised.

"No!" she screamed, seizing a rock. She threw it as hard as she could. It struck him squarely on the temple. He dropped his sword, covering the bleeding gash with one hand. He fell to his knees, his face hidden. Tavia's heart pounded and Melisande wailed louder.

He raised his face, and his sword dropped to the ground out of his suddenly slack grip. "Forgive me," he said in a hoarse voice. "Forgive me, lady. I know not what I did."

She stared in disbelief, not quite trusting what she heard. "You were sent to kill me and the child. He had no intention of letting us go."

"No." He shook his head, tears coursing down his face. "I don't know what he did to me. He has some accursed hold upon us all. But I know the further away we rode, the looser his grip became. I am sorry, lady. I would not harm you or the child for the world. Please, forgive me."

He struggled to his knees, still holding his head. Blood seeped through his fingers and trickled down the side of his face. Tavia tore her kerchief from around her neck and handed it to him. "Down there, I think there's likely to be a stream. We have no supplies."

"No. We weren't expected to need them. Don't worry, though. I can get us to Ahga." He raised his head, staring north, toward Minnis. "We'll have to travel as quickly as we can. Lord Amanander will know something's amiss when I don't return. He'll likely send someone after us, if he thinks he can spare it."

"Then maybe you'd better go back."

He shook his head. "I can't leave you in these woods. There's lycats and worse on the prowl. It would be impossible for you and a child to reach Ahga. And the sooner we get there, the sooner we can warn Lord Phineas what has happened."

"Then let's go to one of the farms. I have this—" She held out her hand and her wedding ring threw off sparks of reflected light. "Surely we can trade this for supplies, horses, whatever we need. Roderic will reward whoever helps us with whatever they wish."

"No doubt, lady," he answered, staring at the emerald. "That stone is worth a King's ransom."

"Indeed," agreed Tavia. "Or a Queen's."

Chapter Twenty-seven

The great hall of Minnis Saul was bright with noon sun when Annandale was escorted in by one of Amanander's personal guards. She shied away from his loathsome touch, trying to concentrate on keeping her wits about her. It was apparent that Amanander's troops were few, that he had a rudimentary, though incomplete, grasp of the Magic, that there was much he did not fully understand. But she also knew that Minnis was built to be impregnable, and that Amanander knew enough about the Magic to recognize her usefulness. She hoped she could control her terror.

Light reflected off the polished surfaces of the wooden floors and glinted off the glass doors leading out to the gardens. The unseasonable heat had diminished somewhat after last night's storm, and inside the great hall, the air was pleasantly cool. Amanander stood, just inside one of the wide glass doors, his arms folded across his chest.

He was dressed, as always, impeccably, his white linen shirt embellished at neck and wrists with complicated black embroidery, his black trousers tucked into high leather boots. His dark hair was drawn back from his face and held at the nape of his neck in a silver clasp, and the length of it cascaded down his back, as lustrous as a woman's. His eyes swept up and down the length of her body as the soldiers urged her forward, a violating look which made her cross her arms over her breasts.

"Good day," he said, when she stood before him. A little smile played across his face, and she knew he sensed her discomfort and enjoyed it. "Will you talk with me, lady?"

"What for?" she blurted.

"The day is fine. You would not want to waste it indoors, surely? You spent much of your life roaming beneath the trees of the forest outside the walls, did you not?"

At that, a chill went through her. She shuddered involuntarily, but he did not notice her reaction. Instead, he continued, "I regret I can't let you out, so instead, will you walk with me in the gardens my father made for your mother?"

She lowered her eyes and nodded her assent, walking past him quickly onto the wide terrace and down the broad shallow sweep of the steps. As her feet touched the graveled path, she was overcome with the desire to kick off her shoes and curl her toes in the green shoots of the spring grass. Instead, she turned and looked at him, a question in her eyes.

He indicated a stone bench where Peregrine and Gartred sat before a small table which held four goblets and a flagon. "Shall we sit?"

"What do you want of me, Amanander?"

He caught her under the elbow, and she realized that once again, he wore those tight black leather gloves. He traced the line of her cheeks down her jaw, and below, all the way to her throat, and a shudder of revulsion went through her. He chuckled. "So enamored of my little brother you don't find me in the least attractive, my dear? Pity. I find you most desirable." His dark gaze fell to her bosom, following the rounded swell of her breasts, dropping to her waist. "Such a delectable captive I have, it would almost be a shame not to enjoy you. And then you could compare—and decide which brother you preferred."

At the thought of Amanander's embrace, nausea swept through her, and as they reached the bench, she sank down, feeling dizzy and weak. If he forced her—rape was bad enough, but incest . . . the thought made her shudder. And she would have no choice but to submit, because she would die before she revealed the secret of her birth to Amanander.

He touched her hair, and she pulled away, drawing herself up. "Is this why you summoned me? To paw at me?"

He dropped his hand and raised his eyebrow. "I know what you are. An empath."

She met his stare and did not waver. "What of it?"

"You will help me."

She gathered the strands of her will about her like a cloak and stared as directly into his eyes as she could, ignoring the other women. "No."

A smile curved the corners of his mouth. "Of course you will."

"No."

They stared at each other while the breeze blew softly in the trees and the scent of the early roses twined about them. Amanander drew a deep breath. "I was afraid you'd refuse."

"Then why ask?"

"Because I wanted to spare you, if I could. I wanted to see if perhaps you would come to your senses of your own volition—but I see you are as stubborn as my twin in your own way." He shrugged. "As you say, lady. I had hoped we would avoid this, but . . ." He let his voice trail off, looked toward the door, and clapped loudly.

Annandale followed his gaze and saw two of Amanander's guards dragging out the wine steward and his wife, plump, middle-aged, and obviously terrified. "What do you mean to do?"

"Watch."

The soldiers dragged the two of them to the broad expanse of the lawn in front of where they sat. As they came closer, their fear reached out to her like the arms of drowning men. She glanced at Amanander.

A little smile played across his face, and with one brief nod, he gestured to his soldiers. While the first held the woman pinioned, the second threw the man on the ground so hard that the air was knocked out of his lungs, and he lay there, looking stunned. Before he could recover, the soldier hauled him up and tore the tunic he wore from collar to waist. The woman screamed, and the soldier who held her backhanded her across the face with a casual cruelty that wrenched Annandale as surely as if she had been the one hit.

When the steward's clothes hung in rags about his waist, the soldier threw him down on the ground like a rag doll. His head struck a stone, and Annandale screamed, "Stop it!"

Amanander looked at her, amusement playing on his face. "So you'll agree to help me?"

"No," she whispered. The residual echo of the steward's pain clutched at her, filtering through her defenses.

Amanander nodded at his soldier, and the guard drew his short sword. Grasping the steward's arm, he carefully peeled the flesh off his arm from his wrist to his elbow, allowing it to hang in shreds. The pain roused the man from his unconscious stupor, and when he saw what was happening, he began to wail, high and thin, the sound a rabbit makes when a hawk's talons pierce its flesh.

Annandale resisted the urge to cover her ears. "Stop it," she said through clenched teeth. "Stop it, now."

"Of course, lady," said Amanander pleasantly. He waved the guard back, and the poor, terrified steward rocked forward and back, that low keening wail issuing from his throat.

Without another thought, Annandale leaned forward and touched the man's uninjured fingertips. Instantly, blue light flared, brighter than sunlight, and beneath the fabric of her gown, her own flesh peeled and split in strips. Before the man's shocked gaze, his skin readhered, the blood bubbling and congealing.

She closed her eyes as the pain lanced through her, hot and

white and searing as a flame. The steward fell back in a faint, and Annandale met the shocked, staring eyes of his wife.

"In the name of the One," the woman breathed.

Annandale looked at Amanander, sweat beading her forehead, and Amanander smiled, a cruel thin smile. "Will you help me, lady?"

She shook her head as she felt the familiar, cleansing surge.

Amanander met her eyes with another thin, cruel smile, and he beckoned to the guard. "Again. But this time, take the woman."

It was close to dusk when Amanander finally ordered the steward and his wife taken away. Annandale raised her head, watching them stumble across the lawn, the red marks of their healing wounds fading into pink with every step.

Sweat rolled down her face, tinged with blood, and every bone, every nerve in her body ached and screamed with residual pain. She slumped upon the ground, pressing one hand against her face, the other gripping the grass, white-knuckled in distress.

She closed her eyes and sought to block out every distraction. The grass seemed to push itself up against her open palm, and beneath the grass, she sensed the surging pulse of the earth itself, alive with insects and earthworms and creatures too small to be seen by the naked eye.

She let her shoulders sag and bowed her head, giving herself over to the peace within. The blast roared out of nowhere, it seemed, a mental assault that ripped through the strained defenses of her mind. She cried out, her body tensing under the onslaught.

Like stinging wasps, Amanander's energy penetrated her mind seeking access to the most protected core of her, the core she thought of as her own, her very deepest self.

Annandale panicked. This had been his intention, she realized, to force her to heal again and again, until, weakened and vulernable, she could no longer resist. Involuntarily, she gripped the grass with both white hands, as though the very earth could help her.

Let go. The voice seemed to come from everywhere at once, within and without, over and around, above and below. Let go. Surrender. Give yourself to the Pattern. You are of the Pattern—your strength is of the Pattern. And the Pattern is All.

A clear white light seemed to flood her mind, an understanding and a comprehension beyond anything she had ever experienced before. The voice was her own and the words seemed to be as much a part of her as her body. Like a child, she obeyed, willfully relaxing, even though Amanander's assault swirled like a maelstrom around the edges of her awareness.

Her panic subsided, borne away by the light, washed away by the words, and Amanander's Magic faded into the frustrated buzzing of a trapped housefly. She raised her face and met his gaze, for the first time unafraid. "You can't win," she whispered.

He was on his feet and moving toward her, murder in his eyes, when a movement in the doorway distracted him. Annandale did not shrink. The knowledge which the voice imparted had given her more courage than she had ever thought she possessed, and detachedly, she recognized the Captain of Amanander's guard.

"What do you want?" Amanander snarled, as the man walked woodenly across the grass.

"Lord Prince, the soldier you sent out with the prisoners this morning has not returned. Is it your will that a search party be sent?"

Rage distorted Amanander's face. "Fool," he muttered. "Fool." Annandale saw him glance at Peregrine, and in that split second, she understood what was meant to have happened.

Amanander had had no intentions of allowing Tavia and Melisande go free. The guard who'd gone had instructions to kill them and return. But something had gone wrong. She closed her eyes and murmured a silent prayer that Tavia and the child were safe.

Peregrine had risen to her feet. "My baby—" she choked out. "You intended to kill her."

Amanander reached across the bench, dragging her to her feet and flung her away. She fell onto the grass not far from Annandale, covered her face in her hands and began to weep. "Oh, lady," she sobbed, "what have I done? What have I done?"

Annandale reached out and drew Peregrine close, cradling her head against her bosom. She raised her chin and addressed Amanander once again. "Something went wrong, didn't it? You aren't in as much control as you'd like us to believe you are."

Gartred squawked, her eyes darting from the two women on the grass to Amanander and the guard.

"You've made a terrible mistake," Annandale went on, as the implications of the one soldier's defection came clear. "You think you have us trapped, but you're wrong. You're the one who's in danger here, you with all your plans. Roderic will come, and when he does, there's no way out for you."

She got to her feet, pulling Peregrine up with her, and, wrapping an arm around the other woman's waist, turned on her heel, leaving both Amanander and Gartred staring after them in the falling dark.

Chapter Twenty-eight

Roderic stared in dismay across what served him as a council table, twisting the little pearl ring between his fingers, as though it offered reassurance. Less than an hour had gone by since the messenger's arrival, who, between bites of food and long gulps of water, told a story Roderic did not want to hear. At the far end of the table, Brand listened with a grave expression, his arms folded across his chest, and Alexander stood by the window, his eyes closed as he listened. His face was creased as though he were in pain, but Roderic had no thoughts to spare for what Alexander might be feeling.

"How long has Amanander held Minnis?"

The messenger shook his head as he bit into a chicken leg. "At least a month. Your lady has been there three weeks."

"But Tavia escaped?" Roderic clutched the little pearl ring tightly.

"He allowed Lady Tavia to leave with your daughter, supposedly as a gesture of good will to the women. But he sent a guard with them, who had instructions to kill them once they got deep in the woods. Luckily, that guard changed his mind. Instead, he helped them get to Ahga." The messenger gulped his food, drinking as he swallowed, and wine ran out the corner of his mouth and down his chin.

Brand frowned in disgust. "All right, messenger. Get some rest. Doubtless we'll have a dispatch for you to take back soon enough." The messenger grabbed plate and goblet and bowed his way awkwardly out of the room. As the door swung softly shut, Brand swore beneath his breath, a soldier's oath so uncharacteristically coarse that even Roderic was surprised.

Alexander closed his eyes and pressed his face against his windowpane.

"He has my wife, too," Brand said.

Roderic leaned back in his chair, knotted his hands behind his head and stared at the ceiling. "And that's not all—even if it is the worst. Phineas says that the Senador of Atland's second son has raised an army against his father. If we can't get some kind of reinforcements to him, and Atland falls, we will lose more than an ally."

Brand was silent, tracing patterns on the table with the tip of one index finger. He shot a glance at Alexander, who had not moved.

"I'm to blame," whispered Alexander, so softly, Roderic wasn't sure he had spoken at all.

"I fell for his trap," said Roderic. He got to his feet and paced to the window. He stood, with thumbs hooked in his sword belt, beside Alexander. Fog was rolling in off the sea, reaching out with misty tentacles to blanket the camp. He was tired of the everlasting rain, the moist salt air, the lonely cries of the gulls which only made him think of the nights he had spent in Annandale's arms. Nights which seemed all too few, and very long ago. "Amanander knew I'd want to preserve our relationship—he knew I'd leave Ahga. He did this deliberately, and I walked right into his hands."

"Don't blame yourself, Roderic," said Brand. "We don't have the time to waste. We've got to get back—Phineas has contacted the nearby garrisons. Hopefully, we'll be able to raise enough troops—"

"Minnis has never been besieged," said Roderic. "Maybe it's not quite so impregnable as everyone thinks."

"It has an independent water supply, arable land in its center, and foodstores to last the entire garrison for years." Brand shook his head. "Dad must have been planning for another Armageddon."

"Something like that," agreed Roderic. "We can try to tunnel beneath the walls."

"The walls are thirty feet thick. And Minnis is built on rock. We could try to starve them out—" began Brand, and stopped.

It was Roderic's turn to swear softly beneath his breath. The presence of the women and children of the court meant that such tactics were out of the question. "It's not a question of *we*," he said.

"What do you mean?"

"I need you to take at least one division and go south. We'll send messengers on to the garrisons in Arkan—in the Pulatchians. But someone has to relieve Atland, and who else is there to do it?"

"You want me to go to Atland?" Brand asked.

"Who else?"

Brand shot a glance at Alexander. In the silence, Alexander looked from one brother to the other and spread his hands, a hopeless, old man's gesture. "This is all my fault. I should go."

Roderic shook his head. "Out of the question. You're only just beginning to recover, Alex. And besides, you still know Amanander better than any of the rest of us. I need you to help me at Minnis."

"Unless you're still not sure you can raise your hand against your brother," added Brand.

Alexander paled and flinched as though he'd been struck. "I deserved that, perhaps. I should have done whatever I could to find Amanander. Brea M'Callaster should have been my wife, and the One only knows what he did to her. But I never dreamt—"

"None of us did," interrupted Roderic. "But there is something else we haven't even considered. Vere said Amanander is able to use the Magic. And he said that the Magic was dangerous, uncontrollable, unless one had an empath to guide it. And with Annandale, Amanander has an empath."

Brand got to his feet and paced to the opposite end of the table. "Surely you don't believe all that? Surely you don't for a moment think—"

"I know what she is."

Brand stared at Roderic, as though at a stranger. "Now what are you talking about?"

"The day we met her—the day Barran broke his leg? It was broken, but she healed it. Tavia—Annandale healed her, too. And me—when I fell off my horse and hit my head, she saved me from bleeding to death or worse. Whether you choose to believe it or not, Brand, the Magic is real, empaths are real, and we can't afford not to believe in it, or in Amanander's ability."

Brand looked as though he had aged ten years in ten minutes. "How are we to fight this thing?"

"We'll have to hope," said Roderic grimly, "that Vere is successful in persuading the Mutens to come and help."

"You'd bring the Mutens into this?" Brand frowned.

"Amanander learned the Magic from a Muten. I'd say they were in it already," Roderic said as Alexander nodded.

There was a long silence. "And in the meantime," Roderic said, "you'll go to Ithan, and Alexander and I'll think of some way to try to get into Minnis."

The hour was late and the candles had burned away to waxy nubs when Roderic dismissed his weary scribe. "Seal those dispatches, Henrode, see that the Captain of the messengers has them, and then go to bed. We have a long march ahead of us tomorrow."

"As you say, Lord Prince," murmured the scribe as he bowed his way out of the room, his arms full of writing supplies and parchment dispatches. As the door closed after him, there was a loud curse and a clatter. Roderic had just time to stand up behind the makeshift desk when the door swung open again and Deirdre strode into the room. Despite the late hour, her step was as energetic as usual and her eyes met his with their customary fire. Inwardly Roderic groaned. Surely her appearance could only mean one thing. The delicate peace, just four days old, had collapsed.

"Good evening, Prince." She dragged a three-legged stool over to the desk and sat down opposite Roderic. "You don't look as though you're glad to see me."

"I shall only be glad, lady, when I know that my lady is safe." He ran his fingers through his hair. "It's the M'Clure again, isn't it?"

She looked puzzled for a moment, then shook her head as understanding dawned. She reached for the flagon of wine and poured the remains of the wine into his goblet. "Not at all, Prince. The peace will hold, I guarantee it."

"Then—" Roderic hesitated. He had no wish to insult her, but he was very tired. The siege of Minnis would demand all he had.

"Why am I here?" She drank, and arched an eyebrow over the rim of the cup. "It occurred to me, Prince, that you're marching into a situation no less ticklish than this one."

Roderic sighed and sat down. There was no use lying to Deirdre, or to himself. His only chance against Amanander at this point was to muster enough men to attempt to storm the walls of Minnis—the walls Abelard himself had boasted were unbreakable. But the lines were stretched thin: the losses over the winter had been heavy; the garrisons in Atland and Dlas and Arkan demanded full complements. Brand needed men to take to Atland. His dispatches were to Senadors like Norda Coda and Phillip in Nourk, and he prayed that he could trust these old allies of the King. He hoped that Obayana would muster enough to make up for their losses in the Settle Islands, but in his heart, he doubted that Obayana would be able to meet such a demand. And without enough men, without the troops to overwhelm the fortress of Minnis and take it by sheer force, his only other alternative would be to starve Amanander out. And Amanander was likely to start killing hostages long before that. "You're right," he said after a long silence.

"I've come to offer you help."

"Help?"

"I will come with you when you leave on the morrow, and I will bring six thousand fresh troops with me."

"What?" He was so tired he could scarcely believe what he heard.

"Two full divisions." She nodded. "At a price, of course."

"Of course." He had learned a lot about the Settle Islanders during the last months. There was always a price. But then, he thought, wasn't there always? with everyone? in every dealing? At least the Chiefs were open about it. "What do you want?"

She drank again and set the goblet down deliberately. Her eyes were dark in the guttering light. The silence lengthened, until Roderic heard the slither of the sand in the hourglass beside his elbow. "I want an heir."

He raised one brow.

"I know you've sworn a vow to your wife. But this is what I want. When your heir is born, or named, and you are released from that vow, I want—"

"There're no guarantees I could father a child on you."

"That's what I want, in exchange."

"Why? Why my child?"

"Because I believe that my kinsmen will make trouble after

my death. If I name an heir, I believe they will try to make him fight for the title, just as I did. I don't want that to happen. If the child is believed to be your son, then you will ensure that his inheritance is secure, and perhaps they will think before challenging his right to rule."

"So even if the child is not mine, you expect me to claim him as my own?"

"Only if there is the possibility that he could be your own."

She waited, and she did not take her eyes off Roderic's face. The room seemed to grow very warm, and his eyes ranged from her heavy coils of hair down her lean throat, as strong and corded as any youth's. He remembered suddenly that it had been a very long time since he had lain with Annandale. "Very well."

"Then swear the blood-oath."

He sat back as she pulled a curved dagger from her belt and slashed it across her palm. As the blood bloomed in a red curve, she gestured with the blade. He took his own dagger and did likewise. He held out his bleeding hand. With a grip as firm and sure as his own, she clasped their hands together, and he felt her hot hand tremble as he pressed her flesh. "You swear, then, to give me an heir?" Her voice was hoarse, her eyes bright sparks in the shadow.

"You swear to aid me in this campaign?"

"I do."

"Then I swear." Their fingers knit together as their blood mingled, her palm as smoothly callused as his own. And he thought of the feel of the hand on his body, and abruptly, he pulled away, unnerved.

She smiled and got to her feet. "Then, together, we ride on the morrow, Lord Prince. Sleep well."

He was not surprised when his dreams were troubled by visions of her body, naked and demanding, pressed against his own. And somehow in the dream, he knew that Annandale was lost to him forever.

Chapter Twenty-nine

Twilight came, a hot, dry hour in that hot, dry season, bringing no relief, no cooling breeze. The trees drooped in the arid air, their leaves parched and curling at the edges. Roderic leaned against the trunk of the tree and stared at the gray stone walls of the fortress rising inexorably before him.

Tomorrow was his birthday—his and Annandale's. They would both be twenty. In all those years, he had never thought of Minnis as anything but a place of respite and ease. Until now. Sweat trickled down his neck in the unrelenting heat, and he stared fixedly at the black shapes of the guards upon the walls. They kept to the shadows for the most part, though whether because of the heat, or for some darker reason, he didn't like to speculate.

He closed his eyes, wondering, hoping, praying that Amanander treated her kindly. He thought of the gardens of Minnis, seeing Annandale walking the wide, even paths, her hand touching the red roses and the pale purple delvynes, her face dappled by sunlight amid the branches of the drooping silver willows. What a fool he had been last summer, he thought, cursing himself. What time he had wasted. He should have listened to the dictates of his body and his heart and taken her to his bed as soon as she'd arrived. Now the thought of losing her cut through him like a white-hot blade. Who knew what that monster did to her? Who knew what devious tortures he devised?

Tavia had told him in great length how Amanander's guard had seen them safely to Ahga and the hapless guard had reluctantly revealed the proof Amanander would have required that the deed was done. Roderic shuddered.

"Lord Prince, the council awaits."

He waved a dismissal to the serving boy and turned away. Late yesterday the great army had arrived at the threshold of Minnis, and now it was time to plan the assault. There was only one course of action, and they all knew it. He missed Brand, missed his older brother's counsel and advice. Brand had parted company long before they had reached Minnis, riding south through what remained of the Forest of Koralane, which still smoked and smoldered. Alexander was still too sick, too riddled with guilt to offer advice, and only Deirdre listened with the same look of concentration he had seen her wear in negotiations. He realized with a start that he had come to rely on her very quickly.

Roderic walked down the low rise, where a path had been beaten down in less than twenty-four hours. A small city of tents and wagons and hastily constructed fences lay before him, and already the engineers had begun the construction of the massive siege towers, which would gain them access to the high walls. Others were engaged in reinforcing the defensive earthworks before the castle. Pennants flew above the tents, barely visible through the trees, the colors of the Chiefs of the Settle Islands, Norda Coda, and Kora-lado. His footprints raised little puffs of dust.

At the entrance of the command tent, he gave orders for food and drink to be brought to them. The group gathered around the table looked at him as he entered. Phineas lay on his litter, near the head of the table, and ranged down the sides were Deirdre, Alexander, and the Captains of the divisions.

The soldiers came to attention and saluted. He acknowledged them all and took his place at the head of the table. "I apologize for being late," he began. "Captain Ulrich, can you tell us what the scouts have discovered?"

The Captain shook his head and spread his hands. "Damn little we don't know already, Lord Prince. It appears the Lady Tavia was correct. Amanander doesn't seem to have a large force behind those walls. Guards are sparse and appear to rotate seldom. The guard duty is rotated but once every twenty-four hours—"

"Once?" Deirdre interrupted. "That's impossible, man. Surely your spies slept—"

"Lady, my men are reliable—"

At the testy edge in the soldier's voice, Roderic sat forward. It would never do to have emotions roused, or have his forces pitted against each other. "There is no doubt of that, Captain. But to rotate only once every twenty-four hours—that sounds unbelievable, you will agree?"

The Captain subsided, scowling.

Phineas leaned forward, his litter creaking as his weight shifted. "Then that tells us one thing for certain. Amanander may not have many men, but those he has have inhuman abilities."

Deirdre shook her head. "With all due respect to you, Lord Phineas, and to you, Captain, you don't know how many men he has. Lady Tavia never got an opportunity to see how many troops are there. And even if what the scouts say is true, we have no way of knowing what the strength of Amanander's forces are. He could be putting fewer guards on the walls to trick us."

Roderic nodded, running his fingers through his hair as she spoke. "I know. I've thought of that."

"Then have we committed, Lord Prince?" asked the other Captain, the Captain of the engineers, who sat beside the other, sweat plastering his tunic to his burly shoulders. The smell of freshly cut wood mixed with the salty smell of sweat. "Are we committed to storming the walls?"

"What other choice have we?" asked Roderic. "It doesn't matter how many men Amanander has, nor how they fight. We cannot starve them out—there is only one chance that we get over the walls, and take the castle—"

A stir outside the tent interrupted him. He looked up in annoyance, but the expression on his face changed when he saw who it was whom the guards escorted. "Vere!" He pushed back his stool and stood up in surprise. "At last."

Vere stood a moment, his face grave, the blue and green swirls of color on his face ghastly in the dim light. He seemed to be taking in the occupants, and he nodded to each of them in turn.

"Gentlemen, M'Callaster, my brother, Vere."

Phineas hissed with surprise, and Vere coughed softly. "Greetings, Captain Phineas. I understand you have been well rewarded for your loyalty to the King."

Deirdre pushed away from the table and leaned back, eyeing Vere speculatively. "I mean no disrespect, Lord Prince, but would this family reunion not be better held after we have determined our course of action and have made our battle plan accordingly?"

Roderic smiled at Deirdre's impatience. "I hope my brother brings us news which may aid our planning. Come, sit, Vere. Tell us. Were you successful?" said Roderic eagerly.

Vere drew a deep breath as he reached for a camp stool and sat at the opposite end of the table. "I'm sorry, Roderic. I did the best I could. The council has decided to put all resources available to them to fight Ferad. They refused to send any help at all to you."

"It's Atland, isn't it?"

Vere would not meet his eyes. "They did not say that."

"But that's what they meant, isn't it?"

Roderic felt as if the air had punched from his lungs. Vere shook his head.

"I am sorry, Roderic. Believe me, I did the best I could. I

tried to explain how dangerous Amanander is—how he has the empath—"

"And what did they say to that?"

"They refused to believe that he would have the ability to work much Magic, and that if he did, at least the empath would prevent him from doing much damage."

"What are we up against?" asked Deirdre with narrowed eyes. She flicked the end of her braid off her shoulder. "What are we talking about?"

"I've told you about my brother and his interest in the Magic," answered Roderic. "The scouts confirm that his men have some sort of inhuman power. So what can we do now, Vere?"

Vere wet his lips. "I am sorry. They did not want me to come back—they ordered me, in fact, back to the College—but I broke my vow to come to you. I understand what's happening here. But the Elders are faced with problems of their own. They have discovered that the traitors who call themselves the Brotherhood are more pervasive among them than they ever thought."

"By the One," Alexander swore softly. "This is my fault."

"Fault or not, it matters nothing now," said Phineas. "The responsibility for this doesn't rest on you alone, Alexander. The guilt is spread thin, believe me. But now—can you help us, Vere?"

Vere looked down at his lap. "There may be one more option."

"What's that?" asked Alexander, with the air of a condemned man.

"Nydia. Nydia Farhallen."

The name settled in the room, and Roderic felt his blood run cold.

"Annandale has said that she thinks her mother might be dead."

"Are you certain of that?" asked Vere.

"No," Roderic shook his head, "but surely, she'd know."

"Why do you think that?" asked Vere.

"She's an empath."

"That means she feels things. But she's not telepathic—she can't necessarily communicate with her mind. Some have that gift, but most achieve it only after long training."

"So you think Annandale might be wrong?"

"She may indeed feel the loss of her mother and doubtless, Nydia feels Annandale's own absence as a loss. But you don't know she's dead. And if she is alive—"

"If she's alive, why hasn't she come to help us?" interrupted Deirdre.

"Because of what she is," answered Roderic. "The way she looks now."

"She was beautiful," said Alexander. "Why would she hesitate to come?"

"She's not beautiful anymore," said Roderic. "She's ugly, inhuman. She goes about veiled—Annandale says she veiled herself when Annandale was very young, that her mother wanted to spare her the pain of what she had become. Believe me, you don't want to imagine it."

Vere's expression was troubled, and for a moment, Roderic thought he might ask a question. But then he shook his head and said, "We should go to her tower as quickly as we can—tomorrow at the very latest."

Roderic hesitated. The thought of returning to Nydia's desolate tower raised the hackles at the back of his neck. But he remembered how his hesitation as far as Annandale was concerned had cost him so much wasted time, and his resolve strengthened. He would not let his fear cost her another moment in Amanander's control. He drew a deep breath to reply to Vere, when the table and the dirt floor beneath it shuddered. Another tremor shook the poles of the tent. Roderic sprang to his feet.

"Earthshake!" cried Vere. "Guards—see to Lord Phineas."

As the guards rushed into the tent in response to Vere's cry, Roderic rushed outside, where he was met by a scene of complete chaos. Men broke into a run as the land buckled and split in a long crack through the whole camp. Before Roderic's disbelieving eyes, the earth rose up, flinging men and equipment in all directions. The rough frames of the siege engines collapsed as if they had been constructed of sticks.

A wide chasm opened up, and men and horses stumbled and fell into it, screaming, and Roderic fought to keep his footing as a crack snaked its way from the chasm up the rise of the little hill he stood upon.

The ground shook once more, and Roderic grappled for purchase. The ground dissolved beneath his feet in a shower of loose gravel and he fell, sliding into the dark chasm before him. Just in time, Vere grabbed his wrist. He clung to Vere with all his strength as the earth shook once more and was still.

Roderic lay still for a moment, feeling the rough dirt beneath his cheek, afraid to rise lest the unnatural shaking begin once more. Vere disentangled his hand and slowly rose to his feet, his face black with mud.

Roderic got to his feet and looked around. Minnis rose, vast and unapproachable, looking no worse for the wear. Men and animals lay on the ground, some wounded, some deathly still, and the remains of their equipment lay in broken heaps. "It looks like the Armageddon."

Vere nodded grimly. A tall, slim shape appeared on the walls. Mesmerized, Roderic broke away from the gathered men. He saw the longbow in the figure's hands, and as he watched, the figure drew the bowstring. Across the long space, an arrow flew an impossible distance and thudded into the ground directly at Roderic's feet.

He looked back at Vere and the others. Some of the men were muttering prayers, others clutched iron crosses to their lips. With steadier hands than he thought he should have been able to muster, he reached for the arrow. Wrapped around it was a piece of parchment. He broke the seal and unrolled the scroll. With a growing frown, he read the words.

"What's it say?" asked Vere.

Roderic glanced up at his brother, at the men clustering close. He crumpled the scroll into a ball in his fist. "He demands our surrender."

The men looked at each other with sidelong glances and frightened eyes. Roderic didn't give them the chance to voice their opinions. "Captains, Lieutenants, order your men. I want a complete assessment of the damage, of the losses we've suffered. Get a burial detail together—I want accurate numbers of the wounded, our remaining supplies. We may be here for a long time."

Chapter Thirty

Before the dawn broke over the trees, Roderic and Vere mounted horses and, skirting the walls of the great keep, rode north into the dense woods.

In the gray first light, the forest was preternaturally quiet, even the birds curiously hushed. Only the dew dripped from the trees, falling like tears on their shoulders as they brushed beneath the branches. Less than three hours north of Minnis, Vere held up his hand and Roderic reined his horse to a halt beside his brother.

There was a heaviness in the air, a thickening as they moved beneath the trees. Roderic found something familiar about the feeling, something he recognized, and he realized with a start that the atmosphere reminded him of the day when he and Barran had made their way to the tower of the witch.

The sky darkened as clouds roiled across the sun. "That day—" Roderic began "—that day there was a storm—"

"Yes," answered Vere, "doubtless it was her doing, calculated to bring you to the tower."

"You think it will happen again?" Roderic stared uneasily at the sky.

"I don't know," said Vere. "I don't know if she put some sort of defense in place—"

Even as he spoke the sky cleared, the clouds dissipating into pale white wisps against the harsh blue glare.

"Interesting," Vere muttered. "Interesting."

"Maybe she's dead," said Roderic.

"If she were dead, I don't think that would have happened at all. She's still alive, but for some reason, she's not using the Magic as she could."

In silence, they rode on. At last, the trees parted, and the path opened up into a clearing at the center of which stood Nydia's tower. Roderic glanced at Vere. His brother did not hesitate. He swung out of his saddle and tied his horse to a tree limb. "Come," said Vere.

Roderic's heart pounded harder as he walked closer to the base of the tower. Weeds choked the clearing, the steps were mossy and overgrown. Ivy twined up the sides, and the whole structure was windowless, blind, more of a fortress than Minnis. His palms began to sweat, and he hoped Vere would not notice when he wiped them on his legs.

At Vere's touch, the heavy doors swung open with a loud creak, and Roderic noticed for the first time how quiet it was in the clearing. Their footsteps echoed as they walked into the hall, the marble columns cracked in more places than he remembered. Dust motes hung in the long shaft of sunlight as it filtered through chinks in the wooden boards covering the windows, and Roderic wondered how many years had passed since full daylight had penetrated more than a few yards into the hall.

He walked further into the cavernous room, right into a faceful of cobwebs. Choking, he brushed them out of his mouth and eyes, and turned to see Vere peering up the listing staircase, one foot on the lowest step. It was Roderic's turn to beckon. "I remember the way."

Cautiously, for the winding stairs tilted at a precarious angle, the brothers crept up the steps. Was it only a little more than a year since he had come the first time? Roderic wondered. He felt years older, decades wearier. He had been Regent for less than a year and a half, and already he had been faced with two of the worst uprisings in living history. As they reached the top of the staircase and started down the long narrow corridor, he remembered Nydia's words: "War, Prince, war in every corner of the realm . . ."

Abruptly, he halted before a door. "I think it's this one."

He pushed gently on the door and stepped over the threshold. It was just as he remembered from before, except the air in the room was stifling and close. Something else was within the room, and the hair on the back of his neck rose in response. He looked at Vere, who put a hand on his arm. "She must be close."

There was a low moan, less than a whisper, more than a sigh, and Roderic with the greatest difficulty suppressed the urge to draw his dagger. "Nydia?" he called. "Lady Nydia? Are you here?"

There was another moan, and this time, the air seemed to shimmer and pulse, and Vere held up his hand. "Don't go any further. Lady Nydia? It's me, Vere. Do you remember me?"

Something moved in the shadows beside the hearth, and Roderic realized that the woman had been there all along, watching and waiting. Some energy, some force swirled through the air and then faded. Roderic let his breath out and realized he had been holding it the whole time.

He touched Vere's arm. "Over there." He pointed. "She's over there."

Vere nodded. "May we approach and speak with you, lady? We would not disturb you, but your daughter is in utmost danger—we need your help."

This time there was a choking rasp, and Roderic realized that the creature laughed. "Help?" she croaked. "Lift up thine eyes. Help is not mine to give. You see help, you see hope, in this place?"

The men glanced at each other, and Roderic took one single step forward. "Please, lady, we would not have troubled you, but Annandale—"

"Fairest of creation! Last and best of all God's works!" Nydia mumbled. "Creature in whom excelled whatever can to sight or thought be formed."

Roderic leaned toward Vere. "What is she saying? Do you understand her?"

Vere nodded. "There's a certain sense to it, I think. She's quoting an ancient poet—someone whose work was old when Meriga was young. May we approach, lady?"

There was a rustle and a heavy, ponderous shifting, as though the creature rearranged her bulk. Suddenly, Roderic felt cold, cold to his bones, and the fire in the hearth suddenly flared and sparked to life.

"You do Magic, lady?" asked Vere.

She made a gesture which might have been a shrug. "Necessity and chance." She extended one disfigured arm, and in the wavering light, Roderic saw again the thickened, fused digits, the long yellow claws and blackened scales. "Stay back," she cried. "What I will is fate."

Vere dropped down on one knee, his eyes above his beard filling with tears. "Oh, my lady. What's happened to you? What made you like this?"

She made another low crooning sound deep in her throat and Roderic felt fear raise his hackles. "What happened to me? Long is the way and hard that out of Hell leads up to light." She rocked and swayed, her veils moving gently flowing around her like shadows. "You come for my help? I cannot help myself, let alone another. Long is the way and hard that out of Hell leads up to light."

Roderic grasped Vere's shoulder. "What in the name of the One is she saying? How can you make any sense of this?"

A tear seeped down Vere's cheek. "How can this have happened?" he whispered, more to himself than to Roderic. "She was so beautiful—no one was more beautiful than she." He shook his head.

Nydia seemed to have heard that, for she raised her head.

"She walks in beauty like the night of cloudless climes and starry skies, and all that's best of dark and bright meet in her aspect and her eyes." She chuckled, low and dangerous, and parted the drapes in front of her face, revealing the misshapen monstrosity she had become. "You see? Farewell hope, farewell remorse. All good to me is lost."

"Lady, you can't believe that," said Vere, his voice choking. "Come with me—perhaps the College—the elders—there must be something that can be done to set the monstrous wrong to right."

She sighed, cocked her head to one side, and Roderic thought she smiled, if such an expression were possible on her hideous snout. "They say that might makes right. And now you say they might make right? You're right, they might. But does right make might?" She shook her head. "No. It doesn't."

Roderic shook Vere's shoulder. "Vere, she can't help us. She's speaking nonsense. Let's go. Leave the poor creature in peace."

Nydia shifted and stirred, her black bulk quivering. "Who are you that dares disturb my dying?"

"Lady Nydia?" asked Vere, his voice quivering with urgency, his mouth working as though he sought to hold back tears. "You knew me once. My name is Vere. Abelard Ridenau's second son. We walked beneath the cellars of Ahgá, you and I—you taught me much, and gave me hope. I have never forgotten you, lady. And this, you know him—this is Roderic, Prince of Meriga."

"Prince?" she whispered. Her voice was even, without the breathy singsong of madness.

"You brought me here last year, lady," Roderic said, as Vere nodded. "I took your daughter with me—I married her as you commanded."

"Married?" She looked down at her lap.

"As you commanded."

"Then you must *go to her*!" she shrieked. "Do you still not understand the danger? You are a child playing at being Prince!"

"Lady," said Roderic, feeling more truth in her words than he wanted to admit, "that's why we're here. Amanander has Annandale. He's holding her in Minnis—at the fortress my father built for you. We need your help—"

"The Magic," put in Vere. He rose to his feet and advanced, his expression carefully neutral as he stared at Nydia's black draped shape. "Amanander has the Magic."

"We came to ask you to leave this place, lady," said Roderic, with another glance at Vere's stricken face. "To use your Magic to help us fight Amanander."

She cocked her head, as if considering.

"He has Minnis," Roderic continued when she did not speak, "and he has Annandale."

"Fool!" she muttered. "Did I not warn you?"

"You did, lady, but I was called away to the North—there was war among the Chiefs—Alexander was besieged. I thought I had no choice but to go."

"There is always a choice," she hissed.

"So will you come?" Vere held out his hand. "Will you help us?"

"Why? What do you look for from me?"

"Amanander has the Magic," said Roderic. His desperation was growing with each passing moment. "He killed my sister Jesselyn, and he tried to kill Vere. He ordered Tavia and my infant daughter slain. If Annandale refuses to help him, he might even kill her. I don't think he'd hesitate to do such a thing if he thought it would work to his advantage."

"What about the Mutens?"

"They refused," said Vere, looking down.

"Refused?" Her voice was breathy with disbelief. "And do they know all?"

"Yes, lady. I told them myself. But they believe Ferad to be the greater enemy, and they will expend every resource available to stopping him."

She shook her head. "They will fail."

Vere sighed, and Roderic went down on one knee, hardly aware of what he did or felt, save only his frustration. "Please—"

"They will fail," she croaked. "Ferad shall live—and you, Prince. Would you like to know what I see? I can give you that. One last prophecy to follow you down the years? I'm dying. I'll tell you what I see, and then you let me go. Let me go, for I've earned my peace and paid for it long ago. All these years I've lived with the results of what the King commanded—"

Vere narrowed his eyes. "Did my father force you to do something which made you like this?"

"Your father? I curse the name of Abelard Ridenau, a thousand, thousand times. When I was young and very beautiful and time meant nothing—'Come,' he said, 'Come live with me and be my love . . .' Didn't I do that? I pledge allegiance . . ." Her voice trailed off into a whispery rasp, and Roderic stared in disbelief as the last vestiges of sanity collapsed like paper walls and Nydia crumpled into a black, shapeless mass, muttering incoherently.

Horrified, he backed away, and Vere caught his arm when he would have gone past. "She's mad, poor thing," Vere whispered. "Come. Leave her in peace. There's nothing for us here."

Vere nodded. They were at the door when Nydia's voice stopped them. "Wait, Prince. Three women—three women must give their lives for you. One already has—she died to give you life. But the second and the third—I cannot see their faces for the choices aren't yet made. But three women shall die before the throne of Meriga is yours. And the memory of each death will haunt you all the days of your life."

Roderic opened his mouth to question, to protest, but Vere

tapped his shoulder. "Come. She speaks in riddles—she's mad, poor thing. Even her visions make no sense."

Silently, Roderic followed his brother out of the tower, the floors creaking ominously beneath their feet. When they were riding through the trees, Roderic turned to Vere. "You think her prophecy was madness? Only that?"

Vere nodded sadly, a faraway look in his eyes, and Roderic knew he must be remembering Nydia as she was when he was young. "I pray she rests in peace, poor soul."

Chapter Thirty-one

He could not sleep that night. As the lamps burned low, and the campfires flickered and died, Roderic rose from the low camp cot and pulled a linen shirt over his head. When a sleepy Ben would have protested, he touched the old man briefly on the shoulder, murmuring a reassurance. The servant turned over with a snore. The guards outside his tent snapped to attention as he emerged, but he looked neither right nor left. He hooked his thumbs in his sword belt and stared at the black walls of Minnis rising before him.

The moon was a pale white crescent high above the trees, and the stars shone with an unearthly light. He glanced up and shivered although the night was hot and no wind moved through the low-hanging branches above his head. We were here long before you were, the stars seemed to say, and we shall be here when you are gone.

He thought of old Garrick, another death at Amanander's hand. So many dead, so many who should not have suffered. Garrick had retired from military duty; he should have grown old by the hearths of Ahga, watching the next generation of soldiers come to manhood. And Jesselyn, a sister he would never know. And Brea, Alexander's beloved. Not dead, perhaps, but scarred in mind and body. And Abelard. Who could imagine what had happened to him? At the thought of his father, the motto of the Ridenaus ran unbidden through his mind: *Faith shall finish what hope begins.*

He felt around his neck for the leather thong on which he kept Annandale's ring. The pearl was warm from his body, smooth and silky to his touch. Almost without thinking, he began to walk.

His footsteps led him through the camp to the very perimeter of the defenses, where the sentries gathered around a watch fire.

"Can't sleep, either?" asked one at his approach.

Momentarily, Roderic was taken aback, and then he realized that there were more men gathered in the fire's glow than was necessary. They thought him one of their own, he realized, and he replied with a nod and a grunt, and squatted down just within the perimeter of light.

"Me neither," came the reply, out of the dark, and Roderic looked up into the hardened face of a man at least thirty years his senior.

They ranged in age from grizzled veterans to men no older than he, and Roderic lifted his head and gazed once more in the direction of the fortress.

"Yes," said another, seeing which way Roderic stared, "you can't help looking at it, can you?"

"What's there, I wonder?" asked another, a boy with a voice so young Roderic thought it might at first be another girl, like Deirdre, snuck into the ranks.

"The Prince's lady, for one," answered the first man who had spoken, and Roderic knew from the way he leaned upon his spear that he was the sentry on duty.

"And what else? That's what I'd like to know. What else is waiting there? What do we go walking into tomorrow?"

"Aye," a heavily accented voice spoke from the shadows, and Roderic realized that it was one of the Settle Islanders. "It's not the dying I mind. But I would dearly like to know what it is I'm dying for."

"You've never seen the Prince's lady?" The sentry leaned forward upon his spear, and the flames made patterns which danced across his face. "Believe me, she's worth fighting for, and dying for, if we must."

"What woman's worth all this fuss and bother?" spat the Islander.

"And why?" asked the boy.

Roderic turned to answer, but before he could speak, the sentry answered. "Because, boy. It's what we're sworn to do—each of us, all of us. My father died for the Ridenau Kings, and I'm certain I'll die for them, too—"

"No," interrupted Roderic. "It isn't about dying." He spoke slowly as all the faces turned to him. "We fight so that others don't have to—so that children may grow up, grow old in peace. We fight, not just for the Prince's lady and the Prince, but for all of us, so that someday our children or our children's children won't have to." Suddenly he understood the Ridenau motto better than he ever had before. "We fight for the law, for the law is greater than one man's desires. The one who holds the lady—Amanander—doesn't care about anything but himself." The men had fallen silent, listening, and Roderic gazed at each man's face in turn. "We believe in something more than ourselves, and we have hope we will live to see a better day. That is why we fight, and that is why we die."

The men stared back at him. Roderic got to his feet. "Until tomorrow, gentlemen. Good night." There was a low murmur around the fire in response, and Roderic paused to look over his shoulder. The other men were talking excitedly amongst themselves, but the sentry met his gaze. The old soldier pulled himself straighter and offered a quiet salute. Roderic bowed in acknowledgment and turned away, fading into the blackness before the others could react.

As dawn flooded over the forest, Roderic gave the orders for the siege engines to advance. Stealthily, through the cover of the trees, the great towers moved, and from his perch on his horse, Roderic watched the troops fall into line and begin the grim march toward the walls of Minnis. In the growing light, he saw the siege towers draw closer, and squad by squad, the soldiers took their places.

Roderic raised his gloved hand, and the herald nodded, paused, then blew three notes upon his horn. With a roar like the surging ocean, the tide of men swept forward. The battle had begun.

Ten thousand men converged upon the walls of Minnis, but still the walls held. Inch by inch, Roderic rode forward, pressing through the men, until at last he, too, stood outside the walls. The ground was covered with corpses, three or four bodies thick, and above him, the sounds of the raging battle were a dull throbbing roar.

Deirdre rode up, her gloved hands covered in blood, and Roderic realized it was with the blood of her men. She shook her head and nodded at the walls. "It's not going well—what's he got up there?"

"There's only one way to find out," Roderic replied. He looked up as a body thudded to the ground. Over the walls, the men were pouring, flung right and left as though by a giant, and Roderic narrowed his eyes as a single line of black-garbed men appeared at the apex. As he watched, he saw them wield their weapons so deftly, so efficiently, there was not one wasted stroke. It seemed that they anticipated the moves their opponents would make, anticipated and met them, or dodged them completely. Their blades whirred and flashed and glinted like knives in the morning light.

Roderic watched horrified. This was Amanander's Magic. Somehow he had welded those men into a single unit, a single unit with many arms, which functioned so efficiently there were hardly any injuries. It was inhuman, terrifying to watch that line of slim, black shapes. They leaped off the walls, into the siege engines, nimbly hacking and slicing, avoiding blows with the grace of dancers, cutting down five or six at a time.

And even though more men rose to take the places of the fallen and the slain, the black figures did not tire, did not slow. Surely it was hopeless, for all the reserves in Meriga could not cut through such an enemy. And then, out of the corner of his eye, he saw a black shape topple soundlessly from the walls, and then another. A cheer arose, spreading across the battle line, and Roderic drew his own sword. "Bring up the reserves—concentrate on that opening—come, we mustn't lose this chance."

"Come, men," he cried, hoping his voice would carry, "to arms—to arms!" With Deirdre at his heels, he charged, leading the regiment up the sloping ramp, leaping across the walls. The scene before his eyes stopped him short. The tide of the battle seemed to turn, at least briefly, and now more and more of the King's men were pouring over the walls. But the black fighters rallied and had resumed their cold, elegant attack. He found himself before one. The man's eyes were dull, the expression on his face slack, but he moved with all the precision of a fighting machine. Roderic tried a double feint and felt the flick of a blade nick his arm. Blood bloomed down his sleeve, and his arm felt as though a thousand needles had pricked him at once. There was no time here for tricks. This was fighting reduced to its most efficient state. There was one chance, he realized: speed. He thrust and parried, dodging the strokes of the sword with a dancer's speed, and suddenly he saw his opening. He rammed the sword straight into the fighter's throat, and the man crumpled, soundlessly.

He summoned all his strength and met the next foe. Deirdre fought beside him. "It's speed," he bit out. "It's possible to go faster."

"True," she agreed, "but the men are tiring—even the reserves."

A cold wind blasted his neck and he glanced up involuntarily. The sun was hidden by a cloud, and the dry, arid heat of the day had given way to a damp, chilling wind which blew through the trees with a rush. Immediately, he realized that these were no ordinary clouds, for they swirled, moving faster and faster. "More Magic!" he cried, pulling Deirdre down with him as, with a mighty crack, a fork of lightning split the sky, toppling one of the towers at the corner of the wall.

The black-garbed soldiers jerked and shuddered, temporarily losing their synchrony, and another lightning bolt burst out of the heavens, this one aimed right at the wooden gates. There was another thunderous crack as the wood splintered and caught fire, the bluish flames eating through the dry wood like parchment.

A cheer went up from Roderic's forces. "Mother goddess," breathed Deirdre. Cautiously, she peered around. "Look there." She pointed down.

The men were pouring through the gates, overwhelming Amanander's soldiers by sheer strength of numbers. "Let's go," he said. Together Roderic and Deirdre fought their way through the last of the enemy to the courtyard. As the last of their men poured through the shattered gates, Roderic saw a squat figure veiled in ragged black which could only be Nydia hovering just outside the entrance. He pushed his way through the horde of fighting men—they outnumbered Amanander's men severely now—and grasped the black squat figure by the elbow. "Lady Nydia," he breathed in disbelief. He wiped his brow and saw the dirt and blood on his sleeve. "You came."

"My daughter." Her voice was so weak he could barely understand her over the din.

"Yes, lady. Come." Unthinking, he kept his grip on her arm, and Nydia allowed him to push a way through the press of bodies.

Finally Nydia gasped and halted, nearly doubling over in

what looked like pain. "I—I can go no further, Prince. The garden—"

She sank onto the steps which led into the hall, her black draperies blending with the shadows. He opened his mouth to protest, and suddenly, Deirdre was there by his side, urging him on. "Come," she said. "If we can find the bastard now, the day is ours."

Roderic ran across the polished surface of the hall, yanked the door into the gardens open and stopped short. Amanander sat on a stone bench, his eyes closed in grim concentration, a deep line etched between his brows. Behind him stood Gartred. Peregrine and Annandale were seated before him on the ground, their wrists bound with chains.

Amanander's hands were twined in Annandale's hair, and her eyes were closed, her face twisted in what could only be agony.

"No!" Roderic cried, gripping his sword. He ran across the grass, and in an instant, Amanander was on his feet, a dagger against Annandale's throat.

"Come closer and she dies."

"What a stupid waste of her life, Amanander," Roderic said. He lowered his sword by a fraction and took a single step.

"You don't think I'd kill her?" Faster than Roderic thought anyone could move, Amanander grabbed Peregrine and sliced his blade across her throat. Her eyes flew wide and he gave a little shove. Her head rolled off her shoulders into the grass, and her body gave a violent twitch and fell to the ground with a quiver, blood fountaining from her neck.

Roderic stumbled to a halt, his mouth working in disbelief. He reached out with one hand, his breath a ragged gasp in his throat.

"Now do you believe me, little brother?" Amanander pressed the bloodstained blade against Annandale's throat.

"What do you want, Amanander?"

"You know what I want. I want what belongs to me."

"There's nothing that belongs to you. You've set your hand against us all." Roderic edged forward.

"Throw that sword down, and you too, M'Callaster. Now, or I'll kill her."

Annandale shook her head. "No, Roderic, he'll kill you—"

Amanander moved his arm back, and in that moment, another fork of lightning split the sky. It sizzled on the very tip of the blade with its full force. Blue sparks arced in all directions, and the electrical surge traveled down the blade, into the hilt, and into Amanander.

His body spasmed and jerked like a puppet on a string as the energy blasted through his body. His eyes popped open wide as if in shock, and then, with one small gasp, he collapsed in a heap on top of Peregrine's lifeless body, his blackened hand still clutching the dagger.

Gartred stared wild-eyed at Roderic, gathered her skirts and ran.

"Let her go." Roderic put a restraining hand on Deirdre's arm. "She can't go far." He hesitated as his eyes found Annandale's. Awkwardly, he walked across the grass, tossing aside his bloodied sword. She looked up at him and gestured helplessly. The chains which bound her to Peregrine made a hollow clang, and he realized she was unable to rise.

Silently, he dragged Amanander's body off of Peregrine's, and Deirdre came forward, automatically understanding what he needed. He drew a deep breath as he gazed into her eyes. "Lady—" He began, then paused as Deirdre touched his arm with a ring of keys.

After a few false efforts, he unlocked the chains around her wrists. She rubbed her hands together, and awkwardly, he helped her to her feet. She sank back down on the stone bench. He looked down at Peregrine's lifeless body.

"I'm so sorry," he muttered. "If I hadn't left you—"

She shook her head and made a little noise of protest.

"Lord Prince?" said Deirdre. "I've got men here to remove this body."

Tenderly, he gathered Peregrine's body in his arms. "Don't move," he said to Annandale. She nodded, and turned away as he carried Peregrine's remains into the hall and laid her down before a hearth.

"Go on," said Deirdre gruffly. "I'll see to what must be done."

The hall was filling up with soldiers, crowding close, some laughing with relief, others quiet and grim. He nodded to Deirdre, and walked outside in time to see Annandale gather up her skirts and run across the grass to a black shape huddled beneath one of the ancient trees.

"Mother!"

Roderic ran to her side, just in time to see Nydia roll to one side, evading her daughter's touch.

"Let me help you," sobbed Annandale, reaching for her mother again.

"No help," rasped Nydia. "No help for me."

"You used the Magic to help us," Annandale said. Tears rolled down her face unheeded as she tried to gather her mother's bulk in her arms.

"Leave me, child." Nydia turned her head away. "Take me out to the woods—"

"No," cried Annandale. "Not this time. Mother, let me help." She reached beneath the wrappings, exposing the ugly snout, and Roderic shuddered in spite of himself. But Annandale ignored him. A thin blue light flared, bright and pure, and Roderic felt something pass through him: some energy, some force. He waited, expecting Nydia's face to change, for the horrible, terrible disfigurement to appear on Annandale's lovely face, but nothing happened. The creature only sighed, shut her eyes. Her head fell back with a little sigh.

Nydia was dead.

A breeze swept through the garden, sweet with the scent of apple blossoms. Roderic blinked away tears. Annandale got to her feet and held out her hand. Something older and sadder looked out of her eyes, something he didn't recognize, but he took her hand and pulled her close against his chest.

He wrapped his arms around her, holding her tightly, his fingers twined in the dark mass of her curls. "By the One, I swear I'll never leave you. Never. Forgive me. I—"

She pulled back, looked up at him and touched one finger to his lips. "You did what you believed you had to do. And you came. I knew you would."

He tugged at the leather cord around his neck. The knot loosened and the ring came free. He took her hand, and pushed the silver band down her finger, raised her hand and kissed it. They might have been alone in the garden, for the look which passed between them said more than words ever could. He raised her chin with the tip of one finger, and would have kissed her mouth but for Deirdre's shout that broke the moment.

"Lord Prince!" There was an odd, strained tone to Deirdre's voice. "He lives."

Deirdre knelt over Amanander. His prone body was twisted and curled upon itself. As Roderic met Deirdre's stricken look, he heard Vere and Alexander call his name, and Tavia cried, "Annandale!"

As the women embraced, the men gathered around Deirdre. Alexander dropped on one knee beside his twin and bowed his head.

"What are you waiting for, Roderic?" asked Tavia behind him, her arm around Annandale's waist. "Kill him."

Roderic sucked in his breath. He looked at Vere. Alexander turned around, aghast.

"No, Roderic!" he cried. "Please, don't kill him. That's not the King's justice. Let him answer for his crimes before the Congress—you know they'll condemn him."

"So kill him now and save them the trouble," said Tavia.

Roderic hesitated. He looked at Annandale, then Vere, as though searching for an answer. Neither said a word.

"Please, I beg you." Alexander put his hand on Roderic's arm. "He's my brother, don't kill him in cold blood. There's been enough killing today. Let him stand trial. I'll not speak for him, if that's what you think. But don't kill him."

"Roderic," hissed Tavia. "He's no brother. He's a monster. Kill him."

"Annandale," Roderic said. She met his eyes evenly. "Can you—can you heal him? Bring him back to answer as a man?"

She went rigid, her mouth quivering, and Roderic thought for a moment she might weep. She glanced around at the faces standing gathered over Amanander's body.

"How can you ask that of her?" Tavia cried. "Have you no idea what he is?"

"I do," said Roderic. "But can I kill someone lying helpless as an infant—"

"He would have killed your infant," spat Tavia, "with no more thought than he would a flea. He's a viper. He deserves to die."

Annandale held up her hand. "Hush, Tavvy. Roderic is right." She knelt in one graceful sweep and touched Amanander's forehead with her fingertips. She shut her eyes. Roderic drew back, expecting to see the healing light flare blue and bright.

But nothing happened, and Annandale drew back with a puzzled frown. "He's beyond my reach," she said, looking up at Roderic. "I can't touch him—it's not his body, it's his mind that's gone. In this state, he's no danger to anyone."

Roderic nodded and helped Annandale to her feet, drawing her close beside him. He drew a deep breath. "We'll take him back to Ahga. He will answer to us all, if he wakes. But I'd say his state is like a living death." He pressed Annandale hard against his side. "Come, lady. Let's leave this accursed place. The forest is cleaner."

Silently, they turned away and walked out of Minnis, arm in arm.

Epilogue

The night was cool. The silver light of the crescent moon filtered through the dark leaves of the great trees and the insects whined in the stillness. Annandale heard Roderic give the orders for the watch and listen to the final reports of the duty officer for the day.

She had bathed in the clear water of the nearest lake, and her hair was still damp. It lay coiled in a loose knot at the nape of her neck, and the thin chemise she wore was one of Tavia's. It was too big, but it didn't matter, for the thought of putting on anything which had been inside Minnis made her flesh crawl.

She sat on the low pile of blankets, spread with linens, which would serve them as a bed. He was shy with her, she knew; he had sensed the changes in her. She stared at her hands, smooth skinned and rosy tipped as always. She was different. Amanander had shown her things she had not wanted to believe existed. And part of her wanted to scream with Tavia to kill him. But the other part, the part of her that was stronger and better, the part that all the suffering and pain had strengthened, knew that such an act would have been wrong, would have violated some deep sense of right and would have changed Roderic forever, even if he had not raised the sword to do the deed himself.

It had never occurred to Amanander that he had unwittingly strengthened her, that the very suffering he had forced her to endure again and again had only toughened her, tempered her will like forged steel, even as her body weakened with the pain.

The tent flap opened and Roderic slipped inside. It was the first time they had been alone together in months. He paused, looked as if he might say something, and then he flung himself into her arms. He wrapped his arms around her, clutching her close, his head buried in her bosom. "Forgive me," he murmured again and again. "I should never have left you. I was a fool not to see his trap—it's what he wanted, surely."

"I don't think he knew what he wanted," she said, raising his head and gazing into his eyes. "Amanander only knew he wanted power, wanted me because he saw me as the means to that power, wanted you dead because he thought you stood in his way. But it doesn't matter anymore. All that matters is that we are together."

"I promised I'd keep you safe. I didn't live up to my promise."

"That's not a promise you can keep." She stroked his face, smoothing back the lock of hair off his brow. "We cannot keep each other safe. We can only love each other."

He drew her close to him, his gray eyes dark in the dim light, and kissed her, his mouth searching and warm. "I won't let you go," he murmured against her mouth. "I'll keep you with me, and I'll die myself before anything happens to you."

She let him pull the chemise off her shoulders, let him lay her down on the cool clean linen sheets, let him feast upon her body, pulling him closer and deeper until they were once again one flesh. But in her mother's dying moment, she had seen the prophecy, had seen the faces of the three women who would die to give him his throne. Peregrine, and Nydia . . . and hers had been the last.

About the Author

Children of Enchantment follows *Daughter of Prophecy* in the Power and the Pattern series by Anne Kelleher Bush. She holds a degree in medieval studies from Johns Hopkins University. She lives with her four children in Bethlehem, PA.